LENA DELATORA DISCOVERS FAME

THE LIFE AND TIMES OF A NORTH SIDE GIRL

D1281724

ROSEMARY DELUCA MCDONALD

outskirts
press

1

"**W**hy the hell am I living here? I'm freezing my ass," I said to myself, out loud.

The lady standing in front of me with a little girl moved a little further from me after I spoke out loud. I was born and raised in Chicago and I still hate the winters.

Paulie and I are good friends. He is also my uncle. I am twenty-one and he is twenty-four. Paulie is the youngest of six brothers: John, Sam, Pete, Mike, Joe, then Paulie. There were three sisters born in between the brothers.

I am the first daughter of the oldest sister, Josie. Paulie has an old junker. He holds it together with spit and wires. Uncle Sam helps him a lot, but he's getting tired of fixing that junk and paying for the parts, too. Paulie has an audition today.

Really, he's just singing for Mr. Riggio. He owns a neighborhood lounge. If Riggio likes him, maybe he'll let him sing for tips. When Paulie was a kid he ditched school to sing on the street. He finally got wise and put his hat out in front of his big feet. Sometimes he would make a few bucks.

He finally got thrown out of school for ditching too much. Then he got sent to Montifieore Reform School for Juvenile Delinquents. He graduated from there. He's still proud of the diploma. Me, I'm going to be an actress eventually. I already been in a thirty-second commercial on TV.

I'm on Chicago Bandstand sometimes, too. I am going to interview for another commercial next week. Meanwhile, I worked part-time at a beauty shop. I was a shampoo girl. I went to beauty school three nights a week. I was waiting for Paulie because I have a car that's running today. He lives with my Nana. He has the house in the back. She won't sell her house, so he stays there to protect her. Yeah, right. He's never home anyway. Nana is probably five feet tall in her stocking feet. Believe me, she doesn't need anyone to protect her. She is dynamite in a small package. I've seen her chase Paulie with a broom and catch him every time. She can throw a slipper and make it turn a corner.

"Hey, Lena! Waddaya doin' with all that makeup on? I didn't even recognize you."

"You know, Paulie, I'm freezing my ass out here. What time did you leave the house?"

Paulie carried a huge radio with a tape player.

"You complain so much it's like having a wife. Let's go. I'm supposed to be there by noon. You hungry?"

"Yeah, but I don't have any money, honey."

"I figure maybe Riggio will spring for lunch."

We drove down North Avenue and parked in the lot behind the restaurant. When we walked in, Riggio hugged Paulie and slapped him on the back. He eyed me up and down like he was buying a pony.

Paulie said, "This is my friend, Lena."

"Lena? Aren't you Josie's kid? Paulie, you should be proud to be related to this beauty."

It was all I could do to keep from rolling my eyes. What a big fat flirt. Paulie put a tape in the player. He sang a bunch of corny songs. The first was "Smoke Gets in Your Eyes."

Riggio told him that the customers want something more "Italian." Then he sang a few Dean Martin songs. Riggio was finally happy with that. He told him to come back at 7 p.m. and sing for the evening crowd. That's when the drinking starts. He would have a better chance at getting tips.

"You kids hungry?" Riggio asked.

Thank God. I was starving by this time. He brought out beef sandwiches and a huge salad. He parked himself in the chair next to me. *I swear if he touches my thigh, I'll pop him. If he's smart, he'll remember my six uncles.*

"You comin' back tonight, sweetheart?" Riggio said.

I looked at Paulie for help. He's too stupid to understand that my look was for him to bail me out.

He said, "Sure, Mr. Riggio. Lena can come back. She has to pick me up anyway."

"That's swell; ask for me at the bar, honey," and he walked away.

"Paulie, I don't need to spend my night here. I was planning to go over by Auntie Lilly's house tonight."

My Auntie Lilly was expecting her fifth kid; her daughter Gemma was expecting her first kid. They were due about one week apart. Gemma lived upstairs from Auntie Lilly. Neither one of them was looking so good. They could hardly walk. I could tell Mama I couldn't go, and then she could go over later today and check on them.

"Be a good sport, Lena. I don't even have a ride to the El. Ma would want to see you anyway."

If I took Paulie home, my Nana would send me home with bags of food again. I'm still living at home.

My ma cooks like she has a dozen kids, and she only has my brother Bobby and me. They were always sending food back and forth. I told Paulie okay, but I wasn't coming back until about 11 p.m. The place closed at 1 a.m. and I didn't want to sit around with all the old drunks.

I went home to take a nap. My Ma asked if I was sick and I told her that I was Paulie's chauffer again. I asked her if she wanted to come with me to Riggio's later.

"No. He's a big flirt," she said Your Dad always has a fit when we go there without him. Tell Nana not to send food home with you. You know she'll get up when Paulie gets home. I'll go spend the afternoon with Auntie Lilly."

When I got up from my nap, my ma had a note on the kitchen table: "Take the bag of food in the fridge that I packed up for Nana."

I knew it. I teased my hair to give it some body after sleeping on it. After I sprayed the heck out of it, I did my eyes for nighttime. I threw my makeup bag in my purse and put on my black dress from my high school dance night. It looked pretty good with my high heels. It fit me better now.

When I walked in to Riggio's, the old man tried to hug me. I saw it coming and stuck my hand out. He shook it real hard, like he was pumping oil. Riggio is really an old friend of my family. I just get the willies when my Mom or Dad aren't here.

"Lena, did you come alone? Where's your Ma and Dad? Paulie did good tonight. He got lots of tips."

All the drunks at the bar turned around to see who Mr. Riggio was talking to. I pretended not to hear the comments. Paulie was at the end of the bar and gave them a dirty look. He finally walked over and put his arm around me as a show of protection.

When we got in the car, Paulie said, "Geez, what the hell stinks in here?"

I said, "Mama made me take food for Nana and you."

"What did she send, something that died yesterday?" I told him it was eggplant and some left over lasagna.

"Oh, I love your Mama's lasagna," he said.

Paulie told me that Riggio liked his singing and he made $22 in tips. He was pretty proud of himself. I dropped him off in the alley behind the house. "Tell Nana I didn't come in because I'm tired. Paulie, are you taking this food in to Nana?"

"Yeah, she'll be waiting up anyway. I'll drop it off before I go to the back house. You sure got dressed up for a girl who's going home to go to bed."

"I didn't say I was going home to go to bed." I smiled a sweet smile.

"You better be careful, Lena. You going to see Nick? That Nick Piccolo is trouble. If you go to that club, make sure he walks you back to your car. Maybe I should go with you. I haven't been to The Club in a long time."

"Go home, Paulie. I have a life too."

When I walked into The Club, Nick looked surprised. He had his arm around some blond bimbo. I walked up next to him and looked over his shoulder. I whispered, "skank." She flipped her hair and

---

4

walked away. She looked old.

"Hey, baby! You look terrific," Nick said.

"Nick, you stink," I told him. I'll have a rum and Coke. Who's the virgin blond?" I asked.

"Oh, she's not a virgin, believe me. She's been around."

"Thanks for the travel report," I said, "I'm hungry. I'm not staying out all night. Are we staying here, or what?"

"No, baby. You wanna pick up a pizza and go back to my place?"

"No, Nick." I said, "Would it ever enter your mind to take me to a restaurant for dinner?"

"Lena, honey, I promise we'll do that. But it's late now. There's no place open at this time."

Just then my friend Mona came over. "Hey, I hear you got an interview at the TV station tomorrow."

Tomorrow?

"Oh, Geez. Is tomorrow Monday? I thought tomorrow was Sunday."

"No, it's Monday," Mona said.

I told Nick that I had to leave.

My interview was at 9 a.m. I decided to go to Nana's house and sleep. It was closer. I could wear this outfit I had on. Good thing I had thrown my makeup bag in my purse.

My Ma knew a lady whose brother was friends with a guy at channel 7. He got me this interview for a small part on another commercial. I had to look my best; this could be my big break.

When I got to Nana's there were no lights on. There was a light on at Paulie's in the back house. I had a key, so I let myself in. I could sack out on his sofa. I could hear someone in the bedroom, so I went to see.

"For Cripes sake!" I said.

"Geez, Lena! What the hell are you doing here?"

There was Uncle Paulie, doin' the wild thing with my friend Theresa Rose from down the street. That's not such a bad thing, but Theresa Rose is married and she has a kid. She pulled the covers over her head, like that was going to make her disappear. I decided to sleep at Nana's house after all.

I went to Nana's door. I turned the handle and the light went on in the bedroom. I swear she has radar. By the time I got in to the kitchen, she was shuffling down the hall, tying her bathrobe.

"Paulie, is that you?" she said.

"No, Nana. It's Lena. I'm going to sleep here, okay?"

"Yeah, it's okay. Sure. What's a matta? You fight wid 'a you Mama?"

"No Nan, I have a job interview in the morning. This is closer."

"Okay." Nana shrugged her shoulders. She usually accepts whatever you tell her.

"You wanna something to eat?"

"No, I'm tired. I'll sleep in Paulie's old room."

Nana cupped my face in her hands and kissed me on the lips and went back to bed.

2

In the morning I borrowed Nana's pearls and her coat with the fur collar. I put my hair up, because I wanted to look sophisticated. I got through the security booth by telling the guard my mother's friend's name, and I had an appointment. I parked in the back of the lot because my car looks like a piece of junk.

When I got inside the front office of the studio, they asked me a million questions. When she finally believed me, she told me to have a seat.

A girl in a mini skirt and tight sweater came out to get me about an hour later. I was busy looking at the cheesy stage sets while I was walking behind her, and I almost broke my neck. She looked very snotty and tried to flip her hair. She wasn't good at it. Finally! I was introduced to Mr. Latmen. He never stopped moving. I had to follow him to talk to him.

He said, "So, what do you do, kid?"

"I'm an actress, Mr. Latmen," I said as I ran along behind him. "But I go to beauty school at night."

He was pulling cables around the worn living room set for the soap opera. It looked much better on TV. He stopped dead and looked at me in the face.

"Can you do hair and makeup? Did you do your hair and makeup?"

"Yes I did, Sir. Yes I can. I go to beauty school," I said again quickly. I could do cartwheels, if that's what they needed.

"Okay. Can you start today? My makeup girl was a no-show this morning. She's fired. The ladies are going nuts in the dressing room. Greg!" he hollered.

The guy named Greg ran over and said, "Yes, Mr. Latmen."

"Take Lorna over to the soap opera queens' dressing room. She's taking Maxine's place. Make sure she gets a studio pass and whatever else she needs."

"That's 'Lena,' Mr. Latmen."

"Yeah, okay, whatever. You got the job."

Okay, I thought, *Nevermind the commercial.*

Greg said, "Let's go, Lena. You don't want to get caught in the crossfire."

The studio was crazy. There were cranes and wires and cameras and lights all over the place. I followed Greg behind a fake wall, down a long hallway. He talked as we walked along.

"These women are used to being pampered. There are two of them: the star and the costar. They share the dressing room. I hope you can handle it."

I walked in with my head high, and said, "Good morning, ladies." I saw a smock hanging on a hook and put it on, just like I knew what I was doing. "Let's get started! Who wants to be first? Let's do makeup before hair."

"Oh, thank goodness," The redhead said. "We were getting panicky."

I must admit they looked pretty snazzy when I got done with them. Mr. Latmen said that I was in the right profession.

I was finished by 3 p.m. I asked Greg what my regular hours would be. He told me nine to three.

I asked, "How much am I making an hour?"

Greg said, "$5.50 an hour."

I was speechless. I had visions of a new car, my own apartment, and some hot-diggity clothes. If I was making $5.50 an hour for doing hair and makeup, how much did a TV star make?

I drove home, pretty excited with myself. My ma wanted to know how the interview went. I told her that I wouldn't be a star for a while, but I got a job at the studio doing hair and makeup.

"This calls for a celebration. Let's all go to Riggio's for dinner. Is Paulie singing tonight?"

"Yes, Paulie has been singing every night. Is Daddy going with?"

"Yes, lets make a party out of it. Tell Dad to get dressed. Go tell your brother we're going out. Tell him to take a shower and put clean clothes on. I'm going to call Nana too."

I said that was just swell. I didn't really want to see the fat man again, but I would be safe if my ma and dad were with me. Nana was thrilled to be seeing her baby boy on stage. You would have thought that she was going to see the Pope. She got all dressed up in her other black dress. She wore the pearls and the coat with the fur collar. We looked more like we were going to a funeral. Everyone wore black.

Paulie sounded great. Everyone was nuts about him. My Nana cried real tears. She said, "My Paulie, he sounds like Tony Bennett."

Mr. Riggio sent over a bottle of wine. Everyone thought I was going on TV. They didn't get the part about me working as a makeup girl. All they heard was channel 7 TV.

They were patting Paulie on the back and kissing my cheeks.

Old friends of my ma and dad came over to shake hands. My dad was so proud that he forgot what they were congratulating him for. He just kept saying, "Thank you, thank you."

Paulie and I decided to go next door to The Club. His car was running for a change, and he would drive me home.

When we got to The Club, Nick was at the bar with that same bimbo. She looked like a burnt-out floozy.

Paulie and I went to the other end of the bar and ordered drinks. When Nick saw me he looked like someone stuck him with a pin. He came running over like he got caught cheating on his wife.

He shook hands with Paulie. Paulie shook his hand and gave him a dirty look at the same time.

I told Nick, "Get lost. I think you and the skank deserve each other."

Nick looked shocked, but he never said a word. He just shook his head and wandered back to the bar like he couldn't believe I would talk to him like that.

The next morning Greg was waiting for me at the door of the

studio. He said the soap opera queens were real happy with the makeup and hair-dos. That made my day. They were excited to see me. I guess they were afraid that I wouldn't show up, like Maxine.

At lunchtime, Greg asked me if I wanted to get a sandwich in the cafeteria. I said yes. He was pretty nice and I didn't know anybody there anyway. He talked all through lunch. He was kind of cute. I think he was a little nervous. He insisted on paying for my lunch. He has blond hair, but he looks a little Italian. I'm not sure. I'll have to ask his last name.

Greg was waiting to walk me to my car after work. I don't know why. It was still light outside. I didn't want him to see my junker, but he didn't seem to mind.

When I told Paulie about Greg, he said, "Maybe he has a crush on you." I didn't think about that. I haven't dated very much. Nick and I have been an item off and on since high school. Even though we haven't been really "going steady" or "engaged," I've only been out with a couple of other guys. They were both friends of Paulie's, and they were afraid of him. God forbid they should get fresh with Paulie's niece. They knew he would kill them.

Paulie came down with an awful cold the following week. He couldn't even lift his head off the pillow. Nana was beside herself with worry. She was lighting candles and asked the priest at St. Michael's to say prayers for him. It was probably a coincidence that Theresa Rose had a bad cold too.

Nana was planning to make a Novena, but that takes nine days. Paulie told her he had to get well by Saturday, so that would take too long. So Nana made soup and covered Paulie with about ten blankets instead. I guess that would be a speed-novena, if you include the priest's prayers from St. Michael's Church. Mr. Riggio was busy explaining to his customers why Paulie wasn't singing tonight.

When Paulie was sick for a second day, Riggio called him on the phone. He said, "Paulie, how about when you come back, I pay you a regular check on Fridays?" I don't know what Nana was praying for, but this worked out real well for Paulie.

I didn't go see Paulie while he was sick. I didn't want to catch his cold. Now that I had a good job, I couldn't miss work or call in sick. I loved taking care of the soap opera queens, even if I wasn't famous yet.

Greg met me at the stage door every morning and walked me to the Queens' dressing room. We went to lunch together every day. He always paid for my sandwich and chips in the cafeteria, except for the days that I brought leftovers from home. He was really loving homemade Italian food.

Did I say that Greg is Jewish? His name is Neuman. Not that this would matter to my family. We are a league of nations. My Uncle Mike was stationed in England when he was in the Air Force. He married a girl there. My Uncle Sam married a Swede from Wisconsin. Uncle Joe married a Polish girl, then Auntie Dolly, who is Italian and Jewish.

When I am in the dressing room with the Queens, whose names are really Beth and Susan, I usually listen to them practice their lines for the day's program. I can usually coach them in the few hours that we spend together.

As fate would have it, Susan was sick as a dog one day. She couldn't stop "barfing."

Latmen said, "What the hell am I supposed to do about this!"

He was going nuts, making phone calls and yelling at people. Greg was following him around and trying to talk to him. "Mr. Latmen, Lena can fill in for Susan." Latmen kept pacing and yelling.

Finally, Greg yelled at Latmen, "Lena knows the script!"

He stopped hollering and said, "What did you say?"

Greg repeated it and Latmen looked at me and said, "Really?"

Greg said, "Yes sir! She helps them rehearse while they do hair and makeup every day."

It's a good thing that Susan, the sick chick, has dark hair like mine. I put my make-up on like hers and fixed my hair in an up-do. It all happened so fast I didn't even get a chance to phone Paulie. I told Greg to call my ma and within minutes everyone in the family knew. When the show was over everyone applauded.

When I realized they were clapping for me, I almost cried. It's a good thing that it happened that way because I didn't have time to get nervous.

Mr. Latmen slapped me on the back. "You did good, Lorna. Real good."

"My name is Lena, Mr. Latmen."

"Well, Lena, I found out that Susan is pregnant. I'm giving you a thirty-day trial on the show. If you do good, we'll talk about a contract."

Wow, I thought, *could things really happen that fast?*

We were celebrating again. Everyone went to Riggio's. Ma invited Greg too. I said, "Mama, It was just one time! I don't know how I'm gonna do for thirty days."

That's all it takes to celebrate in my family. When we got to Riggio's, Paulie was out in front with a brand new car. It was a beauty: a big red and white Plymouth with huge fins sticking out the back like the Queen Mary. I started laughing. Then he started laughing. We both were thinking the same thing. A few months ago neither one of us had real job. He was driving a wreck of a car. I was working part-time at the beauty shop. Now we both had good jobs that paid real good money.

3

On Monday, Mr. Latmen called me into his office and handed me a check. He told me it was a clothing allowance. I thought I would faint!

When I called Mama on my lunch hour she said, "Lena, can you take the clothes home?"

"Yes!" I said. "They are mine to wear whenever I want, as long as I look professional on T.V."

That evening Gemma went into labor. We all rushed to the hospital together. Nana was at the head of the line at the delivery room. The nurse explained that no one could go in but the husband. Nana was very insulted. Auntie Lilly was so pregnant that the nurse kept looking at her like she was going to put her in a bed. She finally asked her to stop pacing. An hour and a half later, they called Memo in.

"I have a daughter!" he exclaimed. We finally got to go in for a short visit. Gemma said her name was Rosina Marie, after our Nana and Memo's dead grandmother. Nana cried and cried, she was so thrilled about the baby's name. "I'm-a gonna buy her diamond earrings!" Well, that's no surprise. It was her first great-grandchild.

The next day after work, I went to see Gemma and baby Rosie. Gemma was propped up surrounded by pillows. Her hair looked perfect. She looked like Annette Funicello. Memo must have bought every rose in town. They were in vases and buckets everywhere in the room. The nurse was not happy. "Too many flowers," she said.

Later, when the whole family came in, she looked frantic, "There are far too many people in this room." Nana gently guided her by the arm, put her in the hallway, and shut the door.

Auntie Lilly came to see her first grandchild too. Uncle Vito was pushing her in a wheelchair. "She's in labor," he announced. They were both very calm. After all, it was their fifth kid.

"I'll let you know when the pains get closer," she said.

By 9 p.m. we had another new baby in the family. It was a boy! They named him Anthony Vito. Anthony was my grandpa, and the name Vito goes far back in Uncle Vito's family.

The babies would be christened together in a few of weeks. I would help Nana make about 200 cannoli shells. Nana would store them in a cool dry place, probably under her bed in baking pans covered in towels. The morning of the christening, we would fill them. If you fill them too soon they might get soggy.

<hr/>

I got to Nana's around eight thirty Saturday morning. She had everything ready and was putting pots of oil on the stove. We were rolling the dough onto the tubes when the doorbell rang. I went to answer it; I had flour all over me. It was Greg. I was so surprised! I was a mess, and Nana's kitchen was a mess from the cannoli stuff.

He said he had called my house to see if I wanted to meet for lunch. I never had a lunch date before, so I was surprised. My Ma told him I was at Nana's house helping her. She gave him directions, and he showed up here.

Greg looked like he was confused when he saw me. He looks confused a lot. I said, "Oh, hi. I'm making cannoli shells with Nana. Come on in."

"I called your house; your Mom told me I could come here."

Sometimes my ma doesn't think right. Why would she tell a guy to come here and see me all messy?

Nana was delighted to see him. She said, "Gregorio! What are you doing here? You come-a to help?"

He looked confused again.

I said, "Greg, Nana just enlisted you to help make cannoli shells."

He said, "Okay, tell me what to do."

I showed him how to pull the hot tubes out of the deep fried shells without burning himself. Nana kept frying, and I kept rolling them out. We had a great assembly line going. There wasn't much talking going on. Everyone had to pay attention to what they were doing.

Greg finally said, "I've eaten these things, but I never knew how much work they are."

We were working like crazy when Paulie came in from the back house. He always gets up at the crack of noon.

"Hey! You guys are doing a great job. Greg, how did they drag you into this?"

Greg said, "I was going to take Lena out for lunch."

Nana heard the word "lunch," and she shut off the flames under the pots of oil and moved them off the stove. "Okay, time-a for lunch. I cook now."

Paulie also knew how to time his visits. Nana pulled stuff out of the fridge. Before you knew it she had three or four things in the oven and a big pot on the stove.

She said to Paulie and Greg, "Come-onna with me. I gotta something for you to do."

The next thing I hear are some loud banging sounds coming from the basement. I looked out the window and saw Paulie and Greg dragging Papa's old wine press up the basement steps out into the yard.

I went out there and said, "What are you going to do with this, Nana?"

Nana said, "I think I take-a to the cemetery and put-a flowers in it."

Paulie rolled his eyes.

Greg just stared at Nana like she had two heads.

I said, "Nana, I don't think you can do that. The cemetery has rules."

Nana put her hands on her hips and said, "Yes, Bella, they have rules. I see flowers all-a time in pots and stuff."

I told her, "Nana, this is too big. They won't let you put it on the grave."

She thought about that for a second and said, "Okay. Then I put-a the flowers in it for my yard. Papa, he would like that. I put over by the tomatoes and basillico."

Now that that was settled, we could eat lunch. Nana was delighted to have two men at her table. She kept filling their dishes. Greg ate like he was going to the electric chair.

Paulie thought Greg was pretty funny. "Hey Greg," he said, "don't think that my ma cooks like this all the time. She's just showing off for you."

Nana waved her hand, dismissing Paulie's comment. "Paulie, he's a-pazzo," she said.

Greg knew by the hand motions that she said Paulie was nuts. But we all knew that already.

NANA DeLUCA'S CANNOLI SHELLS AND FILLING

<u>Cannoli Shells</u>
2-1/2 cups all-purpose flour
¼ cup sugar
1-teaspoon ground cinnamon
¼ teaspoon salt
¼ cup shortening
2 well-beaten eggs
¼ cup cold water
2 tablespoons vinegar
1 beaten egg white
Cooking oil for deep fat frying
Powdered sugar to dust shells

In a large bowl combine dry ingredients. Cut in shortening until mixture resembles small peas. In a small bowl, combine eggs, water, and vinegar. Add to flour mixture, stirring until dough forms a ball. On lightly floured surface roll half the dough at a time to slightly less than 1/8" thick. Using sharp knife cut rectangles approximately

4x5". Beginning with the long side, roll each piece of dough loosely onto a cannoli tube, corner to corner. Seal seam with egg white. Press gently with fingers to be sure edges are sealed. Fry cannoli in deep hot fat (375 degrees) for 1 to 2 minutes. Drain on paper towel. When cool enough to remove, gently pull pastry tube from shell. Shells can be stored in a sealed container for several weeks.

Cannoli Filling

3 pounds ricotta cheese
1 cup mini chocolate chips
2 tablespoons vanilla
2-1/2 cups powdered sugar
Optional: ½ cup diced citron

We cleaned up the mess in Nana's kitchen. Greg had to leave and I was covered in flour. He said he'd call me later.

I got home and went in to shower. Mom said I looked like a snowman, or a snow woman. As soon as I closed the door, the phone rang.

———— ((◦)) ————

"Hey, you wanna come to The Club tonight? I'm only singing until 10 p.m.

because it's slow on Sunday. Meet me in the bar. Call Greg."

When Mona saw me, she hugged me and Greg like she meant it. We ordered drinks and squeezed into the corner booth. When Paulie got there, she pushed me out of my seat and said, "Time to go to the ladies' room."

"Lena, is this serious with Greg?"

I said, "Mona, I don't know. I really like him, but I'm not ready to get serious."

"Oh, I think I understand . . . you're saving yourself for Prince

Charming, right?'

"Yup, you got it. But I'm having trouble understanding my life right now. So I'm holding on to what I've got."

"You've got a nightie and a toothbrush in your purse, that's what you've got. And that ain't nothing to write home about.

"Mona, I can't make my life an open book."

"Sure you can. I tell you everything!"

"Well, when it happens, you'll be the first to know."

4

The new season had started for the soaps. *Tortured Souls* had gotten great ratings. I signed a contract for another six months. Mr. Latmen gave me a small increase and an additional clothing allowance. I now made more money than my father and more than Greg. I tried to remind myself not to get a big head. Money doesn't mean anything without family and friends.

Our program would soon be going "color." I went to Mr. Latmen and told him that we needed to spruce up the set.

He looked surprised and said, "Waddaya wanna do?"

I told him, "We need to paint the sets and get some new furniture for the show."

He called the painters in and had the set redone. He told me to go to the Merchandise Mart and pick out some new furniture and charge it to the station.

He said, "Lena, pick out some doo-dads and nice stuff to decorate the place to go with the new colors."

I was having a great time! Greg teased me about being the real boss at the studio.

Speaking of Greg, he kept trying to get me to spend the night with him. I really didn't have the nerve yet. Every time I was brave enough to put a nightie and a toothbrush in my bag, I would chicken out before the evening was over. I know Greg was getting a little frustrated. I was too, but I always remember what my ma said, "Save yourself, Lena. A woman leaves a piece of her soul with a man. A man shoots in the dark and walks away."

She has a lot of those sayings. I'll keep the nightie and toothbrush in my purse, just in case.

Paulie and Mona were fighting all the time. She was jealous of the girls who flocked around him when he was singing at Riggio's. I always knew that Paulie was a womanizer. When I caught him in the sack with my friend Theresa Rose that time, I knew he was an alley cat. I thought he and Mona were pretty serious and he had settled down, but some men can't be faithful to one woman. Paulie was living proof that some men had a bad case of "Big-Shot Male" syndrome. I think it's from too much of that male hormone.

This is a crazy family. Someone is always fighting and making up, or fighting and blaming someone else. If nobody admits they are wrong, Nana is usually there to make the decision for them.

Let me tell you what happened last week. Nana called our house. She was hysterical. After Mama calmed her down, Nana told her that two women were fighting in the backyard. A blond came out of Paulie's house in the back when a dark-haired girl came to the door. Before you knew it, they were pulling handfuls of hair out of each other's heads. Paulie couldn't break it up. Nana said he was getting the crap beat out of him trying.

Mama and I jumped in the car and drove over there. We figured two chicks fighting over Paulie was worth seeing. It turns out that the two were fighting because the blond-haired girl was cheating on the brunette. That's right. The two chicks were a steady "item." Paulie didn't know until the brunette came looking for her. He was all scratched up, standing there watching them like a dope. I pulled him inside and we gathered blondie's stuff and threw it out on the porch. Mama took Nana inside to explain the situation. At first, Nana didn't believe it. Then she slapped herself in the forehead and said that Paulie better burn the bed sheets. The three of us marched around the back of the house because Nana wanted to see if Paulie was okay. Once she decided he was all right, she slapped him silly while she swore at him in

Italian. When we left, the two chicks were gone.

You gotta love this crazy family. Mama and I had a good laugh over that one. We didn't tell my dad. I don't know if he would have been as amused as we were.

5

Greg and I had made a date to meet Paulie and Mona at The Club. Greg insisted that he was going to fix dinner for me at his apartment. I had never been to his place, so I was looking forward to it.

He picked me up early. He was there by 6:30 p.m. Dad invited him in and they had a little glass of wine in the dining room. That's when you know Dad likes someone. He gives them wine from the good glasses in the china cabinet. We left about 7 p.m. Greg helped me into his car. My skirt was kind of straight, so I had to hike it up a little to get in. He couldn't keep his hand to himself while he was driving. I finally told him, "You're gonna get us killed. Stop it, okay?"

He said, "Sorry, Lena. I can't help myself."

He lived in an elevator building that had a doorman. Very swanky.

The doorman said, "Good evening, Mr. Neuman."

I was very impressed. The elevator doors opened on his floor. I was very impressed, again. Palm trees on either side of the elevator doors. Fake, I think, but they sure looked nice. When he opened his apartment door, a funny little dog ran up to us and was going nuts. He was so ugly that he was cute. Greg said it was a pug.

"What's his name?"

"His name is Goofy."

"That sure does suit him."

Well, Goofy jumped all over me and tore my stockings.

"Oh, Lena, I'm really sorry. There's a drug store downstairs. I can go get you a new pair."

"Oh, thanks Greg. That would be great." I told him what to buy.

While he was gone, I took my torn stockings off and put them in the trashcan in the bathroom.

When Greg came back in to the apartment he said, "The doorman asked how your stockings got runs in them so quickly. I felt my face turn red and that made him laugh. I haven't had too many girls up to my apartment."

"Did you tell him that Goofy did it?"

"Yeah. He said that was a cute nickname for me."

"Oh, I get it. He thought you were Goofy!"

Well, Greg had the table set already. The oven was on low and the baked potatoes were done. He put the steaks in the broiler and poured us both a glass of wine.

We were sitting on the sofa and I had my legs tucked under me. We started to make out and Greg's hands were all over my legs. I realized that I didn't have any stockings on when that little dog stuck his cold nose up my skirt. That was good timing because the steaks were beginning to smoke. They weren't the only things smoking by that time.

We had a very nice dinner. He apologized for not thinking of dessert, but I said that was okay, since I'm on a diet anyway. We cleared the table together and did the dishes. It was very sweet.

I freshened up and put on some lipstick. We started making out again while we waited for the elevator. We heard the bell ring for the floor below us and straightened up real quick. When the doors opened an elderly couple got out.

We said, "Good evening."

The lady smiled a sly smile and the man winked at Greg. That's when I noticed the lipstick all over his face.

Needless to say, we took a big ribbing when we got to The Club so late.

Mona had us all squashed into a corner booth. When the music started, Paulie and Mona got up to dance. Greg took that opportunity to lean over and start smooching me all over my neck. I can't say that I fought him off. When Mona and Paulie got back to the booth, she grabbed my arm and dragged me to the ladies' room.

"Wow! Lena, you and Greg are getting pretty hot and heavy aren't you?"

"Oh, maybe just a little."

We both fixed our lipstick and fluffed our hair and went back to the guys.

—————⟫⟪◊⟫⟪—————

That night when I got home, Ma and Dad were sitting at the kitchen. It looked like my mom had been crying. I kissed Ma and Dad and said "good night" and kept going to my room, but Ma put her hand out to stop me. It scared me that she wanted me to know what was wrong. Everyone has skeletons in their closet. My family has more than its share. Mama has six brothers. Three are average married guys with families. The other three . . . well, let's just say that they get into some trouble now and then—nothing serious really, just a little "trascurato," or carelessness sometimes. They don't think about the consequences of what they do. My dad drives a garbage truck for the city. He also has "side jobs." I've never understood exactly what the "side jobs" were. This time my Uncle Mike was in deeper than usual. Dad had given him a job delivering some "goods." He stopped at his girlfriend's house for some afternoon delight. The truck got stolen because he left the keys in the ignition. It was a truckload of new appliances. Now the stolen goods were stolen for a second time. This was a very bad turn of events. When your family is "connected" there are responsibilities that go along with the privileges. Dad had his little black book in front of him. He was talking to Niko Bazzoli.

"No, I don't think we have competition. I think some punk got lucky and saw the keys in the ignition. I don't know if we'll recover any of it. I'll talk to you later.

Dad looked at me and said, "Mikey is holed up at Zia's house in Michigan. He'll have to stay there for a while."

Uncle Mike's godmother is Ma's great aunt. The realization that Zia's house has been a "safe house" hit me like a ton of bricks. I guess I knew this since I was a kid, but I never made the connection to people in trouble in the family. I use the word "family" in the broadest sense of the word.

We spent a lot of time at Zia's house in the summer while I was growing up. We picked strawberries and stayed up late, watched the stars from the porch and listened to all the uncles harmonize, singing Italian songs. They thought they sang better than Frankie Lane and just as good as Tony Bennett. Between songs, they would argue about what branch of the military was the best, since they had been in the marines, air force, army and navy, collectively.

Zia has a huge farmhouse. There were always people staying there that I didn't know: Uncle so-and-so, and cousin so-and-so. Now I know that the family does special favors. But that means that you have to do your job, too, because somebody is depending on you. Paulie and I would go to Uncle Mikey's house that night and pack some of his stuff. Paulie would drive it up to Zia's in the morning. This was very unsettling to me. I have been very sheltered growing up in this big Italian family. I should have known what was happening around me before this, but I didn't. I was protected. This is the name of the game. Now I know that being "connected" means a lot more than having an extended family.

⟫⟪⟪◉⟫⟫⟪

Uncle Sam

Uncle John

Niko Bazzoli would arrange for the missing merchandise to be replaced. Mama told me later that she would rather have a brother living at Zia's than the alternative, which was dead. I spent a lot of time lying awake thinking that night. Daddy goes out late in the evening several times a week. Mama said he was going to union meetings. I am much wiser now. I have my head on straight and have come to terms with the situation. I need to be a professional and ready for work in the morning. I studied my lines for tomorrow's episode and finally fell asleep. Poor Mama. I woke up during the night and I could hear her crying over her brother being exiled to

Zia's. He wouldn't be at the babies' christening.

The following Saturday, Mom and I had an early appointment at Stella's to get our hair done for the christening. I was even planning to spring for a manicure, since I had discovered fame and was making big bucks. She was in a better frame of mind and seemed to be adjusting to Uncle Mike being at Zia's.

We were getting ready for the babies christening the next day, so we all had a busy evening ahead of us. Baby Tony and Rosie would be christened together on the same day at St. Michael's Church. The party would be at Auntie Lilly's house. Christenings in our family are like mini-weddings. Since Gemma lives upstairs, the christening would be an open house. It was the middle of June and everyone could be outside and inside. The women would cook sausage and beef. Nana was making big pans of lasagna. The cannoli shells were already made. My cousins Gemma and Gia had been sewing little bonboniere bags for weeks. Mama went to DeNatalie's Italian store and ordered fifteen pounds of colored candy almonds for the bags.

One of the ladies at the church made little white tags for the ribbons that said, "God Bless Rosina and Anthony." She writes in fancy letters.

Uncle Joey went to the Holy Store and bought little crosses and tiny plastic shoes. We all went to Auntie Lilly's house and spent an entire evening tying the bonboniere with ribbons and all the cute junk on them. That stuff is really a pain in the ass. Everyone takes the bags home but nobody eats that crap inside. They keep it in their china cabinet or on their dresser. We still do it for every occasion: bridal showers, weddings, baby showers, christenings, first holy communions, and confirmations. For weddings the almonds are white.

I'll bet our family has spent thousands of dollars on that stuff. I didn't even know you could eat the almonds until I was about twelve years old. My Ma had some old bonboniere in her china cabinet. I was snooping around with my brother Bobby and we opened them up and ate them. I asked my ma why we give people these little nuts that taste like rocks.

Mama explained the meaning: "Almonds are bitter. The candy coating is sweet. Most happy occasions are bittersweet events. The woman feels joy in finding out that she is having a baby. Then there is the pain of giving birth. With a wedding, there is the bittersweet experience of leaving your parents. Now you are starting a new life as husband and wife with the person you love. It's a mixture of joy and sadness."

Geez, my ma is full of surprises. I don't think she made this up. How come I never heard this before? Sometimes she says some amazing stuff. I gotta pay more attention to family. I really grew up in a bubble. Sometimes I look back at my childhood and wonder where it went.

The morning of the christening, Mama and I went to Nana's at 7 a.m. We filled all the cannoli shells and packed them gently in roasting pans. We covered them with clean dishcloths so the shells wouldn't get mushy. We loaded them into Ma's car and drove to Auntie Lilly's house. We put some of the pans upstairs and some downstairs, since everyone would be going between apartments. Later we would put them on serving trays lined with paper doilies.

We went home to dress for church.

The week before the christening, I had taken Mama and Auntie Lilly to Mayson's for a special dress for the ceremony. Now that I'm on TV every day, everyone recognizes me. The ladies at Mayson's act like I am the Blessed Virgin when I walk in. When I brought Auntie Lilly and Ma, they were thrilled. The dresses would be my treat to both of them. I have my own charge account now, so I put it on my tab. They both tried on about a dozen dresses before they made up their minds.

Mama picked a red suit. I couldn't believe it. It was pretty low cut in the front. I said, "Wait until Dad sees this." She really looked snazzy. She picked a hat with a red and black feather and a black veil. Auntie Lilly picked out a pastel brocade dress with a wide white belt. A lot of the pattern woven through it was pink and blue, which was appropriate for the day. She picked an off-white hat with a wide brim and a white veil. The seamstress at the shop added small pink and blue flowers in a small cluster near the bow on the side. Auntie Lilly looked pretty good considering she had just had a baby four weeks ago.

We didn't worry about what Nana was going to wear. She went to the little neighborhood dress store that catered to Italian widows and bought another black dress. She would wear her pearls from Italy and a broach with her gold chain with the cross and Papa Joe's wedding ring on the same chain. Along with that she would add all of the gold bracelets that she owned. Nana felt it was appropriate to wear as much gold as possible for special occasions.

The men, well, they wore sharkskin, of course. Some wore black and some wore shades of gray. Even my little brother Bobby got a new suit. His was light grey. My dad wore a black sharkskin suit, with a white shirt with a red tie to match Mama's suit. By the way, he loved her suit. In fact, he couldn't take his eyes off her. She blushed every time he looked at her.

Both of the babies cried their heads off when Father Joe poured the holy water on them. The church was packed with parents, godparents, and friends.

I am Rosina's godmother, so I was up in the front of the church holding her. Memo's cousin, Carlo Bazzoli, was the godfather. Memo and Carlo's families both lived in the same neighborhood. We all grew up together. I have known Carlo most of my life. He wasn't one of my favorite people. I learned to be polite when I saw him, because of the family connections, but I tried to keep my distance.

As a kid in our neighborhood, Carlo used to do rotten things. I heard that he set a cat on fire once. He took his ma's pots and pans and sold them at a flea market for money for cigarettes. He made girls cry all the time. Somebody's ma or dad was always going to his house to tell his dad what offence he committed. Overall, he had a bad reputation. I was told to stay away from him when I was a kid.

Carlo wore a black sharkskin suit and a black tie with a striped shirt. He looked like a hoodlum. He should have gotten a haircut. He was actually very handsome, but there was something about him that looked wrong to me. I couldn't put my finger on it. I think it was his eyes. They never stopped moving. There is a word in Italian, "skiveade," which means something makes your skin crawl, like a dirty bathroom.

Now we are *Padrini* and *Madrine* to baby Rosina . . . for life. Being godparents was a lifetime commitment to be taken seriously.

I was dressed in a beautiful white two-piece suite. The top was long and covered my butt. That's a big concern of mine. The dress had a lace overlay. The sun was shining and the stained glass colors reflected on the white suit as the light shone in. I looked like a saint.

The ceremony was beautiful. The priest held each baby high during the final blessing. Then, he passed the baby to the godparents, and we kissed them and passed them to the parents. My Nana cried through the entire thing. Anthony was her daughter's baby and Rosina was her first great-grandchild. When it was over we went outside to take pictures. Father Joe was thrilled to be in the photos. Nana insisted he come to the house for the party, and he accepted. This was customary and we knew he expected it.

We all went back to Auntie Lilly's house for the christening party. It was a great turnout. There was so much food. We had lasagna, baked ziti, meatballs, sausage, and more. All of the women wore colorful aprons over their dresses. We worked to get the food on the tables, and then we joined the guests.

Gemma and I went upstairs to change baby Rosie out of her christening gown. We were sitting on the bed on either side of the baby when Carlo came in. He said, "Hello, lovely ladies."

I saw him look at Gemma and poke his head toward the doorway, as if to ask her to leave. Gemma said, "Lena, you bring Rosie outside when you are finished changing her, okay?"

I said, "Sure, Gemma." I wasn't too pleased about being trapped in the bedroom with Carlo. I stood up rather than sit on the bed. After that, he stared at my ass while I was bent over Rosie. He finally said, "So, Lena, are you seeing anybody special?"

I said, "I think he's special right now. It's not a lifetime commitment."

"So, is it that guy named Greg, outside in the yard?"

After thinking about this for a few seconds, I wondered what gives here? Since when is he concerned about my social life? I got a father. I don't need another one.

He didn't wait for me to answer. "I don't think he's Italian. Does your dad know that?"

I was speechless.

He went on to say, "I think that a nice Italian girl like you should consider dating someone who is the same ethnic background."

Now, I was fuming. When I finally composed myself, I asked him, "What's this really about, Carlo?"

He said, "Lena, I think it would be nice if you and I dated."

I finally got the message. This was a threat. I was quickly putting the connection together with Uncle Mikey's situation, having the truckload of appliances stolen. I was payback. I was getting really mad now.

I turned around to face him, holding baby Rosie.

I was very controlled when I told him, "Carlo, you don't scare me. If that was your way of asking me for a date, you're going to have to do better than that. Next time you want to ask me out, you can ask me like a gentleman, or better yet, call me on the phone."

I clutched baby Rosie to my chest, and with my head high I marched out of the room, swishing just a little bit.

Out in the yard, my dad was sitting with Joey Scarpella, Myrtle "The Turtle," and Jimmy "Bags" DeMaria. They must have been talking business because they got quiet as I came closer.

"Hello, bellezza," my dad said. "Let me see that beautiful baby." He took Rosie from my arms and held her high. She giggled like the little princess that she was. I kissed everyone around the table. Dad said, "Lena, Carlo was looking for you earlier."

"Oh, he found me. I'm not sure what the heck he's thinking. He followed me into the bedroom upstairs, but he doesn't scare me. Carlo thinks he can muscle me into dating him," I said. "He's barking up the wrong tree. I don't scare that easily. He thinks because his family has a corner on some of the 'goods' that move around and Uncle Mike is in trouble, I'm just going to cave in and say, 'Oh yes,

Carlo. Whatever you say, Carlo.' "

After I said all this, Dad looked a little embarrassed. Myrtle and Jimmy laughed out loud.

Jimmy "Bags" said, "Oh, I think Carlo has met his match."

"You stick up for yourself real good, Lena," Jimmy said. "It's good you're not afraid of Carlo."

Just then Uncle Paulie called my name and I moved on to show Rosie off to all of my uncles who were sitting together: Joe, Sam, Pete, John, and Paulie. Only Uncle Mike was missing. That made me sad.

Memo and Paulie motioned me aside and asked, "What gives with Carlo trying to corner you all day?"

I shrugged my shoulders, "I'm not sure. I don't know if he was trying to ask me out, or if he was showing off because his family has so much muscle in the business. But he doesn't scare me. I'm going to talk to my dad about this. I don't understand why he has this sudden interest in me."

Memo looked very serious.

"What! What do you want to say, Memo?" I said.

"Well, Lena, you know he was moved up in the family recently. I'm glad you're going to talk to your dad about it before you say 'no' to Carlo."

Oh, shit. Now what. This gave me a bad feeling. "Has he been 'made?' " I asked. "Does this mean that I have to kiss his ass?"

Memo said, "No, but it's the next step up."

Memo ruined my day. I picked up a basket and started to clear up some dishes and glasses. Greg saw me and came over to help. He took the basket out of my hands and I continued to load it with dishes.

He followed me around and finally said, "Lena, is something wrong? We haven't seen much of each other today. I know you have been helping Auntie Lilly and Gemma. I know this is a big party. I wondered if someone upset you. You had that look that could kill."

I had seen Greg sitting with my uncles earlier. They looked like they were having a good time and I didn't want to spoil his day by telling him about Carlo.

"I'm just tired, Greg."

He carried the basket inside for me and I walked him to his car. He kissed me good-bye and I went back inside. He was probably the nicest guy I'd ever met. I didn't want to hurt him.

Sure enough, when I went back inside, Carlo was standing in the kitchen, leaning against the doorframe. My stomach turned over when I saw him. The overpowering smell of his cheap aftershave mixed with the food aromas didn't help.

He said to me, "Okay, Lena, you win. Will you please go out with me on Saturday?"

Now I was speechless again. I already had plans with Greg on Saturday. I mean, we weren't going steady, and we were far from engaged, but I have never been the kind of person who could date more than one guy at a time.

"Carlo, I have plans for Saturday," I said.

"Okay, how about Friday?" he said.

"I'm staying at my Nana's on Friday."

"Can you stay with her another night?"

Now I saw how determined he was. Now I have to think about how to handle this seriously.

"You know I'm dating Greg. Why do you think I would date someone else? That's just not nice, Carlo. I wouldn't do that to you if you were dating someone else first."

He said, "Christ, Lena! Why are you making this so hard?"

"I just don't want you to think that you can threaten me in some way. Maybe I'll go out with you, but I need to make my own decisions about who and when. Do you understand, Carlo? Call me during the week and I'll think about this."

"Geez, Lena, It's not a marriage proposal. It's a date, for crying out loud. Whatever you say."

I continued to clean up in the kitchen while Carlo followed me around trying to be helpful. I finally went outside to get away from him. I found my dad and Uncle Pete sitting under a tree.

Dad said, "Well, Lena, I see that Carlo found you again. What did he have to say?"

"He wants me to go out with him, Dad. I have to ask you something and I want you to be honest with me."

"I will, Lena. I'll always be honest with you."

"Am I payment for the shipment that Uncle Mikey was responsible for losing?"

I could see my dad was giving his answer serious thought.

He finally said, "I would never do that to you, Lena. I won't lie to you. But I have to be honest about this situation. It would make it easier on the family if you would consider dating Carlo. There are a lot of things that have happened. I'll tell you that I met with the Bazzoli family before I agreed to let Carlo ask you to go out. They agreed that if you didn't like him, the deal would be off and we would find another way to pay them back. This is up to you, Baby. I explained this to Niko Bazzoli. He agreed that it should be your choice. This is not the old country."

I could feel the lump in my throat starting and I swallowed it hard. I started pacing in front of them. I finally answered, "I'm going to go out with him. If he makes me nuts, or forces me to do anything I don't want to, I'll . . . I'll let you know."

"That's fair enough, sweetheart," Dad said.

Geez, this being "connected" was a pain in the ass. It's okay when you're a kid and you don't understand. I'm understanding more than I really wanted to know.

Carlo called on Monday. I told Ma, "Tell him I'm at the TV station."

Carlo called on Tuesday. I told Ma to tell him I was at Gemma's house. Wednesday, when Carlo called, I told Ma to ask him what time he was picking me up on Friday.

This had really upset me. These obligations were going to kill me. I had to be my best for the next day's TV show, but I knew I'd be tossing and turning all night.

On Monday, the day after the christening, my *Tortured Souls* soap opera was making its color TV debut. There was a lot of pressure on all of us to look our best. I was very stressed out over the confrontation with Carlo and being forced into dating him; I know I didn't look like my usual adorable self.

When I got to my dressing room Greg was waiting at the door. One look from him and I thought I was going to cry. I get like that when I haven't slept well. I could cry over a broken fingernail. I pulled myself together and forced a smile.

"Lena, what gives? You just aren't your happy self this morning."

"Greg, I got up late and didn't sleep well. I need to get myself put together for the show."

He accepted that and I went inside my dressing room. Once inside I put my back against the door and looked over at my dressing table mirror. Geez, I looked like hell. I had a lot of work to do on this face if everyone was going to see me in color today. I had no sooner covered the dark circles under my eyes when Beth, the other female costar, came in. We shared a dressing room with separate makeup tables. She was perky and as cheerful as hell. She just chattered on and on about our first Technicolor show. I was lucky that she was so absorbed in herself that she never looked at me.

"What colors did the director decide we should wear today?" She chirped.

"I am wearing the deep purple outfit hanging on the door. You are supposed to wear the gold suit on the rack by your closet."

"Oh, that's great. Being a blond, I never get to wear the dark colors. I just love that gold suit."

While she chattered away I continued to apply makeup base, powder, eyeliner, false eyelashes, eye shadow, mascara, and whatever else I could find in my bag of tricks. I pinned my hair up and curled the tendrils with a curling iron. When I got done the result wasn't bad at all. I had just worked a darned miracle and turned a hag into a TV star. I silently thanked Max Factor for the miracle of makeup.

We got the "five minutes" call and walked out of the dressing room. When we got on set, everyone applauded us because we looked so amazing for our Technicolor debut. That's a very good thing.

My big scene that day was an attempt to break up with Johnny Roman. In the script, he was a married man and I'd had enough of the sordid affair.

My real life was such a wreck that I had no trouble being an emotional bombshell. I cried real tears and Johnny held me in his arms. He spoke his lines so sincerely because of my outpouring. Then he got his hankie out of his pocket and that wasn't in the script. Thank goodness for waterproof mascara.

6

When the credits rolled, I got a standing ovation from the crew. The director, Mr. Latmen, hugged me and kissed me on the cheek. "Well done, Lena! You were so convincing!"

My life was probably a better soap opera than the scriptwriters could produce.

It was a whirlwind week and the reviews were fantastic. I got a contract locked in without waiting for my six months. Management notified Susan that her job had been filled while she was on maternity leave. I'm sure she had been watching the show and figured that out before the call came from the station.

On Friday, Carlo picked me up in a snappy black car. I pretended that I didn't hear him honk the horn and that made him come to the door. He was very polite to my ma and dad. I could see that Dad was a little sad about this, since I was part of the deal with Niko Bazzoli.

Since I didn't care where we were going, I didn't have much to say. Finally, Carlo asked me if I liked veal. I guess he felt the need to make small talk. I told him that I hadn't eaten veal since I found out that they starved baby cows and only gave them milk so they would be tender.

He looked stunned and said, "I didn't know that."

He took me to the Como Inn: very pricy, very Italian place. He ordered a bottle of Chianti. When the waiter came, he asked if he could order dinner for me.

"Sure, why not," I said. All the while I was thinking he should have got a haircut.

Carlo ordered pork scaloppini, instead of veal, Beef alla Siciliano, and an appetizer of Bracciole. Soup and bread and salad came first. Since I was very nervous, I drank the wine first, and Carlo kept filling my glass. It always makes me talk out of my head. The first thing I told him was that he needed a haircut.

He said, "Lena, that's very forward of you to say." But he was smiling.

"If you're taking a girl out for dinner, you should look in the mirror. That's not a bad suit, but it would look better if you wore a different tie and got a decent haircut."

Then he started laughing and said, "Your father said you have a mind of your own. What else would you change?" Then he ordered another bottle of wine. I should have known that was a bad idea.

Dinner was really nice, as far as I can remember. I know we laughed a lot and the waiters kept bringing more food and filling our glasses. That's all I remember.

When I woke the next morning, I had the covers over my head. Moving my eyes seemed to be a very painful. I didn't feel well. Then I ran my hand along my leg and sure enough, I was wearing my stockings. After further investigation of my attire, I felt my garter belt, panties and bra.

"Oh, shit," I said out loud. I felt for the pillow next to me and there was no one there. Thank God! I think I said that out loud.

When I left my house last night, I was nearly as pure as the driven snow. At least I knew I was a virgin. Yes, still a virgin. Now I wasn't sure. I found my purse under the nightstand and dug out my makeup bag. I stumbled into the bathroom and turned on the shower. I didn't know what to think. I know! I'll call Mona. She's had sex plenty of times I put the bathrobe on and locked the bedroom door. I stretched the cord to the bathroom, dialed her number, and told her what happened.

"How do I know if I've had sex?

"What? She said. You don't know if you had sex?"

"No, Mona. How can I be sure?"

"Check the sheets, Lena."

"Huh?"

"The sheets."

"I don't see anything on the sheets."

"Well, then you didn't have sex."

"Oh, good," I said. "Are you sure? Because when I have sex for the first time, I want it to be with someone I like. This isn't what I had in mind at all."

Mona said, "Where are you?"

When I told her, she said, "Cripes, Lena. You're a mess. That's disgusting," and hung up.

After I got dressed I made the bed and went into the kitchen to find Carlo fully dressed and reading the morning paper. He had a silk dressing gown over his clothes.

"Good morning, Lena. I made some coffee and toast."

Now Carlo was the dreaded kidnapper. How would I deal with this? I didn't go home last night and I didn't call my parents. What else happened?

"What a great evening that was, Lena. I can't remember when I had such a wonderful time. I really needed the laughs. I took the liberty of calling your dad. I told him that you fell asleep in the car and I put you on the sofa to sleep it off. He thanked me. I didn't tell him anything else."

This rotten dog was going to let me think we did the wild thing. I know I didn't. Mona gave me a very vivid description of the physical signs to look for. I wanted to go home now.

"Carlo, can you take me home please?"

"Sure, Lena. Whenever you're ready."

"I'm ready now, Carlo."

When I walked into the kitchen, my ma and dad were sitting at the kitchen table. My dad looked like he was going to cry when he saw me. The guilt he was feeling was written on his face.

I sat down with them and said, "Daddy, look at me." He slowly picked up his head and looked me in the eyes.

"Carlo got me drunk and put me in his bed . . . alone. That's all that happened. He wants me to think that we, well you know. But it didn't happen.

I would know," I said knowingly. "I'm going to take some aspirin and study my script. I'm a soap opera queen, you know."

I could see the relief on my parent's faces—my dad especially. He actually smiled. The worse thing that had happened last night was that Carlos saw my fat ass in my underwear.

I had no sooner closed the door to my room when the phone rang. It was Paulie.

"Hey, you wanna come to The Club tonight?" I'm singing until 1 a.m. because it's Saturday. It's going to be a fun night. Meet me in the bar. Call Greg."

I said, "Not so fast, Paulie. I've got to study my lines for tomorrow's show."

Paulie said, "Tomorrow is Sunday. Take a nap, princess. Be there about 9 p.m.

Paulie was right. Life could be that simple, if I wanted it to be. I said, "Okay, I'll call Greg and see you about 9 p.m."

Greg answered on the first ring and said, "Lena, I missed you last night. I haven't been alone on a Friday night since I met you."

Geez, the guilt that men put us through!

"Pick me up about eight thirty. I've got some stuff to do today, then I'm going to study my lines for a while and take a nap."

Greg was at my door at 8:30 p.m. He always picked me up right on time. My parents were always fond of Greg, but now that they knew I didn't bond with Carlo Bazzoli, my ma kissed his cheeks when he came in. My dad patted him on the back and said, "Greg, how you doin'. Good to see you."

When we got to Greg's car, he planted a big fat wet kiss on me. I said, "Whoa! Thanks for the greeting! I guess you missed me"

He said, "Lena, I really missed you last night. I never realized how much our time together meant to me."

All the way to The Club, Greg kept kissing my hand like I was some kind of real princess. I was feeling so guilty about lying to him about my date with Carlo, and I knew that I'd have to come clean eventually. I'd talk to Mona first.

Paulie was just belting out the last bars of "Jezebel" when we came through the door. The crowd was going wild and most of the ladies were standing, whispering, "Oh, he sounds just like Frankie Lane."

Paulie motioned for us to go next door to The Club. Mona had saved us a spot. She rolled her eyes when she saw me and hugged Greg like she meant it. We ordered drinks and squeezed into the corner booth. Once Paulie got there, she pushed me out of my seat and said, "Time to go to the ladies room"

"Mona, I don't want to talk about last night."

"You called me and told me you were in Carlo's bed! What the hell was that all about?"

"It was a deal I made."

"Yeah, a deal with the devil."

"It was because of Uncle Mikey. Payback for the goods that were stolen."

"Holy crap. Really? You mean you had to have sex with Carlo as payback for the goods?"

"We didn't have sex, Mona. I woke up in his bed after he got me drunk on wine. Mona, I'm thinking he might like guys."

"Oh, and why would you think that?"

"I don't know. Why didn't he take advantage of me? I noticed his manners last night. I'm just not sure. There's something about him."

"Maybe he's a nicer guy than we are giving him credit for."

"I'll tell Greg about this. I'll ask him to dance and we'll have a chance to talk. You keep Paulie busy."

"You'll want Paulie to know eventually. He has to know because he's family."

"Oh, I guess that's true." I said

When we got back to the guys, they looked like they were telling stories of their own. I danced with Greg first and he got all mushy and romantic. Then I told him about "Carlo, The Evil Kidnapper." He got real quiet at first. Then he looked really mad.

"You could have told me, Lena. I would have understood."

"Greg, you would have had time to fester and get mad, then you would have understood. I know it would have hurt you. And I didn't want to do that.

"Give me a little more credit than that."

"Let's go talk to Paulie. I really should tell him too."

By the time we sat back down, Mona had told Paulie the story. He was so mad.

"Lena, if there is anything freaky about this guy, I'll find out. I'll put the word out on the street that I need information. I better not find out that he took pictures of you in your underwear or something. I'll have to kill him.

"Oh, shit. I never even thought of that. Paulie, what should I do?"

"Don't do nothin' at all. I'm gonna take care of this. You just act like it never happened."

For the rest of the night I couldn't think of anything but Carlo in his silk bathrobe and his slicked back hair, with me in my underwear.

Did I see any evidence of photography? Was there a camera anywhere in the room? *Maybe I could kill Carlo myself. That's it! That would solve everything. My boss, Mr. Latmen, is Jewish but I heard that he had some mob connections. Maybe he could get me a gun.* I would probably lose my mind before this was over. No one would have to worry about Carlo, Greg's feelings, or any photographs of me in my underwear. One more drink and a last dance and I had to get the heck out of there.

When I came in through the back door, I saw flowers on the kitchen table.

The card read *"Thanks. Love, Carlo."* I'm glad my ma and dad were in bed so I didn't have to answer any questions. I didn't know what the heck he was thanking me for. Maybe he was thanking me for not telling everyone he's a horse's ass . . .or maybe he was thanking me for not waking up during the night and choking him with my bare hands. That would have been a neat trick since he got me stinking drunk and I passed out. Paulie said, *"Act like this never happened."* Okay, that's what I was going do.

My soap opera show, *Tortured Souls* started at 1 p.m. I usually got to the studio around 10:30 a.m. That gave me time to go over any changes in the script and do my hair and makeup. When I got this job, I was the "Hair and Makeup Specialist." Now that I'm permanently employed I'm pretty sure that somebody should be doing my hair and makeup for me.

I sent Greg to see if I could talk to Mr. Latmen for a few minutes. Latmen knocked on the door and opened it at the same time. That's his style.

"What's up, Lena? You doing okay?" he said.

I said, "Sure, Mr. Latmen. I just wondered if we could hire a makeup and hair specialist, like we had when Susan was here. Namely, me."

"Oh, sure, Lena. That's not a problem. Why didn't you say so a long time ago? You got anybody in mind, or should I call the agency?"

"Let's call the agency. I think we are really in the big time now that the show is in color. I want us girls to look our best."

"Lena, I'm thinking that we should have the guys in the show powder their noses too. I've been noticing that other shows are doing that to the men."

At that moment, I had a brain freeze. My mind clicked back to seeing Carlo's face by candlelight when Latmen said that thing about guys powdering their noses. Did I see traces of face powder on Carlo's cheeks in the restaurant?

Who in the heck would I ask about this? I looked at Latmen and said, "How would I know if a guy is . . . you know, doesn't like girls?"

He said, "Lena, what the hell are you talking about? I'm saying that guys on TV wear makeup all the time."

I said, "Mr. Latmen, I need to make a phone call. Will you excuse me?"

"Broads," he said, and left the room shaking his head.

I called Mona and there was no answer. I called Paulie. Forget it, because he sleeps like the dead. Who can I talk to about this? Just then there was a knock on the door. I peeked out and saw Greg. I pulled him inside and locked the door behind him.

His face got all red and he said, "Wow, Lena. I'm glad to see you too."

"Greg, how do you know if a guy is . . . oh, hell, a sissy?"

"Do you mean queer, as in "likes boys?"

"Yes, that's exactly what I mean"

"Who are we talking about?"

"Carlo Bazzoli, that's who."

"Lena, you're going to have to start at the beginning. I don't know what you're talking about. Carlo is a mob guy's son."

"Greg, we need to go out of the studio after the show for lunch today. I have to talk to you about something."

"Good," Greg said. "That's fine, Lena. You calm down for now and we'll go out right after today's show."

I managed to get through the show. It's a good thing that I'm always supposed to look like a damsel in distress. My character is lovelorn and sometimes forsaken by the married man that she is having an affair with. That overall appearance certainly did apply to my frame of mind.

When the show was over, Greg and I walked down the street to a local deli and sat in the back. I reviewed my sordid story and included the possibility that Carlo might be of another persuasion.

Greg agreed that my suspicion about Carlo being queer was very possible. I told him Paulie knew the whole story.

"What should I do, Greg? I know he's going to ask me out again. What am I going to tell him? What do I tell my dad?"

"If he's queer, he needs you as a cover. You could be very valuable to him. This could also be a benefit to your dad as far as his 'family connections.' I'm going to talk to Paulie about this."

"Greg, I don't want my dad to know about this queer thing."

"Lena, honey, your dad will have to know eventually, but we have to keep it quiet on the street and away from the Bazzoli's. It's better that your dad knows that you're seeing Carlo to cover his male preference than to think that you'll continue to see Carlo and become emotionally involved with him. That would really hurt your dad."

"Oh, Greg, I feel so much better. Thank you for understanding."

"You're not getting off so easy, kiddo. After I discuss this with Paulie, you and I have some serious talking to do."

"Oh, I suspect that would probably have something to do with the nightie and toothbrush that I carry around in my purse and haven't used at your apartment yet."

"You're on the right track, Lena."

I told Greg that I would walk back to the studio parking lot alone. I needed to take a walk and clear my head. I had some thinking to do. My life had gotten very complicated in the last few weeks.

I walked along with no destination in mind. I found myself in front of a beauty shop called "Jen's Den of Beauty." I needed a change.

I walked in and said, "Can I get a haircut without an appointment?"

The girl at the desk looked up and a stunned look of disbelief was on her face. "Aren't you that actress from *Tortured Souls*? Oh, my gosh! Jen, look who's here!"

Jen said, "I am so excited to meet you. Can we get your autograph?"

Someone had a camera and started snapping pictures.

"Is that okay? Taking pictures, I mean," Jen said.

I said, "Sure, that's just fine, but can I get a haircut?"

After much deliberation, I decided to have it cut short. This was a huge change for me. I was going for the "Gina Lollobrigida" look.

When they finished, I thought it looked terrific. I walked back to the studio parking lot to get my car.

When the guard saw me he said, "Wow, Miss Delatora, you look fantastic."

The next morning, when I got to the TV station, everyone saw me and got really quiet when I walked into the rehearsal area. Mr. Latmen looked at me like I had shaved my head.

"What the hell have you done?"

"It's just a haircut. Does it look bad?"

"Jeez, Lena, you can't just go get a haircut. It has to be worked into the script. Somebody get me a fake ponytail! Get the set designers in here. We need a beauty shop front. Lena, go find a way to get that ponytail attached to the back of your head. Don't come out until you look like you did yesterday!"

I was near tears as I turned and walked to my dressing room. A little later, Greg came in with a fake ponytail.

"Lena, don't be upset. Your looks are not your own when you are on TV every day. The public expects you to be the person that they know and love when they turn their soap opera on."

"I guess I wasn't thinking. I just needed a change. I wanted to do something to make myself feel better."

Greg said, "Today when the show ends, we'll shoot you in front of a beauty shop, staring into the window. Tomorrow when your hair is short, it will all fit in.

"I'm beginning to think that I don't have any part of my life that is entirely my own."

After Mr. Latmen's fit about my short haircut, the fake ponytail was attached to the back of my head after it was all slicked down. Later, they filmed some footage of me in front of the mock beauty shop set. It would be part of the next day's show.

The day after that, I could look like Gina Lollobrigida.

7

The following day, I studied my lines, jumped in the shower and headed for the TV station. This new hairdo was the best idea I had ever had. I could towel dry it and it was all big ringlets. By the time I got out of my car at the studio I had a head full of curly hair. Some of my friends are still ironing their hair. Geez, I'm glad I never fell into that trap. I used to roll it in with empty juice cans when I was in high school. That didn't last long because I like to sleep too much. If you used those big cans, you had to sleep with your head hanging off the bed.

But I digress . . .

Everyone at the TV station loved my new look. Mr. Latmen finally smiled. That isn't very common. Usually he has no space between his eyebrows. When he's in a good mood, his eyebrows have a small space in the middle. When I saw him walking toward me I got a little nervous. That's when he smiled and I saw the space.

"They love your hair, Lena. I got tons of phone calls. It's a hit! Before you know it, every woman who sees it will want the "Angie haircut" from *Tortured Souls.*

————)(O)(————

Greg and my Uncle Paulie were on a mission to find out about Carlo's personal dating preferences. We thought he liked boys. I didn't know how they would determine this without ruining his reputation. That would not be good for either of our families—I mean the mob families, of course.

We all met in the lounge at Riggio's just before closing. I drove my own car and Greg picked Paulie up. When I walked in, I nearly doubled over laughing. They were both wearing black pants and sweaters.

I said, "What the heck are you two dressed for? Halloween?"

They looked a little embarrassed.

"Well," Greg said, "If we're going to follow Carlo, we have to be sure he can't see us."

"You have blond hair and you are 6' 3". He knows Paulie. How are you going to disguise that?"

"We have black stocking caps. And we'll scrunch down in the car."

"How do you know where Carlo is tonight?"

"I called his dad and asked if Carlo would like to meet for drinks tonight at the Club," Paulie said.

I said, "Gee Paulie, did you leave your name and phone number, just in case he said 'yes.' "

Paulie said, "No, Lena. I was counting on him telling me where Carlo is tonight. He said, "I'll give you Carlo's home number and you can ask him yourself."

"Then what did you do, genius?"

"I called his house and some guy said Carlo wasn't home," Paulie said.

"Get the car, you dummies. We're going to wait outside Carlo's house."

Sure enough, a few minutes after we got there Carlo and some guy came out and got into a car together. We followed them to some seedy street where they went into the side door of a building. We waited about an hour and Carlo came out with the same guy. They were laughing and they had their arms around each other's shoulders.

"I've seen all I need to see. How about you two?" I said.

"Yep. He's definitely with a guy," Greg said. "They could just be buddies."

I rolled my eyes in disbelief. Could these two be any cornier? What kind of comment was that? It was hard to believe they could function in the adult world.

"Okay, I don't want this to go any further. You both understand that?"

"Sure, Lena," the dummies said in unison.

I wasn't sure what I was planning to do with this information. Carlo was a nice enough guy and I had no desire to hurt him. We had our differences because he was acting like he thought a tough guy should. I had to think about this. My gut feeling told me that I could use my newfound knowledge to my advantage. My street smarts told me to take my time. I was tired. These two knuckleheads were like a Laurel and Hardy comedy act. They dropped me off at my car and I headed for home. I slept so hard that I didn't hear the phone ring. I saw a note on the kitchen table in the morning.

Lena —Carlo called tonight about 10 pm. He wants you to call him tomorrow.
Phone No. AV-3-4649

Ma

Did he see us? Geez, I hoped not. Life was getting too complicated.

How did this all happen?

The followingevening after work, I ran some errands and bought some new cosmetics. I decided to stop by Nana's. I want to talk to her about Carlo. She had known his grandma for many years, maybe she would have some ideas that I could talk out with her.

Even though it was late, I was sure she would be glad to see me. She had that intuition that comes with age. She always knew when family was stopping by, and she always had food. It didn't matter if you were hungry or not, she pulled out all the food out as soon as you sat down. She was also very wise about most matters. I could talk to her about anything. Sure enough, as soon as I touched the doorknob, she opened the door.

"Hello, Bella. I thought it was you. Come-ona inside. You wanna something to eat? You wanna sleep here tonight? Should I call you mama?"

I suspected that my Nana never slept. I've never been able to prove this. I think she changed into nightclothes at a specific time, but she never really closed her eyes.

"Sure, Nana. Are you tired? Let's talk first."

"I'm never too tired for you. Lena, what's wrong? You look worried."

"Nana, do you remember Angelo?"

I need to interject here: Nana came from Italy in 1909. Many of the families who sailed to the United States and arrived at Ellis Island together had remained lifelong friends. My Nana befriended a young man named Angelo. He had no mother or father, and no known family. Angelo was *Finocchio.* In other words, he was queer. Angelo spent a lot of time at Nana's house when I was a kid. They did a lot of baking, cooking, and talking about the old country. No one ever said *Finnochio* out loud. My uncles used to tease him about his dapper clothes and slicked down hair. He took it all with good humor. One day Angelo went to the butcher shop for Nana. No one ever saw him again.

"Yes, Bella. I get sad when I think of him. Whadda you think happed to him, Lena?"

I wanted to say that I thought he met up with some thugs who didn't like his looks, and someone bumped him off, but I kept that thought to myself.

"I don't know, Nana. I think maybe he left town with your $20 and the pork roast." That made her laugh.

"Nana, I think that Carlo Bazzoli *is Finnochio.*"

"Well, Bella I don't think so," she said too quickly. "I see him at parties and on the street and he doesn't act like Angelo."

She got very quiet after that. I could tell that she was giving this some serious thought. I got up from the table and helped myself to some of the food that magically appeared on the stove. I put a little plate of pasta in front of her too.

Nana said, "I think sometimes people are different. Maybe *finnochio,* maybe not. Sometimes people need a friend who can think that they are okay just the way they are."

We both got quiet for a while. Nana finally said, "Bella, why you ask me this? Are you in trouble with Carlo?"

"Oh no, Nana. Carlo and I are friends."

"Oh! That's a-nice! I'm glad to hear that. You wanna some more pasta?"

I knew what Nana was saying. She was telling me in her own way that she suspected the same thing that I knew. Nana's wisdom included not only what she said, but also what she didn't say. Her lady friends, Dona Mariella and Dona Maria, all had plenty of secrets. They played innocent and kept quiet, but they were a wealth of knowledge.

We talked a while longer about family stuff, then she sent me to bed. In the morning, she was up before me, frying bread and eggs. I smelled the fresh coffee as soon as I stepped out of the shower. I started the day with a firm resolution. I planned to talk to Carlo as a friend. I would help him keep his secret. Sometimes everyone needs a friend.

I called Carlo after the show was over the following afternoon. I tried to sound as casual as possible. I had thought a lot about how I was going to approach the subject of his being *finnochio.* Greg and I discussed this with Paulie and Mona. I wanted to be sure that everyone who knew, or suspected Carlo's "choice," was sworn to secrecy, and could befriend him if necessary. I felt confident about my friends and family. After all, the world was changing.

Carlo answered the phone and I said, "Hi. It's Lena. You left a message for me?"

"Lena! I'm glad you called. I was wondering if I could see you Saturday night?"

Oh, I've been thinking about you, Carlo. That's a good idea. I'm really glad you called me."

He was very quiet. I thought I must have said something that he didn't expect. My thoughts were racing. Should I say something? Did I offend him?

I quickly said, "How's your dad? Is the family okay?" I thought, *Lena, you are such a chooch. Why can't you keep your mouth shut?* The biggest problem I have is that I don't have a thought filter that works yet. I'm working on that.

Teachers have told me that, friends and other adults have told me that. I don't have a time delay between my brain and my mouth.

Carlo finally said, "Lena, that's so nice to hear. I was wondering if I offended you the last time we were together."

I wanted to say, *"Oh no, Carlo. Just because I woke up in your bed, alone, in my underwear, why should I be offended?"*

I controlled the little filter trap thing in my brain and clenched my jaws.

"Anyway," he said, continuing his sentence, "I though it would be nice if I fixed dinner for you at my place tonight. Maybe I'll make some lasagna—nothing too fancy. I'll come to pick you up about 6 p.m., if it's okay."

My head did little bleeps and hiccups while I digested his. I felt like a puppet in some bad "Punch and Judy" episode. I was the one getting punched.

"I would like that, Carlo," I said without thinking.

My ma was baking bread that afternoon. I asked her to make a loaf for me to take with me for dinner at Carlo's house. She glazed the top and added sesame seeds. When I came into the kitchen after I got dressed, she had the bread in a basket lined with a napkin. I think she must have seen that on TV.

I said, "Nice touch, Mama. Maybe I should have picked up a bottle of wine." Mama made a dash for the basement door. I knew she was going to bring up a bottle of Dad's homemade red.

Carlo was there at 6 p.m. sharp. He had roses in one hand and some cigars in the other. He handed these to my ma and dad. *Now, this is really making me nuts. What am I supposed to think?* I locked my jaws and smiled. Carlo helped me on with my sweater and opened the door for me, while my parents stood in the kitchen with frozen smiles, as if I was leaving for the army. I know my ma was thinking about my Uncle Mikey. My dad was probably thinking that his mob negotiations had prostituted his daughter. Uncle Mikey had been living in exile in upper Michigan for several months.

We'd had to send him away because of the truckload of stolen goods he was transporting got stolen. I was part of the "payback" to bring him home.

I had the bread and wine. I felt like I was going to have a religious experience. Geez, I hope not. I've had enough surprises lately. I could smell the lasagna when he opened the door in the bottom hall—a little heavy on the garlic. I'll have to bring mouthwash to the studio tomorrow. My leading man already mentioned my breath once before. I brought him meatballs the next day and he hasn't complained since.

The table was set in Carlo's little dinette. *I still feel like I'm cheating on Greg, even though Carlo likes men*, I thought.

He opened Dad's wine and poured us each a little glass. I held my glass up and said, "To friendship." He looked a little surprised when we clinked glasses and said, "salute." I sliced the bread on a plate and sat down while he brought the lasagna to the table.

Carlo's apartment was as neat as a pin. He and Greg could compete for the "Better Homes and Gardens" award. The only difference was that Greg's ma decorated his place. Carlo did this by himself. Very nice, though, I've got no issue with any guy having a nice apartment. Vince's apartment looked as if it had been burglarized.

Carlo said, "Lena, please make yourself at home. You know where everything is."

I wondered, *What the heck did I do the last time I was here, that he thinks I know where everything is?*

This was exhausting. I couldn't continue to work this through my little brain. Maybe I should just relax.

I asked, "Can I have another a glass of wine?" While at the same time thinking, *You must really be losing your little mind, after what happened last time you had dinner together.* But I drank the wine anyway. I broke the ice by saying, "Carlo, I have a confession to make." He tried to interrupt me, but I continued . . .

"Don't be angry, I want to help. I know how hard this is for you. Maybe we could be friends." I said all this after two glasses of wine.

That was the icebreaker that he needed. Carlo cleared his throat and said, "Lena, this is something I've never talked about and I don't want you to say anything until I'm finished. I not the person that you think I am. I am not 'Machismo,' I am not a 'womanizer.' I am not even the person that my father thinks I am. This isn't easy for me. My preference for partners appears to be men, but I really like women too. I know this makes me some kind of freak. I haven't had a lot of experience, but I think I lean toward liking men more."

I stopped him by putting up my hand. "Carlo, I know."

It was his turn to look startled. "How did you know, Lena?"

"I happened to be out one night. I was passing your house. You were with a man when you went out."

His face darkened and he looked down at his plate before he spoke again.

He told me that no one in his family knew about him. Being *finnocho* was not something a tough guy's family could tolerate. He had spent all of his life sneaking around trying to keep everyone convinced that he was the tough son of a mob boss, and ready to kick ass whenever he was needed. The family would expect him to get married soon, since it had recently been decided that he would be "made."

I had been hatching a plan in my head. I told him, "Carlo, what if you had a female roommate? She could come and go as she pleased. Once in a while you could take her to family functions. She could be your decoy."

I could tell he was digesting this while I kept talking.

"Eventually, you could 'break up' with her. Your family would be distracted for a while and it would take the pressure off you to get married for a while."

Carlo said, "Lena, are you suggesting that we live together?"

I wanted to say, *Hell no! I'm trying to get out of this mess.* But the little thought filter that I installed kicked in.

Instead I said, "No, we need to keep our eyes open and make some discrete inquiries for this female companion."

We spent the next two hours discussing several scenarios. We had to find the right girl. She had to be needy, but somewhat independent. She had to be cute, but not a bombshell. We were on the right track. Now I was sufficiently drunk, but still able to request my desire to get the hell out of there and go home.

Mama heard me come in and she said, "Lena, is that you?"

I said, "No, Ma. It's Elvis."

I heard her tell my dad, "I think she had too much wine again."

My acting career was moving along very nicely. Not only was I helping to develop my character in *Tortured Souls*, I was doing live commercials for shampoo at the end of the show. My new short haircut was attracting a lot of good mail. It took some quick wardrobe changing and fresh makeup. Mr. Latmen finally let me hire a girl that was called the "Personal Assistant" to Lena Delatora; she would be helping Beth too. I was making almost as much for the commercial as I was for the soap opera. When I got the job on the show, I thought I was there to audition for a commercial spot. Isn't it funny how things turn out?

Paulie called me when I got home. He wanted Greg and me to meet him in the bar at Riggio's tonight. Greg had family commitments, but he insisted that I go without him. I really didn't need his permission.

Paulie's singing gig was steady and he did longer sets with longer breaks in between. Mona kept him on a pretty short leash since they had gotten engaged. The girls really fell all over him. The pink Cadillac that he bought was a "chick magnet." Mona had a little framed picture of herself hanging from the mirror with a huge red Italian horn. I think she felt like she was staking her claim and the horn was warding off other chicks. I could keep Mona company while Paulie was performing and we always had plenty to talk about.

Mama and Nana were coming to hear Paulie later. I couldn't believe that Nana was going out so late, but Mama insisted that she come.

After two rum and cokes, we were feeling pretty sassy and decided to dance during one of the breaks. Mona and I were dancing and Paulie joined us on the floor. Some other guy joined us that I had never seen before. He was a pretty good dancer. He asked if he could join us in our booth and I said yes. I could tell that Paulie didn't like this very much. He liked Greg and he felt like he was my protector.

He pulled me out on the dance floor and said, "What's with you, Lena?" I said, "Paulie, I'm not married to Greg, you know. We don't have anything in writing and I'm not wearing his ring." His comment was, "Just don't leave with this guy. I've never seen him before."

I've got someone watching out for me all the time. With six uncles and a father, I felt like the president's daughter sometimes, or royalty. There are times that I want to just get crazy and do whatever I want.

When Paulie and I got back to the booth, the new guy stood up and shook hands with us. Mona introduced us all around. It turns out the guy's name is Gianno Bevalaqua, but he uses the name Gino. I could tell that Paulie was making mental notes about the name and he would send the scouts to check him out. Geez, what a life.

Paulie went back on to the stage. He was singing several songs tonight. They included Dean Martin and Tony Bennett hits.

I heard a lot of commotion at the front of the restaurant. We all turned to look and I could see my dad first, then my ma. Then I saw, UNCLE MIKEY! We all jumped up and started yelling and crying. No one cried as much as Nana. She was at the back of the family pack bawling her eyes out. "My Mikey, he's a-come home," she said over and over. It turned out that Gino was the driver who had brought Uncle Mikey home with his belongings. It was my guess that Carlo had put in a good word with his dad to get Uncle Mikey sent back.

Gino hung out with the family for the entire evening. Before the night was over, he had his arm around me. He mentioned that he had seen me on television. They got most of the Chicago stations in Wisconsin. Gino had his own trucking company. My mind was sorting all this out.

No more rum and Coke tonight. It was possible that he owned the truck that Mikey was driving when it got stolen. Gino was a good-looking guy. He was very tall with dark hair and lots of muscles. He was smooth, but not slick, and a nice dresser. He smelled good too. Was it possible that I was losing my mind? I danced with him several times during the evening.

My dad was chatting him up and Paulie appeared to be changing his disposition about this guy, since he found out he was one of the good guys. By the end of the evening, Gino was whispering "plans for the future" in my ear: the future being any time before morning.

Paulie and Mona had left for her apartment earlier in the evening. I had a key to Paulie's place. I still had the nightie and toothbrush in my purse. I had been fighting men off since I was in high school. Was it time to give it up? I was seriously considering this. My parents were busy slapping my Uncle Mike on the back. Nana was hanging on his arm. Mona and Paulie were gone. Gino's hand was at the small of my back while we danced. I could feel the muscles in his back, among other things. We slipped out without anyone noticing. We got in my car, since the truck he drove was the only vehicle available to him.

I was thinking, *It's a good thing I invested in a new car and got rid of the junk I had been driving.* I guess I didn't want Gino to think I was a loser. What did I care? But he already knew that I was a TV star. Did he really like me, or was he just out to scratch that itch? Could be both.

Things were getting pretty heated in the car. The windows were steaming up and he had his shirt unbuttoned. I finally said, "I have the key to my Uncle Paulie's house."

He said, "Lena, you have made me a happy man. I was going to suggest a hotel."

I answered, "A hotel might be better. I won't have to explain why I was at Paulie's house."

I let him drive. We drove out of the neighborhood and picked up the expressway. We checked into the Marriott near the airport.

Gino went inside to register and get the key. I was a confused, overheated mess. He got a room on the hotel's outside terrace. Later he told me he was thinking about me walking through the lobby in the morning. A local celebrity might be recognized.

We nearly undressed each other in the elevator going up to the room. There were no questions asked and no long conversation. We knew what we were there for. Our timing was perfect. It was meant to be. I knew this was the right man. I only had one night of awkward-almost-sex with *Nick*, my high school boyfriend. Now I was glad I never let him push me into having sex with him.

This was the man I was waiting for.

We woke up during the night, a tangle of arms and legs. Finally, we had some meaningful conversation.

Gino said, "Lena, you didn't tell me it was your first time."

I said, "I think it's my third or fourth time, now." Since I was a beginner, we practiced again.

In the morning, Gino woke up first. He told me it was about 7:30 a.m. He got up and showered and I pulled the covers over my head. He said, "It's your turn, babe. I'll get some food and coffee."

I came out of the bathroom wearing the hotel robe and a towel on my head. I smelled the food and coffee. Then I saw a beautiful pink sweater set on the bed. It had a pattern of white pearls on the front. I was so delighted!

"Gino! This is beautiful. Thank you so much."

" I stopped in the gift shop. I couldn't let you leave in the same clothes that you wore yesterday. I didn't know if you were going to the studio, or home. Either way, you shouldn't look like you didn't have a choice of what to wear."

I curled up on his lap and gave him a big smooch. He pulled the robe off my shoulders and I took the towel off my head.

"Easy, babe," he said. "I don't want to be on your dad's hit list. I'd better get you out of here."

Gino drove back to his truck in Riggio's lot. He leaned into the window and kissed me. "Can I see you tonight?"

"I would be disappointed if you didn't. I have to be at the TV station at ten thirty. The show airs at one. Do you have my number?"

"Oh, Lena, I've got your number, babe."

I had time to stop home first. I decided to wear the pink sweater set that I had on. I changed into a burgundy colored skirt. My ma smiled when I came in the back door.

"Hello, bella mia. You want some breakfast?"

I said, "No, Ma. I ate already."

"Daddy and I are trying to find out where that nice guy, Gino, is staying. Dad is going to call Niko Bazzoli this morning. I thought it would be nice to have him over for dinner tonight."

That's when I realized she had no idea where I was last night. She probably thought that I stayed at Paulie's because she knew I didn't like to drink and drive. He was usually at Mona's place anyway. I kept my mouth shut and smiled. Gee, that new thought filter is really working.

"I think that's a good idea. I danced with him last night. He seems very nice. He didn't say where he's staying. The Bazzoli's should know. I think that's who he works for."

"Well, it's settled then. I'll fix a nice dinner to thank him for bringing Uncle Mikey home."

I got to the T.V. station and went to my dressing room. A few minutes later, there was a knock on the door. The door opened a crack and I heard Greg say, "Lena, can I come in?"

I said "Sure. I'm dressed."

He came in carrying a huge bunch of roses. I felt myself panic. I hadn't even thought of Greg. My Personal Assistant, Penny, excused herself. Beth, my costar, smiled and said she was ready to go on, so she stepped outside the dressing room. Greg and I were alone. Then I read the card and it said, "Not bad for a beginner." No name, but I didn't need one. I could feel my face flush. I couldn't meet Greg's eyes.

Greg's smile looked kind of hurt. I asked him to sit down.

"Greg, I met someone. He's very special. I didn't know it was going to happen. It wasn't planned."

"Lena, I'm Jewish. We've always known my family wouldn't approve of our relationship long-term. My family would never tolerate my being serious about an Italian girl. I know your family is more forgiving. You have a League of Nations starting with all of your uncles marrying into different nationalities twenty years ago."

"Greg, I really care about you. I would never hurt you intentionally. This just happened."

"I guess that means that you finally wore that nightie that you carry around in your purse."

We both laughed at that. I didn't tell him that I never even took it out of my purse.

Greg said, "Tell me, Lena, is Penny Jewish?"

"No Greg, she's Italian."

He slapped himself in the forehead and said, "That figures!"

We got the "Five Minutes" call and prepared to exit. Beth met me outside the door and we stepped into the wings.

8

My costar Johnny looked especially dapper for the day's show. Good thing that I wasn't attracted to men with dirty blond hair. My hormones must have been in high gear from the night before. I returned Johnny's kisses with no problem. He was very surprised and tried to keep from smiling.

After the show he said, "Lena, you're not getting a crush on me, are you?"

I said, "You should be so lucky, Johnny."

Ma called me before I left the T.V. station. She said that Dad had called Niko Bazzoli and he asked Gino to call us. He'd be over for dinner about 7 p.m. She said, "Pick up Nana on your way home."

Well, that solved the problem of how I'll get to see Gino again.

He arrived at 7 p.m. sharp. He had pastries from the bakery, chocolates, cigars, and flowers. I know this is crazy, but my knees got weak when I saw him.

When everyone was finished kissing each other's cheeks, we finally sat down to dinner. Dad poured wine and we all toasted to Uncle Mikey, even though he wasn't there. Then my dad toasted Gino for bringing Uncle Mikey back home. Mom made a great meal. We had lasagna, meatballs, sausage, homemade bread, and salad. Dad's wine rounded it out just right.

Gino was charming the socks off everyone. Nana kept pinching his cheek and thanking him. We knew the "homecoming" agreement was struck up with the terms between my dad, Carlo, and me. They were simply thanking the delivery driver.

Nana was sitting between Gino and me, so I couldn't see him. Every so often he would slide his arm behind Nana's chair and rub my back. The wine was making me light headed, and his touch was making me sweat.

The doorbell buzzed. Uncle Mikey surprised us. He was using Paulie's car. He would pick Uncle Paulie up at Riggio's place at closing time. Uncle Mikey was staying at Nana's place until he could rent a place of his own. Paulie was staying at Mona's place most of the time since they had gotten engaged.

Geez, please don't let Ma ask me if I slept on the sofa at Paulie's, because I'll have to lie. No one missed a beat. They just kept on slapping Mikey on the back.

Before too long, Nana said she was getting tired. Gino offered to drive her home, but since he drove over in the truck that he brought Mikey home in, I said I would take her. Gino said he would come with us. Two ladies should not be alone at night. Corny, but it worked.

He walked Nana to her door. He hugged her and kissed her cheeks. When he got back to the car, I was dangling Paulie's house key in front of him. He laughed out loud. We snuck in the side door and raced to the bedroom. Who knew I was such a sex fiend? I can't believe I had waited all this time. Although, I didn't think I had met the right guy until now.

Nana always cleans at Paulie's place when he's not home. It really looked nice. I was glad for that, even though it wouldn't have mattered. The bed was made and all the junk and newspapers were cleaned up. We ran through the house and made a dive for the bed. Clothes flew all over, and we got all tangled up in the bedspread. I left the bathroom light on so neither of us would bang into anything—only each other.

Gino said, "Lena, for a girl who was a virgin two nights ago this is all very natural for you." Somehow, I was flattered that he thought that, even though I was a little embarrassed.

I explained that I had planned this for a long time. The right guy just hadn't come along.

Later, when we were exhausted, Gino said. "What are we going to do about this? I can't be away from you. I can't get you out of my mind. I was really talking stupid today. I wasn't paying attention to anything Niko was saying. He finally asked if I had a hangover. I said, "Yes, I think I do."

"I don't want to pressure you, Gino. This is all very new to me. Let's just take it slow. You'll come to Chicago when you can, and I'll be here. Now we'd better get out of here before Uncle Mikey decides to stay here instead of Nana's. I hope I can walk to the car. I feel like I was horseback riding." He thought that was pretty funny.

I asked him not to call me to say good-bye when he left the next day. I knew I would cry. I stayed in bed late Saturday morning, although I wasn't asleep. I did some ordinary stuff like laundry and changed my sheets. Yes, even a soap opera star has to clean her house.

In the afternoon, I went to the store for Mama. When I got back, I checked the mail before I went into the house. I found two cards: one for Ma and Dad, and one for me.

I sat on the front steps and opened mine. It read,

"I can't believe how much I care about you. I feel like my heart is beating outside my chest when I think of you. My heart belongs to you, Lena. I miss you...
Love, Gino

I slipped my card into my purse.

It was all I could do to keep from crying. I choked back the lump in my throat and took some deep breaths before I went inside.

My ma was at the sink. She said, "Lena, dinner will be read in ten minutes . . . leftovers tonight."

I said, "I don't think I can eat right now."

Ma said, "You'll eat."

Geez, She thinks I'm twelve years old.

I missed Gino already and he wasn't even gone one day. I went into my room and sat on the little chair by the window. Is this what it's like to be in love? Is this what I've been waiting for?

The phone rang and I jumped for it. I though it must be Gino calling from Michigan. It wasn't Gino, it was Carlo. He said he had some good news and some bad news. I said, "Give me the good news first."

"I wanna tell you how glad I am that you are my friend. I need someone to be my girlfriend. Your suggestion was the answer to so many of my problems. Do you have any suggestions? She's gotta be Italian. That's the good news."

"What's the bad news?"

"Lena, I gotta do something . . . something bad, before I can become a made man.

"Carlo, are you supposed to be telling me this?"

"I don't know who to talk to about this. Do you understand what I'm supposed to do?"

I didn't say it out loud, I knew he had to do a "hit."

"I've heard rumors, Carlo. I don't know all the details."

"Before we can be made, we have to do a favor for the bosses. Do you *Capise?* It's a contract. You know what I mean?"

"A contract. You're supposed to fill a contract? Are you telling me you need to eliminate someone? You won't do that, will you?"

"I don't know what to do. I have to. Maybe I should leave town. No, that wouldn't be a good idea," he answered himself. "The *famigila* would just find me and . . . and, if I don't do this, I'll be a failure to my father and to my family. You're the only person who really knows me, Lena. I don't know who else to talk to."

I thought about this on my end of the phone for a long time. Carlo finally said, "Lena, are you still there?"

"Carlo, does it have to be a real person?"

It was his turn to get really quiet. "I'm not sure what you mean. The 'family' has to pick the person. Someone who they wanna punish, like to get even. It can't be some random guy."

"Oh, shit. That kills my idea."

"Well, what was your idea?"

"I thought we could steal a body"

"Sometimes you're pretty funny, but not this time. Do you have any other ideas?"

"Do you *have* to get made?"

"I don't know if I have a choice. I like being connected to the *famigila*. I don't mind some of the stuff, but not the big contract thing."

"Carlo, talk to you father. Tell him how you feel. Maybe there is something else you can do instead of the final contract."

"There has to be witnesses to the execution. Then there is a big ceremony."

I didn't like the word execution. I realized that my dad was a made man. I felt my stomach turn.

Only the men are at the ceremony for the made man. Two other made men perform the ritual. Many members attend too. No women are allowed, but a party usually takes place later . . . like a coming out party.

I snapped to attention. "Carlo, we have to get together this week. I have someone in mind, but I've got to watch her another few days."

"Lena, I owe you. You're the greatest. I haven't had a friend like you . . . well, never. Your friendship means a lot to me."

I almost forgot about my other life. The one that gets so complicated because I'm a "family member's" daughter. I have Carlo in my head, Gino in my heart, and Greg in my dressing room.

My Ma said, "Who was it, Lena?"

"It was Carlo, Ma."

Why did she make the sign of the cross and roll her eyes? She probably thinks that I'm dating Carlo, Greg, and Gino. She probably thinks I'm a tramp. She'll have Nana make a Novena for me tomorrow. I'll know when I see the candles burning when I pull up in front of Nana's house. It takes nine days for a Novena. Maybe I'll ask Nana to make a speed Novena like she did when Uncle Paulie was sick, and Riggio wanted him to sing at the club.

It worked that time. I'll tell her that I need to help Carlo. She knows he's *finnoch*. She knows I'm his friend. That should be enough.

We had an early dinner. I ate even thought I wasn't really

hungry. That's the bad thing about being Italian. We eat when we are happy. We eat when we're sad. We eat when a baby get's it's first tooth, when the roses bloom, and on and on . . .

I went to bed early and tossed and turned all night. One of the things that I decided is that I needed my own phone. Maybe I should also get my own place. Why didn't I think about this sooner? I wonder if Paulie was going to stay at Mona's permanently? If he does, maybe I could live in Nana's back house. That seemed to be the transition place for all the uncles as they came of age. I fell asleep rolling this around in my head and nearly overslept. I hadn't even gone over the script for the next day's show.

My costar, Beth, was in the dressing room when I got to work. She was pondering two different outfits that were hanging on the door.

"What do you think, Lena? Should I wear the green pant suit or the lavender dress?"

Since we went to color broadcasting, every day was a dilemma. She couldn't decide on a color to save her soul.

I said, "Just close your eyes and pick."

She said, "Lena, was that sarcastic? I'm never sure if you are joking or not."

Beth is one of the most clueless people I've ever met. She has no perception of what's going on around her. What a self-centered flake. I was getting better at this "thought filter" thing. I didn't even say it out loud.

Beth continued, "I think it's because, you know, I've been dating Greg. You haven't been acting the same. I know he was crazy about you, but you broke his heart.

"What?" I said, as I sat down in my chair like someone had pushed me. "You've been seeing Greg? How long?"

"How long? About two months. I went to his niece's Bat Mitzvah with him just last weekend."

I could feel my blood boiling. I was dating Greg two months ago! Well, I must really be *stupida*! Am *I pazzo?!* Did I go blind?

"What the hell is the matter with you, Beth? You know I've been dating Greg for over a year!"

"But you're not Jewish and I am. So that doesn't count."

Oh, If I had a gun. Now I understand why Greg was so kind and understanding when I told him about Gino. He hasn't been hurting over me. In fact, I'm the one who lives in a fog. I'm the one who's been self-centered. Poor Greg! I never even noticed he was falling out of love with me. I'm so mad! I think my head is going to explode. I felt like my eyes were going to pop out of my head. Why couldn't he just be honest?

Greg knocked on the door and said, "Five minutes, ladies."

I opened the door and threw a punch at him. I was aiming for the nose. Well, he saw it coming and ducked back and I only caught his chin. I waltzed out of the room with my head high. I thought "one down and two to go." The second one being Beth, the other being Carlo. I'll sort one problem at a time.

I looked over my shoulder and said, "and watch who you're calling a lady." Beth didn't deliver her lines very well during that performance. She was mousey and didn't look at the camera. Mr. Latmen was getting so irritated.

When the show was over he said, "Beth, you were lukewarm today. What the hell is the matter with you?

She said, "I'm Jewish, that's what. And Lena is mad about it."

Beth burst into tears and ran off the set. I saw Greg waiting by the dressing room door and she fell into his arms. He was consoling her when I stormed past him and pushed the door open. It takes a lot to get my "dago" up, as my dad would say. Right now, I'm an emotional mess. I have so much on my mind. I took it out on Greg. He's always been there for me. When I started at the TV station, he's the one who showed me the ropes. He fell for me and I took it for granted. Greg came into the dressing room without knocking. I was about half dressed, and I didn't flinch. I put a robe on over my bra and panties. Greg said, "Lena, I tried to tell you about Beth. You were so preoccupied for the last few weeks that I couldn't find the right time. My Ma has been after me to find a nice Jewish girl and I didn't want to string you along."

I understood what he was saying. I wasn't any better than he was about this "honesty" thing. He put his arms around me and said, "Friends?"

I said, "Yes. Friends."

At that moment Beth, the Drama Queen burst through the door of the dressing room. Her hair was wild and she was sobbing.

She smacked Greg in the back of the head and was reaching for me. Greg was holding her back.

I said to Greg, "Are you sure she's not Italian? Talk to this nut while I get dressed. Beth, get a grip. This has been resolved. The conflict is over."

Mr. Latmen opened the door and said, "What the hell is the matter with her? Did she have some kind of breakdown?"

Greg said, "It's all under control, Mr. Latmen. We have it all worked out."

Latmen said, "Beth, get over this, whatever it is, or you'll find yourself cleaning dressing rooms for a living. And what the hell are you all doing standing around in this dressing room?"

Beth was hiccupping and trying to gain control, "I'm fine, Mr. Latmen. Just a little misunderstanding."

Greg decided to take Beth back to his apartment and calm her down. While she was changing, he told me that she had a history of emotional relationships. She doesn't handle rejection well. He hoped that he wasn't making a mistake getting involved with her.

I rolled my eyes, reminding myself of my mother, and said, "Greg, you can do better than this. She will be a noose around your neck for the rest of your life if you stay with her. She's not the only Jewish girl in the world. She's just convenient."

Beth came out of the bathroom dressed and primped. She looked like nothing had ever happened. Greg put his arm around her and she said to me, "Have a good night, Lena. I hope there are no hard feelings." Then she swished out the door.

Yep, she was nuts for sure.

I called Ma and told her that I was going to stop at Mona's house after work, and she shouldn't hold dinner, I'd probably eat with Mona and Paulie. My plan was to ask Paulie what his plan was about his living arrangements.

I know my family is going to get all crazy when I tell them I want to move out. Living in Nana's back house isn't exactly "moving out." It's just moving further away from my ma and dad. I know that Nana is going to be stopping in most evenings with food and laundry. She thinks she has to be the laundry service for everyone who lives there.

Paulie is the last of her kids to leave the nest. I can't disappoint her. Imagine how she would feel if no one in the family lived in that house? It's a cute place. I could do nice things with it: three rooms with a bathroom and a nice front porch. Paulie would probably leave most of the furniture for me. I guess I should ask him before I mentally decorate the place. It seems that I've practiced my exit speech for Ma and Dad too.

9

I called ahead to tell Mona that I was coming over. She sent Paulie to Felecia's Deli for beef sandwiches with peppers. She was making a salad when I got there.

"Lena! Why do you stay away so long?"

"Now that Paulie lives here most of the time, three's a crowd."

"Most of the time, I want to kick him out."

"It's not working okay for you two?"

"We get along okay most of the time. I don't know if he's ready to settle down. He won't set a wedding date. He claims that he doesn't want to leave your Nana alone. He thinks he's obligated to stay there because he's the last son."

"Oh. I'm gonna talk to him about that. I was thinking that maybe I could live there, in the little back house, if he plans to stay here." Mona's eyes lit up.

Lena!" she said. "This could be a really great idea. It might help Paulie make up his mind about us. Would that be forcing him to make a decision? I'm not sure how he's going to feel."

"You are engaged. Both of our families expect that you will get married. If he's here most of the time, that's okay, but you know your ma won't let him move in here unless you have a wedding date. Even If I move into the back house, Nana has left his old room just the way it was in her house. That's a good decoy for your family. I can't live in my ma and dad's house, with my bedroom off the kitchen any longer. It isn't working anymore."

I didn't realize that I was raising my voice. Mona was looking at me with her eyes bugging out.

"Lena, are you having an affair? Are you having SEX?"

At that moment, Paulie walked in with bags of food in his arms. He stood there like a dummy looking at me.

"Did I hear that right? Lena, are you having sex?"

"Oh, for cripes sake Paulie. Are you having sex? Why is this such a big issue? I'm going to be twenty-two years old."

"Lena, you could have told me. I shouldn't have to find out from my girlfriend."

"Oh, I'm sorry Paulie. I didn't know you were a priest. Since when do I have to confess to you?"

"We have always been close. I thought you always told me everything."

"Be serious, Paulie. Did you always tell me everything?"

"Okay, you two. That's enough. Stop yelling at each other. Sit down and eat. We'll discuss this like adults. No more fighting."

Paulie said, "Who is he, Lena?"

He said this like he was going to go out and bust the guy's head.

I said, "It's Gino Bevalaqua."

All of a sudden he looked pleased.

"Hey, I like that guy! Why didn't you say so. He's really cool. Got a good head. Gonna be somebody someday. Do your ma and dad know?"

"No, I don't think they would like the idea that I'm having sex with a guy I met last week, Paulie. I'll need to break that to them by having Gino come over a few times. I'm trying to line up my own place so I can have some privacy."

"Hey, once they get used to the idea maybe you could move in my place behind Nana. I've been trying to figure out how to break that to her."

Mona and I looked at each other in mock amazement. I slapped my forehead like I was having a revelation.

"Paulie! You are a genius! I wish I had thought of that."

Mona agreed, "Yeah, Paulie. That's a good idea. We were wondering how Lena was going to get some privacy."

Paulie was having a dozen ideas at one time. He was so excited he forgot he brought home the food. Mona and I were watching the bags in his arms as he paced back and forth in front of us.

"We could tell your ma that I'm going to move in with Mona, but she can't let Mona's family know . . . or I could move back into Nana's first while you live in the back house. That way Mona's family would go easy on her . . . or I could ask Mr. Riggio if I could move into the two rooms behind the restaurant. I could fix it up nice."

I saw Mona roll her eyes. She looked like she was going to cry.

I took the bags away from Paulie and said, "Sit down. You're getting off track."

Mona breathed a sigh of relief. Paulie's last suggestions were going haywire.

I told him, "Paulie, your first suggestion was the best. Let's stick with that." "Oh, what did I say first?"

"You said that you could move in with Mona and I could live in the back house."

"Oh, Yea. That's the best one. Let's eat."

Mona was trying not to grin from ear-to-ear while she put the food out on plates. I just shook my head at her. My family has a lot of good men. Nobody ever said that they were smart men.

A long time ago, my ma told me, "When you really want something from a man, you have to plant the seed and let him think it's his idea." *BINGO, MAMA!* You got this right, too. As usual!

I've been rolling this idea around in my head, the one where Carlo gets a "decoy" girlfriend. Since I met Gino, I can't be there for Carlo all the time. The family gets very insistent when a special event comes around. They want all the made men to have a lady in their life. I'm not so sure why they feel this way. Some of the oldest guys are bachelors. They have some old-fashioned notion that a man has got to have a "broad" on his arm to make him look good. Well, Carlo sure puts a spin on that by being *finocch*. He looks the part of a "man's man," but the fact that he likes men more than women complicates things.

I have this idea about Penny, my makeup girl/wardrobe assistant. I've asked Mr. Latmen if Beth and I could have separate dressing rooms. Penny could still help both of us, but not in the same room. Since I've decided that Beth is nuttier than a fruitcake, I really want to avoid her as much as possible. This will give me a chance to talk to Penny about Carlo. Monday will be the best time to do this because Beth will be moving into her own dressing room. I'll call Carlo this weekend and feel him out about this idea.

Sunday afternoon my ma and dad went to the park. Dad plays bocce ball with a bunch of guys from his Italian club. The wives bring food and wine and they set up a picnic. This is a good time to call Carlo.

He answered on the first ring.

I said, "Can you talk right now?"

"Sure. How are you?"

"I'm fine. Listen, I have this idea. There is a girl who works at the TV station. Her name is Penny. She's cute, around our age, and she wants to move out of her mother's house. How do you feel about meeting her as a potential roommate?"

"Does she know about my situation?"

I said, "Not yet. I think that I'll talk to her on Monday. I wanted to be sure you are still keen on this idea."

"Of course I am. I so glad to have you on my side. I sure wouldn't want you for an enemy. You are so clever that you scare me sometimes."

"You wouldn't be the first guy I scared. I'll call you next week and tell you how it went."

When I hung up, the phone rang immediately.

Carlo said, "It's me. Is Penny Italian?"

"Yes! Her last name is Costa."

"You're amazing, Lena. I love you."

"Thanks, Carlo." I thought about Gino. He said that for entirely different reasons.

I hung up the phone and shook my head. I smiled and thought about what a great guy he really was after all.

10

Monday morning I brought some biscotti to work. There was a small table outside my dressing room with papers and stuff. I made room and put the dish there. Everyone gathers like vultures when free food is around. While the crowd was occupied I pulled Penny into my dressing room.

I said, "Are you still looking for a place to move?"

"Oh, yeah, but I don't have the money saved yet."

"Well, Penny . . . I've got a proposition for you."

I explained the whole sordid mess to her. I explained that if Carlo is going to get "made" he needs to have a girl for the party.

"He would also score big points with his dad if he had a girlfriend. I'm not sure if you will share his apartment or he'll find you a place of your own. I think you'll move in with him. I haven't fine-tuned the idea yet."

Penny asked, "Does anyone know about his other life?"

"No," I said. I appreciated the fact that she sounded so diplomatic.

"Let me think about this, Lena. I think I have to meet him first."

"That sounds reasonable to me, Penny. We'll work something out soon. Hey, do you want to go out for a drink some night? My Uncle Paulie sings at Riggio's." I felt that I needed to say something more friendly than the Carlo proposition.

"I'd like that. It's really nice of you to ask."

Wow, that sounded like she likes me as a person. Sometimes people get hung up on the fact that I'm on TV.

"Do you want to go see my Uncle Paulie sing on Friday night? I could pick you up, so you won't have to walk in alone? I know I don't like to go someplace new by myself."

Penny wrote down her address and I said I'd be there at eight.

Getting my own phone was one of the best ideas I'd had. Gino called me about every other night. He told me that he loved me and he missed me. I hoped he meant it, because my mind was on him all the time. He was going to try to come to Chicago the coming weekend. It was my birthday and I would love to see him.

My ma always said, "Was that Gino, again?"

I said, "Yes, Mama," and she looked pleased.

The situation at the TV station was getting a little better—not so much tension, since Beth had her own space. She felt so threatened by everything I said. She still knocked on my dressing room door and asked, "Should I wear this lavender dress or the gold two piece outfit?"

"Yikes, Make a decision." *Nutball.*

I picked Penny up at 8 p.m. on Friday.

We got to The Club around eight thirty. When I walked in, the first thing I saw was balloons. Then everyone yelled "SURPRISE!"

My birthday was the following day, Saturday. I never expected this. Everyone was there, even my ma and dad. Then I saw Gino and started to cry. My ma gave me a little shove and said, "I called him." That Mama of mine never ceases to amaze me.

We all went to the restaurant lounge area connected to The Club. Paulie was singing until midnight, so we moved the party there. I wasn't surprised to see a lot of my dad's buddies, and some of my uncles. I was surprised, however, to see Carlo sitting with his dad at the bar.

He came over and hugged me and wished me "happy birthday". All the other friends and cronies hugged me too.

What a perfect opportunity to introduce Penny and Carlo!

I looked around until I found her and grabbed her by the arm. "Penny, this is my friend Carlo. Carlo, this is Penny."

I knew immediately that this was going to work out for the best. When Carlo turned on the charm, he could be a real lady-killer. At least, that's the appearance he could give since I taught him some manners and how to dress.

I was so overwhelmed by Gino being there that I left Penny and Carlo at the bar together. Carlo's dad went over to sit with my uncles. When I remembered the two of them were alone at the bar I glanced over. They were chatting like two old friends. Gino and I worked our way over to them. I introduced her to Gino and we ordered drinks.

Paulie came over to the bar during his break to join the birthday celebration. He pulled me aside and said, "Who's the chick with Carlo? Did he change from fruits to cupcakes?"

I couldn't help but laugh out loud. I said, "Paulie, you really have a way with words. No, I introduced him to my friend Penny from the TV station."

"What's the point, Lena? I don't get it."

I explained the game plan to him. I added that sometimes he likes girls too. Remember, Paulie isn't the sharpest tack in the box.

He thought about it for a few seconds and said, "What a great idea. Maybe he'll like her and not be *finocch* anymore. Get it, cupcakes instead of fruitcakes."

I rolled my eyes and told him, "Paulie, I don't think it works that way."

"Oh. Well, at least he'll have a nice looking girl to show off to the 'family.' "

"Now you've got it, Paulie. By the way, are you staying at Mona's tonight?"

He gave me that "sly dog" look. "Yes, I am Lena."

I said, "swell," and walked back to Gino.

Later in the evening, my ma and dad were getting ready to leave. I told Ma that I'd probably stay at Mona's place. She looked as innocent as she could and said, "That's just fine, honey." Bless my ma for not judging me. After all, this is the sixties.

Later, when Gino and I were alone he gave me a gold bracelet from Italy. He got it from a little shop that his Nonna told him about. He had it engraved, "I love you, Gino."

Well, I was very grateful . . . to say the least.

———

Early the next morning, there was a knock at the door. I knew it was Nana. She would never think I had Gino in here. I had parked my cark in front and Gino parked in the back.

She said, "Bella, you wanna some breakfast?"

Gino said, "Holy cow! What should we do?"

I said, "I'll be there in five minutes, Nana. I'm gonna put some clothes on."

"Okay, Bella. I'm making some frittata and potatoes."

"I'll help you peel the potatoes."

"Bella, open the door. I think Paulie has my big frying pan."

Gino made a mad dash for the bathroom while I threw his clothes in after him.

I ran in the kitchen and saw the frying pan on the stove. I opened the door and let Nana in. "Here it is, Nana!"

She looked around and said, "Boy-oh-boy, this place is a mess."

I said, "I know, Nana. It could really use a woman's touch."

When I walked across the yard to Nana's, I was thinking about how to break this to her. After that, I would have to tell my ma and dad. They would go into serious drama.

I hugged Nana and gave her a dozen kisses, because she loved it when I did that. I peeled the potatoes while we discussed the babies, Anthony and Rosie. Nana was waiting for summer, then she could walk to my ma's house. It was just a few blocks away. She talked about her garden and all her herbs. She dried most of them for the winter.

When we sat down to eat, I was thinking about Gino, sneaking out the back door with no breakfast, and smiled. He used a lot of energy last night. He would have loved this breakfast.

Nana said, "Bambina, why you smile?"

"I was just thinking about Paulie's house, Nana. If I lived in the back, I would fix it up really nice."

Nana looked me right in the eye and said, "Bella, what took you so long? I thought when you got the nice-a job, you would move here pretty quick. Paulie, he's no come-a home too much now that he's gonna marry Mona."

Could life be this easy? You coulda hit me with the frying pan. I thought this was going to be trauma and drama. After all, Paulie is Nana's youngest.

I pretended to act a little surprised. When I looked at Nana, she was trying not to grin from ear to ear. Then she said, "Bella, after all, you a growin' up woman now—even if you are still my little girl."

"I need to talk to my ma and dad." I said. "They probably will be a little worried about my moving out of the house."

Nana rolled her eyes and said, "Lena, you think you mama and daddy are stupido. They know you a grown lady. You got serious man now. You mama and me, we talk about this already."

I got up and hugged her. I said, "Nana, the women in this family are really amazing."

She said, "I know this. I tell-a you Auntie Lilly all-a time, same-a thing. After we do dishes, we go to Paulie house inna back. Maybe I maka you some new curtains.

I did a slight panic, hoping Gino snuck out the side door while we were eating. Then I remember hearing the car pull into the gravel alley.

When I got home, Mama had all sorts of news. "Carlo called. He wants you to call him back. Penny called. Who's Penny? Oh, I remember your friend from last night! Nana called and told me she's making light blue curtains for the bedroom and red for the living room."

She said this all in one breath. I know my mouth was hanging open.

"Honey, this is going to be so good for you. You're a TV star, making a lot of money. You shouldn't be living with your parents."

She's right. I keep putting money in the bank and I don't bother spending it.

I've been cutting my own hair. What was I thinking? I should be going to the beauty shop. I don't even spend much on clothes, since the TV station gives me so much for my wardrobe. I need to start living it up a little.

First thing in the morning, I drove over to "Jen's Den Of Beauty"

They were delighted to see me. She scolded me for cutting my own hair. I guess it was pretty obvious to the trained eye.

"Lena, you can't continue to chop this curly hair on your own. It will all be uneven. Then I'll have to cut it too short to even it out."

I apologized for my lack of understanding the fine art of beauty culture. I explained that I started to attend beauty school, but never finished. Jen understood completely. She was much more understanding about my chopped up hair when she found out that I was a beauty school drop out. I'll have to remember to stop at the bakery the next time I come for my haircut. Food always makes people feel better.

While I was there, I got a facial, Manicure and pedicure. I am teaching myself to enjoy my new money. Why stop with a haircut?

I left Jen's around noon. I didn't have to be at the studio until one today. We aired at two. I decided to stop at my Gram's for lunch. She loves surprise visits and she loves to feed me.

The door was never locked, so I let myself in. *"Nana, dovi sei? Where are you?"*

"In-a cucina."

Where else would she be?

She was sitting with Dona Natalie. They had scraps of paper all over the table, and they were both holding little yellow stumps of pencils. The scraps of paper had scribbles of numbers and calculations. Nana's cigar box was on the table with the coffee pot and two giant mugs. I was familiar with this cigar box from my childhood. I knew all the important papers for this house were contained in this old wooden box. I could see trouble on the horizon.

I said *buonginorno* while surveying the scene and kissed them both while asking, *"Cosa c'è di sbagliato?* What's wrong?"

Nana said, "I tell you what's wrong, Bella. I pay for this house every month. We buy this house in 1946. Papa give Signore Genardo three hundred dollars down payment. Papa and me, we pay thirty-five dollars each month for sixteen years. I go pay Mr. Genardo last week at his butcher shop and tell him now I finish pay him for house. Papa figured this out before he died. His note is in the box. See? Now Genardo has to give me paper to show I own it. Signore Genardo tell me, 'No Signora. You owe me more because of interest.' *Che cosa*? Interest! We pay too much already."

Signore Genardo owned the biggest butcher shop in the neighborhood. He owned the building it was in as well as several other buildings in the area. He was known to be less than fair when it came to trade—like the time Mrs. Regato caught him putting his thumb on the scale with her beef order.

While she was talking, and piling food on plate in front of me, I was working the same figures.

"Nana, I think you are right. I'm going to take this box to my dad after the show today. He'll figure it out. Okay?"

I barely made it to the studio by on time. I was focused on my lines while my mind was on the figures for Papa and Nana's house.

I drove to Uncle Mike's garage after the show. He always had a few tired-looking mechanics working on cars. I knew my dad and my uncles would be in the back. I went to the side door and knocked. I heard Uncle Mike say, "Who's there?" I heard my dad say, "I think its Lena." The back of the garage is a makeshift "Boys Club." It has one big room that was a catchall. It had a stove and fridge, a couple of old couches, and a kitchen table. They kept some old cots and blankets in the back room for poker nights, or when somebody had a fight with their wife. Sometimes someone in the family had to lay low for a few days.

My dad opened the door and said, "What's wrong, babe? You okay?

I told him Nana's story. I put the little cigar box on the table. "Check the math, Dad. Even if Nana's figures are off a little because of interest, I think she still should own the house by now."

My uncles looked at one another. My dad nodded his head to my uncles. They nodded back. Daddy said, "Kiss your uncles and go home, sweetheart. We'll take care of this.

I knew exactly what this would mean. They would pay Mr. Genardo a visit as family members. They would start out by talking, but if he disagreed with the figures, they would have to persuade him that he was very wrong. Yup! I'm learning the good and the bad of being "family."

It was out of my hands.

11

Five men walked into Genardo's butcher shop. The last one in, Joey turned the door sign from open to closed, and pulled down the shade on the door.

Mr. Genardo popped his head up from behind the butcher's case. His smile quickly turned to a look of concern.

"Hello, gentlemen. Nice to see everybody together. What's the occasion?"

He looked very nervous. My dad was the first one to speak, on his mother-in-law's behalf.

"Mr. Genardo, It has come to our attention that there is a discrepancy in your bookkeeping."

He never gave Genardo the opportunity to defend himself. He simply told him he was wrong, in a very tactful way.

"Oh, Senior Delatora, I explained to Rosina that there is interest on the payments."

That's when three of the brothers stepped up to the meat counter with my dad.

Uncle Johnny said, "My ma's not too happy right now. That makes us all unhappy." He said this while Myrtle "The Turtle" was examining the meat cleavers on the chopping block behind the counter.

"But maybe my calculations are not so good. After all, that was almost thirty years ago. Let me get my books."

He went to the back of the shop and came out with a ledger. He made a big show of scanning the book and running his finger down the pages. Then he went to his adding machine and banged in a few numbers.

"Oh, yes! I see I make a mistake!"

"Oh, I'm glad to see we agree on this Mr. Genardo," my dad said.

"Please let me make a package of meat for you to take to Dona DeLuca."

The uncles were nodding while Genardo was wrapping pork chops, roasts, chickens and ground beef. Uncle Joey turned and pulled up the shade on the door, and flipped the sign back to open.

Uncle Joe asked, "This isn't going to be a problem later, is it? I don't want my mama to worry about this again."

"No, No, Mr. DeLuca. It's my mistake. I will get the deed from the safe later. This is all settled."

They all shook hands. The problem was solved. Sure is good to have family.

12

When I got home I called Carlo. He was very happy that he had met Penny. He said that she's just the kind of girl he was looking for. If he wasn't "that way" he would seriously date her.

I played cards with my ma, took a shower, and went to bed early.

After my show the next day, I went to my grandma's house. I was afraid that she was still upset and I wanted her to know that my dad was going to see Signor Genardo.

I was surprised to see my Uncle Sammy's car in the driveway.

Nana was cooking and while she did so she chattered, laughing and crying. I looked at Uncle Sammy and shrugged my shoulders with my palms up, in a "what's up" gesture.

Nana said, "Bella, you never guess what! Signore Genardo was here this morning. He give me my paper to own the house and a check for five hundred dollars. He say that he figured the interest out wrong and he's-a very sorry. He give me a big roasts and lots of chicken and chops. He send some home for your mama too. You wanna stay for dinner?"

I called my ma and told her the "party" was at Nana's house tonight. I told her that I'll help Nana set the tables in the kitchen and dining room. Round up Aunt Lilly and call Gemma. I asked her to bring something casual from my closet. I had sleep clothes here. I'd stay here tonight to help with the clean up. I could go to work from here tomorrow.

God bless Nana! She was on the phone inviting Signore Genardo to come for dinner with his wife. She never holds a grudge. I'm sure he won't come. You would think that she would be angry with

Genardo for scamming her out of money? Nope, not my Nana. She is the example that shaped my life. *Andare avante!* Go forward! All the women in my family seem to follow this rule. We get angry for a moment then we forgive. The men . . . not so much. I guess it's their job. I've heard my uncles say, "Defend and Revenge. Always."

I had too many irons in the fire. I needed to make a list...

1. Get Paulie out of Nana's back house. I have to do this if I'm going to have any privacy with Gino.
2. Get Penny and Carlo reasonably close to each other before he gets Made.
3. Start packing. I know my ma will do most of it. She was already crying last night when she was sorting some old dishes.
4. Shop for new dishes and don't tell Ma
5. Get a new mattress. That one's gotta go. Too many uncles and too many miles on that old mattress.

Paulie was not helping the situation. He wasn't making any effort to move his stuff to Mona's apartment. I finally had to corner him at Riggio's one night.

"Paulie, what gives?"

"Wadda ya mean, Lena?"

"Why aren't you getting your stuff together to move in with Mona?"

"Ya know, Lena. I'm not so sure that's a real good idea. I gotta take this thing kind of slow."

"What? Slow? You been engaged for a year. You don't even have a wedding date set."

I could see the stupid look on his face and I got a pretty good idea what was on his mind.

"Paulie, are you changing your mind about getting married?"

"Now, Lena I didn't say that. It's just so permanent. I kinda like this arrangement. No pressure, you know. If I want some time alone,

I just come back to my place and hang out for a coupla nights. Mona understands."

"Paulie, you are a worthless alley cat. You're still chasing skirts aren't you? I should tell Uncle Joey and Uncle Mikey. They would knock the snot out of you. Better yet! I should tell Nana. She would straighten you out!"

"Oh, Lena. Don't tell my ma. She'll chase me with the broom. She still does that when she's mad at me. She hits hard. Last time she did that I had a big knot on my head."

"Paulie, that was when you got drunk on your graduation night. Here's what's going to happen. I'm giving you two weeks to make a decision like a big boy. Either you are committed to Mona, or you break off the engagement."

"Lena, I spent a lot of money on that ring."

"Listen, block head, I'm sure she'll give the ring back. I know a lot of guys that would love to date Mona. Don't think you're the only person who's attracted to her. You've got two weeks, Paulie. Break it off, or I tell her that you've been messing around."

"Is that my only option?"

"No dummy. The other option is to move in with her."

As I was walking away, I could here him mumbling, "Yeah, there are lots of chicks who would like to have that ring, too."

I turned and said, "Don't push me, Paulie."

13

Penny and I went out for dinner after the show about a week later. We were discussing the fact that I had plans for my new money.

"If I had a lot of money, I would buy a house. Maybe I'd buy an old house to fix up the way I wanted."

"Gee, Penny. I've never thought about buying a house. I really thought about paying off Nana's house and my parent's house. Nana's house is paid for now. I'll have to ask my ma and dad if theirs is paid for."

"You could ask your Nana if she would sell you her house. You could remodel it."

I looked at her like she was a genius. Why hadn't I thought of that?

I said, "Penny, you really have got me thinking about this."

On Friday, I went to the bank after work. I sat down with a bank officer who was very glad to see me. He had a nice brass plaque on his desk that said:

"MICHAEL SAMUELSON, VICE PRESIDENT. "

"How can I help you, Miss Delatora?"

"I need some financial advice." I pulled my bankbook from my purse and put it on the desk between us. When he opened it, his eyebrows went up.

Oh, I thought, *I know that's a good thing.*

"What kind of advice do you need, Miss Delatora?"

I said, "I'm thinking about buying a house. Not just any house, but my grandmother's house. Do you think I have enough money?"

Mr. Samuelson blinked several times before he spoke. "Miss

Delatora, you have enough money to buy several houses, cash, without a mortgage."

"Okay, here's what I want to do . . . I want to buy my grandmother's house and remodel it, as well as the old back house. I also want to put an addition on my parent's house for my grandmother and remodel my parent's house too."

"Whoa. This is a big undertaking. You'll need plumbers, carpenters, electricians, painters, and you will certainly want an architect."

"Well, I just want you to tell me if I have enough money saved to do this. I'll have plenty of people to do the jobs."

"Yes ma'am, you do have enough to do this project."

"Well, here are a couple of more checks to deposit in my account."

Mr. Samuelson was smiling when I left. He probably wasn't thinking about the money I was going to take out of his bank. He was busy smiling about the money I just put into his bank.

I had big plans. I needed to talk to my uncles. They loved projects like this. They would rise to the occasion! One word about "remodeling," they would pick up the phone and start calling in all their favors from other members of the "family." But it was Friday night, and I wanted to take advantage of the weekend.

When I got home, Gino was sitting in the kitchen having coffee with my parents. My ma pulled out every baked treat that she was hiding. Gino had such a big smile when he saw me come in. I felt my heart skip a beat when I saw him. And that smile . . . well he was winning my parents over, with no trouble at all.

Gino got up and kissed my cheek. I got tingly all over. He pulled out a chair for me. Mama got up and took a plate out of the oven for me.

This would be as good a time as any to tell them what I wanted to do. I would skip the question about my parent's house and whether it was paid for or not, until Gino wasn't here.

We talked about family and Carlo pending promotion. In other words, he was going to get "made" soon. My little brother Bobby came in and Gino pretended to spar with him. He invited Bobby to sit down with us. I know this scored points, too. It made my parents look at him like he belonged in the family. Gino's not a dope either, he knew what he was doing.

After I cleaned the table, my dad brought the wine out. This was my opportunity to start telling my plan. I waited until the second skinny glass was poured.

"Daddy, I have been thinking about something since Paulie might move out of Nana's house." He knows I say "Daddy" when I want something, but it usually makes him happy anyway.

"What? Is something else wrong? The house is paid for, so what's up?"

"No, that's all been straightened out, thanks to you and the uncles. I was thinking of remodeling Nana's house and putting an addition on this house."

Well, it's one thing to do a good deed for Nana, but paying for something for my dad was going to be difficult. An Italian daughter giving her father anything for free is almost an insult, unless it's in payment for a debt. Then he probably wouldn't take it anyway.

I could see Dad digesting this. Mama was silent, but her eyes were huge.

I continued, "I thought it would be nice if Nana could live closer to Ma, you know, now that she's getting older. She could still have her own garden and work in Mama's garden too. You know how she loves to be outside in the summer months."

Dad finally said, "Where in the hell did you get this brainstorm?" He looked at my ma and said, *"Lei e pazza?"*

I could hear the edge in his voice, so I knew that I'd better talk fast.

"Daddy, you know I've been planning to move into Nana's back house. If I can get her to sell the house to me, I would remodel it while I live in Nana's house. First I would have to put an addition on this house."

"Josie," he said to my ma, "I think she has lost her mind. What do you think of all this *stronzate?*"

"Well, Sam, I think this would all depend on what Nana says. This could take a lot of time, Lena. Nana isn't going to leave that house without kicking and screaming."

"Maybe she would, if I live with her while the remodeling of the back house and the addition are being built. She would think that she is doing me a favor. I could slowly convince her to move into the addition after it's done."

Gino said, "May I say something, sir?"

"*Avanti*, go ahead!"

"I'm planning to stay in Chicago for a while. Maybe I could live in the back house while it's being remodeled. I could help the contractors. My dad has a concrete business. When Nana sees all this taking shape, she might be more flexible. The house wouldn't be empty."

My dad really looked pleased. My ma looked like she could kiss Gino. My dad got up from the table and announced, "We're gonna have a family meeting. I'm going to call the uncles and some other members. Lena, meet me in the office tomorrow after you get off work. Gino, you come too. The office was the room behind the garage. I need to see what kind of resources we got in this family. We don't need no outsiders making money off us. Gino, call your dad. Ask him if he's interested in this little project. Josie, when the hell are we having dessert?"

Dad walked into the living room. Gino followed him. Dad sat in the easy chair and Gino sat on the ottoman at his feet. They began an intense conversation immediately. My ma came around the table and hugged me.

She said, "Lena, when you were born, I knew you would be successful. Look what you've accomplished!"

Typically, women are not consulted for major decisions in this family. The men might ask them about colors or style, but not major construction. This was going to be very important in my life. I could tell my dad was almost as proud of me as he was when I got the soap opera role. I was also surprised that he accepted Gino's offer to help so quickly.

14

Paulie was moving in with Mona. *FINALLY!* Nana accepted this as a fact of life. She prayed for his soul, because he was living in sin. She didn't seem to worry about Mona's soul.

Paulie didn't have a lot of personal possessions other than clothes. The furniture was staying in the house. It was mostly cast-offs and rummage finds. Gino was planning to move some of his stuff into the "uncle house" the following weekend. I don't know why I was so excited about this. Oh, I guess I did . . . .he held my heart. I really was beginning to think we would have a future together.

Gino and Paulie were loading their cars, and I was putting a couple of boxes in my trunk. Nana came out of the house with meatball sandwiches for us. She wore her flowered housedress with a bright red apron over it. She always looked the same to me: ageless, white haired and perfect. We all sat on the back porch and had iced coffee and sandwiches. I noticed Nana was very quiet. I asked her if she was okay.

"Bella, I look-a this house, and I feel sad today. Papa Joe and me, we raised nine kids in this-a place. Now the first time in my life since we buy it, somebody who is not my *famiglia* is going to live in it. I'm glad it's gonna be fix up-a for you, but I feel a little *strano*. Maybe is sad."

I nearly cried for her. "Nana, don't be afraid. This is all a little strange, I know. You will be very happy, once I move into the little house."

I got a knot in my stomach. If Nana was so upset about remodeling the little house in back, and having Gino live there temporarily, how was she going to feel about moving into the new addition at my ma's house? I was having an emotional dilemma.

Paulie is a pig. Nana tried to sneak in and clean his place whenever he was at Mona's. She never opened his drawers and she stayed out of his cabinets and closets. I decided to tackle that job while the guys were moving stuff to Mona's apartment.

I found things in that closet I would be ashamed to throw away in the trash. What if Joe, the garbage man sees this stuff? I found a big empty box in the garage. I put a pair of Paulie's gloves on and started throwing junk in it: A huge plastic doll? Oh, cripes! This thing blows up! Girlie magazines by the dozen. Women's underwear that was definitely not Mona's. I couldn't do this! I decided to work on the kitchen cabinets instead. No problem there. Just a couple of cans of sardines and some canned soup, crumbs, and cobwebs. Obviously, Paulie didn't have food at the top of his list.

I heard the cars pull into the driveway and met them on the porch. Paulie took one look at me and said, "Oh no, I guess you were cleaning the closet."

"I'm not touching that crap. You better get in there and throw that nasty stuff out before Nana decides to come back here and help us. I don't know where you're going to put it, but don't throw it in the trash in the alley. I thank the Virgin Mary that Nana never saw this stuff. What if kids found your disgusting magazines in the alley."

Gino and Paulie looked a little afraid of me. Gino was following Paulie. I said, "Where do you think you're going?"

He said, "I thought I'd better help Paulie before you start throwing stuff out the door."

"Take that nasty stuff to the construction site down on Clark Street. It's a big hole and everyone seems to be dumping trash in it. Make sure that nothing has his name on it. If any of the uncles find out what a pervert he is, they will make his life hell."

"Lena, it's a guy thing. It's not the end of the world. Most guys have things like that around their house. Especially if they live alone."

"Stifle it, Gino. Don't make excuses for him. He's a pig. I feel sorry for Mona."

I was still standing on the porch when Gino went inside. I heard Paulie through the open door say, "Geez, she's really mad isn't she?"

" Yep. I tried to explain that it's kind of normal, and you're not a pervert."

"Thanks Gino. We better get busy," I heard him say.

Gino looked in the big box and said, "Wow Paulie. You really have quite a collection here."

"*Had,* Gino. That part of my life is over. I'll never live this down. Lena's going to think I'm a creep for the rest of my life"

"She'll get over it. You'll see. She was just a little surprised to see all this smut."

I reached over and slammed the door for punctuation. I wanted them to know that I could hear them, and they better be afraid.

I needed a morale booster. I asked Penny if she wanted to go to the beauty shop with me after work on Monday. We could have dinner at my Uncle Joey's restaurant. I needed a trim and Penny was talking about a haircut too. I needed to have my *Gina Lollobrigida* hairstyle trimmed a bit. Penny is so good at this TV makeup she does. Now that the show is in color, she is really enjoying matching my eye shadow to my clothes and putting fancy stuff in my hair. I like to limit the hair decorations because my hair is short. She even suggested to Johnny, the leading man, that he use some rouge on his cheeks. He said, "NO WAY!" She told him that the next best thing would be for him to get some sun. She called him "tall, light, and handsome."

We went to Jen's Den of Beauty. Penny is Italian, but has strawberry blond hair. It's got a nice loose curl. Jen wanted to cut it short. We had a group discussion and decided on a cut that was just above the shoulders. It looked fantastic. She commented that she couldn't wait for Carlo to see it. I didn't want to ask her why this would be important to Carlo. We could discuss this at dinner.

When we got to Uncle Joey's restaurant, he wanted to fix us

something special. I told him I was on a diet. He insisted on rolled eggplant filled with spinach and ricotta cheese. The sauce was a light Marinara with lots of garlic. It was great. It might have been low in calorie, but I knocked off half the breadbasket including the butter while we waited. I have no shame and no control.

When we started eating, I said, "So, it sounds like you and Carlo have been getting along really well."

"Oh yes, Lena. We have been seeing each other on a regular basis."

"What are you calling a 'regular basis,' Penny?"

"Oh, about three nights a week." Her face flushed and she put her head down.

"Penny!" I said in a shocked whisper, "Have you done the nasty with Carlo?"

"Well, the first time was an accident."

"Excuse me? How do you have sex *accidentally*? Are you telling me that you have had sex with Carlo more than once?"

"Lena, please don't be angry. We have feelings for each other. Carlo says that he has never felt like this before—at least, not for a girl."

"Oh, Penny. I wasn't thinking about anything like this happening. When am I going to learn to mind my own business?" I thought to myself, *Lena, that thought filter is not working again. What have you done this time?* "I wanted to help Carlo and you too. I thought this would get you out of your home situation and give Carlo the front that he needed. I never wanted you to get hurt. Now I'm afraid that both of you might get hurt."

"Lena, you don't need to worry. We both know that this might not work out. He's very sweet and he treats me like a princess. I've met his family too. They seem to really like me."

"Sure they like you, Penny. You're the first girl he's brought home since high school. They're probably thrilled to see a chick in his life."

"You're so upset. I wanted you to be glad for us. Not angry."

"Oh, Penny. Just be careful. I'm not even sure what I mean by *careful.* What if Carlo starts to see guys again? How will you feel about it?"

I could see Penny thinking about this.

"Lena, he's thinking about getting a bigger apartment. He wants me to move in with him soon."

This life of mine is getting so complicated. Maybe I could ask Paulie for some advice. I know it sounds crazy, but sometimes his logic is so simple. I called him when I got off work. Mona said he was sleeping. I wonder if I should talk to my ma about this. We have discussed Carlo in a roundabout fashion. Everyone knows by now that he's *finnoch.* We just don't say it out loud. I needed someone to listen to me. Ma's pretty open- minded. I called the house and Ma told me that Gino and Dad were at the office with the uncles. They said I should meet them there. The office was simply the back half of the big room behind the garage. I didn't get to talk to her about Carlo, so it would have to wait.

When I got to the garage, I went around to the back door. They had tables and chairs across the back of the room with chairs all around. I had some notes with me about what I wanted to do for the three projects, Nana's house, the back house, and Ma's addition. When I came in the door, the men stood up. I saw a man who I knew was Gino's father. I had seen some pictures. He must have driven down from Detroit for this meeting. Gino came over and kissed my cheeks and brought me over to meet his dad. Gino's dad seemed very formal. His cheeks brushed mine, but he didn't kiss me. I could tell that he was holding back. I could feel it. *One thing at a time,* I thought.

I opened my folder and spread out my drawings and notes for the remodeling. They passed them all around. Uncle Joey was the first to comment, probably because he had built a restaurant from the ground up.

"So, Lena, you want to build an addition to your ma's house first?"

"Yes. If I put an addition on my ma and dad's house, she will have a new place to live while we remodel her old house and the little back house.

Uncle Johnny said, "Gino, are you planning to start remodeling the back apartment at the same time that we're building the addition at Josie's?"

"Yes, I can get a lot done while I'm living there," Gino said. "I can work on the kitchen first, then the bedroom, living room, then the bathroom last."

"My ma will be happy to cook for you. She still cooks like she has six sons at home," Uncle Joey added.

The meeting progressed into the dinner hour. Ma and Auntie Virgie showed up with sausage and meatballs in a huge pan and some lasagna. They went back to the car once more and carried in two skinny bags with loaves of Italian bread bursting out of the top. They put out plates and silverware and left. It didn't matter that I had dinner with Penny earlier in the evening; I ate anyway. When it comes to food, I am defeated before my diet can start. We made several decisions, and I felt like we got the ball rolling.

I said "good night" to everyone and did the usual round of kisses. Gino walked me to my car and got into the front seat next to me. He laid some hot and heavy kisses on me before I could say a word. He always managed to take my breath away. I had to push his hands away to catch my breath.

He finally said, "Babe, I can't get our weekend getaway out of my head."

"Me too."

Just as he reached for me again, there was a knock at his window on his side. I nearly jumped out of my skin. It was my dad. Holy crap. At least we weren't pawing at each other again. He crooked his finger at Gino to motion him to get out of the car. Then he looked at me and jerked his thumb toward the street.

I thought, *Oh boy, now I've pissed him off.*

15

The next afternoon I was in my dressing room when someone knocked on my door. It was my love interest on the show, Johnny. It's a good thing that nut, Beth, had her own dressing room now, or she would have gotten all fluttery and started acting goofy.

I said, "Come in." He looked flushed and sat down immediately. He must have taken Penny's advice and gotten some sun.

Before I could ask what he wanted, he said, "Lena, I want you to know that I'm getting divorced."

I sat there for a moment taking this in. It seemed so personal.

"Johnny, I'm so sorry to hear that. That's sad news. I know I haven't seen your wife at the studio for a while. I wondered why."

"She wants kids. I don't. End of story."

I couldn't help wondering why he felt the need to share this with me. I didn't have to wonder very long, because he went on, "You've become very special to me, Lena. I get significant vibes from you on the set. I know your feelings toward me aren't all an act."

My eyes kept getting bigger and bigger as he spoke. When he finally took a breath. I said "WHOA! *Goombah*! Back it up! Johnny, we work very well together. It's just a job. I'm acting every moment I'm on the set. You are in a confused emotional state. I think you're misunderstanding my performance for real emotion." That sounded good to me, and I'm not a professional counselor.

Johnny looked stunned. He stood up and walked toward me. He was still standing there waiting for me to say something more, but my mind was wandering.

Johnny was a darned good-looking guy: sandy blond hair, broad shoulders, six foot two, eyes of blue, and all that stuff. Not my type at all. That might work for those American girls, but I'm more attracted to Italian guys with hard bodies like wrestlers: dark skin, kind of swarthy. I was lost in my thoughts.

"Oh, I'm sorry, what were you saying, Johnny?"

"I was saying that we should really should try to start a relationship. Maybe what we have in the script could become real."

My thoughts were racing. Johnny needed a reality check. How could I bring him down gently? We had great chemistry on the set.

Maybe we have too many kissing scenes. Sometimes I think of Gino when I'm kissing him. This was not good. It's probably how he got the impression that he was turning me on.

"Johnny, you need to try to work things out with your wife. Relationships have all sorts of ups and downs."

"No, I think the question of having kids has ended our relationship."

"Well, I need to get ready for the show. If you'll excuse me."

I could tell he was going to kiss me when he took a step toward me.

I said, "Just so you know, I want kids too."

Just then Penny came in. She looked at Johnny's face then looked at me. Johnny turned and walked out, Penny said, "What the hell was that all about?"

It was pretty obvious that I was going to have to work some magic into the script. Johnny was going to have a new girlfriend. Wouldn't that be a nice surprise?"

16

I called my ma from the studio to tell her that I was having dinner at Nana's with Gino.

Ma said, "Lena, the surveyors are in the backyard with Vito Lasotta."

"Who's Vito?" I asked.

"He's the concrete guy that did Uncle Joey's restaurant."

'Ma, Gino's Dad is doing the concrete work. Don't let that guy do anything else. I need a list of who's doing each part of this job."

"Okay, Lena, I'll bring them some cookies and coffee and tell them."

In our world, everything is accompanied by food. Whether it's good news, bad news, a celebration or an interruption in the day, food is the common denominator.

Ma called back, "Lena, stop home before you go by Nana's. I have leftover lasagna from yesterday."

I need to make another list:

1. Write a new script for Mr. Latmen and get Johnny a new girlfriend.
2. Get a list of contractors from Dad for the construction project.
3. Talk to Paulie about Carlo and Penny.
4. Take some of my things to Nana's house and start staying there more often.
5. Really stick to my diet.
6. Ask Gino why my dad summoned him out of my car.

When I got to Nana's house my brother Bobby was there. He had walked over from Auntie Lill's house with cousins David and Ronnie. Plates of food were being passed. The boys were shoveling stuff in their faces. Paulie and Mona came in the back door and helped themselves. Nana took some stuff out of the oven and put Ma's Lasagna in. The front doorbell rang and it was Gino. Paulie dragged another chair from the dining room for him. I would not be addressing anything on my list tonight and my diet was going out the window.

When everyone left, Gino was helping me clean the table and put dishes in the sink. Nana wouldn't let him help wash the dishes, though. He leaned over and whispered, "Come to the back door when Nana goes to sleep." He didn't know about Nana's radar. Nobody sneaks in or out of her house.

During the night, I heard something hitting my window. It sounded like pebbles. For a split second I thought it might be Johnny. I looked outside and saw Gino standing in the moonlight wearing sweat pants and a tee shirt. His hair was sticking up all over the place. I started to giggle and motioned for him to wait there. I put on Nana's old sweater and met him on the back porch.

I said, "Do you think you're sixteen years old? Grown men don't throw stones at women's windows."

"Babe," he said as he wrapped his arms around me. "We never have a chance to talk anymore. I can't get you out of my head and I'm tired of sleeping alone."

The porch light went on and Nana said, "Who's a-dat on-a porch?"

"It's me Nana. Gino wants to talk about Paulie's remodeling."

"Okay. You got-a sweater?"

"Yes, I do."

"*Buonannote.*"

We both giggled while we tiptoed across the yard to the *"Paulie House."*

I don't even know what time I climbed into the bedroom window. Gino couldn't believe I wouldn't use the door. I told him

Nana had door radar.

The next morning I heard loud knocking on my bedroom door. "Lena! Bella Mia, what-a you doin' in bed so late? It's eleven o'clock. You gonna be late for TV."

Cripes! I go in at noon today. I had to hustle my hind end out of there pretty quick.

I was very disoriented all day. I hate waking up late and rushing. It makes me emotional, and I can't think clearly. In the script, Beth and I were supposed to have a squabble about some furniture in the pretend B and B that we owned. In that script, Johnny was supposed to interrupt us and pull me away into the foyer to calm me down so Beth and I could settle our dispute. Instead he pulled me into his arms and kissed me passionately.

He caught me completely off guard. I pulled away from him and slapped him so hard I saw his head snap. I heard the closing music for the show begin and then fade out. There was dead silence on the set. Oh boy, this wasn't going to be easy to explain.

When the lights came up I could hear a few hushed whispers from the crew. I saw Mr. Latmen storming in my direction.

He yelled, "LENA! MY OFFICE NOW!"

I held my head up and walked past everyone directly to Latmen's office. He didn't wait for the door to close behind me when he yelled "DO YOU WANT TO STAY ON THIS SHOW? ARE YOU GETTING NUTS LIKE THAT OTHER ONE?"

"Mr. Latmen, I can explain." I told him that passionate kiss was not in the script.

"So, what's wrong with improvising? We do it all the time."

"My slap was improvised, too!"

"That slap turned the entire context of the show around. You and Johnny were always kissing before. Now you slapped him! How does that fit into the script?"

I explained the entire dressing room incident to him. I told him about Johnny's divorce plan and his plan to work me into his life. Latmen listened intently. Then he said, "Here's what you're going to do. You will write a script tonight. It will pick up right where that slap ended today's show. I don't care what you write but I want him to stay on the show. Ladies love him. Get the changes to Sophia and Eddie early tomorrow so they can plug it into tomorrow's show."

"Okay, I'll do that. I'll work it out. I'll talk to him today before he leaves the studio."

I left Latmen's office and marched toward Johnny's dressing room. Greg was walking toward me and said, "That was a heck of a finish, Lena."

"Greg, that was not planned. Please come with me. I need to see Johnny and I don't want be alone with him."

Johnny was sitting in a chair, looking like the dog that he was.

Greg stepped closer to Johnny. I think it was a show of support.

"Here's what's going to happen. I'm going to rewrite tomorrow's episode. You and I are breaking up. You will break the news to me that you are leaving me to go back to your wife, who happens to be pregnant. You've decided that you love her after all, and you want this child too. The slap that ended today's show was good-bye for us as a couple. Be here at noon tomorrow so we can go over the new script."

I went to Nana's and locked myself in my room. It took me all evening to rewrite the script and make it sound believable. I read it, changed it, rearranged it, and I was finally ready to present it to Mr. Latmen.

He was totally satisfied with the changes. He even smiled at me. He said, "Let's get Johnny in here and make sure he doesn't have a fit." Johnny said he could adapt with no problem. I think he was worried I would write him out of the show. Power is a wonderful thing. I could really get used to this. Mr. Latmen had given me liberty with changing the script before, but this change was really important.

17

That night, I was sound asleep in the little bedroom at Nana's house when I heard pebbles hitting my window again. I was sure that it was Johnny tonight. No . . . it was Gino again.

I said, "Gino, my love, I need to get some sleep. I can't do this again tonight. I've had too many late nights."

"Lena, Paulie's here. He crawled in bed with me."

"So what. My uncles always had to sleep together. He probably thought he was reliving his youth. Maybe he had a fight with Mona. I'll come over."

Paulie was sound asleep in the bed. I asked Gino, "Why didn't you just move to the couch?"

"I felt funny sleeping in the same house after he crawled in bed with me."

"He's not *finnoch*, you know."

Paulie woke up and said, "What the hell are you guys doing here?"

"We're wondering what you're doing here, since you live with Mona now."

"Oh, we had a big fight. Then I went to a bar on Rush Street and got drunk."

"How did you get here?"

"I think I took a cab."

Nana walked in and said, "I see all the lights. What's a matta here? Everybody okay? Paulie, why you sleeping in Gino's bed? Gino, you go sleep in Paulie's old bed at-a my house."

I said, "No, Nana, I'm sleeping there."

She shook her head and said, "Everybody go sleep someplace," as she walked out shaking her head.

I could hear her mumbling, "I don't know where nobody belong.

Sleep-a here, no sleep-a here. I'm-a all mixed up. *Chissa, forse sono pazzo. Everybody crazy."*

In the end, Gino slept on the couch at Paulie's and I followed Nana back to the little bedroom in her house. I really needed to get some rest.

Gino called the station before I left the next day. "When am I going to see you?" he asked.

"I can't plan a sleepover right now. I have too much going on at work. Do you want to meet tonight for dinner with Paulie and Mona?"

"Sure, I'll take whatever I can get."

"Well, you'll only be getting dinner tonight."

Paulie picked me up at home so Gino and I could ride back in the same car. Paulie and I used to spend a lot of time together when we were kids. We talked about so many of our problems and helped each other through a lot of tough times. As we got older, I didn't always trust his judgment. Right now, I needed his advice.

Riggio brought us soup and bread. "Geez, can I get away from this bread?" I pushed the basket away from me.

"Paulie, I need to talk to you about Carlo and Penny."

"Gee, Lena you could at least say 'Hi Paulie. How are you and Mona doing?' "

"Just listen, Paulie. This is important. They have become intimate."

"You mean they had SEX?"

"Quiet! Yes, Paulie. That's what I'm saying. More than once."

"WOW! Didn't we find out that he was queer?"

"Oh, Paulie. That's what I'm talking about. What do you think we should do?"

I could see him thinking about this for a few seconds. Then he said, "Why do we have to do anything? Just leave them alone. They're all grown up, you know."

I always think that Paulie is not too smart, but sometimes he says things that are profound. He was right! They were adults. I introduced them, but I am not responsible for the outcome of their relationship. That darned brain filter must have shut down again. I needed to keep my mouth shut and let things happen without trying to control everything

"You're right, Paulie. That's the best way to handle this. I want to ask you something else. You know that I want to build that addition behind my ma's house for Nana. I'm worried that she won't want to move there. I'm afraid she won't want to leave her house after all these years."

He asked, "Did you tell her yet?"

"No. I was going to surprise her."

"Old people don't like surprises. Why don't you live in the new house and just spruce up her house?"

Once again, the knucklehead was right.

I kissed him on the cheek and he looked really proud of himself.

We had time for a really nice dinner with Mona and Gino before Paulie had to sing for his supper.

Gino and I snuck into the back door of the "Paulie House" without turning any lights on. After all, we knew where *everything* was by this time.

18

My ma plays poker with her lady friends. This is usually the last Friday of every month. The women cook all day and bring tons of food to the poker house. They rotate houses so nobody has to have the messy house each time, when everyone leaves. All the kids congregate at that house too. They all go in and out for food and stuff to drink. When the kids get tired, they sack out all over the place. There is always someone's kid staying overnight at the poker house when they can't wake up to go home. Tonight is Ma's turn. I was helping her set up for the party. Gino helped me move tables and set up the food that Ma cooked. The men all migrate over to the *Societa Degli Uomini,* which means that only Italian men can come and loose their money at this club. They play for much bigger stakes than the wives.

"Mangiare! Gino, eat what you want. More food is coming." She slapped Bobby's hands while she said this, but he managed to snag a chunk of bread and a couple of meatballs.

Gino was wearing dress pants and a sport jacket. He wanted to take me somewhere special for dinner. I decided to wear my red evening dress. I bought it to wear on *Tortured Souls* for an episode where Johnny took me out dancing while cheating on his wife. It was a little racier than I would typically wear, but I was feeling a little racier than usual. Gino's eyes lit up when I came into the room. My ma did the eye-roll thing. I was hoping that his dinner choice had a hotel attached. When Auntie Lilly, Auntie Virg, and all the other players arrived we stayed long enough to let them "ooh and aah" over us. Gino and I said our polite good-byes and slipped out the door.

Smart fella that he is, he made reservations downtown at The Drake. We checked into our room first. Needless to say, dinner was late that night. It was a wonderful meal. I am trying to watch my weight, because my ass looks so big on color TV. I ate some kind of Italian chicken dish that Gino ordered for me. We had wine with dinner then we went to the bar for some drinks. People recognized me there. First I was flattered, then Gino decided it was time to go upstairs because I was feeling the drinks, and I was getting sarcastic.

We had really missed each other! We made love in the bed, on the floor, and in the shower.

Gino asked me, "Where did you learn how to do *that*?"

I told him "I read a lot."

"Well, babe, remember how you did that thing, so we can do it again?"

We were catching our breath after the shower when I decided I was hungry again. I was wearing the hotel bathrobe and Gino was wearing his boxers. He put on the other bathrobe and called room service. We had tiramisu, chocolate-covered strawberries, and some kind of cute bits of beef wrapped in dough. I'll diet tomorrow. I was joking about having breakfast in my red evening dress, when Gino opened the closet door and took out a white gift box with a red bow. I started to cry.

"What? You don't like gifts?"

"Gino, you make me so happy. Geez, that sounded so corny."

"Honey, I worked hard on 'happy' tonight! Now open the box."

He brought me the most beautiful black oriental pants suit. He got the right size and he knew my taste perfectly. Reservations were for the weekend, so I guess we'd have to go shopping downtown tomorrow, or I wouldn't have anything to wear on Sunday. I remembered to call my ma and tell her that I was staying at Mona's that night.

How could we top a night like this? We ate breakfast at a little restaurant down the street from the hotel. I kept it simple with fruit and toast and coffee. Gino ate like a lumberjack. He used quite a bit of energy the night before, so I was glad to see him packing the food in.

We shopped on Michigan Avenue. Gino brought clothes with him. I didn't know that he had checked in before he picked me up at home. That's how he got the gift in the closet! I bought a skirt with a fancy top for dinner that night. I felt like I was walking on a cloud.

I called my ma late in the afternoon to tell her that I was having dinner with Gino downtown and I probably wouldn't be home again. I didn't say where I was staying, but she didn't ask.

When I was finished telling her that I went shopping, she had her own story to tell. Apparently the boy cousins were going in and out during the poker game. My cousin Frankie ate something that didn't agree with him or he just ate too much junk. They took bowls of chips and sandwiches and all sorts of soda out in the yard and played basketball into the wee hours. Anyway, Frankie threw up all night and well into the morning. He was so sick that my Aunt Virg was frantic. She had been calling everyone asking if they were feeling sick too. She thought it might be food poisoning. Ma threw all the leftovers away, just in case. We told her to tell everyone how bad we felt for Frankie. Gino groaned when I told him that Ma threw away all the leftovers. He loves food.

We got home on Sunday afternoon and Ma was crying. Auntie Virg had called the family doctor and he was making an emergency house call this afternoon.

I said, "Ma, even if he has food poisoning or the flu, he's going to be fine. They are doing the right thing calling the doctor."

Ma said, "I know. But Aunt Virg is my baby sister, I hate so see her upset."

We usually have so much drama in our family.

When the doctor left, Auntie Virg called my ma. I could hear her yelling on the other end of the phone.

She found out from Frankie that the boys snuck a pint of whiskey out of my dad's basement liquor cabinet. They all took turns taking swigs. Frankie, being the youngest, was showing off. He drank about half the bottle himself. Little Frankie had alcohol poisoning, not food poisoning!

The doctor said, "Didn't you smell the liquor when he threw up?"

Aunt Virg said, "No, he threw up mostly in the yard. The boys threw buckets of water on it so it wouldn't smell."

"Well," the doctor said, "Give him Pepto to coat his stomach and soup. Nothing solid. He should be fine by Monday."

Aunt Virg said to Frankie, "That's good, you little shit, because you're going to school Monday, no matter how you feel." Poor Frankie just groaned.

The phones were busy that afternoon. All the ladies called each other to discuss the "Frankie" situation and the liquor. I was surprised that my dad thought it was funny. He didn't laugh out loud, but smiled and shook his head.

There was a lineup in the yard that afternoon. My Ma was like a prison matron, pacing back and forth in front of the boys. "Who took the bottle? Don't lie! Get this over with! Admit it!"

She marched them over to Auntie Virgi's house to apologize to her and Frankie. It wasn't their fault that Frankie was showing off, but the older boys took the booze.

I didn't think this was ever going to happen again.

I was at my ma's the next afternoon helping her fix dinner. We were making some steak and eggs with green peppers. Dad was bringing home loaves of Italian bread. My brother Bobby was stopping by Nana's to walk with her to our house. Nana was bringing salad stuff from her garden. Ma sat down to cut some peppers. I sat across from her to help.

I said, "Ma, I don't think it's a good idea to move Nana out of her house."

She was quiet for just a few seconds. I could see her thinking about this.

"Lena, what changed your mind? Are you going to stop the construction?"

I could see the concern on her face. She probably thought I was losing my mind. I must admit that I had been doing a lot of crazy stuff.

"No, I'm going to keep it going. I think I'm being selfish. I'm thinking about how much I have and what I want to do with all my money. I haven't really thought about how all this will affect everyone else. Maybe I should move into the new addition here."

I could see my ma's face light up. She never wanted me to leave. Now she would have the best of both worlds too.

Ma said, "Lena, you don't ever have to leave home if you don't want to. Oh, I know you need your privacy. I think building the addition for you is just perfect."

"I have a feeling that Paulie and Mona will wind up living in Nana's back house when the remodeling is done. I'm going to stay with Nana while he's at Mona's. They should be planning the wedding soon. Once they get married, they can move back to Nana's. I'll talk to him about this.

"Honey, you are going to make yourself *pazzo*. Enjoy life. Don't be so eager to change yourself or something else too quickly. You're young and your life is just taking shape. It's all going to work out fine."

She's right. I'm going to put the addition on my parent's house first. Maybe it will be a separate house. Gino will remodel Paulie's place. I will slowly work with Nana about remodeling her house.

I ate dinner that night feeling much better. I skipped the bread and had steak and eggs with peppers and a big green salad. My ass was starting to look like it needed its own zip code in color.

Carlo called me that night. He wanted to talk. I met him at a coffee shop near the TV station. When he saw me, he looked really happy. He kissed me and seemed so glad to see me.

"Lena, I want you to know how grateful I am for everything you've done for me. I'm so glad that you introduced me to Penny. She's the best thing that has ever happened to me. That is, next to knowing you."

I reached across the table and took his hand. He looked at me and blushed all the way up to his hairline. We leaned a little closer, so people around us couldn't hear us. I thought that was very sweet.

I told him, "I think it's wonderful that this has worked out. I know it's not the same type of relationship that our parents had, but if it works for you and Penny, who am I to question that?"

"Lena, I'm going to get made soon. I think I'll get the call in the next couple of weeks. I want to be sure that you will come to the gathering afterward. Please bring Gino. You will get a call from my dad or Jimmy "Bags," or one of the guys. It's going to be a great party. I really am so nuts about Penny. It's even a surprise to me. I don't know how this happened. Could I have been wrong about my feelings about men all these years?"

"I don't know how those feelings work, Carlo. I just know that you can't turn them off and on. It's got to come natural. It's how you feel inside."

"I wonder if you would like to come with Penny and me to see houses. I was going to look for a bigger apartment, but I think she would like a house."

"Holy cripes! You are just moving right along, aren't you?"

"Yes. I guess I'm just trying to make the most out of something good that came into my life."

"Make sure that house hunting is okay with Penny. I'll join you both whenever you want me."

We finished our coffee and walked outside. He kissed me on each cheek, and we went to our separate cars.

When I walked to my car, I noticed a dark sedan on the other side of the street. The car followed me several blocks before he turned off on a side street. I know he was watching me. After a lifetime of being in the "family," I know a tail when I see one.

I wasn't afraid, but I was a little concerned. I didn't know if I should talk to my dad or mention it to Gino. I needed to think about this for now. I didn't want to make a big stir before I observed more. Maybe my dad thought I needed to be looked after right now. He knows I occasionally carry around a lot of money because of this remodeling. He could have someone protecting me.

That evening I worked on a new script for the show. We needed to find another male for the mix. In the script, Beth and I were competing for Johnny's affection. He was cheating on his wife, but

Beth was constantly trying to steal him away from me. Now that he was going back to his pregnant TV wife, we needed a new scenario.

I thought a new guy and a new girl should be added. Beth needed a new love interest now that Johnny would be a "husband" again. I thought my character should be running the soap's Bed and Breakfast for a while with no love interest.

I presented this to Mr. Latmen early the next morning. He blew his top! "ABSOLUTELY NOT! There is no way I'm going to let you take a back seat in the romance department. Think of something else. Find another man for Beth. Call the Actor's Equity and interview a couple of studs. You can't change a show like this overnight. I know you want to push Johnny away from you, but you can't back away from being the star. If you do that, you'll wash yourself out of the show."

"Okay, okay. I'll do that. I'll call the Actor's Equity and have them send a few guys over this week. I'll call today."

I made another list:

1. Find a chick that would play Johnny's pregnant wife.
2. Find a man for Beth.
3. Get myself a new love interest in the show.
4. Stay on this darned diet and buy darker clothes.

Mona and I went to Mayson's's to buy some new clothes for the show. She was shopping for some new stuff too. She came out of the dressing room wearing a hot pink suit. I was speechless. She looked so beautiful. I could see her on TV in that outfit. Her hair wasn't as dark as mine. It was a little auburn. It would be great on camera with all those lights.

I said, "Mona, have you ever thought about being on television?"

Mona was busy checking out her butt in the mirror. She tugged the jacket down and stuck out her chest.

"What did you say?"

I repeated, "Mona, have you ever thought about being on television?"

"Lena, I couldn't even read a paper out loud in high school. You must be kidding."

"Let me ask you this: How would you feel about playing a pregnant wife to Johnny. It wouldn't have to be permanent— although sometimes those TV pregnancies last a long time."

"Ha! You're very funny. I'm supposed to be planning a wedding, remember? I could no more be on TV than your Nana."

"Mona, think about this. I'm still in the planning stages of this next big episode. But this could give you some extra money for you wedding."

"Well, okay. I'll think about this. I'll ask Paulie what he thinks too."

"You can ask him, but this has to be your decision. Women can make these decisions on their own, you know."

My poor brain was getting tired from all this planning and decision-making. I felt like my head would explode. I had been thinking about going away for a weekend with my ma. I knew she would really be excited. I called Gino from my dressing room before I left the studio and got no answer. I decided to call him from my ma's house later and let him know I'd be away for the weekend.

That evening I asked my ma if she wanted to go someplace for a couple of days. I though maybe we could take a drive somewhere and swim in a hotel pool and relax.

The suggestion was no sooner out of my mouth when she said, " Lena, I've always wanted to go to Lake Geneva. We could get a room at the nice place by the water, the big hotel with a view of the lake, Harbor Shores."

"Done, Mama! I'll make reservations today. Plan to go this coming weekend."

My dad didn't like that idea. He didn't like two women going on a long drive alone. Never mind that! I was pretty good at directions. I could read a map.

"Lena, why don't you take Paulie with you? Better yet, invite Gino to go along."

"Dad, I don't want to take anyone but Ma. This is going to be a girl's weekend."

"*Che testa dura*. Whose kid is this with the hard head?"

My ma said, "Gee, Sam, I can only guess she could be just like you."

I asked my dad to call Gino while Ma and I went shopping for bathing suits. What a riot that was. I never saw her in anything less than a slip and bra. She looked just great. She picked out a black and red suit with a red cover up. We joked about modeling it for my dad.

Ma said, "I'm not going to show him at all. He would only make comments that would change my mind, and I'm already having too much fun."

He might decide that the bathing suit was too racy and he would tell her she couldn't go with me. Ha! We were two women on a mission for a good time.

We left early Friday evening. Dad said he'd try Gino again later. We stopped for dinner about an hour after we got on the road. I saw a black sedan pull in the parking lot behind us. I had seen the same car behind me while I was driving. I didn't mention it to Ma because I didn't want her to worry. I was more offended than angry. I thought, *"Geez, Dad. Don't you trust your daughter with your wife?"* But somehow, I knew there was more to this than what I saw. I wasn't going to let it ruin our weekend. I wanted to show Ma a good time and relax.

Dinner was wonderful. We ate what the waiter recommended. It was a salmon dish with some sort of white sauce. It came with soup and salad and the darned breadbasket was wonderful. Ma insisted on tipping the waiter, even though I said that everything was on me.

"He looks Italian, Lena. I'm going to leave him a nice tip." I wondered what that had to do with service, but I didn't say so.

We drove on and got to Lake Geneva late that night. The same dark car was in the lane next to me as I drove into the wide entrance of the parking lot. I went right and he turned left. He parked close to the lot exit. Easier to pull out behind us, I guessed. I parked closer to the entrance of the hotel. I'm smart enough to know it's well lit and safer for two women alone. We were being followed. It looked like the same dark car that I saw when I left the coffee shop where I met Carlo.

We stopped in the bar for a cocktail and sent our bags up to our room. The band was beginning to play in the lounge. We stayed a while and jitterbugged to a couple of songs. We met a nice couple closer to Ma and Dad's age. We chatted with them a while, then went up to our room.

Mama was delighted with the room. "Lena! This is so elegant!"

The next morning we had a great breakfast of eggs Benedict, sausage, and fresh fruit. We spent the morning at the pool. We took a ride in a carriage after lunch and shopped in the afternoon. Then we went to the hotel bar and had a martini. We were having such a great time! The music in the lounge started around 9 p.m. They had a crooner who sang Sinatra. He was skinny and wore a gray sharkskin suit. His hair was plastered flat, just like Frankie. He came to our table and sang for my ma. She was all flustered. "Oh, Lena is this dress too tight? I don't want to seem like a flirt. If he comes over again, should I turn away?"

"Oh, Mama, don't worry. It's his job to sing to the ladies."

On our last morning, we went to the outside pool. The hotel had a breakfast buffet set up in a beautiful tent. After we ate, I picked up some magazines at the gift shop and we sat in the sun and read. We took a dip in the pool and ate lunch outside. While we were having lunch, I looked toward the street and saw the dark sedan parked at the end of the drive. A man with a hat and sunglasses sat behind the wheel.

Di cosa si tratta? I thought to myself. *What is this?*

Ma must have seen the look on my face. She said, "What's wrong, honey?"

"Oh, I was just thinking about the show. I'm trying to relax and it keeps popping back into my head."

"You'll write the new script. Why don't you tell me about it?"

I explained the new ideas that I had for some new cast members.

She listened and made a few comments. Then she said, "There, now don't you feel better? Let's get dressed up and go into town."

We spent the rest of the day wandering in and out of antique shops and trendy stores on Main Street. We stopped at little bar and grill on a side street and had burgers and beer. Ma and I jitterbugged again to some rock-a-billy on the jukebox. We were having such a great time. We took a cab back to he hotel and had a cocktail in the bar. We turned in pretty early because of the long drive home in the morning.

The black sedan pulled in behind us and stayed at the end of the drive when we got back to the hotel. In the morning he was parked out in front. He wasn't really trying to hide anymore. That was just fine. At this point, the game was out in the open. It was time to talk to my dad about this. I couldn't wait any longer.

Dad met us in the driveway when we got home. I could tell that he had missed Ma. He came right over and hugged her. He looked so serious. We unloaded the car and he carried all of our packages in. We made a big show of pulling all the stuff out of bags and boxes.

He was a good sport and said, "Oh, that's nice," and "What the heck are you gonna do with that?" when he saw some of the old books and a vase that Ma found. When we got all the travel things unpacked and Ma went upstairs, I asked Dad to come into the living room with me. He always gets this wrinkle between his eyebrows when he's concerned about what I might say.

"Dad," I began, "Someone has been following us. It's a black sedan with one man in it. I thought it was my imagination at first, but he's been with us all weekend and followed us all the way home."

"Baby, I have something to tell to you."

I smiled and said, "What? You were protecting me. I know, Dad."

"Lena, come over here and sit down."

He motioned for me to sit beside him on the sofa. Dad took my hand and looked like he was going to cry.

"They sent Gino away, Lena. He left for Italy yesterday. Gino has a commitment that his dad made to the family of a girl in Italy.

The deal was made for power and money. The guy tailing you is a member of Gino's father's hired "family." They were hoping that you were going off with some other guy. They saw you with Carlo one night and they thought they had a reason to tell Gino that you were cheating on him. Then they found out that you and Carlo are *padrini* to Gemma's baby and they couldn't use that.

"I don't get it," I said. "This isn't making sense to me." I could feel denial setting in. *This is not real at all.*

"He was looking for a reason to break you and Gino apart. It's a family promise that goes back to when Gino was just a kid. This arrangement has to be honored. He thought that if you were cheating on Gino, it would be easier for him to accept the breakup. Gino is very upset. He's angry with his father. He was furious when I talked to him yesterday."

I didn't know what to say. I felt myself begin to shake. The tears started to roll down my face. Dad tried to put his arms around me and I pushed him away. He kept putting his arm around me, even though I kept pushing it off.

"I know this is hard for you to understand, Lena. Gino is not accepting this very well either."

"What is this, some kind of test, or a joke, Dad? Who does his father think he is, Al Capone? Are we making a movie? Are you sure about this? I know Gino loves me. He would never do this to me."

I know I was raising my voice. I sounded hysterical. It was as if I was watching this and I was someone else . . . like one of those out-of-body experiences.

"Lena, it's over. There isn't any other way. He's gone." I could hear the sadness in Dad's voice.

My ma heard me raising my voice and came rushing into the room.

"What is it? What's the matter? Is someone hurt or sick?"

I wondered why he didn't call me yesterday. I felt like someone had punched me in the gut. I couldn't breathe or speak. He's already gone. How could he do this to me?

After my dad explained the whole thing to Ma, she looked like she was going to be sick. She sat down and cried next to me

Ma said, "This is not 1945, Sam. Those agreements aren't made any more!"

"Josie, this arrangement was made when Gino was just a kid, maybe five years old. It was made between two powerful families."

My life was a mess and I had to accept it. Ma hugged me and we both cried. After I fought to gain control of myself, I said. "What happens now?"

"I'm not sure," Dad said. "I spoke to Gino about this a couple of weeks ago after the meeting at the club. We went back inside to talk with his dad. He was hoping his dad could arrange something else. He hoped the girl in Italy might have met someone else."

It was all beginning to make sense to me now. I understood why Gino and my dad were having intense conversations and why he pulled Gino from my car after the construction meeting. I didn't know how to handle this. I felt numb.

"So, now life goes on," Dad said. "Gino went back to Michigan night before last. He piled all his stuff in his car and called me when he stopped for gas. He left for Italy yesterday. He didn't know how to tell you, Lena. He wants you to know how much he cares about you, but he has to honor the family commitment."

I had to clear my head. I needed to think logical thoughts.

Dad went into the kitchen and poured us each a glass of wine. Mom poured her own wine in a bigger glass.

I asked, "What happens with the contractor work with Gino's father?" I was trying to calm myself down with logic.

"We'll use the cement guy that Uncle Joey used for his restaurant."

One thing I have learned in this family: there is never any shortage of cement workers.

How could my life keep unraveling? How was I supposed to pull this together? I thought Gino was the man of my dreams; it turns out that he was just passing through. I have to get my head straight and get on with the show . . . in more ways than one.

Dad came over to me and put his arms around me. "No matter

what you think, Lena, Gino's feelings for you were real. Some people never know what it's like to really love someone."

Now I see everything very differently—even my dad seems wiser, more worldly. And life will go on.

I will focus on the new cast for the show and find other interests. I have so many good things in my life and I'm not finished growing yet!

19

On Monday I called Actor's Equity. I told them I needed two men and two women to interview for a soap opera. They sent over one fat guy and a tall skinny guy with thinning hair. I sent them away.

The next day they sent over a girl who looked too much like me, and a little girl who looked about sixteen years old. This wasn't going to be as easy as I thought.

I called Mona. "Come to the TV station and just read from the script. You don't have to commit to anything just yet. It will be fun. Can you imagine us working together? It would be great!"

"Fine, I'll come and read. I don't understand why you can't get a professional actress. I know you can find them all over the place."

Mona came in on Wednesday morning before the show. Mr. Latmen and I waited in my dressing room for her. He liked her looks immediately.

She read the lines, *"Johnny, I love you. Please come back to me. Our baby will need a father. You won't be sorry. You need us. Our lives and our hearts belong together."*

There were a couple of more lines. She spoke them even more emotionally. I was so impressed that I didn't have to say a word. Mr. Latmen asked, "When can you start?"

He explained that she would have to be pregnant on the show for a while. He hadn't decided if she was going to have the baby and stay on the show or have the baby and make some infrequent appearances.

"Lena, show her where the fake baby bumps are so she can get used to the idea."

She was so excited that it made me forgot my own misery. We called my ma and told her about Mona's new part. Ma could hear Mona giggling like a schoolgirl. I think my ma was happy for me. She knew that this would be a great distraction from my broken heart.

Now if I could find two men to fit into the cast, I could score some points and make everyone at the TV station happy.

Mona showed up at Nana's house wearing the fake "baby bump." Nana looked like she was going to faint when she saw her. When she lifted her shirt to show her, I thought Nana was going to die laughing. Then we strapped it on to Nana and she paraded all over the house in it. I don't remember ever seeing her laugh so hard.

"I remember my own 'belly bumps.' I had nine of them! All were real. Not fake like this-a one. This is more fun 'cause you can take it off any time-a you want."

We called my ma to come over for a surprise. Nana wore the "baby bump" under her apron and stood sideways at the kitchen door when my ma came in. We had another good laugh. She tried it on and we took her picture with Paulie's Kodak Instant Camera.

Life isn't so bad when you have family. People who love you can make anything better.

20

N ow that my heart had gone to Italy with Gino, I would have to use the same strength that I've always had for other big decisions. That "thought filter" I created will help me sort out the memories I have of Gino and help my broken heart mend. What's that old saying? *"If you love someone, let them go. If they don't come back, hunt them down and kill them."* Not really, but it makes me smile to think about it.

When Gino left without any good-bye, I was hurt and angry. Then I realized that this was not easy for him either. The decision was made by someone higher up in the chain of command. When he went away, I wanted to know her name. I wondered who she was. Was she pretty? Would they ever come to America? Then I realized that it didn't matter. It was over and I had to move on. This was the age of liberation, and Italian families were still bound by the old country ways. This stunk and I hated it.

I need to focus on the things that are critical to my family and myself. I made a list of workers who would complete the addition at Ma and Dad's:

Ask about the guy who did his restaurant foundation.

Windows – Angelo Loca

Plumbing – Mario Ladona

Flooring – Ma's Uncle Riccardo

The structure itself would be designed by me and completed by my dad's friends who have connections everywhere.

That week I would interview more people for the show. It was a great distraction from my own problems. Being in a soap opera gave me the "alternate" life I needed right then. If Mr. Latmen sent

Beth on a little vacation, I would need to call Susan. Her baby was nearly a year old, and she might be ready to work again. Actor's Equity was sending over a few more people for casting. I was pretty specific about the look I wanted.

I really needed to find someone who would fix the mess in Paulie's old house. Gino moved all his belongings out on the weekend when he called to say good-bye to my dad. Now it was time for me to move on.

Once the new addition is completed, I am hiring Mona's sister Jaclyn to decorate the entire house. She does amazing work; I've seen it in magazines. My house will have three bedrooms, a full bath, a half bath, a living room, and a kitchen with the most modern conveniences. I'll have a dishwasher, a stove with a self-cleaning oven, a refrigerator with a frost-free freezer, and an ice holder compartment.

I knew I would have to face the empty little house behind Nana's. Gino tore it apart, anticipating that he would live there at some point. I drove there after work on Friday, talking to myself all the way. "I will be objective," I said. "This is just a house. It's nothing that can't be fixed."

I walked through the kitchen and saw all the cabinets with the doors off. Gino had taken them down to refinish them. All the furniture was in the living room. I walked into the bedroom. The only item in there was the famous mattress. It sat in the middle of the floor, looking forlorn and bare. Was it just last week that we had snuck in the back door? I sat down on it and bawled my eyes out. Darned old mattress'—it's just a used-up hunk of springs and fluff.

I decided to drag it out to the garbage. After I flipped it up on its side, I slid it through the empty kitchen, all the while sweating and swearing. I leaned it against the wall by the back door while I struggled to hold it back with one foot and propped open the back door. I caught my breath and pushed it out the door and across the porch. It bumped down the steps into the yard and fell over flat, just like my life. I looked down at my white slacks and saw that one knee was torn and dirty.

My hair was hanging in a snarled mess, and my deodorant was worn off. I sat on the bottom step and started to cry again.

Nana came bustling out her back door and said, "Lena, Bella Mia, why you do this you self? You gotta six uncles and so many people to help you. Hey, why you cry?"

I told her that Gino left. He'd gone to Italy to fill a family promise. He would marry a girl that the families promised him to. I'd lost him to someone he had never met.

Nana looked at the mattress and then at me. By the look of shock on her face, I could tell that she understood my feelings completely. She knew that mattress was symbolic of my lost love.

She took two hankies from her sleeve. After checking to be sure they were clean, she gave me one and she blew her nose on the other one. She looked at me with shining eyes and said, "I think we gonna burn this-a thing."

We both started to laugh. She hugged me and said, "You young and beautiful, you gotta your whole life in front of you. Common-a, let's throw this away." We dragged the mattress into the alley and stood it up against the back of the house. She brushed her hands together and said "*FINITO*! We have coffee now."

She's so cute, my Nana. She took out her good china cups and saucers. She set out biscotti and some homemade bread. "Lena, don't let a man take your life for himself so early. I'm-a no sure how to say, you just a young woman. You gonna live a long-a long-a time. You don't need to decide on your partner so soon."

She was trying to console me. She was giving me a dose of her wisdom and letting me know how much she loved me. In Nana's kitchen I felt safe. This was where our family gathered when I was a child. It's where we came to be together. This was where we made memories. Paulie was right. I can't take her away from this home where love still grows for our family.

I asked her, "Was Papa the only man you ever loved?

She looked at me and smiled a sad smile and said, "No, Bella, my first love was Bernardo. I was fourteen years old. He follow my family to the dock when we were gonna come-a to America. He cried, 'Rosina! Please donna leave-a me. I love you.' My mother said, 'You a young-a boy. No mix up-a my daughter. You gotta nothing to give-a her. Why she stay with you?' I loved him, Lena. Much as a young fourteen-year-old-a girl could love a boy. I meet your Papa here in America. Our *famiglia* were friends in Italy. They arrange for us to meet. It wasn't exactly a *fidanzata*, how you say 'arranged,' but the *famiglias,* they say you do the old way. I was almost sixteen years old. He was eighteen and very handsome.

"Nana, did you learn to love him?"

"Lena, we had nine children. I guess it was love!" Her face flushed and we laughed again.

NANA & PAPA DELUCA WITH 6 OF 9 CHILDREN

After the show on Monday, Actors Equity sent over a guy and a girl. We had already decided that Mona would play Johnny's wife. Once again, the girl they sent looked too much like me. She was shorter, a little bustier, and had a bigger butt. I needed to be more specific. I would have to ask for a blond, small, American-looking girl. The guy was almost as tall as Johnny, but he had red hair. How's that gonna look on TV? I took him into the studio so I could see him on the TV monitor with studio lighting. I let them both read.

The girl had nothing to offer TV. The guy was pretty good. I asked him to stay. I might be able to use his looks and talent for the comanager of the B and B. He could be a possible love interest for Beth "The Nut."

Now I need to find a love interest for me . . . on the show, that is. I'm not looking for any love interest in my real life.

My dad was more torn up about Gino going to Italy than I expected. He kept asking me if I was okay. I told him that I was going to be fine. I think Dad liked Gino more than I realized. He was already thinking of him as family.

Every evening that I spent at Nana's house, Ma would call and make sure that I was doing all right. She was acting like I just had some kind of serious operation. She wanted to make sure that I ate dinner.

"How did things go at the TV studio today?" she would ask. "Did you interview any handsome men for the show? Lena, you looked so nice on TV today. I love the additions since everything has gone to color."

I knew she needed to hear my voice. I did my best to chatter for a while. I made her feel better for me.

I was ready to get a crew of men over to continue the remodeling on the back house. I needed to do this to let my parents know that my brain was still functioning, even though my heart was broken. I called Paulie and Mona to come to Nana's house for dinner. I needed to be sure that they wanted to move back in after the place was finished. We could talk over dinner.

I told Nana they were coming over and she said, "It's a good thing. 'Cause I make-a too much food today. Somebody bring-a the chairs from the dinning room."

Nana makes too much food every day. Without exception. Someone always comes for dinner.

My brother Bobby came with Uncle Paulie and Mona.

"Oh, Bobby. Kiss-a you Nana! You get-a the chairs for me. You strong boy."

We ate baked penne regati with alfredo sauce. My ma came over with some stuffed hamburgers. She makes big fat ones stuffed with mozzarella, spinach, and olives. They were outstanding. I didn't eat them on bread.

Mona brought a big antipasto salad. Auntie Lilly and Gemma stopped by. They were out for a walk with the babies and saw all the cars in front of Nana's house.

I brought the subject up about the unfinished remodeling in Paulie's old house.

"I can do it, Lena," Paulie said.

"I can help him, you know," Bobby added.

He said this like a statement, not a question.

I asked him, "When did you become a carpenter?"

"Lena, you don't pay any attention to me anymore. I always help Dad around the house with different stuff. I'm pretty good at refinishing furniture. I helped Dad with the bookcases in the basement."

"Well, Bobby, looks like you get the job of refinishing the cabinet doors for the kitchen."

Paulie said, "Lena, I can rip up that old carpeting and start painting."

I went to get more chairs in the dining room and I heard Ma tell Mona, "I'm afraid she is moving at this frantic speed to help her forget about Gino."

Mona said, "She is. I know Lena. That's how she'll survive."

Construction would start on my addition in about two weeks. The foundation had been poured about five days ago. Uncle Joey's guy did a great job. He kept asking me if I wanted a second bathroom. I finally decided on a powder room next to the front door. So, now it's a bath and a half. The plans are on tables in the garage so the men can use the area as a workspace. Dad always parks out in front or in the driveway anyway. Ma always has fresh coffee for them. Dad told her to stop feeding them. "They come too early and stay too late, like squirrels."

I'm so glad this is moving along. It's keeping my mind active and away from Gino. I cry every night, but by morning, I think I look pretty good. No trace of tears and my eyes aren't puffy. Nana asked why the ice cube trays are not frozen? I use the ice on my eyes every morning while I'm in the shower. It's my secret. I told her that she needs a new refrigerator. Good to plant the idea for the new appliances I want to get for her. I'll get past this, but I probably won't get over it.

21

My dad has an Uncle Peppino, or Zio, as we call him in Italian. He speaks hardly any English, even though he came from Italy thirty years ago. Zio has always lived in a little basement apartment in his friend's building. Zio came from Italy with this guy when they were friends. Zio has never been married and has no family other than my dad. Well, Zio fell down the basement steps a few weeks ago. He broke his hip and can't go back to his apartment to live by himself.

My dad came home from the hospital to tell Ma about this.

"Oh, boy. I know where this is going," she said. "Sam, I know if he comes here, this will become permanent. We have Lena's room, but he's not going to like having all these people around all the time."

Ma said she always knew this could happen. We are his only family. I stay at Nana's house most of the time. My room is available.

Ma said, "We could move the TV and sofa into the dining room. We'll move his bed into the living room and he could come directly from the front door into his bedroom."

Dad said, "No way is he getting my living room."

"Just use my bedroom, Ma," I insisted.

I think my ma was afraid to let Zio have my bedroom. If she let someone else have it, it was a sure sign that I wasn't coming back.

Dad is pretty spoiled. He really doesn't want anyone to disrupt his routine. He knows he's obligated to Zio Peppino, but he's struggling with the invasion. It will be like a stranger in his house. My dad has the kitchen clock thirty minutes fast. It's always been that way. If he likes you, he tells you pretty quick that the clock is fast. If he doesn't like you, you can leave a half hour early. People have wondered how they got home from our house so quickly.

Zio gets out of the hospital at the end of the week. I guess he'll be living with us for a while.

When I got to the station that afternoon, I saw Mr. Latmen on the set giving orders to the staff setting up for the day's show. I yelled, "Hey, Mr. Latmen! How's it going?"

"Lena, maybe you can call me 'Jack.' "

"Well, Jack, okay. It's about time."

"Sarcasm becomes you, Lena. Milton is coming in to read again today. I cleared it with the producers and writers. I've included your changes and they approved them."

"Thanks, Jack!"

He smiled and said, "Go look for Milton, Lena."

Milton was really a good fit. I was worried about the red hair, but I think he's handsome enough for it to work out on colored TV. I asked Latmen what part he thought Milt should have in the show.

"Lena, what role do you have planned for him?"

I didn't realize that I was expected to determine that. We have Sophia and Eddie, who are the show's writers. He was asking me to make the call. This was really a big responsibility. I decided to jump at the opportunity.

"I thought he could be Mona's brother," I responded. "They will be starting at the same time, and it might be good to add relatives to the cast."

"He's got to have a purpose. Will he have a job, be a visitor, or something else?"

"I thought he could own a furniture store. That's where I'll buy furniture for the B and B."

"Fine. Feed that idea to the writers so they can get started."

22

I was going toward my dressing room and Greg was coming toward me carrying a princess phone.

I said, "Nice phone, Princess."

"It is for a Princess. It's yours. Mr. Latmen thought it was time that you and Beth stop using the pay phone in the break room. The phone company was here this morning installing the phone jacks. He wants to give you both 'Star Status.' "

"Wow! I'm impressed. I'll have to thank him. By the way, how are you and Beth doing?"

Greg rolled his eyes and shook his head.

"I said, "That really looked Italian. What's wrong?"

"She's really nuts, you know. If she didn't have a script to keep her straight for the show, she would be totally off the wall."

"Are you still dating?"

"If you want to call it that. I'm trying to break it off and have her lose interest in the relationship. She's so clingy and needy. It's not working and I don't know what to do."

"I knew that was going to happen. I heard about her emotional problems before this. Has she threatened to hurt herself if you leave her?"

"No. She's threatened to hurt *me.*"

"Greg, I'm really sorry. I knew she was emotional and high strung, but I didn't think that she was dangerously unstable. Maybe we should talk to Mr. Latmen about this."

"I think I'll talk to her parents first. I have a feeling they've been through this before."

I called Ma to tell her about my new phone and give her the

number. She was very excited that I had my own phone. She couldn't wait to tell the aunties.

I brought up the subject of Zio Peppino. I told her that I had no problem giving him my room. She could leave my bedroom set in there. All we needed to do was move his personal stuff.

I also told her that no one would think badly of her if she found a nice nursing home for Zio.

Ma said, "I thought about this all night, Lena. We take care of our own. A nursing home is out of the question. This is the circle of life."

"I'll help you tomorrow, Ma. We'll take Dad's station wagon and clean out his apartment and get his personal stuff."

The next day I went by Ma and Dad after work. Jimmy "Bags" was there.

Dad said, "Jimmy is going with me to Zio's. We'll make sure the place is clean and there aren't any unusual belongings around. You and Ma have enough to do."

It occurred to me that there was a little more history to Zio Peppino than I first recalled. Mama glanced in my direction and said, "Okay, honey."

When Dad and Jimmy "Bags" went to get jackets in the hall closet, they took a duffle bag off the shelf. When they left she pulled me into the kitchen and out on the back porch.

Her eyes were sparkling. "Lena, when Zio was younger, he was a front man for a lot of stuff. Dad probably suspects that some old dead guys have left stuff Zio has forgotten about."

"What kind of stuff do you think might be there?"

"Guns and money! That's what I always heard. No one could prove it."

Nana came out on the porch.

She said, "Oh, girl talk. I wonder what-a you girls talkin' about. Anybody gonna eat dinner in this house. I bring some eggplant and salad from the garden and *ventriglio de pollo.*"

"Oh, chicken gizzards. It's been a long time since I had those. Did you save some for Paulie? I would have picked you up, Nana."

"Lena, some-a time I gotta walk a little bit. Yes, I left a big dish for Paulie and Mona. What's the big-a piece of concrete in you yard. You gonna have a big cement patio?"

"Ma, Lena is going to build her own little house behind us."

"Madonna Mia! So much money you have to spend for this, Bella. You come to live at my house forever and save your money."

"Well, that would be nice, Nana. Zio Peppino is coming to live here. Paulie and Mona are going to move into the back house now that . . ." my voice trailed off.

"I know, Lena. It's gonna be okay. Don't you worry."

She knew I couldn't say Gino's name.

Ma hustled us inside and said, "Okay, let's get some dinner on the table. Your Dad will think we escaped out the back door. He'll probably bring Jimmy "Bags" back with him. So we better get cookin'."

We all tried to pretend that Gino never existed. Some days I did okay. It was the nights that were so long. I found myself remembering his laugh or trying to remember his smell or his arms around me. I smiled when I remembered him throwing pebbles at my window, that passionate night together at the Drake, the beautiful gifts he brought me in the morning. Some people never experience the profound feelings we immediately had for each other. Nana always *"Che sara sara"*, and then we go forward. *AVENDAMO.*

Uncle Paulie was working like crazy on the little house. He was almost done with the floors. Bobby had enlisted cousins David and Junior to help finish the cabinets. They looked great—the cabinets, not the cousins. Paulie and Mona were excited about moving back into the house. Mona was thinking about wall colors and carpeting. I suggested she use Jaclyn Corona to decorate. Her brother, Dino, got the family okay to do all the windows. Nana was waiting for the wedding plans, although she didn't say anything out loud. She mentioned to Mona that the little alcove in the front next to the windows could be used for a crib.

Saturday morning I went to Ma and Dad's to see if she wanted me to take her grocery shopping. I went around the back door and there was Zio Peppino sitting with his lawn chair in the middle of the concrete foundation.

I said to Ma, *"Che Cos'e questo?"* I laughed, but Ma didn't look too happy.

Ma spun around and said, "I'll tell you what gives. This guy thinks he's at a resort. He thinks that's his new patio. 'Josie, please-a you get me *acqua*. Josie, I'm a little hungry. *Josie, non mi piace questo cane.'* Do I care if he likes the dog? Too bad, right?" Ma was waving her arms like she was ready to fight. The look on her face was priceless. She was very indignant. Her big brown eyes were so wide, that I thought they were gonna pop.

"Don't get upset, Ma. I'll talk to him. We have to remind him that he has to use his legs so they get his hip strong. I didn't know he spoke so much English."

"Me neither. Don't say anything yet. It's his first day home. I'll give him some time to get settled in."

Suddenly, my mouth hung open, "Ma, did you say 'dog'? You don't have a dog."

"Well, we do now. He was in Al's truck yesterday when he came to deliver some of the building material. He got out and ran to me like he knew me all his life. When Al told him to 'stay,' he sat right down. When he told him to roll over, he rolled over and let me scratch his belly. He calls him Joe, but I call him Jojo."

She opened the back door and said, "Jojo, come out!"

Well, there was Jojo the Wonder Dog. I said, "Sit!" and he sat! I said, "Speak!" and he barked.

I said, "Ma, he's really smart. What made you decide to keep him?"

"Oh, the dog decided to stay with me. When Al was ready to leave, the dog walked to the truck, but wouldn't get in. He kept looking back at me. He wanted to stay. Dad really didn't want him, but I couldn't let him go. He's so smart. Al found him running in traffic."

"Well, he can't be too smart if he was running in traffic."

"I think he jumped out of a car or something."

Zio looked over at the dog and said, "*Non mi piace questo.*"

"See, he doesn't like the dog. He'd better not give me an ultimatum, 'cause the dog's staying."

I watched Jojo prance into the house next to Ma as if to say, "So there."

Ma gave him rice with pasta sauce. He licked the bowl clean. Then he gripped the bowl in his jaws, carried it to Ma and dropped it at her feet. "I think he wants more," Ma said.

I watched this with amusement. This dog had my ma wrapped around his paw.

Dad never said anything about what he found in Zio's apartment. I asked Ma about it.

She said, "Guns and money, just like I suspected. Dad found three guns and quite a bit of money."

"How much money?"

Ma said, "I'm getting new living room furniture and the rest is going in the bank for Zio's food and medicine."

"Wow! Good for you, Ma! How much did Daddy find?"

"Three shoe boxes!"

My dad came in from the garage and called "Jojo." The dog came running out of the living room and threw himself at Dad's feet.

Dad scratched Jojo's belly and behind his ears. "Josie, don't get too attached to this dog. What if Al finds the owner? He put up signs around the neighborhood, you know. What did you feed this dog?"

"I fed him rice with pasta sauce."

I wondered who was getting more attached.

With that, he went to the refrigerator and took out a bowl of meatballs. He scooped half of them into the dog's dish. "A dog needs meat," he announced, while he mashed them with a fork.

"Dad, I thought we were gonna have meatball sandwiches for lunch this afternoon?"

Ma said, "I guess we're going to have pepper and egg sandwiches again. I think I have some leftover pork chops."

"Let's go grocery shopping. You can't keep feeding this dog

people food. He's going to get sick. He needs dog food," I said.

My brother Bobby came in the kitchen. He spent the last two nights at Auntie Lil's house with her boys.

"Hey! Whose dog is this?"

Dad said, "Al found him running in the street. Well, we'll see if we keep him."

"What's his name?"

Everyone answered, "Jojo."

Bobby took a butter cookie out of the cookie jar and said, "Speak."

Jojo sat at his feet and barked.

I'll be darned. That dog is really smart. Everyone clapped. My family was so impressed with this silly dog. "Don't feed him another thing!" I said. "Let's go to the store right now before you kill this dog with kindness."

Bobby went with us. He loaded the cart with dry dog food, canned dog food, flavored dog biscuits, a collar, a leash, and some dog toys. Geez, what the heck would they do if they had a grandchild?

When we got home, we saw Zio Peppino sitting in the same spot on the concrete slab. Jojo was at his side. Zio's right hand was scratching the dog's head. When Zio heard the car doors slam, he pulled his hand away and gave the dog a little shove, as if to say, "Move".

I said, "Look Ma. Zio likes the dog. He just wants us to think that he doesn't. He doesn't like the competition."

"I think you're right, Lena. Jojo might make good company for Zio. That would get him to be more independent."

Ma and Auntie Lilly took Jojo to the vet. He determined that the dog was a toy collie mix. He gave him his shots and they had him groomed. Jojo was also very good with the babies, Rosie and Joey, while he rode in the back seat between the two baby carriers.

When Ma got the dog back home, Zio Peppino was sitting in the living room. He looked depressed. "What's wrong, Zio?" Ma asked in Italian.

"I thought maybe you took-a the *cane* to the dog-a place and put him to sleep."

Ma said that Jojo ran in behind her and flipped on his back in front of Zio.

He said, "Hey, *Stupido!* Where you go?"

When I talked to Ma later in the day, she told me that Zio would only call the dog, *"Stupido."*

I said, "I guess he could be calling him worse."

My nana never liked my dad's family. She felt they took advantage of my ma because she had a good heart. Dad had a brother and sister who lived in the suburbs and both had big houses. Neither of them wanted to take Zio, but they all wanted to know how much money he had in the bank. My dad told them Zio had a few bucks, nothing more than that. He barely had enough to take care of himself. He wasn't planning to tell them about the shoe boxes filled with cash. Ma would need that to buy Zio food, clothing, and medicine. No one offered to help pitch in a few bucks a month. Dad kept his mouth shut about the shoebox money. He didn't mention the handguns to them either.

I stopped at Ma's before I went to Nana's house one day and I saw Zio outside on his "patio." Jojo was curled up under his chair.

Ma saw me looking at them and shook her head. "I don't get it. They have a love/hate relationship. In the morning, Jojo only wants to be around me. In the afternoon, he sticks by Zio like glue. Some days, the harder the dog tries to be around Zio, the more he ignores him."

"Jojo is hungry in the morning, Ma. That's why he wants you. He knows who feeds him."

"That's true."

"It's not unusual for animals to follow people who don't show them much affection. Geez, some women are just like that."

"He's been out there for so long, I cleaned the whole house. He's getting around pretty good with his walker now. Do you think I should go check on him?"

"He'll let you know if he needs anything."

I no sooner said that than Zio got out of his chair and rolled the walker in front of him. Jojo stood up, ready to follow him. They both headed for the garage. A few minutes later, Zio came out pulling my old red wagon with one hand. He pulled it up to the hose reel, scooted his chair over with the walker and began to hose the wagon off.

"What the heck do you suppose he's going to do with that wagon?"

"I don't know, Ma. He's sure got something in mind. I'm sure you'll know soon enough."

"You don't think he's going to put the dog in the wagon, do you?"

"More likely, he's going to have the dog *pull him* in that wagon."

Dad came in and said, "What the hell's he doing with that wagon?" We both started laughing.

23

M ilton was at the station when I got there in the morning. I went in early so I could see how Sophia and Eddie worked him into the script. He read his lines for me, and I liked it just fine. We walked over to the employee lounge and sat with Greg. We had some breakfast and lots of coffee. We began chatting about food. Greg was telling Milt about my Nana's cooking.

He asked, "Are you two an item?"

Greg said, "No. We're just friends. Her Nana cooks a lot, and I like to eat a lot."

Milt said, "Are you Italian?"

"No, I'm Jewish. Lena's Italian."

"Oh, I'm Jewish, too."

Greg looked very pleased to have another Jewish guy on the set. I'm sure he was planning Beth's future with Milt.

Actors Equity sent over a blue-eyed, blond female for us to interview later in the day. Her name was Sandra. I gave her part of the script from today's show. She was amazing! Sandra had just finished acting school. Her performance was perfect and we hired her on the spot. She would be written into the script immediately. I decided that I needed a secretary/Girl Friday for my growing business on the show. I had submitted the idea with my cast list earlier in the week. Beth would be assigned the task of purchasing new furniture for the B and B in the show.

"She'll probably think that she's really buying the furniture for herself," Greg joked.

With my last submission for the new script, I gave Sophia and Eddie a list of characters, just so I could keep them straight in my head. We keep adding personalities and the cast is growing.

TORTURED SOULS – CAST

Angie..Played by Lena Delatora
Monica...Played by Beth Eliston
Susan...Played by Sandra Hallerd
Lance... Played by Johnny Roman
Joanna... Played by Mona DeAngelo
Arthur...Played by Milton Beacon

Johnny and I will discuss our "break-up" on today's episode. I will cry and tell him this is the best for both of us. He is devastated and walks off the set.

The scene cuts to Johnny arriving home. His wife, Joanna (Mona) is sitting on the sofa crying. He's afraid that she has found out about his affair. The voice-over tells the story. Then Joanna looks up at him and says, "Lance, I'm pregnant."

He takes her into his arms and tells her, "I'm so happy. I never really wanted a divorce. We'll be wonderful parents."

The screen fades and the credits roll.

When the lights faded, everyone began to applaud. Mona looked more nervous after the show than she did during her performance. Mr. Latmen told her that she did a great job. She will be on the show again next week. She won't be wearing the baby bump until her third time on the show. It will be a smaller bump than the one we took to Nana's house.

Carlo and Penny are looking for a house. This is a little crazy to me, but they seem to be very happy. Penny understands what can happen when you are in a relationship with a man who is "predisposed" to other men. Greg told me that's called bisexual. Oh, this is all too much for me. If she is happy with her life this way, that makes her a very special person. I only want to know they are happy because I really care about both of them.

I heard my dad on the phone. I think he was talking to Myrtle "The Turtle." He said Carlo was sworn in one day last week. They called him and said to put on a suit and tie. He was talking really soft. They picked him up and now it's a done deal. It's a secret ceremony. Then he said something about "they made an exception."

When he came out of his office, Dad looked surprised when he saw me.

"Hey, baby. I didn't know you were here."

"Did you say Carlo was 'sworn in,' Dad? What's that supposed to mean? Tell me about this contract that Carlo had to fulfill."

Dad sat up straighter. He got this stern look on his face.

"You weren't supposed to hear any of this. You *didn't* hear anything. Now go upstairs and see your Ma."

"Dad, Carlo is very seriously dating my friend. How old do I have to be to know what's happening all around me?"

"You ask too many questions. Forget whatever you heard. Lena, it's all private stuff."

"I know Carlo was going to get 'made' but you didn't say that. You said he was 'sworn in.' " Dad could see I was getting agitated. He took me by the arm and sat me on the sofa.

"Listen to me, don't ever repeat this. Exceptions can be made at certain levels. Niko is the top man in our section. Carlo told his Dad he didn't want it. The final commitment to his swearing in is an elimination. Niko asked some of the closest family members to come to a meeting. I was there, so I know what took place. We are low-level family members. What no one else knows is that we can do what we want within limits. We make the rules in this area and we can change them when we need to. We did a swearing-in ceremony. I can't say any more. Everyone who comes to the party will think it's been done, and we celebrate his birthday too. You never repeat this, and you don't know anything. Eventually, Carlo will have to do the deed." He got up and kissed my cheek and left the room.

I was stunned. I was full of questions. The biggest question was the "contract." Somehow they worked it out. I'm not sure how, and I don't want to know any more than I have to. When I had a chance, and my parents weren't home, I'd sneak in my dad's office to see if

I can find some information on the rules of a made man. I knew my dad did a whole lot more than I realized in the "family."

Penny had asked me if there was anything she had to know. I told her the less we knew, the better off we were.

The party will go on as planned in a few weeks. I'm going shopping with Penny. She wants to look like a knockout for the event. We went to several places, but wound up at a hotel gift shop. It happened to be the Drake, and I saw my pantsuit that Gino bought me on the mannequin in the shop. *I can handle this. I can pick out a dress for Penny.* I clenched my jaws and chose a long silver dress for her with a slit up the side. It was bare shouldered, but had one strap that went across the front to the back. She looked so great in it. She said it was too expensive. I knew Carlo was paying for it, so I told her to be serious—start enjoying the family money.

"Lena, what are you going to wear?"

"Oh, I don't know. I'm not even sure if I'm taking a date. I might just go with my ma and dad."

"Why don't you ask Greg?"

"That might be a good idea. But Beth would probably have one of her emotional fits."

"Well, I'm sure you could ask anyone at all. They would be absolutely thrilled to be seen with you."

"You might be right, Penny. But there just isn't anyone that I like well enough. Do you want to go to Jen's Den of Beauty Saturday morning and get our hair done?"

"Yep. That sounds terrific."

"Great, I'll call and make an appointment for 10 a.m. I'll include manicures too."

I decided that I would wear something from my closet. I have a sapphire blue evening gown that I bought for a Christmas party on the show. That should be just fine. I might even turn some heads.

Penny was very nervous about the ceremony. Carlo never told her anything about his swearing in.

Lena, what is my role at this party?" she asked.

"I think that you have to stay by Carlo, unless he tells you

---

differently. If you get left alone for any length of time, come to our table and sit down."

"Okay, that's good advice. I don't know why I never thought about this before. I was so nervous about his duties that I never asked about what I'm supposed to do."

"We are just there as decorations. Everything else is up to the men."

24

Ma called me the following morning on my princess phone. She told me that more of the construction material was delivered. The workers arrived shortly after that and started framing the house.

I was so excited to hear they were beginning. I told Ma that I would come after work.

"Lena, you aren't going to believe what Jojo did today."

"Don't tell me that he used the toilet?"

"No, silly. I went to the store and Dad took Zio to the doctor. Jojo was alone in the house. When I got back, Jojo had stuffed the entire kitchen rug in his water dish, fringe and all. I don't know how he did it. He must have worked on it for hours."

"Ma, you sound proud of him. I think he was mad at you for leaving him alone."

"Well, maybe. But isn't he smart?"

"Yea. He's really a magician. I'll see you after work."

This dog sounded like a pain in the ass to me. Ma and Dad really need a hobby.

I got to my parents house and the workers were pounding away on the framework. Ma was just coming out of the house with coffee and some cookies.

"I thought Dad told you to stop feeding them?"

"Well, these are store-bought cookies. It's not the same as baking for them."

They must have smelled the coffee, because the work stopped and they all climbed down.

"Ma, how many times a day do you do this?"

"Oh, I only do it once in the morning and in the afternoon. Those are the break times."

Four burley guys came over to the picnic table where my ma had cups and dishes set up for them. They were all very polite. They thanked her and took their helmets off. Well, this could be a nice view from the kitchen window. Two of the four men were darned good looking. I tried not to stare, while Ma introduced me to them.

"Lena, this is Eddie, this is Antonio, this is Michael LaSoto, and this is Bianco Bertuci. Gentlemen, this is my daughter, Lena. Bianco runs the construction company that is doing the work on your house."

In that order, they each shook my hand with a polite, "Pleased to meet you," or "It's my pleasure." Bianco put his hand out and said, "Please call me Whitey." That made sense, since his name translated in English to the color white. When he looked up, my heart skipped a beat when I saw his eyes. Holy cow, his eyes were lavender. How could that be? This man had the looks of a movie star.

My Ma said, "Lena, do you want to help me get some cold drinks for the men?"

I didn't say a word about Whitey. Ma pulled some iced tea from the fridge and I grabbed some glasses. Just before we walked out to the yard, Ma said, "That guy Whitey just got his heart broken."

"How do you know that, Miss Nosey?"

"Oh, we talk. All the men talk during their breaks. Whitey just got back from Vietnam. She sent him a Dear John letter about a year after he was there."

"He looks fine to me."

Ma smiled, and said, "He looks fine to me, too."

We were laughing when we got outside.

Antonio asked me if I wanted to see the plans compared to the framework.

He went to get them out of the garage and I cleared off the corner of the table so he could lay them out. Whitey and Antonio stood on either side of me. They were way too close for comfort. I must have been desperate. The smell of their work clothes was a turn on. They smelled like sawdust and metal. I can't explain why that was so nice. They might as well have smelled like aftershave.

They showed me where the windows would fit in and how big the closet was going to be. They pointed out the half bath and suggested we put a shower in there. I don't understand why everyone thinks I need all these bathrooms.

"Is it common for newer homes to have more than one bathroom?"

Antonio said, "More common than you would think. I know older homes like mine and probably yours only have one bathroom."

Whitey pointed to the space behind the wall where the washer and dryer would be. He said, "You still have time to change this wall. I would put a shower in the little bathroom. It won't cost much more. If you have company, or kids, it would be nice for them to have a bathroom rather than use yours."

I smiled at his suggestion that I might have a family in this house someday.

"I'll call the architect and tell him your suggestion. Can you keep going with the framework until I decide?"

They agreed that this was no problem. They went back to work without another word.

25

Paulie called me at Ma's house. He said, "Lena, you need to get out for a while."

I wondered what the heck he was talking about. I thought he meant that I needed to get out of Nana's house for some reason. I asked, "What's up? Why do I have to move out?"

"Lena, not *move* out. Go out for a night on the town."

"Now you're talking Paulie. Should we go to The Club?"

"Let's try someplace new. Do you want to go someplace downtown? I know this really cool bar on Rush Street?"

"Oh, yes Paulie. I seem to remember that you wound up sleeping on the sofa at your old house the night after you found that bar."

"Yea, okay. You always know when to hit me low."

"Let's do it. Do you and Mona want to pick me up?"

"Yep! Wear you dancing shoes!"

I was pretty excited about trying a new place. I needed a change. I dressed at my ma's because most of my clothes were still there. Ma saw me all dressed up and said, "Ooo La La! You look fabulous my dear," in her mock French accent. "Where are you headed for?"

"Mona and Paulie are picking me up. We're going to a bar on Rush Street. Do you like these shoes? I want to be sure that I can dance. Do they look too clunky with this dress?"

"Oh, no Lena. They're perfect for a night out. I think the silver shoes with the dark blue dress look really dressy."

Dad walked into the kitchen and said, "I personally wouldn't be caught dead in those shoes."

"You're a real joker, Dad. But any time you want to go dancing, I'm sure I can lend them to you."

I think my folks were really glad that I was going out. I heard Paulie honking out in front and I told Ma, "I'll stop by tomorrow."

"Bring Nana for dinner. I'm not sure what I'm fixing. Come early and stay late. Tell Paulie and Mona to come to."

I kissed them goodnight and gave Jojo a cookie to say good-bye. That dumb dog fit right in. Zio was still calling him *Stupido*.

The bar we went to was called Ronnie's on Rush. Well, this was a classy joint. No one was wearing khakis or blue jeans. This was a really dressy place. Paulie was wearing a sport coat and Mona was wearing a black dress with a shawl. I'm glad I chose my navy evening dress. The music was great. Paulie went to get us drinks at the bar. Mona and I were standing near the door waiting for a table. I was checking out the clientele, and who do I see but Nick Piccollo. I nudged Mona and said, "Look who's here."

"Holy cow, Lena. He's all dressed up. Do you think he's alone?"

"I don't really care if he's alone. I'd rather not speak to him."

Mona and I were talking to two girls at a table next to us when someone tapped me on the shoulder. I must have jumped. When I turned my head I was looking into those unforgettable lavender eyes.

"Oh, Bianco, how nice to see you."

"I'm sorry if I scared you, Lena. You remember my friend, Antonio?"

I introduced Mona to Bianco, and he said, "Please call me Whitey."

Antonio was shaking hands with Mona when Paulie walked over with our drinks. I introduced him to Paulie. They were all shaking hands when the girls at the table invited us to join them. We all sat down and exchanged names all around. The girls waited a few minutes before they mentioned that they recognized me from TV.

I told them, "I hope that doesn't spoil our evening."

"Gosh no! I hope you don't mind us hanging out with you."

"Don't worry about it. Let's enjoy the night!"

A slow song was playing. Mona and Paulie got up to dance. Whitey touched my hand and said, "Would you like to dance, Lena?

I took his hand without answering the question. He walked me to the dance floor like a pro. I don't know where he learned to slow-dance, but he was so smooth. He had so many twists and arm moves that he nearly made me dizzy. He finally brought me close to him and said, "I see that Paulie and Mona are a couple. I noticed her engagement ring. Are you here alone?

"Yes," I managed to answer him without my voice cracking.

"Well, I must say that I'm surprised. I thought you would at least have an escort."

"I'm not seeing anyone right now. Paulie, Mona, and I go out together quite a bit."

We didn't talk anymore during the dance. I just enjoyed feeling someone's arms around me again.

When we got back to the table, Butt Head, Nick Piccolo, was sitting with Paulie.

"Look who's here, Lena!" like he found the second coming of someone holy.

Whitey tapped Antonio's arm and said, "Maybe we should move to another table. It's pretty crowded here."

I told Paulie, "Please, get another chair for Nick. Put it between the girls there. I'm sure they would enjoy his company. You gentlemen don't have to leave."

I'll be darned if I was going to let Nick interfere with my social life. I spent enough years waiting for him to do the right thing. I had the power now, and I planned to use it.

We were all on the dance floor, except for Nick and one of the new girls. I think her name was Sandy. He was making all the moves that were so like him. That girl would find out how he operates soon enough.

I heard him say that he was there earlier with an older woman. She got bored with the crowd and decided to move on.

Whitey was trying to say something to me, but I couldn't hear him because the music was so loud. He finally took my hand and led me outside. We were laughing because I kept misunderstanding him. He asked if he could see me some evening.

I said, "Do you mean like at real date?" I was thinking about Carlo's big party.

"Yes, a real date! Like I would pick you up and bring you home."

"Whitey, I have to go to a party in the next couple of weeks. Would you consider going with me?"

"Oh, that would be nice. I won't know anybody. Do you think I'll fit in?"

"I think you'll fit in just fine." I explained that the party was for Carlo. I called it a "Family Promotion." I think he understood what I was generally talking about. Whitey was born in Italy.

We were standing pretty close to each other outside the bar without really touching. They had a little patio in the back. It was too cool to stay outside too long. He took his jacket off and put it over my shoulders. We sat outside for a little while talking. No mushy stuff, but he was holding my hand when Paulie came out to look for me.

"Hey, Lena, Mona is looking all over for you."

"Tell her I'm coming in right now."

We danced for the rest of the evening. Some slow dances were sweet.

Whitey whispered to me, "Lena, I don't think I can wait two or three weeks to see you."

"Pick me up at my mom's on Saturday night."

We danced all the fast dances together. Whitey stayed closed to me. I could tell he didn't want anyone to cut in. I bought a round of drinks and whispered to Paulie that I wanted to go home now.

He said, "Am I taking you home or are you leaving with Whitey? By the way, why do they call him 'Whitey'?"

"His name translates from Bianco, *Stupido*. Yes, you are taking me home."

"Oh, that makes sense."

Whitey followed us outside and walked with us to the car. He asked what time he should pick me up.

I said, "Eight o'clock should be just fine." He kissed me on the cheek and said goodnight to everyone. He extended his hand to

Paulie and he kissed Mona on the cheek too—very traditionally Italian.

When we got in the car Paulie asked, "Is he taking you to Carlo's party?"

"Yes he is, Paulie."

"Who is this guy? Where did you meet him?"

I smiled to myself. Paulie will always be my bodyguard. He's been doing this since we were kids. I'm really touched that he still thinks of me as the little girl that he has to protect.

"Whitey owns the construction company that is building the addition behind Ma and Dad's for me."

Mona chimed in, "You keep calling it an addition. It's really a separate house. It's a back house just like Nana has, only it's more modern."

I thought about that for just a moment before I answered.

"I never thought about that. If it were an addition, I guess it would be attached in some way."

"Lena, I don't know if you want to do that. I think it's better to have your house disconnected."

"Yes. More privacy that way."

I was wondering if Whitey had anyone waiting for him in Italy. Then I remembered that Ma told me that he got his heart broken while he was in Vietnam, so I guess that eliminated one obstacle.

Paulie wasn't finished with his ongoing narrative about my social life. "So how come you ignored Nick Piccolo?"

"Paulie, for years you've been telling me that Nick Piccolo is trouble. Now you want to know why I was ignoring him. Make up your mind."

"Well I was surprised to see you pick up with that pretty-boy construction guy, you know."

"What's wrong with a construction guy? He makes good money working hard. Is that so bad?"

"No, it's not a bad thing, Lena. I just want you to be careful, that's all."

"Thank you, Paulie. I promise not to run away and get married without telling you."

"Lena, you're just a baby still, you know. I worry about you. Twenty-two ain't so old. You should have some respect for your elders."

I knew he was joking. He wasn't much older than me. He just turned twenty-four himself.

Mona said, "Paulie, you better watch your mouth. Lena is very important on her TV show."

"Yes, I know. That's the only time that I'm safe from her."

When I was talking to Ma the next day, the subject of Carlo's party came up. She asked if Paulie and Mona were picking me up that night. I told her that I was going with Whitey. I said that Nana was riding with us, so she and Dad wouldn't have to pick her up.

I heard dead silence on the other end of the phone.

I said, "Ma, are you there?"

Ma asked, "Do you mean that guy Bianco from the construction crew?"

"Yes, Mama. One and the same."

"Well, baby, I guess I didn't need to worry about your broken heart too long."

"Be sure to tell Dad, so he doesn't say something stupid, like 'What the hell is he doing here?'."

I saw Whitey several times in the next few days. It was always with other people around, during the day at my ma's. Occasionally, we would walk around the back of the construction site. The excuse was to show me the progress. He would put his arm around me and we would stand close. I could tell he wanted to kiss me, but my mom was in the front yard with the other guys.

It seems like I thought about him all the time. A few more days and we would have a real date.

He picked me up at 8 p.m. sharp on Saturday. He had on tan chinos and a black shirt. This guy was movie star handsome in his work clothes. When he was showered and shaved, he could melt my soul with his eyes. He had the same aftershave on that he wore at Ronnie's on Rush. I am a sucker for good smells on a man.

Sometimes it's just shower soap and shaving cream. It's a turn-on for me. Mom and Dad came out to say hello. Dad was talking to Whitey about trucks and lumber and all that man stuff.

Dad finally said, "Where you kids goin'?"

"I'm going to take Lena to a fish fry near the lake. Then maybe we'll get some ice cream."

"Oh, nice idea. You kids have a good time."

Whitey had his truck washed for the occasion. He reached over to hold my hand as soon as we were out on the street.

"Lena, this has been one of the longest weeks of my life. I always look forward to Saturdays, but I could hardly sleep thinking about you."

"Whitey, that's one of the nicest things anyone has said to me in a very long time."

At the first red light we came to, he leaned over and kissed me.

"I was waiting for that too, Lena."

The Knights of Columbus sponsored the fish fry. We sat at picnic tables near the water. I met some really nice people. Most of them were from other construction crews that Whitey had worked on or the guys had worked for them. There were some very nice ladies and lots of kids running all over.

We ate plenty of fish and decided to take a walk around the area. We ducked behind some trees to grab a little alone time. He had his arms around me and we were smooching up a storm. We saw some little kids poking their heads around the bushes giggling at us.

Whitey told them, "You better go find your mamas because I heard that sharks come out of that water and eat little kids."

They started yelling and ran back to the tables.

By the time we headed for home, all the stores were closed, so we couldn't get any ice cream. I told Whitey to drop me off at Nana's house, since Zio had my room. We sat in the truck and talked for quite a while. He told me that he was pretty sure that he was getting over his broken heart without too much trouble. Then we got into some heavy smooching. I finally decided that I'd better go into the house before we did something we would both be sorry for.

26

We saw each other in the yard nearly every day when I got home. He asked me if I would like to see his apartment on Friday night.

"We could go out for ice cream and stop by my place later."

"Whitey, we both know what's going to happen if I come to your house."

"Lena, I promise you that I will give you a tour, and keep my hands to myself."

We both started laughing.

"Well, we can promise to be strong, right?"

"Yes, we hardly know each other."

I think both of us knew this relationship was taking off. We both wanted to take our time getting it off the ground.

So, we went out for ice cream on Friday. We went to his apartment afterward. We started out in the living room. Every time he kissed me, his hands wandered more. He put the TV on. I'd push him away and he'd go get a drink of water. I was wearing a yellow sundress dress with spaghetti straps. He kept pushing the straps down over my shoulders, and I'd pull them back up.

We watched TV. We raided the refrigerator. We even went outside so he could show me the garden. He lived in his aunt's building.

The little old lady downstairs kept the garden. It was really beautiful.

We tried to watch more TV. It just didn't work the way we planned. We couldn't seem to stay away from each other. I kept finding myself sliding down on the sofa, with Whitey half on top of me and half on the floor. At some point I must have unbuttoned his shirt. My sundress was not covering all my body parts. I'm not sure how we wound up in the bedroom, but I put a halt to the hanky-panky right there.

As much as we had planned to take this relationship slow, it was not working out that way. We both lay there exhausted and frustrated. Just when I decided that it was time to go home, he started kissing me again.

"Holy cow, Whitey! No more! Hands off! Take a break!"

We both laughed like crazy.

"We are consenting adults, Lena. Do you have to go home?"

"Yes, as long as I'm living at my ma and dad's, or staying with my Nana."

"Okay, we'd better get moving, or I won't let you out of here." The following Saturday was Carlo's party. We told Nana that we would pick her up. She wore her favorite black dress and all her gold jewelry for the occasion.

When we got there, I introduced Whitey to all of our friends as Bianco because I felt this was more formal for the occasion. He didn't ask me to say "Whitey," so I didn't. He looked a little nervous at first, but after my dad handed him a glass of wine, he seemed to settle in pretty well

Dinner was in full swing when I saw Niko go up to the microphone.

I heard the clinking of a knife on glass. Everyone stopped talking and looked at Carlo's father, Niko

"I would like you to all congratulate my son, Carlo, who has just been promoted into our family business."

Well, that answered my question as to what would be said about the initiation.

"At this point, Carlo would like to make a speech."

Carlo stepped up to the microphone and said, "I would like to thank my father for this great honor. I would like to thank all of my friends and family members for being here to celebrate. Now I would like to ask my lovely Penny if she would step up here with me."

Carlo extended his hand toward Penny and she looked shocked. I nudged her to get up there. She looked beautiful in her silver silk dress with her hair done up in curls on top of her head.

When Carlo took the small box out of his pocket, I thought I was going to faint. I looked at Niko and he was grinning from ear to ear. I grabbed Ma's hand and she squeezed it.

He opened the box, took out the ring, and said, "Penny, will you marry me?"

She started to bawl her eyes out. Carlo put his arms around her while she sobbed. Everything got a little crazy after that. His father was kissing everyone and Carlo was shaking hands all around. I guess somewhere during the confusion, Penny said yes, because she had her hand stuck out in front of her with this big shiny diamond ring on it.

Now the celebration was really in full swing. I could see this *festa* going on all night. The food kept coming out and more wine was put on all the tables. In the back of the hall, a sweets table was being set.

Somewhere inside my little evening bag, I had copied the "Rules For A Made Man" from my dad's papers in his downstairs office. I decided that Penny would never see this list. It was foolish to bring it with me.

Sometime during all the excitement, I reached inside my little evening bag and crumpled this paper into a tiny ball. Later I would flush it down the toilet and never breathe a word of this to Penny again. I know for a fact that most of these rules have been broken. But, then that's what rules are for. Exceptions to the rules can be made for anyone, right?

RULES FOR A MADE MAN

1. No one can present himself directly to another of our friends from another family. There must be a third person to do it.
2. Never look at the wives of friends. Adultery is forbidden within the Family.
3. Never be seen with cops.

4. Don't go to pubs and clubs. Exceptions are Family-owned establishments
5. Always be available because Cosa Nostra is a duty - even if your wife is about to give birth.
6. Appointments must absolutely be respected.
7. Always uphold the code of silence outside the Family.
8. Wives must be treated with respect.
9. When asked for any information within the Family, the answer must be the truth.
10. Money cannot be appropriated if it belongs to others or to other Families.
11. People who can't be part of Cosa Nostra: anyone who has a close relative in the police, anyone with a two-timing relative in the family, anyone who behaves badly and doesn't hold to moral values.
12. Homosexuality is forbidden in the code of conduct for all Family members.

Dad leaned over when the celebration was winding down. He said, 'Lena, dance with your Old Man."

I jumped when he spoke, I was in such deep thought. It was so sweet of him to ask.

"Lena, you doing okay?"

"You mean because of Gino? Sure, Daddy. I'm fine. He's gone. I don't even want to discuss him anymore."

"I'm glad you brought a guy with you tonight. The family was very worried about you. They talked about some sort of payback for your feelings."

"Holy geez! Dad! Don't let that happen. There is nothing that can be done. It's over. If the family wanted to do something about this, they should have warned me about the girl in Italy when Gino and I first met. Instead, they saw what was happening between us and they let it go."

"You're right, honey. I'm just glad you are okay."

When the dance was over, I got my evening bag from the table.

Ma and I made our way to the Ladies Room. I took the little ball of paper from my purse and flushed. I watched it swirl around and around, and finally go down the toilet. I came out of the stall, washed my hands, put fresh lipstick on, and Ma and I strolled back to our table. Learning to mind my own business was getting easier all the time.

Whitey asked if he could get me coffee. We decided to go to the sweets table, where they had set up coffee and deserts. The table was one of the most beautiful I had ever seen. I almost forgot what kind of party this was. It could have been a wedding.

They had cannoli, bowties, chocolate covered strawberries, wedding cookies, assorted Italian cookies, brownies, chocolates of all sorts, butter cookies, cream puffs, fruit, cheesecake, cream horns, and more. In the middle of this mountain of food, there was a chocolate fountain. There were several different cakes. The one in the middle said, "Good Luck, Carlo." A second one said, "Good luck, Carlo and Penny."

Whitey and I laughed at the extravaganza. I couldn't even begin to choose. He got a dinner plate off the nearby table and began to load it with a little bit of everything. I got the coffee.

My ma and dad were laughing when they saw us coming toward them.

I said, "Nice, huh?"

"Lena, we could make ourselves sick on all this stuff."

Nobody went home empty handed. My cousin Gemma and her husband Memo were passing out containers for everyone to take sweets home.

It was a great party. A good time was had by all.

27

Johnny and I did our big break-up scene this week. Mona had been introduced the same day. We would be visiting the new furniture store in town. Mona would be wearing her small baby bump. Johnny would bring her over to pick out baby furniture.

Beth "The Nut" had quite a big role in today's show. She was going to see Milt, the owner of the store. As I watched her from the wings, I was inclined to think that Greg was right. She probably thinks that she's really buying furniture. She lives a pretend life and this show is part of it.

Milt and Beth were very good together in this scene. Beth explained that she was picking out a collection of furniture for the bed and breakfast in town. She was going to start on the lobby first. Milt, whose name was Arthur in the show, was very cordial and helpful. I was amazed at the convincing banter between the two of them.

I felt someone next to me. It was Greg. He said, "Do you think I should warn Milt about her?"

"I don't know if you need to do that right now. I think you can watch them both and see where it's going."

"Lena, I know Beth. She's going for the jugular. She'll have his head on a platter before he knows what hit him. I see it coming."

"If Milt comes to the cafeteria in the morning, we'll try to find a way to break it to him."

28

I stopped by Ma's after work. Zio Peppino looked a little misplaced. With the construction beginning, he didn't know where to put himself. He had dragged his chair to the back of the cement foundation. Jojo was under it, as usual. Zio looked a little annoyed that the builders were actually infringing on his territory now that the foundation was poured for my house. I saw the old wagon next to the garage door.

"Ma!" I yelled. "What's for dinner?" She loved it when I did that.

"Hi honey! I'm making meatloaf with baked potatoes and carrots."

"Sounds good to me. I'll call Nana and tell her where I am so she doesn't worry. What's Zio doing out there? Do we know what he's doing with the wagon?"

"I asked him about that. He said,'*Maybe some-a time I gonna take a walk with it.'*"

"What the heck does that mean?"

"Darned if I know."

"Well, it looks like he's finally accepted the dog. He's still calling him *"Stupido?"*

Ma said, "Yup. Do you know what that dog did yesterday?"

"No, but I'm sure you're gonna tell me."

"Well, Dad was on the ladder cleaning the gutters on the back of the house. Jojo climbed the ladder all the way to the roof. Dad had to carry him down, because he couldn't figure out how to get his legs to work backward. Isn't he smart?"

"Honestly, Ma, I don't know if he's smart or stupid."

"The vet says that Jojo is part Toy Collie and Welsh Corgi. His legs are like little stumps."

With that, Jojo came bouncing in the back door with Zio trailing behind him. Jojo went straight to his dish, picked it up and dropped it in front of the sink.

"Well, if you would just learn how to talk, you wouldn't have to do that," Ma said.

I guess the dog *is* really smart. I filled his water dish and waited for him to say "Thank you." Well, I half expected it.

I noticed that Zio didn't bring his walker inside. Ma said that sometime he forgets about it. That's really a good sign. That shows he's more independent. I couldn't help noticing how straight and tall he was standing. His white hair and beard needed trimming. He must have been a good-looking man in his younger days.

"Lena, he's been much better at taking care of himself. He even heated up some food on the stove yesterday. He doesn't ask me for much now that he's feeling better."

Zio was looking out the kitchen window.

I asked, "Zio, what are you looking for?"

"Just-a make-a sure those guys don't think the wagon is to use for them."

"They don't need a wagon, Zio. They have a lot of equipment to use."

"It's okay. I want them to know I'm-a watch-a them."

Ma and I smiled behind him. We were a little surprised that he put so much value in that beat up old red wagon. After Zio had coffee and a few cookies, he went back outside. He picked up the handle of the wagon and began walking up and down the driveway.

"Ma, what the heck is he doing?"

"I asked him last week, Lena. He said he's practicing."

I went outside and said, "Zio, you are walking much better. I see you practice your walking with the wagon. What are you planning to do?"

"I'm-a gonna pick *cardone*."

I was a little surprised at this. *Cardone* is a big weed that grows wild. It's a lot like rhubarb. We bread it and fry it and use it in soup.

I don't think anyone has ever made a pie with it, like rhubarb. It's a tough weed. Not too many people know how to cook it, except for the Italians.

Nana decided to walk over to our house for dinner. She saw Zio with the wagon.

"Where you go with the wagon, Peppino?"

"I'm-a go pick *cardone*," he explained.

"Oh. Okay. When-a you go, I would like-a to have some too."

"When I find it, you gonna pay me, Rosina. I'm gonna sell it for money."

My dad happened to be parking his car out in front. He came up the driveway during this conversation. He said hello, kissed Nana, and came in the house.

"What's Zio talking about? Where the heck is he going to find *cardone*? I haven't seen any around here for years."

"I don't know, Sam. He seems determined to pick some and sell it out of his wagon."

29

The furniture store for the show was set up with baby furniture. Mona and Johnny, aka Joanna and Lance, would be shopping for their new baby. They had beautiful cribs and dressers. I ordered some stuff from the Sears catalog for the bedding and curtains. Mona was wearing her baby bump today. She looked so darned cute. We had already got some great reviews from viewers about Lance and Joanna. The women loved the new twist in Johnny's life and the "baby on the way" theme.

Johnny's real wife made a surprise visit to the studio that day. She knew the scene was about Johnny and his pregnant wife. When the scene was over, she was in tears. He came over and put his arms around her.

Wow! What a turn around this was. I'm so glad I didn't fall for his emotional crap. He would have suckered me into his deceitful ways. He's been a womanizer since I can remember. There have always been rumors about him. Maybe this will help him be more loyal to his real wife.

I really think that being nice to other people is good for my broken heart. I just have to avoid anyone who talks about Gino. So far, everyone avoids saying his name when I'm around. They behave like I've been recently widowed. Ma and Dad still quit talking in the middle of a sentence when I come in the room. I still dream about him. Sometimes I think that I still smell him on my skin. I don't want to miss him anymore and I don't want to love him.

One day Mona asked me if I was angry with him and his father.

"I talked with my dad about this, Mona. Gino should have told me about his betrothal. He's known since he was a kid. I think he was about five or six years old. Even if he said it in passing, and not seriously, at least I would have known that it happened some time in his life. It wouldn't have been such a shock. If he really loved me, he should have been stronger. He should have told his dad that he found someone else. This is the sixties, Mona. We are breaking away from the old traditions and threats. The girl in Italy would have found someone else."

"Lena, this was a matter of honor. Not just a promise from him. The families are still pledged together with blood. It wasn't up to him. It was a debt between families."

Now I was angry all over again. I was mad at Gino and his dad. I was mad that I fell in love so quickly. I was mad that I believed that love could be so easy. Next time, I would be much more careful. If something is too good to be true, it probably is.

Mona wasn't finished with this subject. She asked, "Who is this guy Whitey?"

I said, "I thought you'd never ask. He's a construction worker on my house project. He cleans up real nice, doesn't he?"

"Well yes, he does. I got worried when Nick Piccollo showed up at that dance club."

"Nick is a loser. He couldn't accomplish anything in nearly four years since high school, and I don't think he ever will. He's still doing odd jobs and hanging around bars waiting for some chick to buy him drinks."

"Well, Lena, there must have been something good about him. You waited for four years."

"Yes, he's a good kisser and I was young and stupid. He never took me anywhere except his house for pizza. He's still living in his ma's basement."

30

Later in the week, I was over at Ma's house after work. She wanted me to stay for dinner, but I told Mona we would go out to eat that evening. Every time I looked out the window, Whitey was smiling at me from the top of the scaffolding. I was hoping he was watching his footing. I wouldn't want to be responsible for him falling off.

Ma told me that Zio asked her for some of his money. Ma had been cashing his monthly checks and putting the money in her coffee can.

She gave him forty dollars. She asked if he needed something else. He said "No". Ma was worried that he needed something and it wasn't available to him.

I told her, "Ma, I'll ask him if he wants me to take him someplace to shop and I'll see what he wants."

I went outside where he was sitting at the back of the concrete foundation with *Stupido.*

"Zio, I said, "You want me to take you shopping for something you need?"

"Oh, Lena, please you take-a me to that hardware store on North Avenue?"

I noticed his English was pretty good when he wanted something.

"Sure, you have money with you?"

"I go get it!"

He was excited to go to the hardware store. I went inside while he went to the bedroom to get his money.

When he came into the kitchen I asked him what he was going to buy.

"I'm-a gonna buy some stuff for my new business."

Ma rolled her eyes and made the "crazy" hand gesture, twirling her finger around her ear.

I helped him into the car and he said, "*Stupido, Viene que.*"

Jojo, who was now answering to either name, jumped into the car, just as happy as a clam.

Zio bought a pair of long sharp cutting shears, a thick ball of twine, a pad of paper, a marking pen, and some small paper bags. He seemed very happy with his purchases. He held the bag on his lap like a treasured find.

A few days later, my ma got a phone call from her friend, Minnie. "Your Zio Peppino is on the corner, in front of the dime store, selling *cardone* out of his wagon. He's got the red dog with him."

Ma and Dad decided to walk over to see what he was doing. The only people who would know what *cardone* is were the Italians.

Ma and Dad walked over there, and there was Zio. He had all the *cardone* a man could want. It was tied in bundles with little scraps of paper stuck in between the stalks with prices. Each bunch was tagged and ready to be bagged. The wagon was heaped to the top with beautiful red and green *cardone*. Jojo was sitting by the wagon guarding Zio like he was putting important stuff in those bags. Ma and Dad stayed across the street where he couldn't see him. They didn't want to embarrass him or upset him in any way.

That night when Zio got home, he was exhausted. He gave Ma half his money. He said, "Josie, you buy soma- thing nice-a for youself. You work a lot to take care of everybody."

"I can't take your money, Zio."

"No, keep-a this and go to buy soma-thing special."

When Ma called me, she was all choked up. "Lena, I got all this furniture from the money hidden in Zio's house. I can't take this money he worked for."

"Ma, he doesn't remember that money was there. He sure didn't work for it. You're using it to take care of him, except for the new furniture. And that was a bonus. No one else would take care of him but you. You're making him feel better by taking the money.

It gives him a purpose."

"I never thought of it that way, Lena. Maybe I'll put it back in the coffee can. When he needs money, I'll give it back to him."

"Sounds like a good idea. I think he could use some clothes. In the car he smelled like mothballs."

Dad was worried about Zio standing while he sold all his stuff. He could tell that Zio was limping more than usual after dinner. He found a little camping stool in the garage. After Zio went to bed, Dad put it in the wagon.

"Oh, both of you are softies. He's really going to appreciate that stool. I'm glad you're both happy to help him."

"Lena, Bobby is getting older. He doesn't need us so much. It's a good thing to keep the house full of life."

Ma was right. A house needs life. This reinforces my feelings about Nana's house. I know I did the right thing, not trying to move her out. When Paulie and Mona move back in to the rear house, my house will be just about ready to move into.

I wonder where Zio found the *cardone?*

31

found a note on my car window when I left Ma's that night. It was from Whitey.

Dear Lena,
I never asked for your phone number.
Would you like to have dinner with me some night?

Whitey

Well, he is as goofy as I am. He didn't leave a phone number on his note. I have to think about this. I knew he was staring at me when he could see me through the window and in the yard. He was awfully sweet when I saw him at the Rush Street bar. He didn't make a pass at me then or at Carlo's party. I drove my ma and dad home that night because Dad had too much to drink. He walked us outside and kissed Ma and me on the cheek, and shook Dad's hand. Safe. Good so far. I'm taking this one really slow. I break out in a sweat when I think of the night at his apartment. I'll tell my ma to give him my phone number when she brings them the treats at their break time.

After Zio started selling *cardone,* Dad got a little worried about his reasons to need more money. We had a family pow-wow after dinner one night. Zio looked a little concerned that he had done something wrong.

Dad said, "Zio, we want to be sure that you have everything that you need. We found some money when we cleaned out your apartment. We saved it for you, but if you need it now, it's rightfully yours."

"No. Give the money to Josie. She takes care of everybody. She makes a nice house-a for you and me and all-a the family."

"Why do you feel you need to sell *cardone* for money?"

"All my life, I take-a care of myself. Never no wife or kids. Now I can help my family here. I want to *contribuire*."

My ma got all weepy looking. "Oh, Zio. You don't need to contribute any money. You already give me your pension check."

I did the eye-roll thing. We were both thinking about the first few weeks that he took advantage of her kindness. He had been bleeding that "broken hip" for too long.

"Well, Sammy, I wanna ask for some-a thing from you. Not too much a big thing, just-a small favor."

"Sure, Zio. What is it?"

"I wanna make some wine. Does Rosina still have Giuseppe's *vino stampa?*"

Dad looked at me for a response.

"Nana has Papa's wine press in the garden. It has basilico growing in it. It's surrounded by all her flowers."

"Well, Zio, we'll find a new press for you. We can go down to Taylor Street. I know they have stores that sell all the things you will need to make wine."

"Okay. I sell the *cardone* to make money for all my things to make-a the wine."

"Zio, we have to clean out the basement and make some room for you to work down there. I'll put some railings up so you can hold on when you go down the steps, so you don't fall down again."

Ma and Dad knew that Zio needed to feel useful and wanted to keep himself busy. I was amazed at how much Dad was willing to accommodate him. My dad's father died when he was just a little boy. I think Zio was replacing that "father figure" for Dad. This would give my dad a project and keep him and Bobby busy downstairs.

32

D ad went with Zio a few days later to see where he was picking the *cardone*. They took the wagon and *Stupido* and walked down Cleveland Avenue and cut through the alley behind the grammar school until they came to a vacant lot with a worn path. Dad followed behind Zio and Jojo, who both seemed to know exactly where they were going. They finally came to a large patch of weeds growing on both sides. *Cardone* was growing, mixed with the weeds, but nearly taking over the entire side of the lot.

Dad said that he and Zio picked *cardone* all afternoon. Jojo slept in the sun, while Dad cut *cardone* and Zio sat on his campstool and stripped the leaves and tied it into bundles. They came home when the wagon was full.

They told us about their productive day during dinner. Dad said, "Zio's got a good eye. I could see some of the *cardone,* but Zio would point and say, "Sammy, more over to the left. Or Sammy, go behind the tree. I see more."

I asked Zio, "What will you do when the *cardone* is all gone, Zio?"

"It's never all gone, Bella. I know more places to find it."

Zio had never called me "Bella" before. That was Nana's pet name for me. I thought it was really sweet that he was calling me "beautiful" too.

Penny and Carlo found a house. Carlo wanted to get married right away. His ma died when he was four or five years old. Carlo was raised by his grandmother and his dad. His nonna was like a mother to him.

Penny decided that it was time for Carlo to meet her mother.

Her mother was very much alive, but Penny kept her away from everyone she knew. Her mother's name was Galena, better know as Glenny. Her current stepfather's name was Dino. Penny asked me to go with them to her ma's house. I've met her a few times and Penny felt more confident that her ma would behave if more people were there. Glenny drinks like a fish. She'll be no help with the wedding at all, but she'll want to be involved. I want to make Penny comfortable with the fact that I am there to support her. Penny wants to make sure that she keeps Glenny under wraps as much as possible during the planning. Carlo had been warned about Glenny and Dino, so he would know what to expect.

Carlo was driving. Penny was in the front seat and I was in the back. Penny kept a running dialog going on the way there. I knew how nervous she was about Carlo meeting her family.

"My ma was a beautiful woman. I mean, she still is, but she looks kind of worn out. She's had too many years of booze and too much partying. She dresses a little flashy, so don't be surprised at what she's wearing. I didn't call ahead, because I don't want her to start making a fuss. She'll want to cook or something stupid. She's an awful cook."

Carlo reached over and put his hand on Penny's and said, "Honey, don't worry. It's going to be fine. I can handle anything."

Glenny opened the door wearing a shirt cut off to the midriff. She had on tight Capri pants and backless high heels. She held a highball glass in one hand and a cigarette in the other. She looked like it could probably be her third highball. Dino was her forth husband. When she saw Penny with a man, she stood up straight and flashed her brightest smile.

"Oh, Penny, I'm so glad to see you. I see you brought a friend to meet me! What's his name? Would you like a drink? Hello Lena, so nice to see you again. This is my husband, Dino."

She slip-slapped across the floor in her backless shoes, extending her arm to Dino, who was sitting in his recliner. She pulled him up with one free hand, while she transferred her drink and her lit cigarette to the other. Dino shook hands with Carlo and kissed

Penny on the cheek. He nodded a hello to me and shook my hand.

"Sit, Sit! I'm so glad that you're here," Glenny gushed. She clip-clopped from the kitchen with two highball glasses and handed one to Carlo and Penny.

"Lena, can I get you anything?"

"No, thank you. I have to work this afternoon." It wasn't true, but a good excuse.

"Ma, we have some great news to share with you. Carlo and I are getting married!"

Penny held out her left hand to show her the ring. There was such a mixture of emotion that flashed across Glenny's face. I think I actually saw anger first, then sadness mixed with jealousy, and finally a smile of pleasure. Penny always said that her mother treated her like competition. She used to accuse Penny of flirting with all the men Glenny brought home or married.

Dino broke the ice by saying, "Holy Crap! Penny, that's a honker. Glenny, look at this big rock! Carlo, you must be loaded or some kid of big shot!"

Glenny grabbed Penny's hand and said, "Oh, my God! It's beautiful. Carlo what kind of job do you have? You *must* be loaded!"

Carlo smiled and said, "I run a trucking business for my dad."

Penny wanted to tell her ma about the wedding plans. Glenny was so busy fussing and flirting with Carlo, she never even congratulated Penny on her engagement. It should have been Penny's time to shine. Now I remembered why she wanted to move out of her house. Glenny was such an overpowering personality that Penny couldn't grow there. I think she got out just in time.

I finally mentioned the "time."

"Oh, we have to be leaving, Ma. It's getting late."

We said our good-byes. Penny did her best to smile and act like she was delighted with the visit. When we got outside, I suggested treating them to lunch at a little Italian restaurant on Division Street. That broke the tension, and cheered the mood a bit. Carlo wound up paying, because women never pay for anything when Carlo is in the group.

I was getting ready for my date with Whitey. We were going out for dinner. He promised it would be fancier than a fish fry. I asked my Nana what I should wear. She said, "You wear a dress. And don't forget-a you sweater."

I picked two dresses out of my closet and said to Nana, "You pick one."

"Okay. You wear this-a blue one with the poka-a-spots. And wear dark stockings."

I got dressed, and she approved of my finished look. I looked like a librarian. I didn't want to be all flash and glamour. I decided on a white sweater with pearls to perk up this outfit. I didn't want to scare this poor guy away completely.

Whitey rang the bell at 8 p.m. on the dot. Nana answered the door. She looked him over from head to toe very slowly. My nana is about five feet tall. Whitey was at least a foot taller than her. She stood on her tiny little feet with her arms crossed, staring up at him. She never blinked. I saw Whitey's eyes getting bigger. I think he was afraid of her.

Finally she said, "You please come in and make-a youself a house."

That was Nana's version of "make yourself at home."

"*Grazie.*"

He didn't even break into a smile, so I knew he was used to the broken English.

"Where you go with-a my Lena?"

"I am taking her to Alessi's. Maybe we'll have lasagna."

"That's-a nice. Not too late, okay?"

"No, Dona DeLuca. I won't be too late. But tomorrow is not a work day, right?"

"Okay, you are right. Lena no go to TV station tomorrow. It's-a Saturday."

Once we got all the formalities out of the way, we were free to leave.

We laughed when we got outside.

"Your nana is very protective, isn't she? Have you lived with her very long?"

"No, Just a few weeks. I stay with her off and on, but I've been keeping her company since Paulie moved in with Mona. We've always been close. I didn't want her to be alone. Then Zio had hip surgery and needed to stay with us to recover. He'll probably stay with Ma and Dad permanently."

"Well, I'll need to speed up building that house for you."

"Mona and Paulie will move into that back house when the remodeling is done."

"Oh, yeah—I know a couple of guys on that crew. They said it would be done in about a month. Your nana feeds them a lot, just like your ma feeds us."

"I'm not surprised."

We pulled into the parking lot at Alessi's. Whitey reached over and put his hand on my cheek. I leaned into it. I knew I could have feelings for him. I was really holding back.

"Let's keep it casual. I'm so glad we're here, but I have to take it slow," I said. He pulled me toward him and kissed me. This was a very steamy kiss, wet with lots of tongue. I knew I would need to reapply my lipstick before we went into the restaurant.

"Enough, Whitey!"

He knew he was weaving that old black magic, and we both laughed.

When we got inside, we talked for nearly an hour before we ordered. I told him I had thought Gino was my "one-and-only" for life.

He told me about the girl of his dreams who dumped him as soon as he was shipped out.

We talked a little bit about the war, but that seemed to upset him. I could see him clenching his jaws after each sentence. We switched the subject to Carlo and Penny's wedding.

Whitey asked, "Have they known each other very long?"

"No, about five months."

"This is pretty sudden, isn't it?"

"He was waiting a long time for the right person to come along."

"And Penny is the right person?"

"Why do you ask with that strange tone? What business is it of yours?"

"I'm sorry. I didn't mean to pry. Please don't be offended. I heard some rumors about Carlo. Nothing is a secret in the old neighborhood. I know Penny is your friend and you wouldn't want her to get hurt."

"What do you think I'm protecting her from, Whitey? He treats her like a princess. Is there something I should know? Is this why you asked me out?"

Whitey's face flushed and he put his head down.

"This is the wrong subject to discuss. Can I rewind? I was just trying to make small talk. I thought that since you asked me to Carlo's party, and I was there when he asked Penny to marry him, I could speak freely about them."

"I'm sorry, Whitey, I guess I shouldn't have taken offence so quickly. That might be a subject for another night."

I finally said, "I'm really hungry. How about you?"

"What do you feel like having?"

"You mentioned lasagna earlier. I think I would like that. And Whitey, what you heard about Carlo is probably true. It's part of his history. Penny knows about it too."

I looked into those lavender eyes and decided I couldn't be angry with him. I'm a sucker for great smiles, and his was outstanding.

"Lena, you really look nice tonight."

I burst out laughing. "I look like a librarian."

"Yes, you do. But you still look beautiful."

"I let Nana pick out my clothes. I was nervous."

The waiter took our order. As hungry as I was, I only ate one piece of bread from the basket. Whitey filled my wine glass for the second time.

The sweater that Whitey was wearing was really nice. It was a white cable knit with a round neck. It was tight enough to show off his muscles, but not tight enough to look like he was showing off.

33

The waiter brought the lasagna to our table on a cart. It was served family style. He put the big pan on the table, along with another basket of bread, baked vegetables, and a small bowl of extra sauce.

I looked at that white sweater and knew it was doomed. The waiter servedme first. He put a large portion of lasagna on my plate and then the vegetables. He did the same on Whitey's plate. I thought for sure that it was going to splash on the beautiful sweater.

The waiter smiled and left. Whitey waited for me to begin. Once I had started, he picked up his first forkful of lasagna. I watched as he lifted it to his mouth. It looked like slow motion, as it fell off his fork and plopped into his dish. It rained upward like I knew it would. A bystander would have thought he had been shot in the chest. The sauce spread in a splatter in the center of his sweater.

I looked at his face and the laughter died in my throat. He looked shocked. That's when he grabbed his chest. I never heard the gunshot. Someone pushed me to the floor. *Was that another shot?* I remember screaming Whitey's name. At the table behind us, a man was on the floor. It all happened so fast. He was slumped at the table, his chin on his chest. Someone pushed him onto the floor. I crawled to Whitey's side.

His breathing made a whistling sound, like a balloon with a hole in it. I kneeled next to him and put my arm under his head. I could tell he was alive.

"Please, please, don't die, Whitey. Hold on. GET HELP!" I screamed.

Everyone was running out of the restaurant. It was chaos.

Someone was kneeling next to me, applying pressure to Whitey's chest. A man handed me a napkin. I didn't realize that I was crying and my hands were full of blood. I could hear sirens. Once the ambulance got there, they worked fast hooking him up to all sorts of stuff. I rode to the hospital with him. Someone must have called my ma and dad. They showed up at the hospital emergency room.

Dad put his jacket around my shoulders. "It could have been you, Lena. It could have been you.

"I don't understand. Who would want to shoot Whitey?" I began to cry again.

"Wrong place, wrong time. They weren't aiming for Whitey. He wasn't the target, baby. The guy behind him was the mark, and he's dead."

I started crying again. Ma put her arms around me. "He's gonna be all right, hon. The hospital is trying to reach his parents. They need to be here. We can take you home, sweetheart."

"I'm not going anywhere until I can see him. In fact, I'm staying here as long as they let me. In any case, I'm spending the night."

"Miss Delatora, Mr. Bertuci is in Intensive Care. He's asking for you."

I thanked the nurse.

"He's conscious, I have to go in."

My parents waited.

The first thing Whitey asked was, "Are you all right, Lena?"

"Oh, I'm fine. Really, now that I see you're alive." I started to cry again.

"Thank you for staying with me."

He was pretty doped up and he fell asleep immediately.

The nurse came to escort me out. She explained that Whitey would need surgery. They were waiting for all his vital signs to stabilize. Surgery would probably be in the morning.

Ma and Dad were allowed to see Whitey, even though he was asleep. They wanted to be sure he was still alive. They were going to go home and come back in the morning.

After my ma and dad left, I begged the nurse to let me put my chair next to Whitey's bed. She finally agreed, but just for a little while. They must have changed shifts sometime during the night, because no one came to chase me out. I drifted in and out of sleep. Mostly, I watched his breathing . . . in and out, in and out. The machines were helping him and he had oxygen in his nose.

A nurse finally came in some time toward morning. I was dozing.

"Miss Delatora? Two policemen are here to see you."

I thanked her and went into the outer waiting area.

"I'm Officer Milton. This is Officer Dodd." They shook my hand in turns.

I thought, *They sure don't tiptoe around trying to be nice to me. These guys are strictly business.* I asked how I could help.

The older officer started speaking: "Please tell us what you saw last night. We need the entire scenario, from start to finish," the older detective said. "Did you see who did the shooting?"

"I never heard the first shot."

"You mean the one that hit Bianco."

"That's right. I only heard the second shot."

"Why didn't you hear the first one?"

"I don't know. Probably because of the restaurant noise. Dishes clanking and silverware clattering. Just a lot of regular noise for a dinner place."

"When did you know that Bianco got hit?"

"I saw the red spreading on his sweater. I thought the lasagna had splashed his chest. Then I realized that Whitey was shot."

"Whitey? You mean Bianco."

"Yes. It seemed like slow motion. I saw the red spreading on his chest, and for a moment I didn't realize he had been shot."

The younger detective was taking notes furiously.

"But you heard the second shot. The one that followed? Why do you think you heard the second shot?"

"Because suddenly the restaurant seemed to get very quiet."

"Did you see the shooter?"

"These are really ridiculous questions. No, I had my back to the door."

My Dad always said, "Never sit with your back to the door. Sit in a curved corner booth facing the door whenever possible. If you can't get a booth, sit with your back to the wall," I thought to myself. Seems like I forgot all about that.

"Miss Delatora, did you hear me?"

"I'm sorry. What did you say?"

"Have you known Bianco very long?"

"No, only about two months."

"Did you know the other man who was shot?"

I started to cry again. "No, I've never been to this restaurant before. It was our first date."

"You have never gone out with him before?"

"Not alone. Only to a family function, and a fish fry. Never alone before."

"How did you meet him?"

"Detective, why are you asking all these questions about Bianco and me? Shouldn't you be out looking for the shooter? Bianco isn't even out of danger yet. He's really critical at this time."

"Miss Delatora we are simply trying to get a complete picture of the events of the evening."

"It's been a long night. I'm tired. Perhaps you could come back another time."

"Of course. You get some rest. Good-bye." We shook hands all around and they finally left.

I sat down on the sofa in the family waiting area and broke down and sobbed—big, wracking sobs that shook my whole body. I felt a hand on my shoulder. It was Paulie. He had a big bag of food and cups of coffee.

"I brought you breakfast and the newspaper. Check the top of page three."

It said, "**SOAP OPERA STAR IN NEAR MISS SHOOTING**"

I said, "Oh nuts." Why did I think this could be kept private?

It followed with: **Lena Delatora was dining at Alessi's Italian Eatery with a companion, Bianco Bertuci. A shootout erupted at 9:15 p.m. Shots were fired and Miss Delatora's companion was**

struck in the chest, just inches from his heart. It went on.

"Why are they calling it a shootout? Two shots were fired and nobody shot back. What a bunch of dopes."

"Stupid reporters. They've been outside since last night. You must be some kind of celebrity, Lena."

"Yeah, I know, Paulie. It's more than I ever expected."

"You have blood all over your dress, babe."

I looked down. "I didn't even see it."

Some of the polka dots were dark brown now.

"Lena, you sure got some bad 'man' luck."

"No shit, Paulie. I need to change my dress. I don't want Nana to see me this way. She must be worried because I didn't come home last night."

"Your ma and dad stopped over there last night to tell her what happened. She's making a speed-novena for Whitey."

"Nana's speed-novenas usually work. I'll come home with you and change into something of Mona's."

The doctor came out to speak to me about Whitey's injury He said that the bullet ricocheted around his chest, a lot like a pinball machine. It penetrated the chest mass, bounced off a rib, and lodged in the left scapula.

I know my mouth was hanging open.

Paulie said "Jeez, Doc, is he gonna live?"

"Yes, we can fix this. He will need rest. The damage could have been much worse. It was a small caliber bullet.

As the doctor turned to walk away, we looked up just as an older couple came in. They looked very Italian, so I knew they were Whitey's parents.

"Miss Delatora? Thank you for being here with our son." She started bawling and her husband put his arm around her and gave her his handkerchief. Then they both started to cry.

"Mr. and Mrs. Bertuci, this is my Uncle Paulie. He came to give his support and prayers."

"*Cosi dispiace per tuo figlio.*" So sorry about your son, Paulie said.

He shook hands with Mr. Bertuci and kissed Mrs. Bertuci on both cheeks.

I told her that they would be taking Whitey into surgery very soon. Whitey should make a full recovery.

"What's the surgery for, Miss. Delatora? They didn't sew him up yet?"

"Please, call me 'Lena.' They were waiting for him to stabilize to remove the bullet. He is stable now and the surgery should go very well."

She rolled her eyes and made the sign of the cross, "Madre Mia. He's-a gotta bullet inside him still?"

The nurse came out to tell us that they were taking him into surgery now. They rolled Whitey out with all the tubes and IVs in him. I thought Mrs. Bertuci was going to pass out. She started praying in Italian and her husband made her sit down.

The nurse said, "Bianco will be in surgery about three hours. Then he will go into recovery for another two hours. You can either stay here, or go home and come back."

That's when Mr. Bertuci told me that he didn't drive. They waited for a neighbor to bring them to the hospital.

"I'm going to go home to change my clothes. I'll be back and we will get something to eat. I brought them to the family waiting area and got them some coffee.

"*Grazi, grazi, Miss Delataora.*"

"*Non e niente.*" It's nothing.

I explained the events of Friday night to the Bertucis, leaving out the most graphic details. I tried to emphasize the fact that the ambulance came quickly.

"Somebody died. I saw it in the newspaper," Mrs. Bertuci said.

"Yes. We didn't know him. He was the person the shooter was aiming at."

"I pray for him too, Miss Lena."

Paulie took me home with him. Mona was waiting with coffee and food.

"I ate already, sweet girl."

"Okay, you lay down for a while to rest, Lena."

"I've got to call my dad."

I explained that the Bertucis didn't drive. Could he arrange for a car to bring them back and forth to the hospital?

"I only gotta make one phone call. Consider it done. You call when you want them picked up and dropped off. It will be taken care of."

"Thank you, Daddy."

"It's the least we can do."

I wondered how I got myself into all this complicated stuff. I was beginning to think that being a soap opera queen came natural to me. My whole life was drama. Maybe I should be working at the QuickMart or become a beautician, which is what I was going to do in the first place. Maybe I should go talk to a priest, or to Paulie . . . not that they are even similar in their capacity to give me advice. But Paulie still gets me on the right track.

Mona wanted me to stay at her house and rest. I insisted that Paulie take me to get my car. My first concern was to be sure that Whitey got well. I'll call Mr. Latmen—Jack, and ask him if they can shoot scenes around me for a couple of days.

He got on the phone immediately when I called his office. "Lena, Doll, you doin' okay? How is Whitey?"

"I'm okay, Jack. Whitey is going to be all right. I'm going back up to the hospital right now to be with him. His parents are there. I need to be sure he's going to recover okay."

"Lena, I'll talk to the producers. They should be able to get you through Wednesday without an on-camera spot. They mentioned this morning that you might need some time off. They are writing a business trip into the script for you. You are going to look at furniture for the new addition.

"I thought that Milton has a new furniture store?"

"That doesn't mean that you can't shop around. It works."

"Thank you, Jack, I really appreciate that."

"Stop being so formal, Lena. We're like family. We look out for each other. Take care of yourself."

He hung up without saying good-bye. That was typical of Jack.

I breathed a little easier knowing that I didn't have scripts to memorize for a few days. Maybe Greg could drop the Thursday script off on Wednesday night. He loves my Nana. I'm sure she'll want to cook for him.

When I got back to the hospital, Whitey was in recovery. The surgery went better than expected. The bullet was two inches from the heart, but missed his lungs completely. I gave Mr. and Mrs. Bertuci the phone number for the car pickup that Dad had arranged. They were overwhelmed. They couldn't believe they didn't have to pay the driver.

"This is his job. He is paid to drive people when they need to go anywhere."

I didn't bother to explain about the family job that went along with this. There were all sorts of odd jobs that got done. I didn't even ask questions anymore.

My ma and dad came to the hospital. They met the Bertucis. The owner of Alessi's came to see him too. Late that afternoon, Paulie and Mona came and brought food. I was going to take the Bertucis out for dinner, but there was enough food brought in to the family waiting area. Penny and Carlo came for the evening visiting hours.

I could tell that Mama and Papa Bertuci were getting tired. I suggested that I call the car for them. They stood up and put their coats on, so I guess they were ready to go. I went downstairs with them to wait. Benny, the driver, got out and helped Mrs. Bertuci into the back seat.

Mr. Bertuci said, "Are you sure I don't pay the man?"

"No, Benny gets paid by my father's business."

He seemed to be satisfied with that.

When I went back upstairs to the waiting area, Carlo was there.

"Lena, I'm worried about you. I thought your life would get calmer, but it's not looking like that's going to happen."

"I have tried to mind my own business and just live my life. I'm getting better at using my brain filter and trying to be more selective. I try not to make other people's problems my own anymore."

"I'm guessing your brain filter is a female, because she seems to get in as much trouble as you do alone."

"I really try to think things through before I make any decisions. I don't know why my life is such a mess."

"Where's Penny?"

"She's powdering her nose. Here she comes now."

"Hello, Lena."

"Penny, you didn't have to come up here again."

"Well, I thought this might be a good time to say something positive."

"What's that?"

"I know you will spend a lot of time with Whitey, but I'm hoping you will have time to help me pick out a wedding dress."

"Oh, Penny. I'd love to!"

"One more thing . . . I'd like you to be my maid of honor."

"Of course! What a wonderful surprise."

"Good, now let me fix your make-up. You look like hell."

She pulled a huge make-up kit out of her purse and worked on my face until I looked like a soap opera queen.

I must have looked pretty awful before, 'cause Carlo shook his head in disbelief and said, "Penny, you're really a magician."

Carlo decided to leave us alone to discuss dresses and other wedding stuff. "I'm going in to see how Whitey is doing."

I took this opportunity to ask Penny how things were going with her and Carlo. Her smile told it all. "We are so happy, Lena. He says that he can't imagine living without me. I never thought I would meet anyone like him. It's like a dream."

"Penny, you deserve this."

Carlo came out and said, "Whitey is awake and he's asking for you. I'm taking Penny out for dinner. He's looks great. Go in and see for yourself."

When I walked in to ICU, I expected Whitey to look near death. He was smiling and talking to the nurse. He was still hooked up to a few machines, but he did look great!

He looked over at me and said, "Hello, Gorgeous."

The nurse blushed and said, "I'll leave you two alone."

He could see that I was going to cry again.

"Hey, I'm doing okay. I look a little like Frankenstein, hooked up to all these machines, but I feel pretty good. They might move me to a regular room tomorrow."

With that, he flipped his covers back and said, "Get in."

I started to laugh.

"I mean it. It's the least you can do for a guy who got shot trying to buy you a cheap dinner."

I walked around his tray table and climbed right under those covers. He sighed a contented sigh and said, "Thank you for taking care of my parents. They told me about the car that you arranged for them."

He closed his eyes and was asleep immediately. I dozed off too! I didn't realize that we were both asleep until I heard the nurse say, "Miss Delatora! This is highly irregular!"

"Oh, gosh I'm sorry. He looked so pitiful, I just wanted to be close to him."

She almost looked like she was going to forgive me.

"Get out of that bed right this instant before I call the doctor."

Holy cow, you bet I did. She really looked glad that I had all my clothes on. I don't know what she expected.

When Whitey woke up, he saw me sitting in the room beside his bed.

"Hey! When did you get out of my bed?"

"When Nurse Crabass caught me. She wasn't too forgiving. After all, this is Intensive Care."

He tried to laugh, but I could tell it hurt too much.

"It's the first time I slept with a girl before I even made love to her."

I walked over and gave him a big fat wet kiss, and told him, "Your breath smells like a wet dog. Go back to sleep."

34

I know my ma had been worried about me. When I left the hospital, I went directly to her house. She has that same radar thing that Nana's got. She knew I was there before I got to the door. She made me eat as soon as I walked in.

"You're getting too thin. I don't care about that darned TV show. You can't neglect your health."

If a woman in my family doesn't have rolls around the middle when she sits down, they are too thin.

"I gotta use the phone."

My phone was still connected in Zio's bedroom. I called Whitey's parents and told them that the car would pick them up at 1 p.m. the next day at their house. Benny would pick them up at the hospital at 4 p.m. I wanted this to be easy for them. I was afraid they would hesitate to call Benny when they needed him. Prearranging this would be convenient for them. I could come back to the hospital after *Tortured Souls* was over.

"Lena, first you eat, then you go lie down in Bobby's room. You need to rest."

It was 5 p.m. when I woke up.

"Ma! Why did you let me sleep so long?"

"You needed sleep. Your body would have woken you up sooner if you didn't need it."

More words of wisdom from my ma.

Dad was sitting at the kitchen table with the phone stretched over from the countertop.

"Hi, sweetheart. How you doin'?"

"You guys know that I didn't get shot, right? I'm fine. Everyone keeps asking me if I'm all right."

"He smiled and said, "Such a smart ass. You've had several traumatic things happen to you." He got up and hugged me.

"Lena, I don't know why you have so much grief and bad luck in your life."

"You're not going to call Mama Diavilo are you?"

"No. Not the witch. I want tell you that the family is paying all of Whitey's medical bills from the club fund."

"Dad, doesn't Whitey have insurance with his company?"

"Whitey *is* the company, babe. He has those few guys who work for him. They pay for their own insurance. I'm going to pull a few men that I know from another job site. I don't want the construction to slow down on your house. When you go to see Whitey, you tell him that, so he can get well without worrying. I'm gonna make sure that his guys get paid for all the hours they have put in."

"That should be my place to pay them, Dad. You do enough. Please thank the men at the club for all their help."

Suddenly, I realized why I am a "fixer." It's because I've seen my dad do this all of my life. He fixes everything for everyone. I think I understand myself better now.

I stopped at the TV station to check on my script. I knew it was after hours. Maybe the script would be in my dressing room. Latmen always stays late.

I saw a light on in his office. I peeked inside and it was Greg.

"Hi, Lena. How's Whitey?"

"He's doing really well. They might move him into a regular room tomorrow."

"You don't have to come in until Thursday. What are you doing here so late?"

"I'm on my way to the hospital. I thought I'd see if the script is in my dressing room."

"It is. Come on, I'll walk that way with you."

"How's the crazy situation with Beth? Does she understand that you want to move on?"

"Beth doesn't understand anything. She really doesn't get the hint at all. I've tried to tell her nicely that we are not compatible. She won't let go."

"Any chance that Milton, the new guy, would be interested in her?"

"There isn't any point in passing her off like used luggage. I'm afraid she'll have another breakdown. Besides, Milt is a nice guy. He'll hate me and then we have to work with him."

Greg was standing next to me, reading the script with me. I turned my head to say something to him and he leaned over and kissed me. Well, I kissed him back and his arms went around me really easy. He rubbed the spot on my back between my shoulder blades, just like he used to. I pulled away and stepped back.

"Oh hell, Greg. Isn't my life complicated enough?"

"I still miss you, Lena. It was nice to feel you in my arms again."

We both laughed a nervous kind of laugh.

"If you were Jewish, and we had stayed together, we would probably be getting married by now."

"Well, I'm not Jewish, and in my family it wouldn't matter."

"You could always convert, like Sammy Davis, Jr."

"Go home, Greg. And stop making me crazy."

He was walking out the door.

"Okay, but don't forgot about that converting option. It's a wonderful ceremony."

"GOOD NIGHT, GREG!"

"Night Lena."

I never heard Latmen come up behind me. He said, "Thinking about converting to Judaism, Lena?"

"No, Jack. It's a running joke that Greg and I have."

"I didn't see either of you running from the big fat kiss. How's Bianco?"

"I'm on my way up there now. I just stopped in to pick up my script."

"Don't try to come back until Thursday. We've got you covered."

I checked at the desk and the nurse there gave me his room number.

"He's really a tough guy. He's got all the nurses laughing at his jokes. I think it's the pain medication talking, but he's doing very well."

I peeked in his room and he was asleep. The floor nurse said he had been sleeping about two and a half hours. I went in and closed the door. As soon as he heard the click, his eyes popped open.

"I thought you gave up on me."

"I wouldn't do that, Whitey."

He stretched out his arm. I thought he wanted me to take his hand. Instead, he pulled the covers back again.

"Oh, no you don't, mister. I'm not falling for that trick again."

"It worked the first time."

I was leaning over him smiling and holding his hand. The door clicked open. Nurse Crabass looked at me suspiciously.

"I brought you broth and Jello, Mr. Bertuci."

"Oh, thank you," he said.

"Miss Delatora, would you like a dinner tray?"

"That would be just wonderful."

My tray had roast beef, mashed potatoes, and creamed spinach. When Nurse Crabass left, Whitey said, "I'd like some of that stuff. How about a spoon of your mashed potatoes? There's nothing wrong with my stomach, you know."

Nurse Crabass came in with a handful of straws.

Whitey asked, "I guess going home is out of the question?"

"That's correct, sir. You won't be going anywhere for at least two weeks. And that's conservatively speaking." With that, she turned and walked out of the room.

"Two weeks, my ass. I'll bet I'm out of here in three days. I can't drink soup through a *straw* and I'm already sick of that green Jello."

"*Well,* you are feeling better, aren't you."

I kissed him again. I handed him his soup and a straw. He was asleep before he finished drinking it. He had a smile on his face.

I watched his handsome face while he slept and wondered, *Where will this man fit into my life?*

The nurse had told me earlier that he said my name in his

sleep. He's building a house for me. I know he's worried about that. Tomorrow, I'll tell him about my dad getting some guys to help with the construction. I won't tell him about the bill being paid by my dad's connections.

I went directly to Nana's house. Ma was there with Auntie Lilly and my cousin Gemma.

"How's Whitey?" they all asked in unison.

"He's doing well. He looks much better tonight." I didn't mention that I crawled in bed with him or fed him mashed potatoes off my dinner tray.

Gemma followed me into the bedroom while I changed into my robe. She asked about a dozen questions.

"No, I don't think it's serious between us. Yes. His parents are very nice. They are older than Ma and Dad."

"Lena, you're getting too involved by staying at the hospital all the time."

"What would you suggest, Gemma? The man was shot in the chest right in front of me. I know I'm not responsible for his injury, but I'm the reason he was sitting in that restaurant, in that very spot."

"I realize that, Lena. I'm just worried about you, emotionally."

Baby Rosie toddled into the bedroom looking for her mama. I picked her up.

"I appreciate your concern. Just because I've been looking at him sleeping, half naked in that bed, and he's a nice guy, and he's got beautiful black hair like Elvis Presley . . . did I say that his eyes are violet colored?"

We both started laughing.

"Well, Lena, he sure sounds appealing, so far."

"Come-ona you two little chicks," Nana called from the kitchen.

I handed Rosie to Gemma, "She needs a diaper change. Joey too."

I helped put dinner on the table. It didn't matter that I just ate with Whitey at the hospital. When we all sat down, Nana said, "Hey, it's all of the ladies, only! I'm going to get some of Zio Peppino's wine."

My ma looked surprised. "Hey! How did you get that?"

"Zio came over yesterday with his *cane*, Stupido."

Ma and I laughed. That poor dog. He answers to both names. Jojo and Stupido. He's had a family before us. I wonder what they used to call him?

My ma made her eyes real big and said, "You're awfully friendly with Zio Peppino. Has he been flirting with you?"

Nana's face turned bright red. She told Ma, "Wha'd da you talk about? Peppino is joosta friend. Sometimes when he pick *cardone*, he brings some to me and a I give him a-lunch."

Nana has been a widow for a long time. I was only three when Papa Joe died. We used to tease her about Mike the Milkman because she used to give him cake and coffee sometimes. Now that we are teasing her about Zio Peppino, she's very defensive.

"Why did you get wine before me, Ma?"

"I tell you why. Because I tell-a him where to find *cardone*. He go behind the school by the old firehouse."

"Ma, did you go with him, behind the old firehouse?"

Nana swished her hand at my ma. "Never mind you girls. Shame-a to you for wadda you thinking."

With that, there was a knock at the kitchen door.

"Bungorno, Dona Rosina. Stai a casa? What's so funny?"

"Nothing funny, Peppino. You wanna some dinner?

"Bene. It's a nice day for *famiglia to* be together."

Zio looked very comfortable in Nana's kitchen. I wondered how long Zio had been bringing her surprises.

I should add that my Nana is only sixty-two. My Ma is forty-three. I was born when my ma was twenty years old. I am twenty-three and single—a late bloomer in my family.

This would be the last full day I could spend with Whitey. When I got to the hospital, I stopped at the nurse's station. They told me Whitey was moved out of ICU to a private room. He was sitting up in bed when I got there. He gave me his best smile when I walked in. He pushed the tray table away and flipped his covers back, motioning me to get in.

"Oh not you don't! You're not tricking me into feeling sorry for you again."

"Why, have I done it before?"

"Tell me you don't remember that we slept together the other night?"

"I don't remember that at all. Maybe that's why I got well so quick. Sure you don't want to climb in?

"No, but I can feed you your lunch."

"I'll take whatever I can get."

"Whitey, do you remember that you got shot three days ago?"

"I sure do."

He was still very pale and his hand shook just a little when he picked up his spoon.

"I'll do that. You're not ready to do everything by yourself."

I took the spoon away from him.

"Lena, I have to get back to my construction business. I have to finish your house."

"Whitey, everything is under control. My dad put extra guys on the crew. A company that he has connections with does work for companies under unusual circumstances."

I didn't dare tell him that my dad was "connected."

"Oh, I guess that's good."

I could see him thinking about this. He was still too weak to argue about the "circumstances."

I finished helping him with his lunch, and he looked exhausted.

"Whitey, it's time for you to rest."

"Right, I'm pretty tired."

He flipped those covers back and I slid right in beside him. I am such a pushover.

"I want to feel your skin, Lena."

I slipped out of my slacks under the covers. Nurse Crabass will have a heart attack over this.

He was asleep when I moved slowly out from under the covers. Without opening his eyes he said, "Kiss me good-bye, baby."

35

When I got to the TV station, Frank Latmen was at the parking lot door, looking upset.

"Lena!" He looked completely frantic. "We got a big problem."

"What could be so bad? You look like you're nuts."

"You have no idea. Beth has locked herself in her dressing room. She's been in there all morning. I can hear her sobbing. I think Greg broke up with her. He's been talking to her through the door for an hour. She won't even answer him. She just cries, quiet or loud."

"Okay, I'm heading that way. Calm down. It will be all right."

"Cripes! I'm so glad you're back, Lena."

I walked down the hall to Beth's dressing room. Greg was standing outside her door. I could hear him pleading with her.

"Beth, open the door. This isn't the end of the world. You are really overreacting. Let's talk about this."

I said, "Move over. Let me talk to her."

"Beth, open this door! There is a show to do today. You can't stay locked in there all day. I need your help with today's script!"

"Lena, if I let you in, don't let Greg come in, okay?"

"Agreed. Greg will stay out here. Open up."

Beth opened the door, just a crack to be sure that I wouldn't trick her into letting Greg in. I nudged the door and walked in.

You would have thought that a bomb went off in that dressing room. There was tissue all over the place with empty candy wrappers all over her dressing table.

"Where did you have all that candy hidden?"

I guess that was an unexpected question. She stopped crying

and said, "I had it in the closet in the bin with the wigs. I'm surprised that it didn't melt with all the lights overhead."

"Are you ready for today's show?" I asked her.

"Yes. I should be okay. I looked at the lines last night. How about you? I heard about Whitey. How is Whitey?"

"Oh, I'm fine Beth. Whitey will be okay." I was simply playing along with her mood swing.

Latmen knocked on the door. "Can I see you, Lena?"

"I'll be right out."

After I stepped into the hall, Latmen asked, "What did you say to her?"

"I asked her about the show. I diverted her attention. I've seen her behave this way before."

"Was that all? What the hell was she so upset about?"

"I'm pretty sure that it was because Greg broke up with her."

I waited for Greg to come back down the hall and motioned for him to come into her dressing room. I asked her if she wanted me to stay or leave.

"Please stay, Lena."

"Okay. What's going on with you two? If the relationship is over, then it's over."

"Greg," Beth said, "I understand that you broke up with me, but I think it was the right thing to do. It was for your own good, and I want you to know I can take it."

This is how crazy Beth is. She tries to have relationships, but she destroys them by smothering the person with her possessive nature. Greg was speechless at her comments. I looked out the open door and saw Latmen throwing his arms up in resignation. I couldn't help wondering if our little Beth had her sight set for a new man. She could change her loyalties on a dime. Time will tell. It wouldn't take a *lot* of time either.

"Well," Beth said, "we've wasted enough time kicking this old blues song around. Let's get to work."

Greg and I looked at each other with complete amazement. The show must go on! She really had some kind of personality disorder.

It was Mona's day to wear the bigger baby bump. She was supposed to look like she was about five or six months pregnant; Johnny, her husband, had just purchased a new home for her in this episode. I don't see Mona as much as I used to. Paulie is pretty busy with his singing gig at Riggio's and Mona has started to move some of her belongings into Nana's back house. The other night, when I left the hospital, I stopped at Riggio's to pick up some dinner for Ma and Dad. I saw Paulie in the bar area, sitting with an older woman. They didn't see me. Riggio offered to go get Paulie for me. I told him I couldn't stay long, so he didn't need to bother. Mona seems to be taking her role with Johnny pretty seriously.

I studied the script last night. I knew that Mona and Johnny were supposed to be happily married on the show. I know happy when I see it. They were both looking way too happy off the set, too. I reminded myself about that brain filter. It's not a good practice to take my personal life to the studio. Something was rotten in Happyland. In fact, this entire cast of characters was a mess. Paulie was flirting with some old chick at the bar; Beth has lost her mind because Greg broke up with her; Mona and Johnny seem to be gazing into each other's eyes too long after the scene is over. I knew I was an emotional wreck right then. Maybe I was not receiving the right messages. My brain filter and my radar must have been off.

I am on camera in about ten minutes. My lines were very easy that day. The writers knew that I would be coming back from a business trip. The purpose of the trip was to find new furniture for the bed and breakfast that Beth and I owned. The entire show was only thirty minutes long. It's not unusual for some of us to improvise lines when things go wrong and to cover someone else's mistakes. This day, Beth improvised twice. She was throwing me off with her goofy comments. At one point she was supposed to say, "How was your visit to the furniture manufacturers?" Instead, she said, "How was your pretend visit to all the furniture stores?"

I managed to cover with, "Oh, I pretend that I have lots of cash to spend and they pretend that they have the best furniture ever made."

I was a little uneasy about the last few minutes of the show. We managed to end with her flirtatious comments about the men at the furniture stores. I said that they were handsome and perhaps she should come with me next time. The producers could use that to write an episode for her to travel and give her a break away from the show.

When the scene was over, Latmen said "In my office, Beth."

Beth was acting very strange. She was too upbeat and flippant. This was the way she behaved when I first met her. I think she's wound too tight. I'm not sure how to read her, but what I see isn't good. I think Latmen could sense that something was not right with her.

Greg was outside my dressing room waiting for me. He spoke first.

"I'm taking bets on the next meltdown. Her parents said that she behaved this way when she had her last breakup. Do you think she's going to blow her top? I don't get it. Her mood swings are crazy."

"I was hoping you had some conversation about her emotional state with her parents. I didn't know that you spoke to them. I'm glad that you had some insight to this situation. I dropped the line in about her visiting the furniture stores to give the writers the option of giving her the opportunity to take some time off. I'm worried that the time that I spent with Whitey in the hospital was too much pressure for her here."

"You might be right about that, but I think this started when she realized our relationship wasn't working out."

Just then the door opened and Beth burst in.

"Well! I can't imagine why you two are in this dressing room alone! Have you decided to rekindle your relationship?"

I stood there with my mouth open. I was startled because she didn't knock. Secondly, I was taken aback by her rude comment. The earlier, flippant casual tone in her voice was gone. Now she sounded like she was going to snap.

"Well, you'll never guess what Latmen told me! He is thinking about writing me out for a few weeks! Can you imagine? He thinks that Susan is ready to come back. Her baby is a few months old. I never thought he would write me out. I thought it would be *YOU!* You're the new kid. Susan and I started with the show. I'm really insulted."

Greg and I looked at each other, both examining each other's face. I spoke first.

"You could be mistaken. Maybe he just has a soft spot for Susan. I've been away for a few days because of my personal situation and you had to work harder. He probably just wants to give you a break, too."

Greg finally spoke up, "Don't you think it would be nice to get away with your folks for a while? You said you used to go up to the Dells every year at this time."

Beth suddenly looked like she had a revelation. "Yes! That's right! I'm going to call them right now. I have a phone in my dressing room too!"

She turned on her heel and walked out, slamming the door.

Greg sighed and looked at me. "Lena, that's it, she's getting ready to blow."

"Yep. I hope her parents will recognize it, too."

"I think they will. I called them this morning to let them know about her behavior. I know they will see the signs. They know what to look for."

"How long does it usually take for her to get herself stable?"

"She won't be able to do it herself. They will put her into a "spa." He rolled his eyes, indicating that it wouldn't be a spa at all.

"Greg, how could you have gotten involved with her, knowing that she was such a . . . nut . . . err, unstable person. And don't tell me it was because she was Jewish."

"Well, it was. I think her parents were grooming me. They still think I'm just taking some time away from her. I talked to my ma about her, and she asked, 'What happened to that nice girl, Lena, that you were dating?' Suddenly being Jewish isn't all that important."

"Are you kidding me!? After you dumped me and turned to darling Beth? What the hell, Greg? Are you telling me that your ma approved of me after all? That's kind of mean. Is she mean? Or did you read her wrong?"

"Gosh, Lena, you really seem upset. I didn't mean to hurt your feelings. She has always said that she expected me to marry a Jewish girl. My dad never commented one way or another before he passed away."

"Maybe you played with my feelings too. Maybe this is the way you treat the women that you date. If they don't fit your criteria, maybe you use your mom, or the girl's mental health, as an excuse."

"Lena,that's not true."

"Leave now, Greg. I have enough going on in my life."

He didn't question me, but turned and left.

I had such mixed emotions. I needed to see Whitey. I needed to see Paulie, too. I felt like life was changing too fast all around me. I want to ask Paulie how things were going between him and Mona. I needed to see Mona and ask her about the goo-goo eyes between her and Johnny. Maybe I should mind my own business. I was getting pretty good at that, for a while.

36

I went home to my mama. That's what a kid's gotta do when the going gets tough.

She took one look at me and said, "Bella Mia! What's wrong?"

I started to cry and she put her arms around me.

"Lena do you understand what you've been through this past year? You broke up with Greg. Then you met someone and fell in love. He left you for someone you've never met; you introduced Carlo to your friend Penny and they are getting married; you are the star of a television show; you are building a house, remodeling Nana's house, and your new love interest was almost killed. Please come back home. Bobby can sleep downstairs in the family room. I need to know that you are all right. Just think, you can wake up every morning and check on the progress of your new house."

"Mama, I think I will do that. I'm feeling a little disconnected. Something is going on between Paulie and Mona."

"What do you mean?"

"I think there is trouble in paradise. I think she has eyes for someone else, and I saw Paulie with some older chick in the bar at Riggio's."

"Well, that makes sense. Nana said that Paulie slept on the sofa at her house the other night."

"I'll just keep my eyes open at the TV station and see where things are going. I'm not even going to ask Paulie what's going on. I don't think I want to know right now."

"Let me fix you something to eat. I'm afraid you're getting too thin."

That's our family. It's not typical for women to be too thin.

"Ma, what's that smell in the house?"

"Oh, that's Zio's wine fermenting in the basement. He made another batch."

"I'll have dinner. Then I'll call Whitey." I was beginning to miss him.

Zio Peppino came home in the afternoon. I noticed that he didn't even use his walker anymore. He had a cane that was all carved and painted in beautiful colors. It looked familiar to me. I asked Ma where he got it.

"Oh, that was Papa Joe's cane. Nana gave it to him."

"Well, for heaven's sake. Does Nana say much about Zio?"

Ma smiled, "Just that he comes over nearly every day for lunch. She's always got plenty of food cooked. He hasn't been eating here very much. Just dinner."

"Well, I see another wedding in the near future."

"Oh, I don't think she would ever get married again."

"Ma, be serious. Don't you see the little smile she has when she comes here for dinner?

"Her eyes light up like a teenage girl. Do you think the brothers and sisters can handle it? I never gave it serious thought. I'll talk to Dad tonight. He'll have to talk to the uncles at the men's club.

I called Whitey at the hospital and his mother answered the phone. "Hullo."

"*Bongorno, Senora Bertuci.* How is Whitey today?"

"Uno momento. I give-a to him-a the tela-phone."

Geez, she has a much thicker accent than my Nana. I'm surprised she answered the phone. Of course, she would realize that whoever it was would speak Italian.

Whitey whispered, "When did you put your pants on and leave?"

"It's a good thing that your parents don't speak much English. You should just be glad that Nurse Crabass didn't catch me."

"We didn't do anything obscene. You had your panties on and I had this attractive hospital gown on. Enough chitchat. When are you coming up here to feel sorry for me?"

"Well, the car is picking your parents up at four. I have a few lines to study for tomorrow's show. I'll be up around five thirty, okay?"

"That sounds great. I can get out of bed now, you know? I can brush my teeth and go to the bathroom too."

"Well, don't push your luck, Whitey. I don't want you to open up all the stitches by trying to be a tough guy."

"We'll see how tough I am when you get here."

I loved to talk to him on the phone. He always seemed so at ease. It was almost as easy to talk to him as Gino. There, I thought about him by name. I didn't even call him anything vulgar in my head. I usually thought about him as, "The Jerk," or "The Shithead." The bad thing about thinking about Gino was once I let him in my head, I couldn't get him out.

37

Nana came for dinner that evening. Bobby and Zio walked with her, because Bobby was at Auntie Lilly's house next door. He was carrying a big pan, and Zio was pulling the faithful wagon. It had a big pot with a lid. Nana had put foil on the pot under the lid.

"Hurry, Bella—this is getting cold." It was a big pot of minestrone soup.

My ma came out and said, "Mama, everyone in this family drives. Why do you torture yourself carrying heavy stuff like that?"

"I don't carry it. We walked with Peppino. He gotta the wagon. He come over with Stupido this afternoon."

My ma looked at me and smiled a knowing smile.

Dad came out and asked, "What's in the baking pan, Ma?"

"I baked some mostaccioli with sausage and peppers."

"I was going to make some eggplant. Bring it all inside and we'll put it all together. Lena, get a big pan from downstairs and we'll fix some for you to take to Whitey and his parents."

"Ma, his parents will be gone when I get there."

"Then you can drop it off at their house."

"Fine. That's what I'll do. Keep it in the oven for me."

We put the board in the kitchen table. Zio Peppino brought up some wine. We had a nice dinner together. I think we'd better get used to all this togetherness. We could tell that Zio and Nana were flirting with each other when they thought no one was looking.

Why should anyone grow old alone?

When I got to Whitey's parents house, they insisted that I come inside. I had the pan of hot food from my ma and Nana. They were delighted, and they were hungry too.

Mrs. Bertuci said, "Oh, Lena, we are happy that you are such a nice-a girl. Bianco is very happy that he meet you. I didn't see him so happy since he had the other girl that he give-a the ring to."

His dad said, *"Grazie, Grazie.* It was such a lucky day when Bianco met you."

I thought to myself, *He was so lucky that he nearly got killed taking me out to dinner.*

"Siete i benvenuti. You are very welcome. I cannot stay long. I want to take some food up to Bianco before it gets cold."

We said our good-byes and they both kissed me.

When I got to the hospital, Whitey was wearing his own pajamas and sitting in a chair. His face lit up in a smile when he saw me. Those eyes really melt my heart. I could tell that he was feeling better because his eyes were clearly violet. When he was really sick, they were very dark blue.

"I'm sorry I got here so late. I stopped at your parents to bring them some food. My nana brought so much stuff over tonight that I thought it was a good idea to share it."

"I'd rather share my bed with you."

"For a guy that I've never really fooled around with, you sure are confident."

"We've slept together. I remember that clearly."

"That was just to make you feel better."

"Now that I'm really feeling better, I can thank you properly."

By this point in the conversation, I had pulled a chair up next to him. He managed to lean over and put one arm around me.

He announced, "I brushed my teeth and took a shower all by myself. I was hoping you'd get here earlier and help me."

"Your parents were here earlier. I'm sure they wouldn't have been too happy about that."

"Believe me, they are so happy that I've met you that they might have approved."

The nurse came in to see if Whitey was ready for his dinner. I told her I had brought food; I asked if she would bring a plate and silverware for Whitey. I told her that the remaining food would be at the nurse's station to share with all the wonderful ladies who had been taking care of Whitey. I could tell that she appreciated that. Sometimes it's a good idea to bring good food to people who do good things. My Ma always taught me that the best favors are paid back with a good meal.

Whitey and I went back to smooching as soon as the nurse walked out.

He said, "Lena, I have to get out of here. I feel pretty good. I'm going to talk to the doctor today about releasing me."

"Whitey, where will you stay? Do you plan to stay with you folks?"

"They want me to, but I think I'll be fine at my place."

"I thought all Italian men lived somewhere near their parents?"

"My apartment is not far from my folks. It's around the corner in a building that my aunt owns, but she doesn't live there. I take care of the two-flat for her. My Ma can stop over every day to be sure I'm all right. You know she'll bring food when she comes."

"I'll come by after work before I go home and see how you are doing."

"I was hoping we could have a sleepover for the first few nights."

"Lets see how this work out with your folks first. I don't want to steal your ma's thunder. She's going to want to take care of you. It's what ma's do. I want you to get back in bed and I'll get some food ready for you. You are beginning to look tired."

Whitey ate quite a lot of food. I moved the tray table away and tucked him in.

"Aren't you getting in bed with me?"

"Not tonight. You need to get a good night's sleep."

38

When I brought the food to the nurses' station, I asked if Whitey's doctor was there.

"I'll see if I can reach him. Are you a relative?"

I was going to tell her that I was his sister, but I don't think she would have believed me, since I'd been under the covers with him. I know Nurse Crabass must have shared that with the rest of the staff. I could tell by the sideways glances and the sly smile.

"I'm his fiancée."

"I'll page him for you."

Sometimes I forget that my face is on television every day. Everyone knows who I am. It controls my behavior to a great extent. I have to behave in such a way that it does not reflect badly on the TV show or the industry. Sometimes I'd like to be invisible.

The doctor met me in the family waiting area.

"I'm pleased to meet you, Miss Delatora. Bianco is healing very well. There is no permanent damage. The bullet missed the heart and the lungs. He has quite a way to go before he is completely healed. He won't be able to return to work for at least one month. He can only stay on the job site for four hours each day. I understand he has a construction company. He can only supervise. In three months he can stay on the job site for the entire day. No heavy lifting for six months. When he leaves, he will get extra medical supplies to change his dressings every day. It's been a pleasure to meet you."

He shook my hand and walked away. No fanfare, no further instructions. He didn't even say when Whitey could go home. I guess I'll check with the desk nurse when I leave.

I was surprised to find out that Whitey was scheduled for release in two days! I got butterflies in my stomach. I think knowing he was going home forced me to think of where our relationship was headed.

39

got to Mona's apartment around five thirty. She looked surprised to see me when she opened the door. I don't think she was going to ask me in until I said, "Hey! What's new? Are you busy?"

"Oh, Lena," she said, "Come on in. Johnny is here. We were just going over some of our lines."

This is not a good thing. I'd gone over lines with coworkers at the TV station after hours. I'd never brought anyone home with me.

"Mona, can you come outside for just a minute?"

"Oh sure, Lena. Is anything wrong?"

We walked outside to my car and I said, "Get in."

"I know what you're going to say. This is not what it looks like."

"It looks like exactly what it is. You're sneaking around with Johnny. Does Paulie know about this? You aren't even trying to keep this a secret, are you?"

"Okay, Lena, stop right there. Paulie and I split up. It happened about two weeks ago."

"When were one of you going to tell me? This is really upsetting. Does Nana know?"

"Of course she does. Paulie has been staying at her house for a couple of weeks. He's waiting for the house in back to be done so he can move back in."

"Holy cheese, Mona. Who did the breaking up?"

"Well, I guess it was mutual. He started flirting with an older woman who has a horse farm. I started having some feelings for Johnny."

"Mona, Johnny is an emotional leech."

"Maybe I need someone like that. I don't have to struggle to keep him interested in me. He's an awful flirt."

"Oh, I know that, for sure. I worked with Johnny first, remember? I thought Paulie was done with all that skirt chasing."

"He may never change. I don't think I can spend my life wondering where he is or who he is with. It's just too much pressure. I need to be able to count on someone. I need to know he's there when I need him. You have been through a rough time with Gino. You know what it's like to be afraid all the time. Johnny and his wife have split up. She wanted a baby. Even after he told her that he wanted a baby too, she got really removed from the situation. He couldn't seem to reach her, emotionally. She finally asked him to start the divorce proceedings."

"Mona, is Johnny living with you?"

"No. He found an apartment in my complex. It's one floor up and around the corner. He's just fixing some dinner for us. Do you want to stay and eat with us?"

"No. I don't think it's a good idea. I'd be uncomfortable.

I said my good-byes and drove over to Riggio's to see Paulie.

I wasn't surprised to see him sitting at the end of the bar with the blond from the other night. She still looked skinny and burnt out. I walked toward them and said to myself, "This chick is way older than I thought." Paulie saw me, and his wide-eyed look indicated that he didn't want me to interrupt. That's too bad. You see, I could read him pretty well. I understood the raised eyebrows and surprised look. I just kept walking toward him.

"Hey! Lena! What a nice surprise!

"Good to see you too, Paulie."

"Helen, this is my niece Lena that I've told you about."

"Please to meet you, Lena." Helen stuck out a limp hand and I shook it.

"Lena, Helen is a record producer. She has been listening to me sing for a few weeks. She thinks I have a very professional skill and she likes my voice."

I know where Paulie's skill lies with women. I wish I could say that I felt good about this, but for some reason this woman was making my skin crawl. Paulie is a stupid slug when it comes to intuition. He has no "thinking" organ when women are involved. That's how he gets in so much trouble.

"Well Helen, that's very kind of you. Paulie, can I talk to you alone for just a moment?"

"Please excuse us, Helen."

Paulie and I went into the empty restaurant side of Riggio's.

"Are you nuts, Paulie? This woman is over forty; you are twenty-four years old. She's a bloodsucker. What are you doing with her?"

"Lena, this could be a big break. She has some songs that she wants me to record. Let's go back and I'll sing one for you."

"Geez, okay. I don't feel good about this."

"Helen, would it be all right if I sang the 'Fantastic' song for Lena?"

"Sure, Paulie. Do you remember the lyrics?"

She handed him the song sheet anyway and Paulie got up on the stage.

Paulie started the boom box and began to sing:

"Fantastic, the world that we live in
Fantastic, the things that we do.
While rockets race to outer space,
We keep our rendezvous..."

The song was all right—a catchy little tune with a cha-cha beat. I smiled at Paulie and turned to Helen.

I asked, "Helen, has Paulie signed a contract with you?"

"Well yes, Lena. In fact, we begin recording next week."

I felt myself wanting to slap her, really bad. I looked at Paulie and he had a stupid grin on his face.

"Well, good luck to both of you."

I got up and walked out. I was physically shaking, I was so angry.

"Lena, wait. I want to talk to you."

Paulie was chasing me through the parking lot.

"Are you nuts, Paulie? You signed a contract? Who is this woman? She smokes like a chimney, smells like old butts, and she drinks all day into the evening. Does this sound like a professional person to you? Did you have a lawyer look at the contract?"

"Lena, she has a lot of connections. I could have a real career in the record industry."

"Does Mr. Riggio know you're leaving?"

"No, I didn't tell him yet. He sees that an older woman has taken interest in me. He doesn't like it. He warned me that she could be trouble. He says he's worried about me."

"Paulie, he's a good judge of character. He sees people come and go all the time. He doesn't like her and I don't like her. What are you going to do for money while you are waiting for your career to take off."

"She owns a horse farm out in the country. It has a recording studio. She says I can stay with her until things get going. She'll pay me to work around the farm."

Now I was making the sign of the cross. I felt like this woman would be paying him for a different service. This situation was headed for hell. I hugged him and got in my car. Paulie was an adult—a stupid adult, but an adult just the same. I couldn't control him. I promised myself I would stop trying to do that. He was waving to me and saying, "It's going to be okay, Lena. You'll see."

I watched him in my rearview mirror and felt really sad.

The next morning I got ready to get Whitey from the hospital. I mentally reviewed my friends and family to myself while I was driving. *Mona is messing around with Johnny; Paulie is headed for hell with Helen. Penny is going to marry Carlo. Somewhere in the back of my head, I think that Nana is gonna marry Zio Peppino. I'm going to wind up in the nut house.*

Today I will focus on Whitey coming home. I was excited, but a little anxious. I still didn't know where this relationship was going, and I didn't know how I felt about him. I picked his ma and dad up around 9 a.m. I insisted on taking them out for breakfast. It was something that they wouldn't typically do. They though it was a big deal, but it was just a little diner near the hospital.

We went to the discharge area on the ground floor. They signed all the papers. When they walked away, I wrote a check. They didn't seem to notice that. I paid the hospital bill in full. It was something I wanted to do. When we sat down, Mr. Bertuci asked if the bill for the hospital would come to the house. I said, "Yes." The fact that they signed everything indicated that they thought they would be billed. This was all new to them and they were a little overwhelmed.

Whitey was dressed and sitting in a wheelchair when we got to his room. He smiled and said, "They won't let me walk to the car."

"That's what they usually do, Whitey. They don't want to take any chances that you might pass out or fall down."

"Let's get out of here," he said.

His parents and the nurse were leaving his room. I went to pull my car out in front for the pick-up. When I pulled up, Whitey was standing at the curb. I could see the nurse scolding him. It wasn't Nurse Crabass, and this nurse didn't know who she was dealing with. I hopped out of the drivers seat to help everyone get into the car. Whitey got the front seat, his parents got in the back. I tried to tip the nurse, but she forcefully declined. I would make arrangements for Riggio to bring lunch up to the nurse's station for the rest of the week.

40

Whitey's Ma had cooked all sorts of food. She thought he was going to stay with her, but I explained that he wanted to go home, so we packed up all the food and put in my car. "It's okay, Miss Lena. I'm gonna stay at his house tonight, just in case he needs some-a thing."

We all piled out of the car in front of Whitey's apartment building, except for Whitey. His dad and I each held an arm to get him up the front steps. Mama followed behind carrying some of the food.

When we opened the door, the entire building crew was there. They had set up a recliner in front of the new color TV. My dad had said, "Let him think his buddies bought it." They brought food too. Beef sandwiches, sausage with peppers, and pizza. Mama sent them out to the car for the rest of her food. I wrapped some of the stuff and put it into the freezer. Mama fussed over Whitey in his recliner, made all the crew sit down, and fed them. She fixed a special plate for her Bianco with soft food. No Italian bread, just sausage, beef, and lasagna. That was the equivalent of a soft food diet in her world. The guys stayed for about an hour

They could see that Whitey was getting tired. I sat with Whitey while his ma and dad discussed the sleeping arrangements in the guest room.

Whitey said, "I guess you won't be spending the night."

"No, you handsome devil. Mama is taking care of you tonight, and probably tomorrow. I have to let her have her time, you know. It wouldn't be right if I bumped her out of the picture. You are her only son."

"Then will you spend the night?"

"I promise that after Mama stays a couple of nights, I will try to convince her that I will sleep in the guest room and be here if you need me."

"Guest room, my ass." He pulled me into his lap and kissed me.

I quickly stood up. It wouldn't be a good thing for them to find me in his lap.

I was planning to drive Papa Bertuci home, but when they came into the living room they announced that they would both be staying. The double bed in the guest room was just fine for them. Papa could go to the grocery store around the corner, if Mama needed anything. I know that I saw Whitey roll his eyes.

Mama Bertuci said, "Time-a for you to go bed, Bianco."

He looked at me and said, "Do you believe this? I never thought I'd hear that again."

I kissed everyone on the cheek and made my exit. It was only seven so I stopped at Ma's. I couldn't believe the progress on my house. It looked beautiful. The outside was nearly finished. The flooring was partially done, and the walls were going up.

I went into my ma's kitchen and said, "Holy cow! My house looks really great!"

"Daddy wanted you to have a nice surprise when you came over. He's been very worried about you both."

"Whitey's doing okay. His ma and dad are staying with him for a couple of nights."

"Are you two getting serious, Lena?"

I started to laugh. "How the heck should I know? I haven't even had a real date with him. The only time we've had alone was at the hospital when he was in serious condition."

Ma started to laugh too. "I haven't even thought about that. You have spent so much time with him. I never considered the fact that it was all sick time."

I didn't bother telling her about the night at his apartment, when we almost went further.

I could hear Zio thumping his way up the basement stairs. He had a bottle of wine in one hand and held the handrail with the other. "Bella Lena. How's you friend Bianco?"

"I think he's doing okay, Zio."

"Give-a to him this wine. It will help his blood get strong."

"Thank you, Zio. That's really nice. I will be sure he gets this."

"I go to bed now. *Buona notte.*"

"*Buona notte*, Zio." I kissed his cheeks.

I smiled at Ma and said, "Well, at least we know where he's sleeping at night."

"Lena, do you think it is getting more serious between him and Nana?"

"I'm no genius, Ma. But I have pretty good instincts. I'm seeing sparks of some kind."

"How do I ask Nana about this?"

"You don't. Just wait and see what happens. We're all together so much anyway. We're bound to see when things get serious."

Dad walked in from the living room. "I hope Zio is more than a little deaf, cause I can hear every word you both said."

I could hear Zio snoring by this time, so I wasn't really worried. Dad said, "That's not Zio. It's Stupido."

"Poor Jojo. He gets blamed for everything."

"Where are you staying tonight, Lena?

"I don't want Nana to be alone."

"Bobby is sleeping there tonight. There's no school tomorrow and he's helping Paulie in the back house."

"Is Paulie sleeping by Nana?"

"No. He bought a new bed and he's sleeping in the back. Bobby is sleeping on the sofa at Paulie's house."

"I'll sleep in Paulie's room."

Someone was always sleeping in someone else's bed. We were worse than the three bears. Bobby had been helping Paulie fix up the old house since he and Mona had split up. I guess he hadn't broken the news to anyone that he was moving to a horse farm with "Helen From Hell."

The next morning, Penny was doing my makeup. She was

happier than usual. She was chatting about a new restaurant that Carlo had taken her to.

"On the way there, we saw the cutest little bungalow! Carlo stopped and wrote the number down from the 'For Sale' sign. If we make an appointment, do you want to go with us to see it?"

"Penny! How nice! Why don't you both go see it first. If you really need my opinion, I'll go with you to see it a second time."

"Oh! That's great, Lena.

41

O h, that baby bump! I was glad that it was between Johnny and Mona when I saw them backstage.

"Hey! You guys better save that passion for the set. You might get mixed up. This is the scene that you two are reconciling in, right? Thank goodness. I'm glad it's not the breakup scene. You'd never be able to pull it off."

They both laughed nervously.

I wanted them to know that I was watching them. I didn't care what the heck they do in private; I like to see some form of professionalism in the studio. I had become very protective of the *Tortured Souls* production. I wanted it to be "right" all of the time.

Latmen was very happy with the changes I'd been making in the script. All of the scenes that I write have to be approved by the producers. They seem to like them very much.

That day's episode went very smoothly. Johnny and Mona had great chemistry on the set. I hoped that they both were smart enough to know that they were acting. I didn't know where their feelings were going and I was pretending not to care

When I got off work, I went to Nana's house. My brother Bobby and Paulie were at the kitchen table. Nana had made some stew and pasta and Italian meatloaf with tomato sauce.

My little brother Bobby was looking very grown up. He had on a pair of chinos and an old shirt of Paulie's. He had his legs stretched out and his ankles crossed. He had a pair of Paulie's old work boots on. He really looked full of himself.

He saw me smiling at him and said, "Okay, so I'm wearing Paulie's old clothes. Is that so bad?"

"Oh Bobby, you look so cute, dressed all grown up."

Paulie said, "Leave him alone, Lena. He's been working really hard."

My brother Bobby was sixteen years old. I looked at him and he sure looked it today. I looked at Paulie and I could see a strong family resemblance. I thought to myself. *What is he in for, hanging around with Paulie?*

I asked Bobby, "Have you been going home at night or staying here with Paulie?"

"Lena, why you asking him that?"

"'Cause I don't know what you do at night anymore, Paulie. Does Helen come here to keep you company? Do you go there and leave Bobby alone in your house?"

I could see I had hurt Paulie's feelings. I knew Bobby didn't have any idea why I was concerned.

"Paulie, come outside with me. I want to show you something." When we got outside, we got into my car.

"Why are you making me feel like I've done something wrong around Bobby?"

"Why do *you* make me feel like you're doing something wrong?"

"Lena, we're not kids anymore. I have a life of my own."

"Paulie, let me tell you something that I heard from Mona. She heard that Helen is the same chick that Nick Piccolo was seeing. People saw him all over town.

"Lena, Helen told me that. I'm not concerned about that. It was a fling for both of them."

42

"What's in it for you, Paulie? I'm sure that there's more going on with you two, besides her coaching you at her little recording studio. I'm gonna say something to you, Paulie. After that, I'm not going to discuss her anymore. Helen is the kind of woman who uses young men. She couldn't find anything more to use Nick for, so she moved on to you. You have a good singing voice, you could be fine entertainment for her. You might even be a meal ticket. How soon is your move to the farm?"

"I'll probably move out there slowly, beginning in about three weeks. I'm going to record the "Fantastic" song there next weekend. Lena, she really wants to help me. Will you give her a chance to show me what she can do?"

"Yes, Paulie. Now I'll watch you both and mind my own business."

I looked over at Nana's porch and Bobby was leaning on the railing waiting for us. I put on my best smile and said, "Okay, I know you're hungry. Let's eat!"

My nana was a saint. She never said, *What's the matter?* Or, *Why you go outside?* She just kept on moving along, trying to make everyone happy. Cooking, smiling, and loving everyone, in spite of any faults they might have.

I missed Whitey. I was going to bring something to sleep in and a different outfit for the next day. His parents had stayed there nearly a week. I'd stopped over there a couple of times. He still slept a lot and his Ma had cooked so much stuff that the freezer was packed. I'd see if they wanted to go home that night. I would drive them back to their house. It was only around the corner, but they had brought so much stuff with them, it might take two trips to get everything back to their house.

Mama Bertuci opened the door, wearing an apron and wiping her hands on a dish towel. I saw Papa Bertuci was in the recliner reading the Italian newspaper. Whitey was stretched out on the sofa, dozing. Mama B. kissed my cheeks and hugged me tight. She whispered, "Bianco has been asking for you since yesterday."

Papa B. started to get up from the recliner, and I motioned for him to stay seated. I walked over to kiss his cheek. He smiled and held my hand in both of his for a moment. He said, "Lena, I'm-a so glad that you come."

I was touched by their behavior. They made me feel like I was part of their family. We went into the kitchen, where Mama B. was cleaning like a crazy woman. She said, "Joosta momento. I'm-a gonna finish-a wipe the cabinet doors."

She finally sat down and poured us each a cup of coffee. "Lena, you a very special girl. I'm glad for my Bianco. I don't think that you gonna break-a his heart, right?"

"Oh, Mrs. Bertuci, I don't think that's going to happen. We haven't known each other very long, you know. I care about him very much. We have to get to know each other a little more before we make any lifetime decisions. If we don't stay together, it will be because we both made the decision."

I tried to keep my English uncomplicated. I wanted her to know that I cared about Whitey, but we hadn't made any commitments yet.

"You gotta some other boyfriends?"

"No. I have no one but Bianco."

"Okay. You a good girl. Only make-a one boyfriend at a time."

She patted my hand and got up to take some cookies from a tin and put them on a plate.

Whitey walked into the kitchen and his face lit up when he saw me"I thought you were going to leave me here to wallow in Italian leftovers for the rest of my life."

Mama said, "Whad-a you say . . . leftovers? You no like-a my food no more?"

He kissed her cheek and said, "I love your food, Ma. I'm just glad to see Lena."

She smiled and said, "Maybe is time for Mama and Papa to go home."

Geez, I thought she'd never say it out loud. I was going to offer to drive them, hoping they wouldn't think I was rushing them.

Mama went into the living room and said, "Papa, we go home today."

Papa B. smiled and put his hands up in a hallelujah gesture, "I'm-a gonna sleep in my own bed tonight."

"I can take you both home whenever you're ready, Signore Bertuci."

"Come-onna, Lena. You help me with the kitchen things?"

"Of course, Signora Bertuci. I would be glad to help you."

She went to the back porch and came back with a carton. She pulled some big baking pans from the cabinet that she had brought with them. She added a few containers from the freezer and some from the refrigerator. I carried the box out to the car. One more trip with their clothes and extra blankets and they had their coats on.

It was a short drive to the Bertucis' house. They insisted I stay for lunch, since Mama B. brought food home. I helped set the table while she heated some meatballs and pasta in a frying pan. I didn't want to rush, but I finally said, "I don't want to leave Bianco alone too long."

Papa helped me with my jacket and we all kissed and hugged again.

━━━►«❰❱»◄━━━

When I got back to Whitey's apartment, he was in bed naked, except for the patch covering the wound on his chest. He was sound asleep.

I stood there watching him sleep. He was really a beautiful

guy, even when his lavender eyes were closed. He must have felt me staring at him. His eyes opened and he put out his hand without saying a word . . . just like he had when he was in the hospital.

I crawled right into bed with him, just the same way. What a pushover. This was our first time alone, except for the short visit to his apartment the night of the fish fry. I didn't know if Whitey could hurt himself if we did the "wild thing." I just let it happen.

Making love with Gino was fireworks, all colors and passion.

Making love with Whitey was sweet and slow. I'll take the sweet and slow any time. We stayed in bed most of the afternoon.

"Lena, I love you. Don't say anything. I can't help the way I feel. Now that I know I'm going to live through this bullet hole in my chest, I can say things that I've been thinking about. When I suggested another bathroom at your house, I was being selfish. I wanted it for me. I hoped I would be living there some day."

"Whoa, cowboy! Slow down. Let's not move too fast on this subject."

"I can be slow. Do you want to do it again?"

"I didn't mean slow sex, Whitey. I meant slow on the relationship."

"Okay, Princess. I won't mention the future until tomorrow. But I have a question."

"Go ahead, cowboy."

"Do you think that I'm the kind of guy that could be married to a television star?"

"What the heck does that mean?"

"You're famous. I'm a construction guy. My hands are rough; I don't feel good in a suit. I didn't go to college; my friends are all construction guys and guys who work on cars."

"First of all, your hands are *just fine*. I didn't go to college either. My dad drives a garbage truck and my uncles own a garage and fix cars."

"That's all I wanted to know. Let's see what kind of food my ma left before the next round."

I stayed through Sunday and went to work directly from Whitey's house. He said he would be fine until I got back after work. I told him that I was going to stop by my ma's and check on the progress of my house. The floors and walls should be finished.

44

Okay, I'm probably in love . . . again. I didn't think this would happen so soon. I'm still not sure if I've gotten over Gino. It's been months. Was it just passion? I can't make any judgment right now. I'm still glowing.

Greg delivered flowers to my dressing room that afternoon with a note that made me blush. It was signed, "Cowboy." Thank goodness it was sealed. When Greg saw me blush, he started to laugh.

"Wow, Lena. I know what red roses mean. He must think you're quite a girl. Who is he?"

I made my eyes wide. "None of your business, mister."

"C'mon, Lena. I was a good boy and I didn't even peek at the card."

"Lucky that you didn't, Greg. I wouldn't have forgiven you."

I had to set some ground rules for Whitey. I wanted him to get well. We had to slow the physical stuff down a little bit—at least until he got his bandages off. I was going to sleep in the guest room that night. I called his ma and told her that I would stay with Whitey. She asked all the right questions about his bandages, and how he was eating and sleeping. She was glad to hear that he made it through the weekend without her.

When I got to my parents house, I got out of my car in the driveway. I almost cried with joy when I saw my house. I had picked out pale yellow siding. It was complete, as well as the light gray roof. The window frames were light gray too. I had picked all this stuff out, but I never imagined the finished project looking like this. When I went inside, a crew of four men were cleaning up drywall dust and sawdust. One of the guys, Joe said, "Hi, Miss Delatora. How does it look?"

"It looks just beautiful, Joe. I can't believe how quickly you finished the inside."

"Just a little bit of wiring needs to be completed. The underlayment for the floors is done in each room. The tile floors in the kitchen and bathrooms are done. You might want to get all the painting complete before you decide on your carpeting."

"Holy cow! What's on the walls now?"

"This is just white primer and sealer. You could live with this, but I'm sure you want to pick out your own colors. Most women do."

"I'll do that, Joe. Thanks!"

I went into Ma's kitchen through the back door and yelled, "Hello!"

"Hello, sweetheart! Isn't your house beautiful?"

"Oh, Ma! I can't believe how fast it was done. Now I have to call Jacki Corona and get some decorating ideas from her. I have to order carpeting and drapes. And furniture. I have to get furniture.

Someone knocked at the back door. Ma went to open it and said, "Bianco! How are you?"

He had the greatest smile on his face. I got up from my chair and kissed his cheek. I got warm all over just seeing him. My ma might have suspected that I spent the night with him last night, but she never said a word.

"I feel really good, Mrs. Delatora. Lena has been taking very good care of me."

Ma said, "Your color is great. Any pain?"

"No pain. I can't lift anything over twenty-five pounds for about a month."

It's a good thing that I was standing behind Ma. Whitey smiled at me and I gave him a big-eyed stare, as if to say, *"Yeah, if only everyone knew."* I was getting cups from the cabinet for coffee. Ma took some biscotti from the tin on the counter.

"Sit, sit, Bianco. Tell me how you feel. Are you very tired?"

"I've been getting so much rest! I'm getting stronger every day. The bullet was a small caliber and it didn't hit any vital organs or arteries. I was very lucky."

Ma made the sign of the cross and got up and put her hands on his cheeks. "God was with you, Bianco."

"No, Mrs. Delatora. It was Lena who saved my life. If she wasn't there, I probably would have died. I stopped at the restaurant on my way here. The owner told me that Lena's quick reaction got everyone's attention immediately. She kept yelling, *"Help him! Help him!"* That got the attention of a doctor who was having dinner a few tables away from us. He's the one who applied pressure until the ambulance got there. He knew the man behind us was already dead, so he focused on trying to control my bleeding."

I didn't realize that I was crying until Whitey got up from his chair and kneeled down to put his arms around me. I thought the guy in the restaurant who had helped Whitey was a waiter. I had no idea that he was a doctor. Everyone kept thinking that I did Whitey a favor. He nearly died because he took me out to dinner. I couldn't help thinking about that.

"It's okay, Lena. I'm okay. I think this brought us closer together."

Ma saw the tender moment and left the room. She was probably listening from the dining room. I know my ma.

Whitey continued, "I don't ever want you to think that you owe me anything. If our relationship doesn't work out, then it wasn't meant to be. I'll always remember this time we had together."

By this time, I was sobbing. Now my ma came into the room. "Lena, honey, why are you crying?"

Whitey said, "Lena has been strong through this whole nightmare. She has taken care of everyone: my parents and me. She has worked the TV show, planned all the stuff that goes along with it, the scripts and the people and whatever else she is responsible for. She has been holding it all in. Now it's time for her to cry it all out."

And I did. I blubbered for about ten minutes. My dad walked in the kitchen door. He took one look at me and said, "What the hell happened now?"

"Nothing, Sam. Lena has been holding in all her emotions. She is finally crying them out."

He looked at Whitey and said, "Good luck. These women are so darned emotional. How about a glass of wine? You can have a little wine, right."

"Sure, Mr. Delatora."

"Dad, I want to take Whitey through my house first. We won't be long."

I linked my arm through his and we walked out the back door. His crew was still working on the outside trim and the porches.

"I thought you would stay home and rest today. You should be exhausted."

"I am, but it's the good kind of tired."

When the guys saw him they started to applaud and chant, "Whitey! Whitey!" The team inside the house came out and joined them.

Whitey gave them the boxer's salute: two hands in the air over each shoulder.

My dad stuck his head out the back door and yelled, "I'm gonna go get that wine now."

My ma came out of the house behind him with a tray of glasses and bread and cheese.

She said, "I'm gonna cook. I have *cardone* and eggplant. I made some sauce. I'll boil some pasta."

I said, "Ma, there must be twenty guys here."

"We'll manage, Lena."

Of course we would. My ma was a food magician, just like my nana. Did they have anything to do with the loaves of bread and fishes in the Bible?

The crew set up sawhorses in the yard and put wood planks across them. My dad and Joe took the long table from the garage. Ma and Dad brought all the chairs into the yard. Zio Peppino came from the basement with two more bottles of wine.

I told Ma, "I'm going to get Nana. She will want to see Whitey."

"Oh, that's a good idea, Lena."

Well, Nana had a big roasting pan of chicken and potatoes in the oven when I got there. She had baked bread in the afternoon. We put it all in my trunk. That was added to the feast.

When Nana saw Whitey, she kissed him and hugged him—a little too hard, I might add.

When we got back to Ma and Dad's, someone had started the fire pit. Dad made this out of bricks to grill steaks outside. That took the chill out of the air, as the evening was turning cool.

Angelo and Vince went to Mr. Genardo's butcher shop and got a bunch of steaks. When he heard they were for Bianco Bertuci, the guy who got shot, he contributed a few extra steaks and some pork chops.

Mike LaSoto asked my dad if it would be okay to drive over and get Whitey's parents.

Dad said, "Sure, I'm glad you thought of that!"

Ma had to call Auntie Lilly and ask her to bring over more plates. Auntie Lilly and Gemma came over with the plates and some sausage and meatballs.

Uncle Paulie showed up with a case of beer. I still don't know how he found out that we were all together. He must have been in the back house at Nana's. It was twilight. Dad turned the yard lights on. This scene was "one for the books," as they say in the movies. I looked around the yard. Nothing could compare to this. I was sitting next to Whitey. His parents were chatting with my parents. Some of the construction guys were sitting around the fire pit. A few of the men went over to the grass and sat on tarps while they drank beer and ate. I watched Zio go into the kitchen to get Nana a chair. They sat talking with Auntie Lilly and Gemma. After a few moments, Nana walked over to Whitey's parents. We watched them introduce themselves as they stood up and kissed and hugged each other. Whitey saw this too. We smiled at each other. He reached over and took my hand. We sat like that for a long time. We were alone in the middle of the party, and that was just great.

I asked Whitey what made him show up at the construction site.

"I couldn't stay away from you, Lena."

45

aulie called me at my ma's house on Thursday. He invited me to come out to Helen's farm to spend the weekend.

"Lena, come on Friday night after work. I'll drop written directions off at your Ma's house."

I said, "Paulie, I won't spend the weekend, but maybe I'll stay overnight."

"Lena, you gotta at least stay overnight. It's too long a drive to do in one round trip."

I said I'd let him know after I saw the directions.

"Oh, by the way," he said. "Helen is having an informal party. Don't wear anything fancy. Slacks are fine."

The more I thought about this, the more uncomfortable I got about going out there alone. I was gonna ask him if I could bring Penny with me. Before I got to make that decision, Penny called me from Carlo's apartment. They had put a bid in on the house they were looking at. They wanted me to go with them to see it that evening. This would be a good chance to ask what they thought about going out to Helen's horse farm alone.

When I told them about it on the drive to the house Carlo said, "Not a good idea at all, Lena."

"Carlo, I drove to Lake Geneva. That was further than the farm."

"Yeah, but wait until you see the directions. It's all dark country roads. Ask Paulie if Penny and I can go with you. It's too deserted for two women to drive that distance alone. If you had car trouble or a flat tire it would be bad news."

We pulled into the driveway of a cute little ranch house with a white picket fence in front. Penny and Carlo had the biggest smiles on their faces. I knew I'd love the house before we got inside.

"Oh, Penny! This is adorable! It's perfect."

They gave me a little tour. It had three bedrooms and one and a half baths. It was all freshly painted in off white. The kitchen had white cabinets. They were metal, but Carlo said they would replace them with oak. The carpeting looked new. Carlo looked really proud.

"Lena, we can close on the deal within the next few weeks. I don't need financing. I'll pay cash for it. Penny can decorate it any way she wants."

Penny asked, "Do you really like it, Lena? It's a sweet little house, isn't it?"

"I love it, Penny! It looks like you two have already made up your minds. I hope you'll both be happy here."

Carlo came over to hug me. "We have you to thank, Lena. Without you, we never would have met."

I was really thrilled for them both. If I had any reservations about their relationship, I was keeping them to myself. They really seemed happy.

Penny asked if I'd like to help her decorate. I said, "Sure! Don't forget I'm going to be working on my place too. Maybe we can pick stuff out together. Then Jacki Corona can come when we're ready to put everything together."

I already had ideas in mind for my place. We would start shopping soon.

It occurred to me on the way home that I don't have any way to reach Paulie. He never left me a phone number for where is staying with "Helen from Hell." I would have to stop by Riggio's place to see if he had any way to contact this *lady,* and I use the word loosely.

When I got to Riggio's, he was in the restaurant. It was too early for The Club to be open. He saw me and waved for me to take a seat near the end of the bar. When he came over, he looked worried. I asked, "What's wrong, Mr. Riggio?"

"Lena, I don't want to start any trouble, but your Uncle Paulie don't sing for me no more. He was supposed to come on Friday and Saturday night. Now he doesn't come at all. He hangs around with the old cat, Helen."

"I gather that you don't like her, Mr. Riggio."

"What's to like? She snags up young men and uses them up. That's what she did to your friend Nick."

"What could she take from Nick? He had no usable talent and no money."

"Nick's talent was his carpentry and skills to fix stuff up. She made him think that she cared about him. She just used him to fix her fences and stuff around the farm. I think he put a bar in her basement and some other stuff. Now he lives in his mother's basement again. He's got nothing but bills from trying to impress her."

Now I was nearly physically ill thinking about Paulie and Helen. I asked Riggio if he had any idea how I could reach Helen. Did she ever leave her number?

"Sure, Lena, I got it. She hands it out to anyone who wants it." He took a cigar box from under the bar. "Here, she has a business card. She gives them away every time she comes in. I think Paulie is headed for trouble living at her farm. I hear she has wild parties and some crazy people hanging out there."

"Thanks, Mr. Riggio. I might go there this weekend."

"Don't you go by yourself, Lena. That's a bad place for a girl alone. I know your family a long time. I only want to help Paulie. I don't care if he don't want to sing here no more. I could find someone else. I just don't want him to get hurt."

I was really touched by his concern.

He came around the bar and kissed my cheek. "Say 'hello' to your ma and dad. Tell them to come in sometime."

I got into my car and sat there a few minutes. I was trying to collect my thoughts. I'd had a bad feeling about Helen the first time I laid eyes on her. I'd tell Carlo about this. I'd call Paulie first and tell him that Carlo and Penny wanted to join me that weekend.

When I called the number on the card, Paulie said, "Hullo."

I said, "Hullo, yourself, dumbass. You sound really stupid. Did I wake you up?"

"Uh, no, Lena. We were just sitting around having a few drinks."

"Paulie, it's two thirty. Why are you drinking in the afternoon?"

"Oh, it's no big deal, Lena. Say, I got a friend coming by with the directions. He'll leave them with your mom, okay?"

"Listen, Paulie, I'm thinking about Carlo and Penny coming out with me. Is that okay?"

He yelled across the room with his hand over the mouthpiece, "Hey Helen, is it okay if Lena brings a couple of friends?"

I heard her say, "Yeah, we got plenty of room."

Paulie said, "Sure they can come."

"All right," I said. "We'll probably leave around this time tomorrow."

"Great, Lena. I can't wait for you to see the recording studio."

"Me too, Paulie."

Somehow he sounded sad.

I went to see Whitey after work. I wanted to be sure that he had everything that he needed for the weekend. I explained that I was going to see Paulie with Carlo and Penny. We were staying overnight at "Helen From Hell's" horse farm.

He said, "Not without me, you're not!"

I told him, "Let's get something straight. I am in charge of my life—both my private life and my social life. You are in charge of making me happy. End of explanation, okay?"

"Cripes, Lena, you sure are tough when you want your way."

"Whitey, there is no 'my way.' It's simply what's right for the situation at the moment."

"I know it's a long drive, but I could ride with you guys. I would be just fine."

"Whitey, you shouldn't have even driven to my ma's the other night. I'll be back the following afternoon."

"Promise that you'll call me when you get there."

"Yes, I'll do that with no problem. I want to let your parents know that I won't be around this weekend so they can check on you."

"Holy cow! Won't that be great! I get to spend the weekend

with my mom. She'll be fluffing my pillows and making soup with all sorts of unidentifiable stuff in it."

"You know you'll love it. And it's good for her too."

I went into the living room to use the phone. I dialed Mrs. Bertuci and she answered, *"Buonasera."*

"Buonasera, Dona Bertuci." I spoke in Italian: "I want you to know that I'll be away for the weekend. I'll be back on Sunday afternoon. I thought you would want to know."

"Oh, Miss Lena, thank you for tell-a me. I'm gonna come-a tomorrow night to stay with him. Then I cook on Saturday so he has enough to eat."

"Oh, I'm glad, Dona Bertuci. I'm going to see my Uncle Paulie at the place where he is making a record."

"Oh, nice-a Lena. Your Nana told us he sing joosta like Tony Bennett."

"Yes, he has a very good voice."

When we hung up, Whitey was making a snotty face, making fun of me.

"My mom has enough food in that freezer to last until the next ice age. She's gonna cook more? Holy crap. We better eat some stuff tonight. Her feelings are going to be hurt if she sees all that food. Maybe you could take some food to your Uncle Paulie. It should stay frozen on the drive, right?"

We had lasagna, cannalone, and veal scalopini. There was enough lettuce for us to have a salad and we had some wine. There wasn't as much in the containers as we thought. Some of the containers were only half full or they had some other food combined in them. I rearranged the freezer and cleaned it up a little, so Dona Bertuci could load it up again.

46

We got the directions to Helen's farm that Paulie's friend left with Mom. I was glad that it was still light outside when we left. Mom made sandwiches for us to take on the drive. We drove to North Avenue to Route 59. Route 59 took us all the way into Algonquin and Algonquin to some other dark road. I was glad that Mom made sandwiches. Carlo had six Cokes in a little cooler in the back. This took us nearly two and a half hours—that's counting the twenty minutes that we drove past our last landmark turn into the farm.

We saw a big house that was all lit up from top to bottom. We guessed that was the place. It had a white picket fence as far as the eye could see. A huge sign was on two big fence posts out in front. It read, Sunrise Acres Estates. Under that it read, **"BOARDING, RENTAL, SALES, AND BREEDING."** I didn't want to be impressed, but I couldn't help it. After we pulled into the driveway, we could hear loud music and people laughing and talking. Carlo banged the brass doorknocker three times.

"Get a load of this doorknocker, ladies," Carlo said. It was shaped like a galloping horse. The head was turned toward the guest. You held on to the head to bang on the door.

The girl who answered the door was dressed like the flower child that was so popular at the time. She had long, blond, straight hair. She was barefoot and wore a goofy headband. She was holding a cigarette and a drink in one hand and a bag of chips in her other hand. I'm sure it wasn't an easy task to open the door.

I said, "Hi. I'm Lena. We were invited here by Paulie." She looked kind of blank. I finally said, "Paulie DeLuca."

"Oh, you mean Paulie Dee! Sure, come on in. He's waiting for you downstairs in the recording studio."

I glanced at Carlo and he rolled his eyes. Penny just looked wide-eyed and terrified at the chaos in the room. We saw all manner of party people: short dresses, long dresses, loose tied, tie dyed, and untied. Helen must have had this party catered, because there were beef sandwiches on the long table in the center of the room, cheese and crackers of all shapes and size, bottles of booze, soda, salads, and many things I couldn't identify.

Our door-opener girl introduced herself as Sadie. She led us down a long hall to an open outside deck. There was a stairway in the center of the platform. We followed her down the steps.

Carlo whispered, "Lena, Paulie must have changed his name."

"I'm thinking that I should kick the snot out of him at some point while we're here."

The studio was really huge. I saw two glass walls and a control room with all sorts of panels, switches, and levers. Helen was in the control room wearing headphones.

Uncle Paulie

There was a guy wearing headphones, too. He was fooling around with controls. Behind the second glass wall, I saw Paulie with a bunch of musicians. There were two guitar players, a drummer who was doing what drummers do with those cymbals and sticks, and there was a trumpet player. Behind the trumpet player I noticed a guy playing tall bongos. Paulie was singing his heart out. He was doing his best stage antics, adding a couple of little shuffle dance steps and a spin during the drum portion. We sat in leather chairs that were at the side of the control room. I saw Helen take off her headphones and nod to the engineer.

She came out and shook hands with us. She kissed my cheek and said, "Lena, I'm so glad you came out. I know this is far from the city. Can you spend the weekend?"

She was very gracious, even though she still looked like a blond burnout. After I introduced her to Penny and Carlo, she extended the invitation to them also. "Oh, please stay! You've driven so far. We always have plenty of room for guests. Maybe you would like to ride tomorrow?"

We were all expecting to stay overnight. I assumed she meant ride a *horse.*

We all smiled and answered, in some fashion: "Maybe; I don't think so; Perhaps."

"Well, you don't have to decide now. I'll show you around the ranch tomorrow. Paulie is doing great. I think this might be his final take on the 'Fantastic' song. We'll play it back when he's done with this session. He can't see you watching on either side of the booth. It's one-way glass. The front is clear glass. That's my husband at the controls. His name is Leonard. Producing music is one of his hobbies. The big hobby of course, is horses."

Carlo asked how many horses they had. Helen answered, "We have about sixty right now. It varies as the seasons change. We board some horses. We own around thirty of them. The rest are being boarded or are here for stud services.

Paulie and the band were giving each other high fives all around. I knew they must be finished for the night.

When Paulie saw us he looked really pleased. He came out and hugged and kissed me, and Penny too. He was grinning from ear to ear. Helen looked very proud too.

"Would you like to hear the finished recording?" She tapped the glass and did a rolling hand motion to her husband.

"Fantastic, the world that we live in. Fantastic, the things that we do . . ."

Well! It sounded great. I really felt like this could be Paulie's big break. The song sounded good a Riggios, but this was amazing. Helen and Leonard looked like proud parents. I watched her face while the song was playing. Maybe I misjudged her. My mom always said to go with your first impression, but she also said, "Don't judge a book by its cover." Helen's cover was sleezy, but maybe she was nice after all.

Helen's husband came out of the sound booth and was

introduced all around. He said very nice things about Paulie.

They suggested that we join the guests upstairs. Helen said, "Paulie, take your guests upstairs and show them where the food is. They must be starving." Once we were mixed in with the party people, Helen and Leonard wandered off.

The three of us walked in a cluster like cartoon characters. We saw Paulie go ahead of us and he was talking with some people he obviously knew.

We saw buffet tables down the center of the entire room. Everything was on warming trays. I grabbed a beef sandwich and some chicken livers wrapped in bacon. There was a server carving ham off the bone. We couldn't imagine anyone living in a home this size. Carlo has seen some pretty ritzy places, but not this size. This was an enormous ranch house with an upstairs and many additions.

I saw timbers on the vaulted ceilings that must have been around twenty feet high. The far end of the room had skylights. You could look up and see all the stars.

"Okay," I said. "I'm impressed and I've only seen two rooms on this level."

Paulie came over to tell us that our rooms were ready. "I want to take you upstairs and show you the décor. The whole place is 'Western.' I had your stuff brought up there. You can go to bed any time you want.

Did he just use the word *décor*?

The upstairs was a wide hall with Western blankets on the walls and wagon wheels. There were light fixtures made from wagon wheels too. All the rooms had names. My room was "The Palomino." Penny and Carlo's room was called the "Chickasaw," and another room was called the "Mustang." Paulie told us that all the rooms were named after horse breeds. He stretched out on the bed while I unpacked my suitcase. I was talking up a storm when I looked over at him and he was fast asleep. I think he'd had a really long day.

All the furniture in our rooms was made from wooden cowboy stuff. They used a lot of barn wood and parts of trees. Even the bathroom vanity looked like a barrel cut flat in the back, with a sink in it. Who thought up all this stuff? Old lanterns hung from the ceiling, but they were electrified. Everywhere I turned I saw something different and hinkey. They even had old barn signs hanging on one wall. At first I thought it was strange, but when I realized the full scope of a horse farm I could understand how it could encompass their entire world.

Penny knocked on my door and said, "Are we going back downstairs? I could use some food."

I poked Paulie in the foot and said, "Hey, buckaroo! You gonna come downstairs with us?"

"Huh? Yeah, I'm gonna introduce you to all the Hot Shots."

"That will be just swell, pardner."

He rolled his eyes and punched my arm. "Let's go, bambina."

Paulie introduced us around to a few people. When people saw him they came over to introduce themselves to us. Some looked like straight business people in suits. Others had starched cowboy shirts and jeans. A few looked like "Helen from Hell," in that they were a little overdone on makeup and had big hair. Then there were the young kids that didn't look like they should be away from home without an adult.

I asked Carlo, "Do you smell skunk?"

"I think that smells like burning rubber from outside," Penny said.

"Do you smell it, Carlo?"

"Uh ladies, that's grass, as in marijuana."

"No, I know what grass smells like. It smells like watermelon."

He motioned for us to come closer.

"For city girls, you sure must have lived in a bubble. You smell marijuana. Everyone here must be smoking it."

Penny's eyes got big. I said in a very knowing voice, "I knew that. I used to smell it on the bus on my way to school all the time."

We all laughed. Carlo told us, "We will all probably get a contact high just from smelling it."

I realized that's why everything seemed so funny. Just a moment go I was cracking up looking at a guy with tie-dyed pants and no shirt or shoes.

Carlo was having a discussion with someone who told him that this ranch had been used to film several western movies. I could believe that because they wouldn't have to do any decorating to get it ready.

The crowd seemed to be moving in one big mass toward the buffet tables. I tried to find Paulie, but I decided I would have more food first. I found the biggest plate and began to stack food in a circle around the edges. I put colored fruit in the center and some white stuff on top of the fruit. A guy in a suit asked me what I was doing. I told him, "I'm gonna eat some of this cute food."

"Okay. Me too," he said. "Aren't you that chick from TV?"

I avoided that question and suggested that he get me a drink.

"Okay, I'll get you a rum and Coke."

He was pretty nice. Before you know it, we were discussing my new house and eating off of each other's plate. He was using his own fork.

"Have you tried any of those little wienies wrapped in bacon?" he asked.

"Here, try these cheese balls," I said.

I got the strange sensation that I was watching myself in slow motion and had no control over any of it.

His name was Eddie. When he went to get more cheese balls, I worked my way through the crowd and walked upstairs to my room. I decided that I was high as a kid on Christmas morning from smelling all that Mary Jane and drinking all night. From the balcony stairway I could look downstairs at this wacky party. I thought, *This looks like some kind of B-grade movie, or a bad dream.*

I put my plate of food on the dresser and got into my pajamas. It was my plan to pig-out and go to sleep, when there was a knock at the door.

"Hey, Lena! It's Eddie. I've been looking for you, Pretty Filly."

"Oh, brother, you should go to sleep. That's what I'm gonna do."

"Come on, open up. I brought those cheesy things that you

liked, and they just put out some fresh fried octopus."

"Oh, calamari. I can't say no to that."

Eddie and I sat on my bed and ate everything on both plates while we chatted up a storm. We fell asleep across the bed with the plates between us.

Someone was knocking on the door. When I opened my eyes, I thought my head was on fire on the inside. I opened the door to Penny. She looked over at the bed and I said, "Don't say a word."

"It's noon. I was getting worried about you. She looked over at Eddie. He was snoring with his head hanging backward off the bed. "Is that guy alive?"

"I think so. Go shake him and see if he moves."

She poked his arm and he moaned.

"That's just fine. I don't need to see him this morning."

I grabbed my clothes and ducked into the hall.

"Penny, I'm going to shower in your room, okay?"

"Sure, Lena. Meet us downstairs in the dining hall."

We were sitting down to our food, which was probably considered brunch. Eddie walked over and looked at me with big doggy eyes. "I'm really sorry about last night, Lena."

"It's okay. Nothing happened. You look like hell. Did you even look in the mirror?"

"No, I thought I'd better find you first."

"No harm, no foul, Eddie. You're free and clear." I was trying to get rid of him, but he wasn't taking the hint. My food didn't look too appealing to me, so I grabbed Penny by the arm and snuck off while Eddie went to the buffet. Carlo followed us.

We snuck around the side of the house and made our way to the barn where everyone seemed to be gathered. I happened to look at Carlo and his eyes were a little downcast when he returned my look.

"Oh, stop looking at me like that! Northing happened!"

Penny smiled and said, "Lena, you are wearing your pajamas."

"Oh, they look just like my black pants."

I finally made them laugh about Eddie's enthusiasm last night.

They thought he was pretty funny when I told them about him piling food on plates and getting me to open the door.

A man came over and asked us if we were going to ride. We all said, "Yes." He found some button-down shirts for us. We didn't have any boots, but there was a bin with high top sneakers and some old worn boots.

We rode with a guide. We saw a lot of people from the party last night on horseback. They didn't look much better than I did. Most of them looked like they were going to throw up. I didn't feel very well myself. I think our guide could see that we were not seasoned riders. He didn't keep us out long.

When we got back to the barn, we were told that a lunch buffet was ready for us in the main dining hall. We saw Paulie and Helen riding toward the barn as we were going inside. What's up with those two? They seem to be together all the time. Where was her husband?

The food in the main dining room was amazing. It equaled the last night's party with no problem. I thought my family cooked big. Who was gonna eat all this stuff?

Paulie came in with Helen just as we all sat down. They saw us and came over and sat across from us. They were very pleasant and friendly.

"Lena, I hope you had a nice ride. I could have sent some clothes up for all of you to wear for the ride. Were you comfortable? Did you find what you needed in the stable?

"Oh, we made out just fine. We had a nice ride earlier today. Thanks."

"Oh, Lena, Eddie asked me to give this to you."

She handed me a business card that said,

**EDWARD HOFFMAN,
VICE PRESIDENT—MARKETING
HANOVER RECORDING STUDIOS**

"Oh, thanks, Helen."

"He wrote a note on the back for you, Lena. He also told me that he was sorry if he put you in an awkward situation."

"He fell asleep on my bed. He was a little tipsy and ate himself into a stupor."

Helen left the table and went to speak to the servers.

I punched Paulie in the arm. He flinched and said, "Whaaat?"

"What the hell are you doing with Helen all the time? Do you spend every moment together?"

"Lena, I live here. Yes, I go with her whenever she wants my company."

"Well, that sounds like a real freaky situation to me."

Just then Helen came over and handed Carlo a big box.

"This is food and sodas for your ride home. I'm so glad you all came this weekend. I'm sure we'll get together soon."

Thank goodness this was over.

Carlo went upstairs and got our overnight bags. We all hugged each other good-bye. Helen's husband made an amazing appearance to say good-bye to us.

On the drive home, Penny and I discussed the assorted nuts that were at the party. None of us could figure out what the heck was going on with Paulie and Helen. I don't think I want to say out loud the words that I was thinking.

We got home around 9 p.m. I went directly to bed and had dreadful nightmares. I dreamed that Eddie was sleeping in my bed. When I woke up, I was very relieved to see it was Jojo. What the heck was he doing here? I was sleeping at Nana's house.

In the morning, I went into the kitchen. No sign of Jojo or Zio—but I'm betting the rent that they were both here.

Monday at work was hell. I was blowing too many lines. I can improvise pretty well. The problem is that Beth starts to improvise too, even if she remembers her lines. That makes it difficult for me to fake the continuity. I had a pounding headache by the time the show was over.

Mr. Latmen said it seemed just fine. Next Monday Susan was coming in to talk to him about a return for her character. He and

I would meet after the day's show to discuss working her into the script. If that works out, Beth's next appearance will announce her vacation to a spa. In reality, her parents will be sending her to a real spa for people who are emotionally distressed. It's called Spring Meadow Estates. I spoke to her parents regarding Beth's leave. They explained that they have done this for her in the past. She gets emotionally unwound when she is under too much pressure. They medicate her on a daily basis. She will stay several weeks and come out a new person

Red, that's Milton, seemed very concerned about Beth. They had been dating and she had been able to keep her private life private for a change. I hoped it worked out for her. She was really nuts.

Penny and I are going to look at wedding dresses and bride's maid's dresses that evening. I called ahead for an appointment. They were so excited when I said my name that I told them, "This is the bride's special time. Her name is Penny. Be sure you treat her royally. Remember, I am only a brides maid."

When we got there, the attendants had several dresses hung out and ready for Penny to try on. Three of the dresses made her look like a kid playing dress-up. Penny is really small. She doesn't need this much fluff and ruffles. I explained that we were just beginning to look at dresses and we would come back another time. We were going to look at bridesmaid's dresses too.

On the way home, Penny was very quiet.

"What's wrong with the little bride tonight?"

"Lena, do you think that Carlo would be offended if I asked for a small wedding?"

"I don't know what the two of you discussed. Did he ever say how many people his family expected?"

"No, not exactly. About two hundred, I think."

"That sounds typical for someone in Carlo's position. His family has a lot of connections."

"Lena, I don't think I can do it. It's overwhelming me already. I hear him talking to his dad on the phone. They're inviting people from out of state. Even a few from Italy."

"Penny, talk to him about it. Maybe if he knows how you feel, he could talk his dad down to a smaller amount.

"I'm going to do that tonight. I'll make a nice dinner and open a bottle of wine. Then I'll tell him how nervous I am."

47

Whitey left a message with my Mom. He never knew where I was going to be. My ma said he told her to say, "Where are you? Am I ever going to see you again?"

"Ma! It's only been four days!"

"Lena, that's a long time when you're in love."

"I'll call him tonight."

The phone only rang once. He answered with such an urgent tone in his voice. "Hi Whitey."

"Lena, I really miss you!"

"Whitey, are you all right? I miss you too. Is something wrong?"

"I haven't seen you for days. Can you come over tonight?"

"Oh, Whitey, I'm so tired. I had a meeting after work." I explained about the crazy weekend and looking for dresses with Penny. "I really need to sleep tonight. I promise I'll come tomorrow."

"Okay, I understand. Promise me you'll come tomorrow?"

I could hear the anxiety in his voice and I got really worried. "Okay, Whitey. Now that I've heard your voice, I really need to see you too."

I told Nana where I was going. She said, "Okay. Lena, you watch-a you driving, okay."

When I got to Whitey's apartment I let myself in. He was sitting in his recliner. When he turned his head to smile at me, I was shocked at his appearance. He was sweating and his skin looked gray. He tried to smile at me, but it was more like a grimace. I knew immediately that something was very wrong.

"Whitey, you're sick. What is it?"

He began jabbering, but not making sense. I called an ambulance immediately. I opened the front door and sat with Whitey while I waited. He buried his face in my hair and said, "Lena, do you have any idea how much I love you?"

By the time the ambulance got there, I think he was unconscious. When we got to the hospital, I called his parents and my parents.

We were all there when the doctor came out of surgery.

"What's wrong with him?" I asked. I'm sure we all looked terrified.

"Bianco is bleeding internally. We had to make a small opening to stitch an artery behind the breastbone. We drained blood from the chest cavity and he seems to be stable. We used the same incision, so there will be no new scar. I expect he will recover completely in about four weeks."

I blamed myself for Whitey's condition. If we hadn't been so eager to please each other, he may not have opened this internal artery.

His parents were thanking me again. These poor people, who nearly lost their son again, kept thanking me for helping him. I would take care of him. I would not let him persuade me into any more extra curricular activity.

My parents took the Bertuci's home. I would stay with him that night. Geez, this guy's got nine lives—. Lucky for me.

I was asleep in the chair when I heard a voice. Whitey was speaking to me.

"Lena, I'm hoping your Nana is making eggplant Parmesan. That's what I was dreaming about."

I sat up straight and said, "Holy cow, Whitey! You sure know how to scare a girl to death!"

I sat on the edge of his bed and said, "You have become part of my heart. When I am away from you, I feel lost."

"Lena, promise me that you are not attached to me because we were together the night I was shot."

"Whitey, don't ever think that, please. But one thing I have to make very clear."

"What's that?"

"No wild and crazy stuff until the doctor says it's okay. I mean that. I won't take any more chances with your life."

"Are you always gonna be this bossy?"

"Yes. Sleep now *mio amore*."

The following morning, my mom came to the hospital to see how Whitey was doing and to spend some time with me.

I started to cry when I saw her. "Lena, honey, it's going to be okay. You are under so much stress. It's not as bad as it seems."

"Oh, Mom, I feel like I'm falling apart. I don't know where my head is. I feel like my heart is breaking. I feel so bad for Whitey. He can't go through much more."

"Lena, Whitey is going to be just fine. He's young and strong. Do you think that you need some time off work? You have been staying with Whitey, trying to keep Nana company, and worrying about your new house. Maybe you should stay at home with me and let me take the pressure off you for a while."

"I guess I could talk to Frank, about taking a few days off. I have the show to do this afternoon. I'll talk to him later."

"Lena, remember what Dad always says:. '"Work to live. Don't live to work. Do what you love, but be sure to stop and live your life.' "

48

The telephone installers are coming to my new house. I placed the order today.

Mom said she'd wait there all day until they were finished. I want one in the master bedroom, living room, and the kitchen. Mom suggested one in the laundry room. I don't think I need one there. It's right off the kitchen.

Mom called when they were finished installing.

"Hi honey! I'm so glad you have phones. Now I can call you before I come over. I don't like coming over unannounced. You stop here after work, Lena."

When I got there, Ma was standing at the sink. I went up behind her and hugged her.

"I love you, Mama. You and Daddy always made my life simple. I love you both for that."

Mom turned and wrapped her arms around me and held me close. I always feel like a little girl when she does that. It always makes everything better. The show went very well the next day. The ad libs were cohesive and well placed. Frank was smiling when I walked off the set.

"Good show, Lena. I think you perform well under pressure."

"Funny you should say that, Frank. I need to talk to you about something."

I spoke to him honestly about the way I was feeling and that I was under too much pressure. I said all of the things that I told my mom. I didn't even cry. Wow! That's pretty good, considering I was an emotional disaster.

He actually put his arm around my shoulder and led me over to a chair. "Lena, you have been the best thing that has ever happened to this show. You are an important part of the staff too. You are taking on too much. You're working on scripts, taking care of Whitey, worrying about your grandma and your house. I'm going to make a suggestion. I want you to know I'm talking to you like an uncle.

I said, "Okay, I'm open to listening to anything you suggest."

"I think you should take two solid weeks off. We'll script out something like a trip to New York to visit your mom's only sister. We can even do a shot of you on film, visiting an old sick lady."

"Wait, I'll grab a note pad! We can get Susan back for the new material. Mona and Johnny are scripted already. Do you think that Beth and Red can carry on for two weeks?"

Frank laughed, "Why not. They have been carrying on behind everyone's back for the last two months. Just because I choose not to acknowledge stuff doesn't mean that I don't see it. Liaisons off the set always help the chemistry on the set."

"Well, I must really be wearing blinders. So you think she'll hold it together until I get back?"

"Sure, I'll talk to Red. She seems pretty infatuated with him. I know Beth. When she knows someone is counting on her, it makes her feel like she's in control."

"Okay, I'll work on an outline the next several nights. After Friday, I'll be out for two weeks. Frank, I can't thank you enough."

"Forget it. You know how much we need you. I want you to get it together for all of us."

I went to the hospital after work. Whitey was sitting up in bed: no tubes, no oxygen, only an IV line.

He smile, but looked really sad.

"Hello, handsome!" I said. "You need to stop trying so hard to get my attention, because I'm all yours."

I think he got tears in his eyes. "Lena, how long will you wait for me to get well? Eventually, you'll get tired of babysitting."

"Whitey, I'm not going to leave your side for the next two weeks. I'm going to make sure that you are healthy and strong. I'll know what you're doing all day, and I'll be sure that you're eating and resting."

Now the smile on his face was the one that I loved.

"How are you getting two weeks off?"

"I know the boss, so don't worry about it."

49

I met with the doctor before I left the hospital. He gave me a written list of "do's and don'ts" with all the instructions on cleaning and dressing the wound itself. The doctor said that since I would be staying with Whitey, he would allow him to go home on Saturday.

I went to see Mrs. Bertuci on my way home. I told her that I would be taking care of Whitey for several days. I didn't tell her two weeks, because she would feel left out. I showed her all of the surgical supplies that the doctor had given me. I had a box of bandages and some iodine and ointments.

"Oh, Lena, I'm-a so glad that you gonna stay with my Bianco."

She took me by the shoulders and looked into my eyes, "I trust you with his heart and his health, beautiful girl."

I realized how tired she looked. Her only son had been shot. Her daughter lived far away. She was old for her age. I don't mean that in an unkind way, but some people are sixty-five and old and some are sixty-five and young. My nana was young for her age.

I promised to call her every day to see if she wanted me to pick her up to see Whitey.

I called Mom to tell her that I got two weeks off. She was so glad that it was that easy.

"I'm going to send Bobby over by Nana to stay. I'll have him stay several times each week. It will work out just fine.

When I got to Nana's that night, Bobby had my clothes laid out on the bed. He had already hung his clothes in the closet. He was sitting in Nana's kitchen eating a huge bowl of bowtie pasta with sausage. Nana looked pleased to have him at her table.

"Gee, kid, you're like a hobo. You'll sleep anywhere."

He looked at me and said, "Look who's talking. I never know where you are."

I showed him the back of my hand and said, "Watch it, kid!" He laughed.

"Did Nana tell you that Gemma is having another baby?"

"For crying out loud! Those two are like rabbits. Do you think they know what causes that yet?"

Nana and Bobby both laughed. I taped a list of phone numbers by the phone so everyone would know where to find me. I included the Bertucis' phone number too.

When I told Ma about my plans she said, "Maybe we'll see more of you too!

I hadn't realized how little time I was spending with my ma and dad. It would be nice when my house was ready. I could see them more often.

Greg called me to see if I wanted him to bring me some dinner to the hospital. I thought that was such a nice gesture. I said, "Sure, Greg. Paulie is at 'Helen from Hell's' house. I can't count on Mona anymore."

Greg brought sandwiches and sodas. We went into the cafeteria.

Greg was very concerned. He held my hand and kissed my cheek.

"Please, Lena, anything you need, I'm there for you. Whatever I can do. I mean that."

"Thanks, Greg. I really appreciate that."

We went back into Whitey's room and he was awake. They made small talk for a few minutes. Greg wished him a speedy recovery, shook his hand, and left.

Whitey was very quiet. I said, "What's wrong?"

"Lena, I don't trust this guy. I saw the way he looked at you. I know that look. He still cares about you."

"Oh, Whitey. You don't need to worry about him. We're just friends."

"Just watch him anyway."

50

I am bringing Whitey home today. I knew I could do it without anyone helping me, but I didn't realize how shaky he would be. He never has complained about pain. Not even the night of the shooting. I sat him in the big recliner by the window. I pushed up the footrest and he fell asleep immediately.

I watched his handsome face while he slept. I could see what a toll this had taken on him. The dark circles and the sunken cheeks said it all. He was probably worried about his business, among other things. He had good workers that would keep the ball rolling until he could get back to work. I'd have to ask my dad to check on his business, just to be sure everything is okay.

I made myself busy in the kitchen and changed the bed sheets so everything would be fresh. I picked up newspapers and magazines. I sat down on the sofa and watched Whitey's breathing for a little while. When I started to yawn, I got up and covered Whitey with a light blanket. I knew he would be okay in the chair. I went to sleep on the sofa, so I could hear him if he needed anything.

Carlo and Penny came by around three o'clock with some sausage sandwiches and a big container of minestrone soup. Whitey ate a big piece of the sandwich and a bowl of soup. We talked for a while about the wedding.

Carlo said he talked to his dad about a smaller wedding. Penny was freaking out about the 250 to 300 people they were originally discussing. Niko said that he could cut the list to 150. Penny was hoping for closer to 100, but 150 was a good compromise. It scared her that it would be all Carlo's Italian family with the exception of her ten or twelve family members, who were all mixed nationalities.

Since I wouldn't let Whitey get up from the recliner, we all sat around in the living room like he was the prince. I brought out some cheese and crackers and a bottle of wine. I gave Carlo the "eyebrows." As soon as they saw Whitey yawn, they said their good-byes.

Once Whitey was asleep in his own bed, I took a shower and crawled in next to him. How else would I know if he needed me?

My mom called at Whitey's the next morning. She said, "Eddie Hoffman called you. He's from some recording studio."

"Oh, crap. Did I give him my phone number? That guy's a pain in the butt. If he calls again, tell him I'm not interested."

"What if it's about Paulie's singing?"

"Paulie knows how to take care of his own business. Don't give Eddie this phone number."

51

By the third night of sleeping with Whitey, he got happy hands. I thought it would be best for both of us if I slept in the guest room. He was well enough to call me if he needed something. He didn't like that one bit.

"That seems unnatural. I can't let you do that. I promise I'll be a really, really good boy."

"Unnatural! We're not married, you know? Listen cowboy, I know you well. I've gone to work exhausted too many times. If you could control your urges, you might not have wound up in the hospital again."

He was faking a dejected, hurt expression. "Do I at least get a goodnight kiss?"

"Sure, how can I say no to that?"

He had me flipped on my back into that bed so quick that I didn't know what hit me. I'm pretty quick too. I jumped out of that bed like a five year old on Christmas morning.

"Good night, Whitey. And don't try to follow me!"

Thank goodness he listened that time because I didn't know how long I could resist him.

On Thursday, my mom and nana came over. They brought homemade pizza bread and soup. I was finally working my way through most of the homemade food in the freezer from Whitey's mom.

We all sat around the kitchen table like family, except that Whitey was in his robe and pajamas. Whitey's parents were at the door. My mom said, "Oh, I forgot to tell you they were coming."

We ate more food and laughed a lot. Whitey speaks Italian

better than I do. He is second generation. His parents spoke Italian at home. I am third generation. My parents always spoke English.

Mama Bertuci was trying to tell me something in broken English. I thought it was about Penny's wedding. I finally told Whitey to ask her what she was saying.

"She wants to know if you will marry me."

We all started laughing. "I'm not ready to marry anyone. I think you have to ask me yourself, and you would be first in line when I decide."

There were days that I felt like I was on autopilot. I lived my life in a few square miles. When I fell for Whitey, he was in my mom's backyard building a house for me. Gino fell into my life through my dad's acquaintance with Niko Bazzoli.

I knew I was falling in love with Whitey. Did I let myself fall, or did I fight what my heart told me?

52

Penny wanted to take her mom for a "mother's dress" for the wedding. She knew that her mom, Glenny, would pick a dress that made her look like floozy. She would pick something backless and wear sling-back shoes. Glenny's current husband, Dino, would wear a tux, so that would be safe.

I told Penny that I'd go with her after work. We'd pick Glenny up and take her out to dinner, then to the dress shop.

When we got there, she was wearing what passed as a dress in her world. It was silver and gold stretch fabric, and she had added a wide silver belt, silver backless shoes, and a silver evening bag. The darned dress was so short that I was afraid to see how high up it would rise when she sat down. We got lucky because the sun was going down and the restaurant turned down the lights and lit candles. That was a plus for us.

Poor Penny. Her mom talks so loud. Her laugh could shatter glass. We began to relax after we ordered our dinner. We had a very nice dinner. I was very glad for Penny because she was very apprehensive about taking her mom out in public.

When we left the restaurant, I walked in front of Glenny because I was paying the bill. Penny walked behind her mom out of courtesy. It worked out well so no one really noticed her dress.

We were the last appointment at the bridal shop. I wanted to be sure that Penny was the "Star of The Show." Too many people were beginning to recognize me. I didn't want the attention taken away from her. This shop was doing the dresses for the entire wedding. The colors for the wedding were silver and blue. The dresses were blue with silver threads running through it. My dress was a little darker and slightly different because I was the maid of honor.

Every dress that Glenny liked was the wrong color or style. If one could be made in another color, she didn't like the colors available.

Penny said, "Mom, any color you want is fine except for red, white, or black." She would be the only mother in the wedding party. Carlo's mom died when he was little. All of the grandmas would wear black or black.

We found yet another really nice dress. Penny pulled it off the rack and it seemed to please her. It was rust colored, but they could make it in purple, Glenny's color of choice. It wasn't too low in the front or back. The fabric had a little sparkle to it and it was just below the knees. Penny suggested dyed-to-match shoes and a bag. Glenny was holding out for gold. Penny agreed to gold, if they weren't backless. Deal!

I went to see my mom. She was in the living room watching TV with Dad. I leaned over to kiss her. Dad was snoring with his mouth open, so I skipped that kiss.

Mom took out cups for coffee. I decided on a Coke instead.

"Ma, how did you know when you'd love someone for the rest of your life?"

"Lena, your father was only the second man that I dated. He told me he loved me after our third date, and said we should get married. After one month we told our parents and they thought it was a fine idea. It didn't seem like a difficult decision."

"Did Nana give you any advice?"

"Yes, she said, 'Watch the way he treats his mama, and the way his dad treats his mama. That's the way he will treat you.' That's important, Lena. You watch that carefully. Does he raise his voice to his mama, or any other females in the family? Is he respectful to them?"

"Wow, Mom! You've been paying attention to life in general. I know Whitey loves me. I think he might be a little clingy right now because he's not feeling well. I think I'm falling for him. It worries me that he might keep me from doing some of the things that I like to do, like he'll want me home all the time. I want to be independent."

"Lena, he's been so sick. He's not himself. Give him time to get back to his normal activity. You can't judge right now. He's not mobile and he gets lonely."

"You're right, Ma, as usual."

"You give me too much credit, honey. Life is always a test. Everything is always changing."

My ma, she's amazing. She knows so much about life. She's such a good teacher, because she never gives advice unless I ask for it.

53

Paulie called me at work. "You gonna come by Nana tonight?"

"Well, it would be nice if you said, 'Hello, Lena. How are you? Why aren't you at Helen's farm?' "

"I need you, Lena, please come."

I could hear the desperation in his voice. I was instantly worried. I felt my heart lurch into my throat.

Paulie's car was in the back of Nana's house in the alley. When I got inside, she was treating him like royalty. She had all different kinds of food lined up in front of him. But he wasn't eating.

"Hi Lena, I'm glad you're here! I want to talk to you!"

I looked at his face and knew something was very wrong. His skin looked yellow.

"What brings you to the old neighborhood, Paulie?"

"Lena, let's go to the back house. I want to see how much work needs to be done."

I started to feel sick. I knew it was serious. My mind was swimming. Paulie seemed agitated. He was walking back and forth holding his arms crossed.

"Lena, I'm in trouble."

"What? What kind of trouble? Money, an accident, murder?"

"It's bad. It's drugs, Lena. Heroin."

"Oh, no! Paulie."

Somehow I wasn't surprised. I could see all sorts of odd behavior at Helen's place. Those musicians were all cranked up on something. I was hoping it was marijuana. No matter what I suspected, this was really bad.

"I need you to help me, Lena."

"What do I do?"

"First of all, don't start crying. I know what to do, but I can't do it alone. This is a good place for me to go through withdrawal."

He looked around the little house and he kept talking. "I need someone with muscle—maybe a couple of guys with good body strength. I was thinking of Carlo and maybe your dad could come with him tonight."

"Paulie, does it have to be tonight?" I had tears running down my face while I followed him around the house.

"Lena, it has to be within the next six to ten hours. It's gonna get messy and ugly."

I grabbed his arm and pushed up his sleeve. I saw the tracks. I covered my face and sat on the floor. "How could this happen, Paulie?"

"Lena, It's the music industry. I thought I could do a little and be tough enough to pull out whenever I wanted. It doesn't work that way. When you're in, you're hooked for life."

"No, Paulie. Not for life. We'll help. We'll do whatever it takes. Does Helen know?"

He laughed a bitter horselaugh. "Well, some friend she turned out to be. They played my record a few times. When Helen found out I was leaving to get my life back, she pulled it from the stations. She said if I don't come back, I'm finished. A few stations wanted to keep it, even though she bad-mouthed me. It might get some air time."

"Paulie, I'm going to call Carlo and tell him to come at 5 p.m. What else can I do to help?"

"Tell Nana that I'm working on this house. I'm trying to get it ready to move back in. I'm getting things organized so I know what I need. That should make her happy. Maybe you should tell her that I've got the flu, so I might stay here tonight."

I looked at Paulie. He was a good-looking guy. Now his cheeks were sunken and his hair and clothes were a mess. He'd be okay. I knew he would.

"Lena, promise me you'll go to work tomorrow. It has to be

business as usual for everyone else. I don't want you to come in here."

"Okay, Paulie. I hear you."

Nana knew that something was wrong. She was very quiet. I called Carlo from the bedroom phone. He was well aware of what he needed to do.

Nana looked at me and said, "Should I make-a some soup?"

"Yes, Nana. If Paulie has the flu, he will need some soup."

She took out her rosary, then she got the soup vegetables out and put water on the stove.

My dad called me at Nana's. "Carlo called Niko. Niko told me what's going on. That Helen broad, she ditched him like he was a mangy dog. This is her fault. She didn't think of protecting him. She's got a bunch of used-up druggies living at her place. Paulie couldn't compete with them without joining in. I heard his song on the radio a few times. She'll axe him now."

"She already did, Dad."

"I'm on my way to help Carlo and Paulie. I'll stop in by Nana first."

When my dad got there, Nana was happy to see him. "Sammy! I fix you some-a-thing to eat!"

It wasn't a question. Since Nana had got new appliances, she cooked more than ever.

After we ate, I walked out the back door with my dad. He wasn't shocked about Paulie, but he looked disgusted.

"Your Nana raised six sons. Paulie was four years old when Papa died. I did the best I could to help Nana with the younger boys. Paulie was always a little wild. I'm glad he's close to you, Lena. You are a good balance for him."

"Dad, this isn't your fault. It's the people he met through that, 'Helen from Hell.'"

"I'm gonna stay with Paulie and Carlo. He won't go through this without family."

No one was ever alone in my family. That was a good thing about my life.

I was a wreck the next day at work. I ad libbed way too many lines. I got through it, and it didn't change the story line. Latmen was concerned.

"What's up, Lena? You okay?"

"I got a lot on my mind right now, Frank."

He wanted to know about Whitey. He asked about my folks. "How is your nana doing?"

He asked about Paulie, too, but that wasn't a problem that I wanted to share.

"You know, Lena, we can talk about anything. If ever you need to discuss life, I'm a good listener."

I hugged him and he looked surprised. "Thanks, Frank. I know that. Maybe I can talk about this another time."

Carlo and my dad told me to stay away. I picked Nana up and brought her to my mom's for dinner. I told her the guys were bonding while they worked on the little house in the back.

She seemed concerned, but she also knew when NOT to ask questions. Zio came up from the basement. Nana and Zio greeted each other with a kiss on each cheek. Mom and I smiled at each other. We were clearing the dishes after dinner when Zio said, "I think I walk-a Rosina home after coffee tonight. I stay with her 'cause nobody is-a home so she no be alone tonight."

My mom rolled her eyes. Jojo nearly fell over his four doggy legs when Zio got his jacket off the hook in the back hall.

Zio said, "Come-ona Stupido, we go now."

Mom and I laughed so hard when they left. Nana didn't even appear to be awkward about Zio announcing he was spending the night.

We cleaned up the kitchen without saying much.

Finally Mom said, "Do I ask what's wrong or pretend everything is okay?"

"It's going to be okay. Ma. But not tonight."

"It's Paulie, isn't it? I saw him a couple of weeks ago. He ducked in the back bedroom when he saw me. I knew something was wrong. He's the baby, Lena. He felt my dad's loss most of all the boys. He doesn't even remember his father."

I took Dad's Jack Daniels out of the kitchen cabinet. I poured us both a shot with a water chaser.

"Mom, tomorrow we will talk about it. No more talking tonight. Drink this and go to bed."

"Salude!" We knocked it back and chased it with water. Not another word was said that night.

Nana said that my dad came over for towels and clean clothes the following morning. A little later he came back for soup. She never asked any questions. I guess when you raise nine kids you don't need to know every single thing that's going on. Dad and Carlo were still in the house with Paulie.

I went to see my ma before I went to Whitey's house. My mom was crying. "Daddy told me about Paulie. It was awful. He had bad stomach pains, fever, all sorts of stuff. He said everything hurt him. He thought he was going to die."

"That's the worse part about heroin, Ma. Getting off is really ugly."

Ma said that Mrs. Riggio had called her. She heard that Paulie had been at Nana's house for a few days. "Would Paulie like to sing for us on Saturday night?"

When I told Paulie, he was so happy he looked like he was going to cry. He's going over to see Mr. Riggio tomorrow morning if he feels all right.

My dad and Niko were thinking about paying a visit to Helen's farm. I persuaded them that it was none of our business what goes on out there. They finally agreed that I was right, as long as that lifestyle didn't interfere with any of our families. Geez, what a bunch of gangsters.

The interior of my house was finally finished. Nana was almost done with my kitchen curtains. I was using black and white checkered curtains with chrome and red accessories. My countertops were white.

My decorator Jaclyn had made the final decisions about my living room furniture. I was using black and white and gray. I loved the clean look.

I was taking Whitey shopping with me that night. I'd pick up my bridesmaid's dress for Penny's wedding, and then we'd go looking for household stuff.

We went to the House & Home Store and I loaded my cart. I got towels, cups, dishes, wall art, a coffee pot, blender, and an electric can opener. When Whitey saw the total on the register I thought his eyes would pop out.

Whitey whispered, "Lena, are you sure that you can write a check that big?"

"Whitey, I make a lot of money. Some day I'll discuss this with you."

"I was just thinking about the big investment you just made in building your house."

When we got outside, I told him, "Whitey, I paid cash for my house, all the construction supplies, and the workers. I plan to move in next weekend, so I need all this stuff.

He was very quiet. Then he said, "Holy Shit."

We went to dinner at Riggio's. Mr. Riggio sent some wine over then he came and sat with us.

"Lena, Paulie is going to come back and work for me! I am very happy. Will he stay with Nana or get his own house?"

"Well, Mr. Riggio, Paulie will live in the house behind Nana. All the uncles have lived there. They don't actually live in the house with Nana, but they are close enough in case she needs anything,"

"I'm so glad that Paulie got away from that woman, Helen. She's bad news. I never felt good about her."

"We are all glad that he is rid of her."

Whitey and I brought all the new stuff to my house. We went in and turned on all the lights. I was going to need lamps besides the overhead lights.

Whitey said, "Are you going to show me your dress?"

"Oh, sure."

I took it out of the bag and he scrunched up his face.

"Has your mother seen it?"

What? You don't like it?"

"Lena, it looks like a coffin lining. It's just not you. Why don't you try it on for me?"

I was in the bedroom trying on my dress. I was in my bra and panties when he walked in and said, "When does your furniture come?"

He had this big stupid grin on his face. In a split second he had me down on the carpet with his arms around me.

"It's really nice soft carpeting. Who needs a bed?"

Just then the doorbell rang.

"Lena, honey, open up. It's Ma."

Whitey scrambled to his feet and I shut the bedroom door. The first thing that popped into my head was, *She forgot I have phones now.*

"Hi Whitey! Did you and Lena go shopping?" She surveyed all the bags and boxes.

"Hi Mrs. Delatora. Yes, we did. And Lena picked up her dress for Penny's wedding. She just went in to try it on."

On cue, I came out of the bedroom.

Mama looked at it and smiled. "It's a beautiful color, hon."

"Oh crap, you don't like it either?"

"It looks like draperies."

"Well, Whitey said it looked like a coffin lining."

We all started laughing.

"Maybe Nana can take some of that gathering out for you. I love the color and the basic style is great. It's got too much crunchy stuff up and down the sides."

"I'm going to have to try to have it altered."

They both nodded in agreement.

"Mom, can you spare some detergent. I think I'll wash all these towels and linens that I bought."

"I'll go get you some from the house."

Whitey smiled that million-dollar smile, "I'll walk over with you and bring it back."

By the time he came back I had everything out of the bags and boxes.

Whitey said, "I had a glass of wine with your Dad."

My phone was ringing. Mom said, "I forgot to call you before I came over. I'm sorry."

I couldn't help smiling. I said, "Ma, you are welcome at my house any time and you can call any time."

"Thank you, sweetheart. But I *will* look for Whitey's truck in the driveway.

She's a wise woman.

The following day, Mom said, "I showed Nana your dress. She said, "Why Lena take-a this dress? It's a not good for her."

"Well, Ma I wanted this to be Penny's choice. It's her day. All the other bridesmaids liked it, so I just went along with it. Maybe I'll stop by Mona's after the show today and try it on for her."

"I think that's a good idea. You still have time to make changes."

My costar on *Tortured Souls*, Beth "The Nut," was on sabbatical. Her parents had arranged a one-month stay at her favorite spa. She thought she was staying for two weeks. Her parents had extended it, but she didn't know that yet. Milton, that's the new guy we call Red, had become very attached to Beth. He planned to visit her as soon as her parents said that it was okay.

Susan would step in as assistant manager of the bed and breakfast. Johnny and his pretend-pregnant-wife Joanna, who is played by Mona, were going strong. Mona was up to the eight-month baby bump this week. The fact that they are getting along so well is excellent chemistry on the set.

Mr. Latmen thinks I'm a genius. I keep forgetting to call him Frank. He wants me to write some ideas for the producers. They will develop the scripts. I'll put together some ideas with the baby. We might be able to use Susan's baby for a couple of shots. We'll improvise for now.

I've interviewed another girl as a receptionist for the show. She has dark hair, but I like her delivery of lines. Her butt is smaller than mine, but she will be at a desk or behind the counter of the store for the most part. Her name is Sabra Smart. What the heck kind of name is that? She will be Pattie on the show.

Mona and I went out for lunch after the show. We ate at that little café where we saw Johnny when I first started on the soap. We had such a nice time. I really missed her, since she is so close to Johnny now. They didn't live together, but they spent most evenings together.

I carried my dress inside her apartment. A little cat came over and rubbed my leg.

"Oh, Mona! I didn't know you got a cat!"

"Isn't he cute?"

"Oh, he is. What's his name?"

"I call him 'Frankie' after Mr. Latmen. He's really funny and good company. Johnny doesn't like him and Frankie knows it."

"Try your dress on for me, Lena."

I took the plastic bag off and laid it on the bed. I took off my skirt. I was pulling my sweater over my head when I heard Mona yell, *"Frankie, NO!"*

That cat had sprayed all over my dress. I never had a cat. I didn't know what cats do.

"Mona, that's really bad isn't it?" She looked like she was going to cry.

"Lena, that won't come out. That dress is ruined. Oh, Frankie. You bad cat."

"I guess Frankie doesn't like *me* either."

I started to laugh. Then we were both laughing.

"My Mom and Whitey hated that dress. I guess the cat didn't like it either. I understand dogs, Mona. Cats never made any sense to me."

"Lena, I'm so sorry. What will you do?"

"I guess I'll buy another dress! No one liked this one anyway."

I called my Mom from Mona's and asked her if she would like to go dress shopping. I told her what happened. She laughed too!

Our first stop was the dress shop where we all picked out our dresses. We didn't have time to order the dress custom made. I couldn't find anything there "off the rack" that I liked. My dress could be a little different because I was the maid of honor.

We stopped at three other places before I thought of Mayson's. They greeted me like royalty. I told them what color I was looking for. They pulled out six or seven dresses in a variety of silver-blue. I tried on a straight dress with a sheer overlay of netting. It had some beading and rhinestones at the neck. We all agreed that it was perfect. I would get shoes dyed to match and we would be ready to party.

I dropped Mom off and drove Mona home. I headed for Whitey's house.

I let myself in and saw candles and wine on the table. He was in the kitchen heating up his Mom's scaloppini. He looked terrific. He was wearing a blue sweater that matched his lavender-blue eyes. His smile made me warm all over.

After he kissed me I said, "Have you tried to call me? I've been running between Nana's house and my ma's."

"No, I talked to Carlo this morning. He called about some work on Paulie's house. I guess Paulie is going to move back in there."

"Oh, I'm glad he made that decision."

He drew me close and said, "The worst is over, babe."

"Carlo told you?"

"Yes, he needed some advice; I'm not sure what he thought I knew, but we talked about some stuff regarding Paulie. We agreed that we'd keep Paulie busy and watch out for him. It's easy to relapse and look for a source to buy drugs in the beginning."

"Thank you, Whitey. I never thought about that. I figured that once he was clean, that would be the end of it."

"Far from it. It's just the beginning. Lena, on a lighter note, I went to the doctor today. He took me off light duty. I can go back to work!"

I said, "Yippee!"

"And you know what else he said?

"I've got a pretty good idea from that grin on your face."

"He said, 'No hanging from the light fixtures or funny acrobat tricks.' "

"That's a good thing, Whitey," I said, smiling.

"But, Lena, I want to say something first. I have been behaving like a spoiled brat. I wanted you with me all the time. When you weren't here, I felt sorry for myself. I love you, Lena. I don't want my folks or the guys from my crew. Only you. I'm sorry I was so demanding. I'll get better at this. My last relationship was a disaster. I couldn't be here for her because I was in Vietnam. I kept thinking it was my fault. I wanted to be sure I didn't loose you."

"Whitey, don't say any more. Our relationship got off to a bad start when you got shot on our first date. Now we have to get to know each other under normal circumstances. We can take our time."

And that's just what we did, for several hours with a nap in between.

54

The next day I went to Nana's. Paulie was sitting in his favorite spot at the kitchen table. He looked really good—more like his old self. He was singing at Riggio's that night. I wanted to wish him luck and see what kind of mood he was in.

Nana said, "Call-a you Mama and Daddy. I make a big frittata. You call Auntie Lilly and Gemma too. If the husbands wanna come-a too, it's good."

"Should I tell Ma to bring Zio?"

"No gotta call Zio, he's in my basa-ment."

"Well, okay then. No need to worry about that."

Paulie and I snickered and Nana narrowed her eyes, warning us not to get too sarcastic.

Paulie and I were dragging chairs into the dining room when Auntie Lilly and Gemma got there. They brought their husbands and babies too.

Gemma said, "What's going on today? When did we start doing Saturday morning brunch? I brought extra eggs and bread. I figured if we are all going to be here we might as well have enough food."

Auntie Lilly brought a whole stuffed meatloaf. She puts spinach, Parmesan, and mushrooms in the middle. The only way I'll ever loose weight is to lock myself in my new house and not open the door. I guess it's similar to what poor Paulie went through with heroin, only my addiction is food.

The following day, I went to Nana's after work. She was in the kitchen cooking, as usual.

"Hello, Bella!" She kissed me sideways, because her hands were in a huge bowl of ground beef.

"Are you making meatballs?"

"Yes, I make-a meat-a-balls and we gonna have some sausage from Signore Genardo's butcher shop. I have to take everything from my freezer because it's no working. I bring in my grocery cart to put-a in you mama freezer. I make pasta sauce this morning too. I bring it in-a big pot. I tape the lid on the top and put it in my grocery cart with the meat on top."

I was trying not to laugh, because I was getting a visual of Nana pulling this grocery cart with the pot and all the stuff piled on top. She was bustling around the kitchen, but she wasn't happy.

"Nana, don't be upset. It's a very old refrigerator. I can take you out this weekend and we'll get a new one."

"Bella, it's not just a refrigerator. It's-a my stove, too. All week I have to light it with matches. It's no stay lit. Only one burner works. The other ones, no."

I was amazed that everything was going wrong at the same time. Now I only had to persuade her to go to Sears with me.

She was still upset. "Paulie, he turn off the gas. He say, "You gonna blow youself up, Ma."

"Oh, Nana, I'm sorry." In my head I was thinking, *I wonder if Paulie sabotaged the appliances?*

"Nana, maybe it's time for you to replace your stove and fridge?"

"No." She said calmly. "I'm gonna have somebody to come-a fix it."

"Maybe it's too old, Nana."

"Bella, old is good. Look at me! I'm still pretty good. Now you help me with the meat-a balls."

My nana could be pretty funny. I loved to hear her laugh at herself.

We loaded all the food into my car and went to my ma's. I called to tell her about Nana's fridge and stove, and we were bringing all this food for dinner.

During dinner, all she talked about was her appliances. "I'm a-lucky they work for so many years. Maybe Mama Diavalo, she could fix them."

Nana was referring to a woman in the neighborhood, who's name was really Dona Triena. Because she was known to dabble in magic, she was better known as Devil Mother.

Dad nearly choked on his food. "She knows how to fix stoves?"

"No, maybe she can make a little magic like years ago when people get sick."

"I think you better forget about her fixing appliances. How the heck old is she now? Shouldn't she be dead by now? She was old twenty years ago."

Nana made the sign of the cross and looked up to the ceiling, as if she was expecting to see Mama Diavola's face there.

Ma looked at Bobby and at me. "Do you remember when Bobby was a baby and I called her when he kept having nightmares?"

"I remember Mama Diavola," I said. "She always scared me when I was a kid. I remember when she did that spell thing on Bobby."

Bobby said, "Was it really a spell, Ma? I remember you talking about it."

Mom began telling the story again, directly to Bobby.

"When you were a little baby, you had awful nightmares. Really bad ones. You woke screaming and waving your arms and legs. You were soaked in cold sweat when I would run to take you out of your crib. Nana said that Mama Diavola could help you. This was the only time that Daddy and I had a cross word. I wanted to let Dona Triena come to help you. Daddy said 'No!' He said that no 'Lady Witch Doctor' was going to experiment on his kid. I took you to our doctor. He couldn't find anything wrong. You kept waking up screaming during the night. Finally Daddy said, 'Call Mama Diavola.' She came with Nana. She wore a big sweater with huge pockets. First she pulled out a long string of garlic."

"No surprise there," Bobby said. I slapped his arm to shut him up.

Mom continued.

"She said we could stay and watch, because Daddy didn't want to leave her alone in your room. We watched from the living room so we could see her at your bedroom door. She said, "Nobody talk." She snapped off one head of garlic and peeled it. She rubbed it all around the doorframe. She was mumbling some weird stuff I couldn't understand. Nana said it wasn't Italian. She rubbed some of the garlic all around the frame of the crib. She broke up two heads and scattered the cloves under the crib. The rest of the string of garlic, she hung from the curtain rod above Bobby's bedroom door. She stepped back and looked at the hanging string of garlic and turned her hands palm up and mumbled some more goofy stuff. She brushed her hands together and said, 'finito.'

"She reached into the pocket of her big sweater and gave me one very large head of garlic. She told me, 'You take one clove and peel it. Rub on you baby's chest, over his heart. With the rest, you make soup tonight. Give some to the baby. Everybody eat the soup and sleep good.

"I made pastina with chicken broth that night. I chopped the garlic up fine in the soup. Bobby, you never had another nightmare after that."

Nana made the sign of the cross again and looked up on the ceiling again. I looked too, half expecting to see Mama Diavola's image there.

"What did she charge you, Ma?" Bobby wanted to know.

"Oh, you never pay with money. I baked bread for her. I bought a bottle of wine from Mr. Natalie. I picked vegetables from my yard and cleaned them. I put it all in a basket and brought it to her house. I saw her look out her window, so she knew it was me paying her back. I left the basket on her porch. I saw her nod. I think there's some kind of rule about not giving payment directly into her hand."

Dad said, "That's some weird shit, huh, Bobby?"

Nana rolled her eyes, but she didn't make the sign of the cross again.

"Oh, Lena! I forgot that Whitey gave me a note for you today."

She dug into her apron and pulled out a clothespin, a cap from a spice jar, a hankie, and Whitey's note. I read it while they watched. My private life had become public property lately.

"Well, what did he say?"

"I know you read it, Mom."

"Yea, I did. Are you going to his house tonight?"

"I don't know yet, Miss Nosey."

"Geez, will you two quit the talking. Let's have dessert first. Then you ladies can chat all you want."

"Fine, Sam," Ma said. We both laughed at Dad. He still gets embarrassed when we talk about girl stuff in front of him.

Nana was still thinking about her appliances and Dona Triena. We could tell she wasn't even listening to us.

We put some cake and cookies on the table and Nana said, out of the blue, in the middle of her thoughts:

"When I married your papa and we bought the house, Dona Triena had a husband and four young daughters. The first one was beautiful. The second one was beautiful, but had ugly hair; the third one was beautiful too, but she was fat and getting fatter alla time. The last daughter, Daniella, her nose was too big. She had bad skin and one crossed eye, like this." She crossed her eyes for emphasis. "I think her head hung down a little bit too. They loved all-a daughters the same, but got no more good looks left when Daniella was born."

I looked over at Bobby, he was laughing so hard that he had tears running down his face. Ma and I started to laugh too. Dad picked up on this and he couldn't stop laughing either. Zio had been silent through dinner and all the story telling. Now he began to laugh.

Between fits of laughter he said, "I think that Dona Triena tried to pay me once, to go out with Daniella."

Nana looked indignant and said, "I'm no finish my story. Be quiet everybody. Well, all the daughters met nice husbands. Daniella was getting old and her mother was worried that no man would want her."

Zio said, "I tell-a you that's the truth."

"Mama Diavola wanted to send to Italy for a husband for Daniella. Her husband said, 'No,' his daughter would find a nice man here and he would love her because she was beautiful inside.

Now she had us on the edge of our chairs. We had never heard this story before.

"The husband and wife fought about a husband for Daniella for many years. The Triena's had a little grocery store in the neighborhood then. One morning a deliveryman find Senor Triena in the alley behind-a the store. Somebody beat him to death. His pockets they turned inside out and his wallet, watch, and his wedding ring is-a gone. They had a funeral and all the daughters were there with the husbands and babies. Only Daniella was alone. She didn't look sad. She didn't even cry. Her Mama didn't cry either. Only the other daughters cried.

"One month later, a man came from Italy. Everyone said that it was *Mama Diavola* who had her husband killed and she sent for a husband for Daniella before Senor Triena died."

We were all speechless. We had heard a lot of family stories and stories from the old country, but this was a new one for all of us.

My dad finally said, "Ma! Don't let this lady ever look at your stove. I think she really is a witch. This had to have happened fifty years ago. She must be about one hundred years old now."

"I don't know, really. It could be. Sometimes I think she has always been old."

I spoke up, "Nana, that settles it. Tomorrow we go to Sears and buy new appliances."

55

I called my ma the following day after work.

"Is Nana there? There's no answer at her house."

"She's here. Hold on."

"Nana, let's got look at stoves at Sears this afternoon. Mama can come with, and she can give you her opinion."

"Oh, I don't think so, Bella."

"Why?"

"Paulie turned the gas back on and it's okay. He said only use the burners in front. Keep the back ones off."

"You only have one burner."

Ma heard me, and she went into my old room to call Paulie and tell him to shut the gas off, and don't turn it back on.

"Nana, Paulie told Ma that there is a gas leak. It won't work. You are going to blow up your house."

"Oooh, that's too bad. I really don't want a new stove."

"Nana, we should replace your refrigerator too."

"It's okay now. The ice is good now. Only the little bit of fat on the meat is soft."

"I'm going to see Whitey for a little while. I'll be at your house by four o'clock."

I hung up before she could argue with me. I knew this wasn't going to be easy. I was hoping Ma could help with the transition.

We went to Sears on North Avenue. Nana marched into the appliance department and announced that she didn't like any of the stoves.

The salesman's eyes got big and he tried to keep smiling. We walked up and down the aisles. Nana was wandering into the refrigerator aisle. She opened the door on a huge monster of a fridge.

She had her head stuck so far into the freezer section that the salesman was trying to get my ma to pull her out.

"This one is frost free," I said.

"Ma'am, could you please persuade your mother to get her head out of the freezer compartment. That unit is running."

"Nana, come to look at the stoves."

"How much-a dis one cost?"

When the salesman gave her the price, she made the sign of the cross.

"Maybe Mama Diavola could fix this price a little bit."

I said, "Nana! Don't even joke about that."

The poor salesmen looked confused. He wasn't sure if he should go back to the stoves or stay with us.

Nana wanted this refrigerator. For some reason she had attached herself to this model. She was so fascinated with the frost-free feature that she didn't want to leave it.

"Nana, this might be bigger than you need. Let's look at the same kind, only a little bit smaller."

"Okay, just-a the same, little bit smaller is okay. Do I pay when they bring to my house?"

I decided to leave out the part that I was paying for the appliances. We could have them delivered, and tell her that the bill would come later.

"Now you have to pick out the stove. Come follow the salesman over this way."

I had to keep her moving. This was a milestone and Ma and I had to strike while the salesman was hot on Nana's wishes.

In the end, Nana ordered a stove and refrigerator. I paid for them while Ma took her out to the car. I scheduled the delivery date for late on Friday. I wanted to be there for the delivery of the new appliances and removal of the old ones. I don't even think that Nana thought that far ahead, regarding the removal.

When I got in the car, Nana was settled in the front seat next to

Ma. She had on her shawl, and her headscarf was tied tightly under her chin. Nana didn't like drafts. I explained to her that I would be at her house after work on Friday for the delivery.

Mission accomplished!

I missed Mona. She was very involved with Johnny. Since they live in the same apartment building, it's a very convenient relationship. I remember the first time she saw Johnny. We were sitting at a little table at the street café near the studio. He saw us and came over to say "Hello." She was so impressed seeing him in the flesh that her mouth hung open. Who knew that she would be playing "hot potato" with him?

I finally called her to help me get my house ready for Penny's bridal shower. It would be fun, since she was in the wedding party too.

We put away all the towels and hung some pictures. I was looking for some cute bathroom decorations and pictures for the bedroom. We decided to do a shopping run.

When we got back from the store, my mom and nana were putting up the kitchen curtains.

"Hi! This looks great!"

Nana saw Mona and she came over to hug her. "Why you no come-a to see me? I miss you, Mona."

"Oh, Nana, since Paulie and I broke up, I feel like I might hurt your feelings if I come. I thought you might be mad at me."

"Mona! Wadda you talk about? It's okay that you don't marry Paulie. He's a pazzo anyway."

Ma had coffee made in my new coffee maker. Nana pulled biscotti from one of the many bags that she brought with her. We sat down at my new kitchen table for the first time. Nana said, "*Buona fortuna e tanto amore nella vostra nuova casa,*" which translates to "Good luck and much love in your new home."

We all said, "*Salude*" and tapped my new red coffee cups together.

The doorbell rang. It was the rest of my furniture being delivered. Now we were all excited!

The delivery guys set everything up. They brought the bedroom furniture in first. I ordered complete rooms, including the tables and lamps. I pulled out all my new linen and the bedspreads. I didn't order any furniture for the smallest bedroom, only the two larger ones. I was not sure what I'd do with the little bedroom.

Jaclyn was having most of the pillows custom made. I picked out the fabric and she designed them.

The living room furniture came in next.

Ma and Nana were chattering away while they made the beds and put stuff in place. Mona was washing out the coffee cups and straightening up the kitchen.

I stood in the kitchen doorway and looked at the scene. I was so happy I thought I would cry. Nana came and stood next to me. She put her hands on her hips and said, "Lena, you make a me so proud for you! Looka-a 'dis beautiful house you make!"

I laughed and hugged her.

Ma said, "We all need to get some sleep, or we'll wind up in Lena's new beds. Lena and Mona have to work tomorrow."

Mona offered to drive Nana home. Ma said, "Thanks Mona. You're a doll."

Mona kissed us all good night. Ma hugged me and asked, "Are you staying here tonight?"

"Yes, I think I will. I have all my makeup in my bag. I'll walk back to your house with you and get slacks and a blouse for tomorrow."

I looked back at my house from Mom's porch. It was an amazing sight. The lights were on inside and I left the porch light on in the back. I could see into my cute kitchen with the checkered curtains. What a great night this had been.

That night, I took a shower in my new bathroom and climbed into my new bed with my new sheets and comforter. I left the little light on over the sink in the kitchen. I could look through the house and admire the finished work. I finally dozed off into a peaceful sleep.

I heard a tapping noise. It took me a moment to remember where I was. Ma's house? Nana's house? Whitey's house? Oh, I know! It's my house. I heard the tapping again. It was on the garden side of the house, not the "Mama" side.

I peeked under the shade. There was Whitey holding a bottle of wine and something I couldn't identify in the other hand. I motioned for him to go to the back door.

"Hey, beautiful! I parked in the back so Ma and Dad wouldn't see my car—yet"

I pulled him inside and gave him a giant smooch. He was holding a bottle of wine and a brass lamp. He put the stuff down and hugged me. He had his nose buried in my hair, taking big sniffs.

"What are you doing?" I said, laughing. "You sound like a puppy."

"I missed your smells." His hands were everywhere.

I said, "That's a beautiful lamp. How did you remember that I needed a bedroom lamp?"

"I remembered you said it when the house was empty."

By this time he had me stripped down to my panties.

"Thank you very much."

"Oh, I don't think you're finished thanking me just yet."

"Guess you're planning on christening my new bed?"

"No. I'm going to leave you standing in this kitchen in your panties." He picked me up and carried me into the bedroom.

"What time do you have to be at the TV station tomorrow?"

"Not 'til ten."

"Well, if I'm not dead by then, I'll certainly be exhausted."

"Whitey, if you're staying the night, I don't have any food in the house."

"Focus, baby. That's not the kind of nourishment I came here for."

We never plugged in that brass lamp. Oh, what a night.

The next morning, around 9 a.m., I asked Whitey how he knew I was at my house.

"I called your mom and asked if you were there or at Nana's house. She told me that your furniture came today, and you were spending your first night in your new place. I wasn't going to let that happen without me!"

I made a pot of coffee for us. After he had a cup, he said, "I better get out of here before your mom brings breakfast over." He snuck out the back door, which was actually the side door. That side door was one of the best ideas I've ever had.

The phone rang a few moments later. It was my mom.

"Hi, honey. How was your first night in your new house?"

"It was great, Ma."

"Lena, get dressed and come over to eat. I know you haven't gone grocery shopping yet."

As soon as Ma said, "Get dressed" I looked down at my naked self and did a quick window check. Yup, everything was closed up.

56

At the TV station, Penny asked me during my makeup session if I would go to the bridal shop with her. She was bringing her dress in for some alterations. She had picked it up after the final fitting.

"Every time I try it on, I feel like a lampshade."

"Penny, it's a beautiful dress. What don't you like about it?"

"I'm not sure. You tell me when we get there, okay?"

"Sure. I'll be honest with you."

Penny tried the dress on for the seamstress. She was trying to explain that the dress was too full. It was too much dress for Penny. She was a little girl. I could tell she was nearly in tears trying to make her understand what she wanted.

"Lena, you explain, please!"

I looked at the apron that the seamstress was wearing. I said, "Give me your scissors!"

"Oh no! Miss Delatora, I can no do dat."

"What's your name, dear?"

"My name is Velda."

"Well, Velda, this isn't going to be a bad thing, you'll see."

"No! I won't give you my scissors."

"HAND THEM OVER, VELDA!"

She looked terrified, but give me the scissors.

I calmly lifted the top layer of tulle and began trimming the fluffy layers out. I thought Velda was going to pass out. I grabbed the second layer and slowly cut it away.

By this time Velda had to sit down. She had her hand on her forehead and was moaning, as she fanned herself with Penny's paperwork.

I stepped back and let Penny have a look.

"Lena! This is perfect!"

Velda opened her eyes and peered at the dress with a pained expression. "Vell, I think this is very unusual behavior. I have never seen any-vone alter a designer vedding gown with chopping of the scissors."

"Calm down, Missy."

"Velda. My name is Velda."

"Yes, I know. Velda, come around the front of this bride and take a look."

"Ohhh. This is good. It's very good!"

"Good!" I exclaimed. You can tell your boss how happy we are with your original alterations."

Velda said, "I vill put a white sash around the waist for the bride. Thanks so much Miss Delatora!"

Penny was beaming. "It's perfect, Lena. Thank you so much. I love it."

"Oh, good, Penny. Then I hope you won't be upset when I tell you that Mona's cat sprayed my dress and I bought one off the rack at Mayson's."

We both started laughing. "Lena, you've been so kind through this entire dress ordeal. I expected a lot more of your opinion on most of this stuff."

"It's your day, Penny. I want everything to be your idea. It should be exactly what you want."

"Well, you're my maid of honor. Your dress should be exactly what you want, too."

"Well, Nana was going to take some of the gathering out of the sides. When I tried it on for Whitey and my mom, they agreed that it resembled the lining of a coffin."

"Lena, it's probably a good thing the cat didn't like it either."

We both burst out laughing. "Come up to the house with me. Carlo will be so glad to see you."

We were still laughing when we walked into the house.

"Somebody made you girls laugh. I was going to offer you some wine, but I think you might have already had some."

"No wine for me, Carlo. I wouldn't mind a Coke."

"Okay. Coca-Cola, with cheese and crackers for my ladies!"

We snacked on cheese and crackers. Carlo cut some salami and prosciutto with melon.

I couldn't believe how quickly the evening went by. Penny and Carlo seemed so happy. I prayed that they would always be as content with each other as they were now.

"I want to propose a toast." I raised my glass of Coke and said, "To my dear friends. I hope your love will grow with time, and you will always be this happy."

Penny looked like she was going to cry. They both hugged me. "Please stay the night, Lena." They both tried to encourage me.

"No, I still look forward to going to my new house."

Not a day went by that I didn't find fresh meals in my refrigerator. My mom had her own key. That day she had made chicken cacciatore. I was glad to see that she went easy on the potatoes. She had left a fresh loaf of Italian bread on the table. I took a quick shower and hit that bed. I was out like a light.

Penny's wedding invitations had gone out weeks ago. I was planning the wedding shower at my house. It would be filled with fun and food.

Nana was crocheting little dolls for all the bridesmaids that would match their dresses. I don't know how she can style her crocheting to be like their dresses. She found some silvery blue colored yarn to match.

We were going to put the dresses down the center of the food table. I noticed the dolls all had the same flat circle around the hips, but were really cute and perky. I picked up the silvery blue doll and looked underneath. I laughed out loud. The little dollies each had their legs stuck through a roll of toilet paper.

I brought one over to show my Mom. "Nana has been crocheting these for weeks. A lady at her church makes them. Nana was crazy about them. She borrowed one to use for a pattern and made her own alterations to it."

I could see Mom was very proud of Nana's skill. I wasn't sure how I felt about all those rolls of toilet paper lined up on the buffet table. If it made me laugh, I knew all of the girls would love them too. I was going to get some silver ribbon to tie around the waist of each doll. I'd get silver and blue decorations. It was going to be beautiful!

Besides the dolls that Nana made, each guest would receive a set of six crocheted coasters. They would be in a satin bag with the almonds for each of the guests.

"Nana! That's a lot of coasters. That's a lot of crocheting!"

"It's what I like to do, Bella. Maybe I make-a you some dresser scarves for you new furniture."

"Oh, Nana. That would be great."

I found out later that Nana had sent Zio Peppino all around the North side to find yarn that color. She bought every skein that Woolworth's and Kresgee's had in stock. He climbed on and off busses to far away places like Pulaski Road and Damen Avenue.

When I asked Susan to come back to fill in for Beth "The Nut," Susan nearly cried. She thought the studio had branded her a "Scarlet Woman" when she had a baby and wasn't married. We all knew the baby's father was a married man. Latmen said, "It's a modern world. Who gives a darned what people think?"

The story behind Beth's going away was this: She was visiting a small bed and breakfast in Lake Geneva to consider a second establishment for us to purchase. As things progress through the series, I would have phone conversations with her on a split screen to get an update on the progress. They would arrange a film crew to visit her at her "spa."

We decided to have a little luncheon catered in to welcome Susan back. Johnny introduced Mona to Susan. They chatted as if they had known each other forever.

The other new girl I decided on would be joining us for the first time today. She would be the desk clerk at the B and B. Her name was Tammy Russo. I figured that I could keep her behind the desk, then I wouldn't have to worry about her butt being smaller than mine.

The luncheon was going great. Everyone was mingling and chatting up a storm. I watched like a mother hen as people mixed and enjoyed each other's company. I noticed we were running out of ice. I snagged Greg to come with me to fetch and carry.

As we walked down the hall to the ice machine next to the cafeteria, we passed a little office used for interviews and contractors. I saw two people in an embrace. Greg was looking at me, and the office was on his right side. I tried not to react. I am an actress, after all. It was Susan and Johnny. I did a mental head slap: THE MARRIED MAN!

Greg was speaking to me, waiting for an answer to something he had asked.

"What did you say, Greg?"

"Lena, you look like you saw a ghost."

"I saw a couple of ghosts, Greg."

He shook his head at me, just like he always does when he can't figure me out.

By the time we got back to the gathering, Susan and Johnny were speaking with other people as if nothing had happened.

I don't really care what Johnny does, but I don't want Mona to get hurt. Paulie was a womanizer. Now Johnny was reliving his past.

At some point, I wanted to tell Mona about Susan and Johnny. Maybe he really has feelings for Susan. They have a child together. He and his wife, in real life, are getting divorced. Maybe he wants to be a father to his baby.

I shouldn't care so much about other people's lives. I know this, but Mona and I are very close friends. We were practically related when she was engaged to my Uncle Paulie.

There was a knock on my dressing room door. Then it opened. I had learned to dress behind the screen. It seemed to be standard procedure for people to just knock and walk in.

"Lena, are you in here?"

"I'm changing behind the screen, Milton." When I stepped out,

I couldn't help but notice he was all smiles.

"Lena, call me Red. Everyone does."

"What's up, Red?"

"I saw Beth last night. The doctor gave her an evening pass. I took her out to dinner. We had a nice stroll around the spa grounds. It's a beautiful place. She says to say hello."

"How do you think she's doing, Red?"

"I think she's doing really well. She's on some new meds and she's really funny. I mean her humor is great. I didn't know she was such a comic."

"When Beth is on her meds, she's a real laugh riot. Then she thinks she doesn't need them. When she stops, she begins a downward spiral and gets goofy."

"I need some advice, Lena. Do you think she can maintain a serious relationship?"

Let me take a step back here. I'll need to check the sign on my door. What the hell does it say? Counselor? Advice to the Lovelorn? Big Sister? NO! It says "LENA DELATORA—STAR." And by the way, Susan's door will say "COSTAR."

I turned back to Red.

"I don't know if I'm qualified to give you advice. I can only tell you what I know about her. As I mentioned, if she stays on her meds, I think she should be fine. But Red, I am not a professional. I don't have a medical background."

"I just needed your friendly advice regarding previous behavior. Greg won't say anything negative about her. He's been a real gentleman."

He kissed me on the cheek and left. I said, "What the hell? Why's everyone asking me for advice."

It was two days before Penny's bridal shower. Latman was kind enough to fix the script so I did not have to be on the set for Thursday and Friday. That gave me three days to get the house ready.

I called Penny to be sure that all the girls on Carlo's side were coming. People always forget to RSVP and that makes me nuts. His little nieces were in the bridal party. They were so cute. Lugina was really going to be beautiful. She was fifteen. Little Tessa was thirteen. I was so glad I'd get to see them on Sunday. Our families all know each other and I have seen these little girls grow up.

Mom had been cooking for days. She'd made mountains of meatballs and sausage with green peppers. Today she was making pans of lasagna. I wanted to have all this food catered from Riggio's, but my mom and dad still act like I'm a kid and don't have enough money.

Nana and Zio were in the kitchen cutting blue and silver fabric to cover the tables. Nana was planning to put a silver ruffle around the blue toppers. I was laughing to myself when I saw she was trying to show Zio how to make bows to put on the backs of the chairs. He wasn't pleasing her.

Dad and Uncle Sammy were cleaning the tables in the garage when Ma called them to come in for lunch.

Suddenly I heard crashing and banging coming from Ma's kitchen. Uncle Sammy came running out of the house. "Your Mom's lost her mind. She's gone *pazzo* again!"

I know my ma has a temper, but she only gets mad every five or six years. So I'm guessing he said something to make her mad.

"What did you do?"

"I didn't do nothin'. She gave us some sausage sandwiches. Your dad said her sauce was a little sour. She started throwing cups at us off her rack on the wall."

"I'll go see what I can do," while quickstepping toward the house.

By the time I got there, Ma had finished throwing cups and Dad was hugging her and telling her what a great cook she was while Mom was crying. I started picking up the broken cups and Dad was covering the pans of lasagna to put in the garage refrigerator. "Not a good idea to hurt her feelings when she's been working so hard," he said.

I said, "Right!"

Tomorrow he will bring her a little gift. That's how he apologizes.

Uncle Sammy popped his head out of the garage and asked,

"Do you think it's okay if I go back in for a sandwich?"

"Sure, Uncle Sammy. She'll act like nothing happened."

"Lena, your Ma's got her Papa Antonio's temper."

"No, she has her own temper. She bottles it up too long."

Whitey wanted to take me out for dinner that night. I told him, "Come to my house and bring a loaf of Italian bread. You have your choice of meatballs, sausage, or lasagna. My mom cooked enough food for one hundred people. Nana and Zio are in her kitchen right now filling about 100 cannoli shells. There is enough food between these two houses for a small army. I think Nana is making *cardone, too.*"

All day, we were all walking between my house and Ma's. By six that evening, I was putting the finishing touches on the decorations at my house; I was really tired.

Whitey got there with the loaf of bread

My dad called and said, "I saw Whitey come over. Can I stop by? I said, "Sure, Dad."

Dad walked across the yard to my door and let himself in.

"Hi, Whitey. How you doin'?"

They shook hands and Dad sat down. He took a small box out of his pocket. "Lena, I bought your Mom a little present. Do you think she'll like these?"

He had bought pearl earrings with little diamonds around them. Do I know my dad? Yes!

"They are beautiful, Dad. They match the ring you bought her last Christmas."

"Yes, I know," he said, with a smile.

I poured Dad a glass of wine and we talked for a while. Then he said goodnight. "I'll leave you kids alone. Have a nice evening."

When Dad left, I told Whitey, "After the 10 p.m. news, you're out of here. I've got a ton of stuff to do."

"Lena, how can I help you, babe?"

'Well, I'm going to cover all the tables with blue cloth. Then they will all look the same, and I don't want to worry about spills or scratches on my new tables. You can fill the candy dishes and put these little dolls along the back of the table, close to the wall."

When he finished, he kissed me goodnight and gave me a big hug and said, "Get a good night's sleep, babe. You look tired already."

⟫«❋»⟪

The morning of the bridal shower, Carlo called. He insisted on sending over ten pounds of beef with gravy and a dozen loaves of bread. Holy cow! Now I had enough food for 110 people. That's okay, because I won't have to worry about not having enough food for the guys in the garage. Dad said most of the husbands would drive the wives and daughters. Instead of going to Mario's Tavern around the corner, they'd hang out in Dad's heated garage and eat and drink the day away.

The guests would begin arriving around one. Carlo's nieces wanted to come early and help set out the food. Sweet girls! It'd be nice to see them. I could find plenty for them to do.

Carlo's Uncle Nino would drop them off. His Auntie Gemma, the girl's mother, had lots of health problems. I, personally, thought she had a drinking problem, too.

When I opened the door, my first thought was, *They look like little Italian hookers! What happened to these kids? They are a little more advanced than they should be at this age.* Lugina looked like she was twenty years old. Tessa looked a little less brassy. They both were dressed too trashy for their ages. Lugina was wearing a peasant blouse that was pulled way down off the shoulders. I'm sure she did that after she got out of her dad's car. I hugged them both. My mom and nana came in to greet them. We all hugged and kissed.

Nana said, "Lugina, Madonna Mia! You got so big!" Ma rolled her eyes at me. Little Lugina got really big in one visible area.

I whispered in Lugina's ear, "Could you please pull the shoulders up on your blouse?" She smiled and did as I asked.

Tessa trailed off into the kitchen looking for something to drink.

The doorbell rang. I could see the florist's truck. "Lugina, could you please let the florist in. The flowers are all paid for. Have him put them all around, centered on the tables. The biggest one goes on the gift table."

I went into the kitchen and Lugina went to the door. I was taking cold trays out of the fridge and helping Nana with the pans from the oven.

About twenty minutes later, Ma said, "Lena, where's Lugina?"

Nana said, "Oh, you mean the *piccola putana?*"

We all laughed.

"Nana! Bad girl." She had called Lugina a little whore.

"Well," Nana said, "that's whadda she look like."

I couldn't argue with that. "I'll go see where she went. We could use her help."

As I walked through the living room, I glanced over at the snack table. There was Tessa, with her face practically in the bowl of spiked punch. "Hey Little Trouble! Get away from that punch. How much of that have you had?"

Our neighbor lady said from her perch on the arm of a chair, "Lena, she's had four or five cups since I sat down. She was drinking cup after cup."

"Why didn't you stop her, Doris?" I said.

"Well, look at her, Lena, I thought she was old enough!"

"Tessa! Put that cup down and see if you can help Nana in the kitchen."

I saw the florist's truck was still in the driveway. That puzzled me.

I went outside and pulled open the back door of the truck. There was Lugina with her panties around her ankles and her shirt completely off one shoulder, surrounded by flower arrangements. She really is a *piccola putana!*

"LUGINA!" I shouted. "Pull your pants up right now! Get back in the house!"

"And you!" I pointed at the delivery boy, "I'm going to call your boss!"

"Oh please don't, lady. He's my uncle. He'll beat the crap out of me."

"Yeah, you should have thought about that before you decided to do the 'cha cha' with this underage girl."

"She followed me out to the truck. Honest. All I did was smile at her."

"Get back to work, *Stupido!* Get going!"

After scrambling around the flowers in the back of the truck, he jumped into the driver's seat and screeched away. I glanced around for Lugina and saw her doing a running walk through the side door. She was taking baby steps because she probably didn't have her panties pulled up past her knees yet.

I went in the same door, hoping to keep the attention to a minimum. I saw Tessa in the far corner of the living room with her head down. Several ladies were clustered around her. *Oh, for God's sake! She's puking! Stay calm, don't smack her.*

Unfortunately it was a red punch. I grabbed a bathroom towel and threw it over the puddle. I pushed her into the bathroom and told her, "Clean yourself up!"

Tessa said, "I don't feel so good. Please stop yelling. My head hurts."

"You're lucky that Penny didn't see what you or your sister did. She wouldn't hesitate to tell your Uncle Carlo!"

Tessa rolled her eyes at me and said, "I hope you're done talking because I'm going to be sick again if you keep yelling. I need to lie down."

Lugina was now standing with the other ladies looking at the towel on the floor.

"Lugina," I purred, "please help Nana in the kitchen, and don't forget to wash your hands." *'Cause we know where they have been,* I thought.

Fortunately, the majority of the people in the house weren't even paying attention to what was going on with the two darlings. I scooped most of the mess up with my new bathroom towel and threw it in the outside garbage. I didn't have any carpet cleaner, because my carpeting was new. I scrubbed the best I could with soap and water and threw the bathroom throw rug on top of it. Problem solved for now. I put Tessa, or "Little Trouble," as she would be known to me forever, in the guest room. "If you throw up in here, I'll kill you."

"Lena, stop talking."

I put a wastebasket next to her and I think she went right to sleep. I threw my hands up in the air and walked out of the room and said, "Madonna Mia!"

Nana asked, "Where is Tessa?"

"She's in the guest room. Cramps."

"Oh, *povero bambino*," she said.

"Yeah, poor baby," I repeated.

Well, I guess I better refill the punch bowl. I went a little easier on the Jack this time. More guests were arriving. I told Lugina, "Bring this bowl back in the living room. And don't drink any!"

I figured there were about sixty people milling around. Everyone was checking out my new house. Penny was showing people around. She was glowing with all the attention. The gift table was overflowing.

Mom asked, "Do you want to serve the food now or after the gifts are opened?"

"Now would be good, Ma. People will digest while the gifts are being opened. Then we can have desserts afterward."

Nana was already filling the trays with all the sweets. They looked beautiful. Ma brought over her big coffee pot. It was a 50-cup monster, and I think we will use the full pot. In between watching the gifts being opened, Ma was carrying food out to the men in the garage. After the gifts were opened, the desserts were brought in and placed on the buffet table. When Ma looked outside, she announced, "The groom is here!"

Carlo came in, grinning from ear to ear. He immediately scanned the crowd for Penny. He walked over to her and gave her a big smooch. Everyone applauded. He reached in his pocket and pulled out a little box.

"These are for the bride-to-be."

He had bought her the most beautiful diamond earrings. They were wires with dangling diamonds.

"These should look beautiful on our wedding day with your dress! Put them on, honey. Let everyone see them."

Penny was holding back happy tears. She put the earrings on and they really were beautiful.

"You don't have to wait until our wedding day to wear them, Penny. I want you to enjoy them now."

She held up her head to kiss him and I could see tears in his eyes.

Mom said from behind me, "Whitey is in the garage with the rest of the men. He brought his truck to help haul this stuff back to Carlo and Penny's house."

Carlo asked, "Where is Tessa? I see Lugina in the kitchen. Where is the little one?"

I told him that Tessa had cramps and I had put her in the guest room.

"Thanks, Lena. You really are great. I hope the girls were some help to you with this big crowd."

"Oh, yes Carlo. They were a big help!" Not too many people would know that it wasn't true.

I went out to the garage to see Whitey. I finally got to him, after I kissed my way through all the uncles, all the husbands, and everyone else's fathers.

"How are you holding up, sweetheart?"

"I'm doing okay, Whitey. I'll tell you about Carlo's nieces later."

He smiled and said, "Okay." Somehow I think he had an idea about Lugina. Depending on how long he had been in the garage, he might have seen her go out to the florist's truck.

I told the men that I would bring out desserts. Whitey came to help me with the heavy trays. Between the garage and my house, Whitey said, "Lena, hold up. I need to tell you something."

I never liked it when I hear a phrase like that. Immediately, I thought something really bad had happened. As it turned out, it was bad enough.

"Lena, last night I met some of my guys at a bar by Lincoln Park."

"Whitey, you don't have to tell me every move you make."

"I'm not finished, Lena. I saw Carlo in a car on the side street with a guy."

I felt my stomach flip. I knew this could happen. I was hoping it wouldn't.

"They were talking real serious stuff with their heads close. I didn't see them do anything else, though."

"Maybe he was negotiating the diamond earrings. Whitey, we're gonna have to ignore it. Stuff like this is going to happen. I think it's part of who Carlo is. I really didn't think he gave up that life completely."

"Lena, I thought you were gonna flip when I told you."

"The wedding is six weeks away. I don't think Carlo will call it off. He probably thought he was far enough away from home that no one would see him. I hope he keeps Penny safe and happy. Come inside, we'll get the desserts."

Carlo spotted us coming in the kitchen door. He hugged Whitey and shook his hand.

"Thanks for bringing your truck, Whitey. We got a lot of really great stuff. We're gonna have to get rid of some of the old stuff once we unpack all this."

"No problem, Carlo, glad to help. Why don't we bring some of it out to the truck while the ladies are having dessert?"

I stopped Whitey at the door and let Carlo go ahead of him. I put my arms around him and stood on my tiptoes to whisper in his ear. I wanted it to look like I had something private to say. I said, "Don't say anything about what you saw to Carlo, okay?"

"Got it, babe. I really like the guy. I don't want to see him or Penny hurt."

The party was breaking up and most of the people were gone already. I was saying good-bye to people and passing out desserts for them to take home.

Penny insisted that she was staying to help clean up. We carried everything into the kitchen. One of the long tables worked well for the stack of dirty dishes. I lined another table with clean towels to drain dishes that were washed. We all switched off drying and putting stuff away. We loaded the plates into the dishwasher and pitched in, washing the other stuff when it was full.

I heard a man's voice at the front door: "Hullo! Hullo!

It was Carlo's Uncle Benny. He had come to fetch his darling daughters. "Lena! It's so nice to see you!"

"Uncle Benny! Come in the kitchen and have something to eat."

"No. No. I was already in the garage with the men. I ate and drank and had dessert, too!"

Lugina said, "Hello, Papa," and kissed his cheek.

"Were the girls a big help, Lena? They help me and their Mama all the time."

I was imagining Mama having some homemade wine in her pantry and Tessa helping herself while she helped Mama.

"I put Tessa to bed in the guest room. She was having 'lady' problems."

"Oh, gosh!" He said, looking flustered. "I'd better go see how she's doing. With her Mama being sick all the time, I understand a lot more about those things from my girls."

I kept seeing Lugina staring at me, giving me big eyes. She was more or less asking me to keep her secret.

When her dad went in to check on Tessa, Lugina said, "Lena, I'm really sorry I upset your day."

"Little girl, you should be more upset about your own behavior. You didn't apologize for doing the *fandango* in the flower truck. You're apologizing for upsetting me. You better watch yourself. If you behave like this at the wedding, I will personally throw you in my car and take you home. And if that happens, I *will* tell your father. Understood?"

She nodded without speaking.

The dad came into the kitchen with Tessa and said, "She looks pretty bad, doesn't she? Do you think she needs a doctor?"

"Oh, I think a good night's sleep and a couple of aspirin should do the job."

"It's hard caring for the girls with their mom being sick all the time."

Poor guy. They must really have him fooled.

I went into my bathroom and sat on the toilet seat lid. I put my head on the cool enamel of the sink. What did all this mean? Would it get easier? Why did I feel like I was everyone's consultant or guardian angel?

My mom knocked on the door, "Lena, are you all right? Gemma is still here. She wants to say good-bye."

"Be right out, Ma."

When I came out, Gemma said, "Do you think I'm blind? I saw Lugina go out to the truck with the flower guy."

We both started laughing. "What a little *Puttana* she is," I said.

Gemma asked, "Did Nana know what she did?"

"No. Nana called her a *Puttana* because of the way she was dressed and all her makeup. I made her pull the shoulders up on her blouse when she got here."

"This was a great bridal shower, Lena."

"Come on, Gemma, I'll pack up a bunch of food for you to take Memo. We'll use a big foil pan."

"Nana is way ahead of you. It's in my car already."

I was so glad I had taken off on Monday. It gave me a chance to put everything back where it belonged, vacuum, and get the fruit punch out of my rug. Yuck! Now I have to deal with old vomit.

My mom came in while I was cleaning the rug and said, "Oh, Lena, I didn't know you had a spill!"

"Yeah, that fruit punch was a killer. I'll use apple juice or pineapple juice next time."

"Oh, but it was so pretty with the sherbet floating in it."

The phone rang. I asked Mom to answer it.

"Hi! How are you, honey? Lena, it's Penny. Oh, yes. It was a beautiful shower. No. She's right here."

"Hi, Penny."

"Lena, I want to thank you again for the beautiful bridal shower.

No one could have done this like you. It was really spectacular."

"Oh, I had lots of help Penny. I couldn't have done this without my mom and Nana."

"Lena, I wanted to ask you if Paulie is still moving into the house behind your nana?"

"Yes, I think so."

"I have to get rid of so much stuff. I have small appliances and bedding and decorative stuff. Do you think he'll want it?"

"I'm going to say yes for him, Penny. I don't think he has anything from the old place he shared with Mona. He moved his stuff to her place and when she moved, she took it with her."

"Why don't you come over to see all my gifts? You were so busy yesterday, you didn't see everything. We'll go through the old stuff. Carlo can load whatever you want for Paulie into your trunk."

My gosh, Penny and Carlo had a lot of stuff to give away. He had bought a lot of new stuff when Penny moved in with him. He helped me load my trunk with everything and I brought it to Nana's house. Paulie helped me unload it into the spare bedroom in the little house. He was really happy with all the loot.

I got to the TV studio around noon on Tuesday. I always try to get in early after I have a day off. I want to have time to prepare for any last-minute changes. I picked up my script from the editors and went to my dressing room.

When someone knocked at my door, I thought for sure it was Red, He usually wanted to chat about Beth after I've had a day off. When I said, "Come in," I was surprised to see Johnny stick his head in.

"Hi, Lena! How are you?"

"I'm fine, Johnny. What's up?"

"I understand that this is the day that Mona's baby bump gets bigger."

"Yes. The script doesn't indicate how much further along she will be. That allows the writers to make her pregnant for as long as they want."

"Oh, that's pretty creative writing. Good idea."

"Johnny, since you have popped in to chat, there is something I want to ask you."

"I know what you're going to say, Lena."

"I don't think you do, Johnny. I saw you and Susan in the office the day of the party."

"Lena—"

"Wait, Johnny. I'm not finished. I've concluded that Susan's baby is yours and you are now available, since your wife has decided to divorce you. Have you told Mona?"

"Wow, I was just going to ask you to meet me for dinner so I could tell you that Mona and I have decided to split up."

"This seems to be a *real* soap opera. I think your life is a better scripted than the TV lines that we use. Exactly when did this happen, Johnny?"

"It was a mutual decision. Mona went to see your Grandma a few days ago. Paulie was there and they started talking about their past and the relationship that they had. One word led to another and they decided that it was worth trying again."

I sat without speaking for a few moments. I was thinking of the turmoil that accompanied the relationship between Paulie and Mona. I wondered how this new agreement really took place. It occurred to me that Mona might have sensed the connection between Johnny and Susan. Maybe she didn't want to be left high and dry. *Why didn't Mona say something to me about her and Paulie at the bridal shower?*

"Lena? You haven't said anything. Do you want to have dinner and discuss this?"

I think I really saw red. I looked at him and said, "Who do you think you are? You are just a used-up Romeo. You're so busy *banging the gong* with every woman who bats her eyes at you, that you don't even know when it's time to grab the brass ring and run like hell."

"I don't know what you mean, Lena."

"Let me explain, once and for all, since I seem to be everybody's psychiatrist or counselor! Susan is back. She had your baby. You should be happy that she still cares about you. When your divorce is final, you should ask her to marry you so that kid will have two parents."

"Lena, I care a lot about Susan, but I don't know if I want to spend the rest of my life with her."

I thought my head was going to explode. I walked up to him until our noses were almost touching. Well, they would have been touching, if he wasn't a foot taller than me. "Get out of my dressing room, Johnny. I don't think there will ever be any reason for us to be in a room alone again, ever."

I needed some chocolate, or a shot of Amaretto. I picked up my phone and used the pager button. "Greg, please come to Lena's dressing room," I said.

He knocked at the door and said, "Chocolate candy bars or ice cream."

I yelled through the door, "CHOCOLATE!"

He came back in five minutes with my choice of three. I took them all and sat down at the dressing table. As I chowed down a Three Musketeer bar Greg asked, "Do want to talk about it?"

"How did you know I wanted chocolate or ice cream?"

"You only paged me once before, and that's what you wanted."

"You're a pretty smart guy. You'll make someone very happy."

"It's not too late for you to have a second chance with me," he said.

"No, I've got a great guy right now. You missed your chance," I said as I unwrapped a Snickers Bar. "You'll need to find a nice Jewish girl who isn't nuts and doesn't work in television. Don't you go to Jewish Church or something?"

"It's called a *Synagogue*. I don't go very regularly."

"You must hang out somewhere where there are girls of your own persuasion."

"You make that sound a little hinky. I think I like it. We always had fun together. And the make-outs weren't too bad either."

We had to get ready. The show started in ten.

"I gotta go right after the show. I can't be late for dinner at my

Nana's house."

My dressing room phone started ringing.

"Lena, do you want me to get that?" Greg said.

"No! I'm going to see everyone tonight anyway."

The show went without a hitch. I couldn't wait to leave the studio!

I wanted to stop at Whitey's house on my way to Nana's. I hadn't seen him for a few days and boy-o-boy, did I have an itch for him to scratch.

I picked up a bottle of wine and some salami and cheese on my way to his house.

When I got there, he had the door open before I could get the key in the lock. After he kissed me, he said, "Your ma called."

"Did it sound important?"

"They are all frantic because they can't find Jojo."

"Geez, Jojo The Wonder Dog. He goes where he wants. Did she say if she called Nana? He might have found his way there. He goes all the time with Zio."

I called Ma. She was half nuts. "Oh, Lena, where could he be?"

"Ma, when was the last time you saw him?

"Zio brought some tomatoes and zucchini from our garden to Nana early this morning. He thought Jojo was outside. When he came out, he could find him. Stupido is his buddy. He's really upset.

"Ma, Stupido is everyone's buddy. That's how he came to live with you. It seems to me that he goes wherever he can find food. Are you sure he's not inside Nana's house somewhere? If she fed him, he's probably sleeping it off under one of the beds. We'll drive over and help you look."

Ma was going to call Nana and tell her to look around.

"Whitey, let's take a ride. They are really making themselves a little crazy over this missing mutt."

"I'll take my car back to the house. You can drive me home later."

"Okay. Lena, will we ever have an evening alone without a crisis?"

By this time it was dark outside. I called Nana to turn on the front and back outside lights, and asked her to tell Paulie to turn on his porch light, too.

We checked at Nana's house first. Nope, no dog there. I opened Nana's fridge and asked if I could take some leftovers.

"Bella! You hungry?"

"No, Nana. It's for Jojo."

She looked a little puzzled. I planned to use the leftovers for dog entrapment.

I piled two dishes high with roasted vegetables, chicken, and a little pasta. Whitey watched me longingly, since he hadn't even gotten to eat cheese and crackers.

I handed Whitey a dish and told him to put it on Paulie's porch. The other would go on Nana's porch.

"Knock on Paulie's door and tell him we're looking for Jojo when you bring the dish over."

When Paulie opened the door, Jojo came bouncing out with his head and his tail high. He ran right to the dish of food and ate like he was starving.

I looked at Paulie and rolled my eyes. "I'm not sure why they call him Stupido. You and the dog could compete for the title."

"Whaaat? I didn't do nuthin."

"Didn't you know everyone was looking for him?"

"No, I took out the garbage and he followed me inside. We had some pizza and took a nap."

"Dopey, everyone's been looking for him for hours. Zio has been frantic."

Whitey and Jojo were waiting for me at Nana's back door. We called Ma to tell her Jojo was taking a nap with Paulie and he was fine. Nana would keep him overnight. Zio was delighted.

Nana warmed up the rest of the leftovers and took out some bread. We ate everything she put out. Whitey was a happy man.

We got in Whitey's truck and he was pawing at me like a teenager. I told him, "My house is closer, babe."

"No way, Lena. I will race you to the front door at my place. There will be no breakfast wakeup call from your mom."

I had his key in my hand and I raced him up the front steps. I jumped into the bed with all my clothes on. He stripped off his clothes while running through the house.

That's when we heard his mother singing an Italian song in the kitchen.

Since I had the good luck to have left my clothes on, I jumped out of bed and ran into the kitchen. Whitey took this as a sign from heaven and pulled on some pants and a shirt. Then he slowly, quietly, walked through the house and gathered up the clothes he had thrown all over.

"Hello, Mama Bertuci!" I said.

"Oh, Lena! I thought I hear somebody come in the door. Where is-a Bianco?"

"He's getting something out of the car."

"I make some-a soup and I got some cheese and capacole. You eat now?"

Whitey came in and sat down like he hadn't eaten in a week. First he kissed his mama on both cheeks, asked about his dad, then pulled a chair out for his Mama.

I smiled at him and whispered, "I told you we should have made that other choice."

"You're right, babe. I owe you one."

He didn't have to say what he owed me, but he knew I was keeping score.

I visited with them for a little while. I said goodnight and Whitey walked me to the door.

It was pretty funny when we both realized that I got there in Whitey's truck.

"Ma, I gotta drive Lena home. I drove her here."

"Oh, it's okay, Bianco. I wait for you to come-a back."

I looked at Whitey and said, "Well, sport, I think my Mom's wake-up call might have been better!"

The next day's show was a huge success! Milt opened the new furniture store, just in time for Mona to shop for baby furniture with Johnny. The stage set was beautiful. The furniture was selected from Sears & Roebuck. We picked it all out and had it delivered to the station. Sears delivery personnel assembled the furniture on the set. We would, of course, give Sears credit on the screen: "Compliments of Sears & Roebuck," or some such thing.

Our cameramen are getting very sophisticated. They put footage together so polished and professional. We'll shoot some footage of Mona and Johnny in the furniture store. The rest will be televised live.

Johnny told me that he and Susan probably wouldn't get married. He said he doesn't love her like he should. I think he's a slimeball. He divorced his wife because he couldn't decide if he wanted to have a child with her. He has a child with Susan, and he doesn't want to marry her. What a pig. He still stands too close to me and makes remarks that I don't feel comfortable with. I guess I mean that he's too nice to me. The word I think I'm looking for is "smarmy," kind of syrupy and fake.

Beth is going to be released from the Spa this weekend. Red will go with her parents to bring her home. He said they'd stop for a nice lunch along the way. That will make it feel more like she's coming home from vacation, rather than an emotional assistance retreat.

Greg had a serious talk with Red regarding Beth's emotional problems. He explained to Red that if Beth stays on her meds, she does really well emotionally. Red understands that she needs someone to guide her constantly. Greg told me that Red has some deep feelings for her.

The producers will give Milt Beth's script in the next few days. They will give her several days to learn her lines. She should be ready for the show next Monday. She is invited to Penny's wedding, along with the rest of the cast. Red will be her escort, of course. He needs to be sure that she doesn't drink with all this medication that she's taking.

51

The people in the wedding party had gotten together several times to get to know each other. Lugina and Tessa were always invited with their father and mother. Their dad always came, but their mother stayed home, because of her health. The wedding was just two weeks away. My dress looked great. Velda, the seamstress, added silver blue ribbon at the waist. Penny's dress looked beautiful. She looked like a doll. She was very petite and thin. She looked like she belonged on the cake.

THE BRIDAL PARTY
    Lena –Maid of Honor and Whitey- Best Man
    Gemma and Memo
    Lugenia and Anthony
    Tessa and Bobby
    Mona and Paulie
    Rosie – Miniature Bride
    Tony – Miniature Groom

The rest of the bridesmaids would look like lampshades in those dresses, but they all seemed to be happy with them. Lugina kept pulling the shoulders off her dress. I was planning to keep an eye on her.

All the guys were going for a tuxedo fitting with Carlo on Friday.

They would have a dinner at the men's club, *Gli uomini del club Itaian una.* It should be a festive evening. They would have tons of food and wine. I was sure they would slip Bobby a fair share. I made Paulie promise to keep a close eye on him and not let him drink too much.

Whitey called me in my dressing room today. He thinks we should give Penny and Carlo a wedding gift. I can't imagine that we could buy them anything that they don't already have. He suggested a case of wine. Carlo had a temperature-controlled room installed in the basement of their house.

"Great idea, honey!"

He said that Paulie and Mona were having a meat package made up at Genero's butcher shop: steaks, roasts, and chops. Genero would freeze it all separately and package it in dry ice for Carlo. He would have it delivered the day before the wedding.

"You fellas thought of some great stuff. My head is so full of information, between the show and the wedding preparation, that I can barely remember who I am. After work, I'm going to stop in at my folks to see how they're doing. I've really ignored them this week."

"Lena, I'll come by around eight tonight, okay? That will give you some time to unwind after work."

———•《◎》•———

I got to Ma's and yelled "Hello" when I walked in the back door. Like so many old houses, you can see straight through the middle of the house from the back door. I could see a man bending over in the living room. He was scratching Jojo's belly. It only took me a second to realize that it was Gino. My heart began to race and my legs locked. My brain refused to accept what I saw.

At that same moment, my mom stepped in front of him. I saw Gino straighten up and they both begin to walk toward me.

I became so red hot angry that I could have choked him. I said,

"Wait! Stop. Both of you! Don't come any closer." My dad stepped out of the shadows somewhere in the living room.

Before anyone could speak, I said, "Get out! Don't say a word. Don't speak! Any of you! How dare you come here! How dare you even consider trying to see me? You can't step back into my life. That chapter is over. Move on. I have!"

I turned to walk out and Gino said, "Lena, wait! Please."

"Leave right now, Gino."

I walked to my house. I locked the door behind me and pulled down the shades. At that moment the phone rang. I knew it was Mom and would rather die than answer it.

It took me so long for my heart to begin to mend after Gino left me. I couldn't even pretend to see him without being angry.

I could hear Mom at my door. "Lena, honey, open the door."

"Mom, go away. I won't speak to him. Make him leave."

I locked myself in the master bedroom and went into the bathroom. I turned on the water to drown out the knocking and the ringing phone.

After a while she gave up trying to get through to me.

I laid down on my bed and cried quietly. Tears were running down my face into my ears.

I finally got up and looked in the mirror. I had black stripes from my eyes to my ears. I looked like a raccoon. I was calmer now. I took a glass from my china cabinet and poured a glass of my dad's homemade wine. I sat on the sofa and took deep breaths.

I was thinking about Whitey and what a great guy he was. I knew I loved him. It was a different kind of love than I had with Gino. He was my first love. My emotions were open and passionate. My feelings were raw and real. We were good together. If Gino really loved me, he couldn't have left me so easily. He could have fought for me, but he didn't. He could have tried to plead with the families in the name of love. He could have talked to the girl in Italy to see if she might want to marry someone else. But he left me instead, without a fight.

Then I found a man who nearly died for me. When I nearly lost him, I realized how much we belonged together.

I decided to have another glass of wine.

I heard my mom at the door, "Lena, honey, he's gone. Can I come in?"

I opened the door. "Why didn't you use your key?"

"I was afraid you were too angry at me. I didn't know he was coming, Lena."

"You shouldn't have let him in, Ma."

She was quiet for a few moments. She finally said, "Lena, he still loves you. He thought you might still love him. The girl he married, he doesn't love her. He knows she loves someone else."

"Ma, It's nearly 1968! He didn't fight for me. He left like a thief in the night. My love for him is dead. I only feel anger now. There is a fine line between love and hate."

"Lena, I'm sorry. I never thought you would react like that. I've never seen you so angry."

"What did you think I would do, Ma? Shake his hand and say, "Hi honey. Glad to see you!"

"I don't know what I thought you would do. We all cared about him. He was almost family."

"When Gino left me, I cried every night for weeks. That's why Nana didn't have any solid ice in her freezer. I put ice on my eyes every morning so I could step in front of the cameras."

Ma put her arms around me and said, "You are so strong, Lena."

I got another glass out of the cabinet and poured us both a glass of wine.

We sat side by side on the sofa, with my head on her shoulder for a long time. She finally said, "Do you feel like eating?"

"No, Ma, I'm not hungry."

A knock at the door signaled Whitey's arrival. When I opened the door, he took one look at me and said, "Is this a bad time?"

"No, Whitey. It's perfect timing."

Ma kissed my cheek and left.

"What is it, Lena? Did you and your ma have a fight?"

He wrapped his arms around me before I could answer.

At first I didn't want to tell him about Gino's visit. Then I decided he needed to know. I'm not sure how Whitey felt, but I could see all the mixed emotions flash across his face.

He smiled at me and said, "Now that you're calmed down, why don't we talk about this."

"Whitey, I know how I feel about you. Seeing Gino only brought back bad feelings: hurt, anger, and betrayal. I thought that if I ever saw him again, my heart would sing. Instead the only thing I felt like was a heart attack from anger, not burning love."

Whitey smiled a sad smile. "You know, they will probably be at Carlo and Penny's wedding next week."

I stamped my foot and said, "Oh, Shit!"

He laughed out loud. "You did that like a ten-year-old kid. Do it again, Lena."

He made me smile. He always made me feel better. I think he can see into my soul.

"Babe, you need to have something to eat. You've had too much wine and not enough food. Do you want to go out?"

"No. I don't feel like redoing my makeup."

"Yeah, you do look like a cat burglar or a bandit."

"Geez! I still have eye makeup all over my face?"

"Yup, you do. Go wash your face. Then pull up a chair and watch the master at work. I'm going to fix us some steak and eggs. Got any hot sauce?"

"Yes. Two kinds"

58

had to accept the fact that Gino and his wife were going to be around for a few weeks. I was bound to see him somewhere besides the wedding. I wouldn't let him invade my life or my thoughts. I was going to be very busy all that week. I could handle this. I had been strong and independent. This was not the first time I'd been on autopilot. Whitey was my future. We would come face-to-face at the wedding next Saturday.

We would pick up our dresses Tuesday evening. Penny had her dress and it was finally perfect. We needed to get stockings and a garter belt. She took her mom with her to get all the other undergarments. She said Glenny was as nutty as usual. Penny was calling this the "Wedding of the Century." She was probably right.

She was still a little nervous about being the center of attention. I told her to pretend that she was a princess, and this was her coronation.

She told me, "Lena, I wish I had your confidence."

"Carlo loves you, so his entire family will love you too. Most of them will go back to Hoboken or Cincinnati, or wherever they came from. All they will say is, 'What a lucky man that Carlo is. What a beautiful little girl he married.' "

Penny threw her arms around me and squeezed me. "If I could have a sister, I'd want her to be you, Lena."

Mama and I picked up the table decorations from Jaclyn Corona. She was decorating the hall in the wedding colors—blue, silver and white—the night before the wedding. The rehearsal dinner was at the same hall as the wedding, but in a different room.

Carlo called me the night of the rehearsal, "Lena, Penny needs to talk to you. Here honey, it's Lena."

"Oh, Lena," she whispered. "I feel sick. I don't think I can walk down that aisle twice."

St. Michael's Church has a 100-foot aisle. I knew Penny would realize she would have to do it the night of the rehearsal.

"Let's see what Father Joe says when we get there. Maybe you won't have to. Maybe you can step in from the side altar. We'll get there early and speak to him."

"Okay, okay. That's really a good idea. Let's do that."

I breathed a sigh of relief. Father Joe expects every bride to walk that 100-foot aisle, no exceptions.

I fell asleep that night thinking about Whitey. I missed having his arms around me. When I woke up in the morning, he was the first thing that popped into my head. I had no control of my thoughts anymore. I had let Whitey into my life. Did I have to let him move into my house? He was taking over my thoughts and built my house. I had to talk about this with my mom. She always had perfect understanding about what was going on in my head.

———※◦《◑》◦※———

The morning of the wedding was chaos. I guess they always turn out that way. I'd never had one of my own, yet.

Penny was getting dressed at my house. She was really a wreck. We spent the evening before getting all her stuff together and loading it into my car. I insisted that she spend the night before at my house. The groomsmen were all going to be drinking with Carlo at her house.

Mona was at my ma's next door with the rest of the bridal party. She was in charge of getting the rest of the girls organized. They took over my old bedroom and Bobby's room.

Niko was sending limos to Whitey's house early in the day so the guys could decorate them. Two limos were picking up the bridal party at my house to go to the church.

Everything was planned to the smallest detail. What could go wrong? PLENTY!

Penny's mom and stepdad both showed up drunk as skunks. Both had to be sobered up before they could get dressed. I was helping Glenny, Penny's mom. Whitey was trying to get her stepdad in the shower at Carlo's house.

He thought it was pretty funny. I was having a nervous breakdown at my house.

I had lunch catered to my house and to Whitey's place. I knew there would be a lot of drinking and I didn't want anyone getting sick. Large quantities of black coffee were administered to Penny's mom and stepdad.

Penny and I were finally ready and waiting for the limo. We were getting frantic, but I pretended I was calm. *BUT I WASN'T!* We were already twenty minutes late.

I called the limo service. They told me that both limos had been dispatched. Mona called me from Ma's next door. Three limos had been sent to Whitey's house. I thought there were only two? He was sending two to my house at this moment. All the guys were on their way to church in the other limo.

Stay calm, Lena. Don't let Penny see that you're upset, I thought. Penny already looked like she was going to cry.

"Here it is, Hon! The limo is here!" Thank God and St. Michael. The driver hopped out just as Penny and I stepped outside.

"Wow! What a beautiful bride!" He knew what to say to a nervous bride.

The bridesmaids came out of Ma's house and piled into the second limo. We were finally on our way to the church. We went in through the side entrance to the bride's room. We showed Penny to the inside door where Dino, her stepdad, was waiting for her. When the wedding march began, he took her arm and walked her toward the huge double doors. Glenny was already seated with my mom and dad on the bride's side of the church

The bridesmaids lined up perfectly behind them.

I think I heard St. Michael breathe a sigh of relief where he stood on a cloud above the altar. It was the most beautiful ceremony I have ever seen.

I never saw Gino at the back of the church with his new bride. We exited the church to the applause of family and friends as they lined the sidewalk. Rice rained down on the beautiful couple.

The wedding party went back inside for photos in front of the altar. St. Michaels is such a beautiful church; most bridal parties want those memorable photos.

The guests went ahead to the banquet hall. The splendor that greeted them there was breathtaking. The blue, white, and silver theme was just short of gaudy. Well, maybe it was just a little gaudy. But what the heck, why not?

Each place setting had a silver pen and pencil set imported from Italy. It was tied to a light blue pouch filled with imported chocolates. The tags attached to the bags had the couple's name engraved with the wedding date.

The bridal party entered in couples. The names were announced by the host and owner of the banquet hall.

The grandest entrance, of course, was the announcement of "Mr. and Mrs. Carlo Bazzoli." Everyone was on their feet applauding. It was so exciting that my heart was pounding. The hall looked like a fairyland. Yards of blue, silver, and white netting were strung everywhere. Silver and blue stars were suspended from the ceiling. Jaclyn Corona had outdone herself.

Whitey only let go of my hand to applaud. I think he was afraid that I would faint or something. We were finally seated at the bridal table. That's when I looked around the banquet hall. Holy cow! There were a lot more than 150 people. I think it was closer to 250. There were at least twenty five tables of ten people each. I do believe that Niko told a white lie about the number of people he invited.

Waiters were walking around with trays of appetizers as soon as everyone was seated. I said my own private prayer of thanks that we had gotten through the ceremony. I was scanning the crowd, looking for my mom and dad, checking out all the beautifully dressed people.

We were getting ready to toast the bride and groom. I turned toward them. I recognized Gino's profile as soon as he turned his head. He sat at a table with friends of Niko Bazzoli. I knew that his wife was next to him. My ears started ringing.

"Lena, look at me," Whitey said. "You're shaking."

I turned toward him and faked a smile. "Babe, your face is white as a ghost. Take a sip of wine. I know you see Gino. You're bound to react this way. I'm here for you, Lena. I'll always be here for you."

"Whitey, I feel sick. What do I do?" He leaned over and gave me a quick kiss. I glanced at my mom. She saw Gino too. She gave me a nervous smile.

I never heard Whitey's best man's speech because the ringing was still in my ears. I applauded when everyone else applauded.

Whitey was doing his best to make me laugh. He finally saw a fat lady in a pink dress get up and head toward the rest room.

He said, "I don't think those shoes were intended to hold that unbalanced load. Just then the spiked heel snapped off her left shoe. We both shook with silent laughter. I knew I would be all right for the rest of the evening.

Dinner included steak with mushrooms and onions, chicken Marsala, and Giambotta. There were too many side dishes to keep track of. Waiters kept changing the dishes to make room for more. There was more bread and rolls than I have ever seen. It was stacked in pyramids on trays and in baskets on each table.

During dinner an old guy played the concertina. I could see a band setting up in the back of the hall.

I happened to glance over at Lugina. She was looking a little disheveled. The fabric flower on the shoulder of her dress kept flopping over. None of the groomsmen were missing, so I guessed they were safe from her right now. I looked across the bridal table and everyone appeared to be having a great time. Lugina's younger sister Tessa was seated next to my brother Bobby. He was flirting like a pro. What a little stud. I was glad to see that Tessa didn't have any wine in her glass, but she was enjoying herself anyway.

A little while later, I noticed Lugina missing from the table. Oh well, it was really not my problem. I think some young waiter might be missing this course. Lucky him. I glanced around and found her dad. I could tell he had his hands full. The mama looked sickly, but she was obviously drinking too much.

When I spotted Lugina at her place at the table later, part of the fluffy bun on the back of her head was hanging down. It looked like she tried to pin part of it up, and now she looked like a unicorn. I poked Whitey to look at her. He said, "Her dress is a mess. Didn't it have a flower on the shoulder?"

"Yes, I think I see it in her dinner plate."

Italians take a long time to eat. The dishes kept coming. Every occasion is about how much food is on the table. I think it's a throwback to the Romans. We were all waiting for the music to start.

Penny motioned for me to follow her. I knew she was going to need help in the ladies room with all her ruffles and stuff. It was definitely a two-person job. What an ordeal. All the snaps and unfastening the hooks was quite a project .We were trying to keep from swearing at the dress or keeping it from dipping into the toilet bowl. We had to touch up our makeup after we assembled her dress back together.

We were still laughing when we were heading back to our table, hoping the music was going to start soon.

I heard someone say my name. I knew it was Gino. The sound of his voice, the way he said my name, sent shivers down my spine. "Don't leave me alone, Penny."

I turned and smiled sweetly. He told Penny how beautiful she looked. His wife was at his side. He introduced me.

"This is my wife, Adriana. This is my friend, Lena."

"How do you do, Adriana? It's so nice to meet you." I thought to myself, *Frankly, I don't give a darned how you're doing. I'd like to see you melt like the bad witch in the Wizard of Oz. He's got a lotta nerve calling me his friend.*

She smiled, tilted her head like a puppy, and said, "I'm pleased to meet you too, Lena," in nearly perfect English.

I looked at her closely. She was pretty, but not as pretty as me. She had slightly crooked teeth, but nice eyes. She was a little too thin and her shoulders sagged. I hoped she was entertaining in the sack. I knew he would never again experience what we had together. His eyes were sad. All this took place in less than a minute.

"It was so nice to meet you. You'll have to excuse us. The bride and I have to return to our guests."

They nodded and smiled.

"You can breathe now, Lena. You did great."

When we got back to our table, Carlo was waiting for Penny. His dad wanted to see them in the outer vestibule. We knew he was going to present them with a month-long trip to Italy as a wedding gift.

The crowd was standing around waiting for the music to start and Whitey was standing with my parents.

He said, "You okay, babe?"

"I couldn't be better, Whitey."

The band was announcing the bride and groom's first dance. She had asked them to skip the father/daughter dance. They looked so in love. I was all choked up. Whitey put his arm around me and smiled. Penny's new father-in-law, Niko, cut in and danced with Penny. That was really sweet, since she didn't have a real dad in the picture. I was really surprised and touched when her stepdad, Dino, stepped in to dance with her. Carlo had coaxed his grandma onto the dance floor. It was really cute, since she came about up to his elbow. He led grandma back to the table and asked Glenny to dance. He had to wait for her to put her shoes back on.

When everyone was invited to dance, Whitey pulled me into his arms. He always buried his nose in my hair. He whispered, "Umm, babe, your hair smells great but it feels like plastic. I think I hurt my nose."

"I know! They did that at the beauty shop. I guess they wanted to make sure it lasted all day and all night."

"Oh, what about later tonight. I'll bet I can mess it up pretty quick."

I said, "Your place or mine?"

"You name it, Beautiful."

I felt a tap on my shoulder. It was my folks. Mom wanted to dance with Whitey. Dad always tries to get a dance in before the fast music starts. Then he feels his obligation is filled.

When the fast dance music started, all the friends who went to

The Club together were out on the floor dancing the night away. All the high-heeled shoes were kicked off at the edge of the dance floor. Glenny, Penny's mom, had lost her shoes once again, but she didn't seem to care.

I felt someone's arms circle around my waist. First I thought it was Whitey. I glanced around and was a little surprised to see it was Nick Piccolo. He was really loaded.

"Lena, I sure miss you. I never stopped caring about you."

"That's pretty funny, Nick, since you have been an alley cat all your life."

"I've changed, Lena; I really would like another chance. I've grown up a lot."

"Oh stop it, Nick. You're drunk."

He wandered off the dance floor looking sad and sorry.

The bride was going to toss her bouquet. All the single ladies lined up in the front of the stage. I made sure that I was at the back of that line. I sure didn't want to be anywhere near the next to be married.

The crowd shouted, ONE! TWO! THREE! Penny tossed the bouquet and the girls scrambled to catch it. Lugina's head popped up in the middle of the tangle of arms and legs. She stretched out her arm like the Statue of Liberty. She had the bouquet! Thank goodness, life could go on.

Next came the garter toss. Penny gave Carlo a separate garter so he wouldn't attempt to remove hers on the dance floor.

All the single guys crowded to the front of the stage. My brother Bobby hung back. He was a little too shy and a little too young. On the count of three, Carlo tossed that garter. It hit Bobby right in the face and he put his hand up just as it fell. He put it on his arm like a pro. He looked so proud of himself!

Typically, the bride and groom try to sneak out early. Penny and Carlo were having such a good time that they stayed until the end of the celebration.

Whitey and I snuck out the side entrance and headed for my house. He insisted on parking his truck on the side of the house so he wouldn't embarrass me. My parents could see if they looked to the left when they pulled into their driveway. He wanted to be as respectful as possible.

We started to walk toward my front door and saw a form at the end of the walk.

Whitey said, "What the heck is that?"

I started to walk closer and he stopped me. "Wait, someone is lying there."

He turned and said, "It's that guy Nick." Whitey leaned over and shook him. "I can't wake him. He's really drunk."

"We have to get him out of here. I'm not bringing him inside."

"We can put him in the truck and take him to his house. You do know where he lives, right?"

"Yes, smart ass. I know where he lives."

Whitey spread a tarp in the truck bed. I hiked up my dress and took his feet. Whitey got him under the arms. We lifted him in the back of the truck and scooched him onto the tarp and slid him into the truck bed. Whitey slammed the hatch.

"Holy cow, he never even woke up. Whitey, we need to get out of these clothes."

We ducked inside and pulled on some old clothes. I had one of my dad's old sweatshirts and a pair of slacks.

Whitey tried to get amorous when I stripped down to my fancy undies from the bridesmaids collection. "Couldn't we leave him in the truck for a little while," he said.

"No! I don't want him to wake up here."

"True! I wouldn't like that, either."

When we got outside, Nick was sitting straight up in the truck bed looking around like a long neck goose. Just as we got closer he laid back down with a loud "thunk" when his head hit the truck bed.

"Oh, shit, Lena, do you think he got hurt?"

"We'll find out when we get him to his house."

When we drove away we noticed that the lights were on at my mom and dad's house.

"I wonder how much of that they heard and saw."

"I'm sure we'll hear about it later."

When we got Nick to his house, I hadn't considered that I didn't have a key. He lived in his Mom's basement.

Whitey said, "I can get him in. Don't worry. Let's bring him around the back."

We wrapped him in the tarp and carried him like a dead body and set him by the back door. Whitey tried the door and the lock held firm.

"Whitey, can't we leave him here wrapped in the tarp? His Mom would probably find him in the morning."

"Lena, I'm not that heartless."

"Well, we would leave him wrapped up in the tarp so he won't get cold."

Whitey was trying the window to the side of the door. Locked.

He went to the truck and came back with a little tool.

"It's a glass cutter," he said. He carefully cut a piece of glass near the lock. He stuck two fingers in, unlocked the window and crawled in and unlocked the back door. By this time, I was laughing pretty hard. I nearly wet my pants. I had my hand over my mouth to keep from waking Nick.

"How drunk is this guy that he isn't awake yet?"

I told Whitey, "As I recall, he can pass out for a long time."

We carried him inside and put him on the sofa. Whitey rolled up the tarp and said, "No evidence."

"What about the missing chunk of glass in his window?"

"No problem." He went to the truck and got a tube of something.

"What's that?"

"Clear silicone sealer."

He fixed the window so neat you would have to look really hard to see the cut marks. "Someday, if he ever washes his window, he'll wonder how he never noticed the window had been patched."

We laughed all the way home. I headed for the shower to get the hairspray out of my hair. I knew it would take more than one shampooing.

Whitey showered in the guest bathroom.

By the time I came out of the shower he was sound asleep. I watched him lying shirtless, in his BVD's. I looked at the deep scar in the center of his chest as it moved slow and steady while he slept. I thought about how lucky he was to survive the shooting, and how lucky I was to love this man.

I curled up next to him, pulled the covers up over us, and fell into a sound sleep.

The next day, I was at Ma's. She said, "Did you and Whitey have a fight?"

"No, Ma. Why do you ask?"

"Well, I saw his truck when we got home, then it was gone for a while, then it was back later."

Geez, my mom missed the part about us hauling a body into the truck. I'm really surprised.

"I had a taste for ice cream. Whitey went out to get me some."

"Oh, that was sweet. What did he get?"

"Chocolate Ripple."

"Did he get a pint or a half gallon?"

"He got a pint, Mom. I ate a lot at the wedding."

"Yes, we all did."

Thank goodness, the phone rang. "It's for you, honey. It's Penny."

"Hi! How are the bride and groom doing?"

"Lena, can you come over and help me pack? I don't have any idea what to bring. Carlo says I can buy whatever I need in Italy, but I have to bring some outfits with. I've never traveled. I don't know what to do,"

"You need to take a deep breath. When do you leave?"

"Tuesday morning."

"I'll come over later today. We'll get it done. I can come after work tomorrow too, if you need me."

When I got there, it looked like her closet had exploded. I shook my head.

"I'll show you how I pack, Penny."

I started by laying out matching outfits. Then she got the idea.

"Now put changeable matching tops on top of those outfits. Then put the shoes that you're going to wear with those outfits on the floor in front of them. Next put the jewelry in the shoes that match each outfit."

"Wow, you make it look so easy!"

"When you have everything together, you can roll each item in tissue paper and start tucking it in your suitcases. Put the shoes around the edges to protect any breakable stuff."

"You are brilliant! Carlo! Honey, could you please go to the store and get us some tissue paper?"

He came into the bedroom and said, "What's tissue paper?"

"That's the white stuff inside gift boxes."

"Oh, I didn't know you could buy that. Penny, where am I going for that?"

"Go to Woolworth's or the drug store. Be sure to get white only."

"Okay, honey."

Now that I had got Penny and Carlo and the right track, I went to Ma's for dinner.

She asked what I was doing at Penny's. When I told her that I left them rolling their clothes in tissue paper, she really laughed.

I called her late Monday to say good-bye. They told me they had two suitcases each. They would probably buy two more in Italy to bring back all the stuff they buy.

It occurred to me when I was washing my hair that night that I'd better get to work early for the next month, since I'd have to do my own hair and makeup. I was really spoiled now.

59

I was in the process of doing my makeup in my dressing room when someone knocked at my door. It was Red/Milt. I had to pick a name and stick with it. I think he prefers 'Red.'

"What's going on, Red. What do you need?"

I just wanted to tell you that Beth loves the script. We went over it several times yesterday and again this morning. I think she's doing really well.

"Red, her lines should be pretty easy. The scene takes place in the main dining hall of the bed and breakfast. When the couple asks about buying baby furniture in the area, she can talk about the new stuff in the dining room."

"Lena, thanks for being so patient with her. She really wants to do well, and she's been taking her meds."

"Red, keep in mind that I have no controlling voice in her part in the show. I have some input with Frank Latmen, but he's the one who she needs to please in the end."

"I know, Lena, but she really needs your approval."

"Okay, Red. When she gets here today, tell her to stop by my dressing room and I'll give her a pep talk."

"Oh, thanks! That would be great!"

After Red left, I sat and looked at myself in the mirror.

I don't look like a saint. I don't have a degree in psychology. I'm not "smarter than the average bear." So, why does everyone think I make all the decisions around here?

My phone rang. It was Greg. "You busy?"

"I've got some time. Come down to my dressing room."

He knocked and opened the door. "Gee, Greg, you did that just like Frank."

"What?"

"You walked in after you knocked."

"You knew I was coming, right?"

"Okay, you win."

I waited for him to tell me what he wanted.

He asked, "What's up?"

"You called *me*, Greg."

"Oh, yea. Have you talked to Beth?"

I rolled my eyes. Beth and her men! She has them all wrapped around her finger. I can't help but wonder if she's as fragile as she appears, or it's a bit of an act.

"Not yet. Red just left. He's sure that Beth is doing great and knows the script."

"Lena, I got a copy of the script too. I'm thinking that it's not good for her. There isn't enough interaction for her. She's going to want to say more."

I pulled out my copy:

Joanna & Lance come into the B and B restaurant/dining area. Joanna looks upset.

Lance looks as if he's trying to be patient.

Beth/Monica: Hesitates when she approaches her guests. The girl is obviously pregnant. Monica doesn't want to step into an awkward situation.

Beth/Monica: Hello, my name is Monica; can I help you select something from our complimentary menu?

Lance/Johnny: We're not ready.

Joanna: Yes, I would like some orange juice.

Beth/Monica: At this point, Beth smiles at the couple, trying to diffuse the situation.

"Greg, the writers are trying to ease her back into the show slowly. She has more lines when I come in to see the new furniture."

"Whatever you say, Lena."

"Greg, it's not what I say. It's the way the writers rolled it out. Call Latmen. Let's ask him how he wants it to fly."

Latmen knocked and entered, as usual. "What's up, kids?"

"Frank, Greg is concerned that Beth doesn't have enough lines in the opening scene today. Read her bit and tell us what you think."

He read it and said, "So, I don't get it. What's the problem?"

Greg looked nervous and said, "Don't you think she's going to improvise if she doesn't have enough to say?"

"Look Greg, we protect her as much as we can. If she wants to improvise, that's what she'll do, as long as she stays in the story line. Now let's get ready. It's almost show time!"

"FIVE MINUTES! Places, Please!"

We all walked on set to our assigned spots. I was behind the desk at the B and B. My new assistant, Pattie, was at the computer. She and I were working on a new billing schedule for the clients.

Beth entered. "Good Morning Ladies"

"Hi Monica," I said. "Are you hostess this morning?"

She gave me a blank stare. I improvised quickly.

"Well, we have some early risers at the first table."

Again, Beth gave another extended stare. She was looking so blank, I kicked into autopilot.

Again, I took her by the arm and said, "Monica, let's go into the dining room together. I want to see the new furniture."

FINALLY! It looked like a light went on in her eyes.

"Good Morning! My name is Monica. Can I get you something from our complimentary breakfast menu?"

The remainder of the scene was acceptable. Beth rambled on about the new furniture until the script turned to the scene with Lance and Joanna discussing the new baby's arrival. They were reconciling their marriage and welcoming their baby.

In the real world, Johnny and Mona broke up, but play the part of this swell married couple. Mona's baby bump was a fake, and Johnny and his real wife were getting a divorce. Susan and Johnny have a baby together, but don't plan on getting married. Susan is being introduced back into the show as my sister.

We aren't sure yet what kind of life crisis she's going to have.

Meanwhile, back in my world I pulled into my driveway to find Whitey and my dad loading stuff into the back of Whitey's truck. Since my brother Bobby is still too young to leave, I wondered out loud what they were loading.

"We're taking some of Zio's belongings to Nana's house," Dad said.

"Why, Dad? Are you throwing him out?"

"He spends most of his time there anyway. He asked if we could move some of his personal stuff."

"Dad, this is more than some of his stuff. You have a dresser and boxes and suitcases."

I thought this would eventually happen. I've even joked about the possibility of Nana becoming my dad's Zia. But this is *my* Nana. She belongs in her house alone—mostly in the kitchen with her hair in a little twisty bun and an apron with a splash of pasta sauce on the front. I feel like a little kid. I am the first grandchild. Will I be able to let myself in and sleep in the spare room? Can I walk around in my shortie pajamas? No, probably not. My dad was staring at me like I was crazy.

Nana DeLuca

"What's wrong, baby?"

"He's gonna live there?"

Whitey laughed out loud. "Lena, don't tell me you're embarrassed for your Nana?"

"I think I am. I don't like it."

"Would you feel better if I told you he wants his stuff in the spare room?"

I thought about that for a couple of seconds. *Where would I sleep when I went there? Oh, yeah, I have a house now.*

"To answer your question, yes, I would."

I turned and went up the back steps into Ma's kitchen.

When she saw my face she said, "What's the matter?"

"When did Zio decide to live with Nana?"

"Lena, they are adults. Nana is only sixty-five years old. She could live another twenty-five years or more. Why should she be alone? Why should Zio be alone?"

"I guess I never thought of it this way. Do you think they will get married?"

"They probably will get married, because Nana won't want a man living in her house *"in sin."* At the same time, she's not going to want a big deal made out of it. Father Joe said they can get married at the side altar. He will make it a simple ceremony."

"What the heck? Sounds like this has been a plan for a while."

"Zio has talked to us about marrying Nana. He felt like he should ask for her hand in marriage. He figured we were the most likely people for him to talk to him about it."

"Right?"

"That's right. It's just going to be us, the immediate family. I'm going to make beef and sausage and we'll keep it small."

"Okay, when do we start planning this?"

"We go to the church Saturday at two."

"WHAT!?"

"Yup, no planning. No fanfare. They made the decision. They also decided that they each keep their own money. They had a lawyer draw up papers. Zio's money goes to us when he dies, Nana's money goes to everyone on her side of the family. But neither of them gets the other's money."

I guess I was quiet for quite a while. I was thinking about how simple this was for them. After Penny and Carlo's wedding, this was like going to a tea party.

"Ma, can I get Nana flowers?"

"Yes, and you can get Zio a flower for his button hole too. I can use help in the kitchen fixing the food."

"So, are they going on a honeymoon?"

"No, smarty pants. Maybe they will take a train to Milwaukee in the summer to the State Fair."

"Oh, I thought maybe they could go to Italy and visit both families."

"They want 'simple,' remember?"

I went to my house and got ready for bed. As I lay in bed, I tossed and turned. I thought about this "simple" wedding. Nana has nine kids. *All together I think she has thirteen grandkids. Each of her kids is married, except for Paulie. He'll still bring a guest, Mona, if they are still speaking. Nana will want her lady friends to come with their husbands. That's Dona Natalie, Dona Maria, and a couple of more old friends. What about the Generos?*

I got out of bed and dialed Mom. "What's wrong, Lena?"

"Do you know how many brothers and sisters you have?"

"I know exactly how many I have."

"Did you make a list?"

"I haven't written it down."

She was quiet for a few moments. I think she was calculating on paper.

"Oh, that could add up to a lot of people."

"Yes, I made a mental list. I'm coming up with close to fifty."

"Oh, honey, that can't be right."

"Ma, are you going to invite all Nana's children to the wedding?"

"Of course. They would all have to come."

"How about all the grandchildren?"

"Yes, grandchildren too, Lena."

"Well, that's around thirty right there, without family friends."

"What have I gotten my self into?"

"You're going to have to call a caterer. And where are you having this little wedding party?"

"I was going to have it here at the house. Between the upstairs and downstairs."

"Mom, you can't do this by yourself. You'll need to rent a hall, or maybe a tent in the yard between our houses. We could have Riggio do it. Ma, we'll have the whole thing catered. It will be my wedding gift to Nana and Zio."

"No, Lena, that would cost too much money."

"Mom, I have the money. Let me do this. By the way, do I have to call him Papa? No, never mind. I'm calling him Zio."

"I'm sure that's fine, Lena."

I asked Ma if she wanted to make the arrangements for the catering.

"Who should I call, Lena?"

"You decide, Mom. I'm sure whatever you choose will be fine."

I thought I would step away from that decision. I'm trying to be less controlling.

"Oh, I can do it. Maybe I'll call that new place on Cleveland off North Avenue. Or, maybe I'll just call Reggio. We're familiar with his food and he knows what we expect."

"Good, Mom! Go with it. Tomorrow I'll start calling about the tent and the tables and chairs."

While I thought we had everything under control, no one bothered to ask Nana.

The following evening after work, Mom and Nana came over.

"We didn't see Whitey's truck, so I thought I would be okay to come over without calling first."

"Sure, that's just fine." I leaned over to kiss Nana. She turned her cheek away, so I could tell something was very wrong.

"Nana, what's the matter?"

She went off like a little machine gun. "Whadda you think you doin'? I tell you no party. So you make a party anyway. I tell you what I do. I get married to Peppino and you have a party without me or the husband."

"Oh, Nana, don't be upset!"

But she wasn't done yet!

"You no the boss!" She was pointing her sharp little finger at me.

"And you no the boss, either!" Pointing at Ma.

"I am a grown up woman, not a young girl. I don't want a party for my wedding, and that's-a that!"

Well, I guess we got told without a doubt that there would be no party on Saturday. Ma was trying not to smile. I got busy and made some coffee. I wanted to stay out of the line of fire.

There was another knock at the door. It was Zio. He took one look at Nana and said, "What's a matta you?"

Nana started rattling off in Italian, telling him that we were *ficcanasos,* or busy bodies. We should mind our own business and no party was going to take place. "*Fineto!*" She brushed her hands together.

"Nana, you made your point and we got it. Please sit down. Have some coffee." I put out some cookies and made everyone have some coffee.

Zio left with Nana to walk her home.

Ma said, "Well, are we going to skip the party?"

"No, we'll just do it the weekend after the wedding."

"Ha! Lena, you and I definitely think alike! I'll call Riggio in the morning."

60

The day before the church wedding, we took Nana to get her hair done. It's always been long and straight. She always wears it up. Her hair color is almost black with some grey streaks in it. I really wanted her to have it cut, but she wanted no part of that.

I told her she had *"dead ends."* That scared her a little, since she didn't want anything dead on her person, so she agreed to a trim. I wanted her to have it cut and curled. She said, "No, just fix it up a little bit."

The beautician said, "We're going to put a little rinse in it to make it shine."

Mom and I grabbed some magazines and went to the outer waiting area.

Before too long we heard Nana yelling, *"Cosa hai fatto? Sembro un pagliaccio!"*

I jumped up and ran to the back, with Ma right behind me. Nana was yelling that she looked like a clown.

"Oh, shit," I said. They had made her hair blue. All the white streaks were blue streaks. She looked like she was from Mars. "Are you going to be able to get that out?"

The owner looked like she was going to cry. "Hurry!" she said, "Don't let that color set," She told the girl, "Start shampooing!"

When they got done, it was more silver than blue, and I guess that looked okay. They fixed it with finger waves in the front and a cluster of curls in the back where her bun usually sat. She said it looked too fancy, but she seemed happy. So we got the heck out of there while she was smiling.

Now we were on our way to the store where all the Italian old ladies shop. The trick here was to get her into a dress that was anything but black.

Nana went directly to the rack with the black dresses. Mom and I headed to the rack that had beige, blue, and white dresses.

The saleslady asked Nana, "What's the occasion?"

"Mio matrimonio. I get married."

The saleslady made her eyes look like an owl, "Well, Dona DeLuca, who is the lucky man?"

She looked the lady in the eye and said, "I'm-a marry Giuseppe Delatora"

For some reason, when I heard her say Delatora, my heart skipped a beat. Of course she would be *Rosina Delatora* now.

"Ooh," the lady said. "Peppino is a very handsome man!"

Nana's face flushed and she looked proud. "Yes, I think-a so too."

Ma and I smiled and looked proud too.

"Nana, try these two dresses on." One was light blue and the other was a silver gray color.

The silver dress was beautiful with her hair. She liked it too. It had a big collar and rhinestone buttons down the front. I took Nana over to the case in front of the store. They had a small selection of jewelry. She picked out matching earrings and a necklace. Everything looked so nice together. Ma and I stepped back and let her decide on the pieces herself.

Nana smiled and said, "I think Peppino will like these."

We agreed and I wrote the check. Nana didn't even try to stop me.

Now we had to buy shoes. She wanted to go home and fix us all some dinner. We persuaded her into getting shoes first, and agreed to go to Riggio's afterward.

She looked at shoes that were so ugly, I nearly cried. They looked like they should come with a walker or a cane. "Nana, you are too young to wear these shoes! Look at the ones with the little strap in the back."

She wanted the pair that had a strap across the front and the back. We all agreed on those. They had rhinestone shoe clips that were perfect. Then she could take them off and wear the shoes any time.

Now we were all tired and hungry. When we got to Riggio's I went to the kitchen to remind him not to mention the party next weekend.

After we got our food, he came over to congratulate Nana.

"Dona DeLuca, *bona fortuna!* I wish you all the best in your new marriage! I guess I'll have to call you Dona Delatora from now on."

First Nana looked puzzled, then she said, "Oh, yeah. Sure, you gotta do that!"

Riggio sent over a bottle of wine and some cannolis. We all ate and drank and stuffed ourselves full. Finally, Nana said, *"Andiamo.* Let's go!" She'd had enough excitement for one day.

My dad and Uncle Johnny took Zio out for a new suit. So simple to be a man.

That night we wrapped Nana's hair in a hairnet so it would look fresh in the morning. We told her that we would come back to help her dress for church. Auntie Lilly and Auntie Virg would want to come too.

"Why you make-a so much fuss? I know how to put my clothes on. Whas-a matta? You think I'm gonna forget to wear underpants?"

She was making us laugh, and she was laughing too. We could tell she was excited.

Ma told her, "How often will I get to help my mother dress to be a bride?"

"This is true, Josie." She patted my mom's cheek and sent us home.

When we got to St. Michael's Church, sixteen adults and seven of the oldest grandchildren were lined up on either side of the walk.

"Oh, too many people!" She said.

Ma told her, "These are your children, Ma. You can't tell them not to come to your wedding."

"I know, but it makes me a little bit *timoroso.* I get nervous."

It was a sweet and simple ceremony. The priest actually looked very touched. He had tears in his eyes. He kissed Nana's cheeks and shook Zio's hand.

We all waited outside to throw rice and applaud for them.

We all went to Ma's for cake and coffee. I was secretly hoping that Nana wouldn't be too angry next week for the big party. Nana and Zio sat at the table and looked pleased with all the attention. My family can never keep anything simple. We were supposed to only have cake and coffee. Auntie Lilly brought homemade pizza bread. Ma baked it and cut it up like little appetizers. Auntie Virg had tray after tray of cheese and crackers with olives and gardinière. Uncle Mikey and Uncle Joey had picked up salami and fresh bread. This was a simple gathering in my family.

The little party lasted all day into the evening. Around 8 p.m., Nana said, "Enough food and drink. We go now."

Zio helped Nana on with her sweater and took her by the hand. They walked out the door to a round of applause.

The uncles followed them outside and helped them into Uncle Johnny's car. They could have walked, but the sons had something else planned for the evening. We didn't know that all the uncles had arranged a special surprise. They booked a room at the Marriott. Ma packed a bag for Nana and my dad packed a bag for Zio. Uncle Johnny had the bags in the car.

When he got back, he said that Nana was not too happy. She tried to make him turn the car around and go home. She smacked him in the back of the head and told him to mind his own business. "What-s a matta wid my kids. They don't know how to mind they own business."

He made sure they got checked in. He told them he would pick them up at 11 a.m. Breakfast was included in the stay. He also put some wine, cheese, and salami in Zio's overnight bag.

On Monday, Niko phoned me in my dressing room to tell me that Penny and Carlo got to Sicily safely. The family lived in Palermo. They picked them up and insisted they stay with them in the villa that they owned. It sounded like the family all had some big bucks.

I didn't usually have any reason to speak directly to Niko Bazzoli.

The family usually communicates through my dad. I felt like there was another reason for his call. I was right.

"Lena, Penny and Carlo are going to spend a little more time in Italy than they originally planned. Carlo has some unfinished business that he has to take care of in another town. My cousin Vincenzo will be staying with him. I don't want Penny to be alone. If you can take any time off work, you might want to join her. It would be my special vacation treat for you, of course."

My first instinct was to say, "Hell, no!" Because I was pretty sure what the unfinished business was. It was the "hit," the kill, the end of the line for some poor slob. Now I was nervous for Penny. I knew she wasn't aware of what was going on around her in Italy. She only spoke a few words of Italian.

My head was spinning. "I don't know when I can take any time off from the show. I took a lot of time when Whitey was shot. That put a big burden on everyone. Niko, can I let you know in the next few days? I'll go talk to my boss today before I leave. Can you give me any idea of when you would need me to be in Italy?"

"Well, I can arrange it as far out as two or three weeks."

Well, I guess some poor guy has about three weeks before he dances with the devil. I can't leave Penny alone in Italy.

"Thanks, Niko!" I tried to sound excited. "I'll call you as soon as I get some firm dates."

"Thanks, Doll. I knew I could count on you. They left a key to their house with me. I'll give it to your Mom. Just in case anyone needs to get in there."

This stuff all stunk. All this warped family loyalty was sucking my brain cells out of my head. I know that once you are in, there is no getting out.

I couldn't focus on Niko right now. I needed to plan Nana and Zio's wedding party. In my heart I knew that I would have to go to Palermo to be with Penny. I just couldn't figure out how I was going to get away from *Tortured Souls* for any length of time.

61

Mom was making arrangements with Riggio for the food preparation and the delivery and setup. I was calling different places for the tent and tables and chairs.

It was going to be difficult to keep Nana away from the house while the tent is being set up. They needed a couple of days. Ma said she was going to make it a point to go there instead. She was making briccole with penne pasta. She called Nana and told her she made too much. Ma and Dad will take it over and have dinner with her and Zio.

I was going to Nana's after work on Friday to eat leftovers. That would keep her from going to Ma's during the day.

Mr. Riggio was so glad to be doing the catering. He and his wife were guests also. He would come early in the evening to be sure that everything was going as planned. I remembered to call Whitey's parent to extend the invitation to them.

The week was flying by. I hadn't had a chance to ask Mr. Latmen about time off. I really didn't know how to approach it. He was very understanding, but there was no way I could ask him for time off to oversee family business. I was going to have to fabricate a story of some sort.

It was so great to be close to my parents and have my privacy too. I was up early to help Mom put all the tablecloths on before the food arrived. We had all the blue and silver decorations from Penny's shower. They were just perfect. We kept the party favors simple. Mom ordered party cups with nuts and candy and matching ribbon. We clustered them in the center of each table, since we were serving buffet style there weren't any actual place settings. We were still feeling guilty having this party without Nana's approval.

Nana and Zio thought they were coming over for a barbeque. We said that Mr. Genero sent steaks over when he heard about Nana and Zio getting married.

We saw them coming down the street. Nana had her arm linked through Zio's. When she saw the tent she had a puzzled look on her face. Then she saw Dona Triena and Dona Maria.

"Peppino, looks-a like somebody is having a circus. Why they gotta tent? Is it a *compleanno?*"

Then she saw the banner, "Congratulations to Mr. and Mrs. Delatora!"

Gemma went up to them and hugged them both,

Nana said, "This family is so *stupido.* Nobody listens to me." She was laughing and crying. Zio looked pleased. After everyone greeted her, she calmed down. Zio and Nana wanted to go home and change into their wedding clothes. My dad and mom said they looked just fine. We had a corsage for Nana and a flower for Zio. Nana was so surprised to see the gift table.

"Sona una donna vecchia?" What do I need?

"You're never too old for new things, Mama," Auntie Virg told her.

Everyone settled in to enjoying the evening. Mr. Genero brought his concertina and cousin Paul played his saxophone. Uncle Sammy played his harmonica and Uncle Joey played the ukulele.

Niko Bazzoli danced the tarantella with my mom and Nana. Everyone danced and sang Italian songs. There was light in the sky when the party started to die down.

I tried to get Nana and Zio to stay in my guest room, but they wanted to go home. Uncle Mikey drove them back to Nana's.

Whitey was picking up beer bottles and putting them into the empty cases. Dad said, "You kids turn in now. We'll finish up in the morning."

I kissed Ma and Dad goodnight and Whitey and I headed for my house.

Once we settled into bed, we talked about how nice the party had turned out. Whitey mentioned that he saw Niko Bazzoli talking to me. "It looked serious," he said.

I said, "Niko asked me if I would go to Palermo and spend some time with Penny. He asked me last week if I could get any time off work."

"Where is Carlo going to be?"

"Carlo has a commitment to something elsewhere in Italy with Niko's cousin, Vicenzo."

He sat straight up, "What? Do you know what that means, Lena? You understand what he's gotta do, don't you?"

"Yes, I do. I'm pretending that I don't understand, but I'm sure it's part of his ceremony."

"That's right. And you're going to be there? That's not good as far as I'm concerned. I don't think that you should go."

"Whitey, we have discussed this type of thing before. You can't tell me what to do. I'm not nuts about going to Italy under these circumstances. This is family business. I need to talk to my dad about this. You have to stay out of it."

Now he was pacing around the bedroom. "Lena, this *family* business is starting to rule our life. I thought it was only the men in the family."

"No, Whitey. It rules all of us. If we stay together, that's part of the deal."

"Lena, I can understand your father's commitment. I'm not sure I understand why your life is consumed with this as well."

"Whitey, sit down." He perched on the edge of the bed. I was quiet while I gathered my thoughts.

"Do you know if your family has any Mafioso ties?"

"No. Not here. I think maybe someone in the old country."

"Honey, it's all or nothing. There is no pulling away when your father is a *soldier.*"

"What do you mean, a *soldier?*"

"That's what my dad's title is. It's his rank in the family. Dad and I have had some long talks. He has finally explained a lot of things to me."

"Then this would be our life? There would be no getting away from it?"

"Yes. This is how it is."

I watched his face. I had never seen this look before. I had a rock in my chest. My mouth was dry. I knew this was seriously bad.

He said, "I'm sorry, Lena; I can't do this. I love you, but I can't live this life. It rules you, and it would consume our lives. It's over between us." Then he walked out.

The sun had come up. I looked at the bedside clock: 6 a.m.

I crawled under the covers and pulled them over my head. I couldn't even cry. How could Whitey have been this close to my family and not understood what it meant to be "connected?" I felt numb and dried up.

I was eighteen years old before I began to realize what how strong the commitment was in my family. I thought Whitey was my knight in shining armor, but I guess his armor had a few chinks. First he got jilted then he got shot. I guess that would damage anyone's armor. It was a month before he recovered physically. I think that I am pretty strong emotionally. Maybe Whitey needs a counselor—the kind that talks a lot. Like $50 an hour. He couldn't use a counselor without telling him about the *family*. I needed to talk to my Mom.

I dozed off at some point because the ring of the phone woke me.

"Hullo."

"Oh, honey. It's Mom. Did I wake you? I'm sorry."

"Yes, I guess so."

"I see Whitey's truck is gone. Are you hungry?"

"I was going to come over anyway. Is Daddy there?"

"Sure honey, he's in the yard."

I got dressed and put a little makeup on so I wouldn't scare anyone.

When Ma saw me she rolled her eyes.

"What happened? Are you all right? Sit down."

I got right to the point. "I think that Whitey and I are through."

She looked blank.

I kept talking; "He can't handle the family connections."

"You mean the *famiglia?*"

"Yes, that's what I mean."

"Bastardo! What should it matter to him? No one has asked him to take part in anything."

"He feels that the *family* has too much control over me. As a result, they will control him and our life together."

Just then my dad came in from the yard. He looked at our faces. "Are we having another crisis?"

"Sam, Whitey walked out on Lena."

I could see his jaws tighten. "What's that supposed to mean?"

I explained the same thing that I had told Ma.

First Dad looked angry. Then I could see him struggle with several emotions. Sadness and hurt were there too.

"I'm gonna talk to him. I shoulda done it sooner."

I explained that Niko wanted me to go to Italy. He stopped me before I finished and said, "Niko talked to me already. I know all about it. I should have talked to you about it before he did."

"Whitey has to make up his own mind, Dad. This is a big decision. If he wants me, he has to accept the whole package."

"Honey, I've thought about having a talk with him for a long time. There are some things he needs to be more aware of in the long run. He would have to be more accepting, but not necessarily more involved.

"Let it go, Dad. I won't chase him. I need breathing space. I feel numb. This is where I should be right now. I need to talk to my boss about time off for Italy. I don't know what's going to happen. I know the show will go on without me, that's for sure. I'll talk to him tomorrow."

"Let me know when you need me, Lena. If you want me to talk to Niko or try to reason with Whitey, I'll be glad to step in. Maybe we could have Niko talk to him. Whatever you need, I will be there."

"The last thing I need is to have anyone try to persuade Whitey. This is a decision he needs to make on his own. Thanks, Daddy." I kissed him and Mom.

62

I spent the rest of the day helping Mom get the house and yard in order. The tent would come down the next day.

"Come for dinner later, honey. Nana and Zio are coming over."

"Thanks, Ma. I'll see how much I get done today. If I've got to go to Italy, I'll have to start getting my things together."

I really needed time to think this out. Could Whitey really walk out on me too?

Paulie and the construction crew were finally finished with the little house behind Nana. When he asked Mona about moving in with him again, she said that she needed more time, even though she wasn't seeing Johnny anymore.

I went into the studio early on Monday. I walked into Frank's office. When he looked up from his desk and saw me he got that deep wrinkle in his forehead.

"What's wrong?"

"Frank, I've got to talk to you."

"You aren't pregnant, are you?"

"No. Not pregnant."

"Can't be worse than that, can it?"

"Frank, I have to go to Italy. It's family business." I didn't plan what I was going to say. It just came out in one sentence.

"Lena, this isn't a great time to do this. Our ratings are great. I'm afraid if you do this now, our ratings will take a nosedive. How long will you need?"

"I'll probably need several weeks, Frank."

"After today's show, I'll talk to Sophia and Eddie and see what they say about a plot or a plan of some sort."

"Thanks, Frank."

"And don't look so worried. We'll work something out."

Beth was finally getting into the swing of her role. I think her meds were finally kicking in. Greg watched her like a hawk. Red really had a crush on her. How did a fruitcake like her have two men falling all over her and I couldn't keep one man interested? I was hoping that she could adjust to a slightly bigger role. Her life was filled with so much drama. I think they underestimated her ability for acting. When she stays on her meds, she does just fine.

Greg knocked on my dressing room door and walked in, again.

"Hi, Greg. What's going on?"

"I was going to ask you the same thing. I just left Frank's office. He's got Sophia and Eddie in there. I heard them talking about *Lena's situation*. Are you pregnant or something?"

"It's the 'or something' part. Not pregnant. Why does everyone think I'm pregnant? I gotta stay away from those bread baskets."

We both started laughing. Greg remembered how much I love bread. We'd had so many dinners together.

He walked up behind me as I sat in my dressing table. He massaged my neck. He was always really good at that. He's got great hands.

Before I knew it, I was leaning back against him while he moved on to my shoulders and back.

"Hey!" I said. "Knock it off! I know where this is going!"

He gave me his most appealing smile. "You're really tense, Lena; I can see it in your face and you have knots in your neck and shoulders."

"You just never mind my knots, buddy. I'll take a hot shower for that."

"You're still my best girl, Lena. I'll help you get the kinks out any time. Are you really okay?"

I told him the same thing that I told Frank about family business.

He narrowed his eyes and said, "Are you going to see Penny and Carlo?"

"Yes. I'll probably stay with Penny. Carlo will be away on business."

"Oh. Somehow I think there's more business to this trip than honeymoon."

"You're very wise, Greg."

"Let me know if there's anything I can do for you, Lena. I really mean that."

"Thank you. I really appreciate that, Greg."

He kissed the top of my head and left.

I didn't stop at Ma's when I left the TV station. I went directly to my house. I felt like I needed solitude.

63

had a meeting with Frank and the directors after the day's show. Frank left a message on my dressing table. *"My office, 3:00. F."* The "F" is for Frank. He has as much finesse as a ditch digger, but he's really a good guy. He must have forgotten that I have a phone.

When I got there. He said, "Okay, kid. We got three scenarios for you. Read them to her, Eddie."

Scenario #1: Lena goes to Italy and meets a rich wine merchant; you fall in love and bring him back, and we work him into the show. We tape ahead of time to work it into the show while you're gone.

Scenario #2: You go on a ski vacation, break a leg, and go to the hospital. It's a bad break. You need to be in traction. You fall in love with a handsome doctor and bring him back from you ski vacation and he becomes part of the show. We tape ahead of time to work it into the show while you're gone.

Scenario #3: Lena goes to Italy to see her Nana. She talks her Nana into coming back with her and we have her in several episodes when Lena returns.

"I like this one the best," Eddie said. "We tape before you go away and we can use your real Nana."

"I don't think Nana is going to be an option," I said. "Do I get to pick the one I like best? Or will you guys decide?"

Frank said, "You pick, Lena. But you decide now. Whatever scenario you choose is fine with us. Sophia and Eddie have a lot of logistics to work out and you have to start calling the casting companies."

"Okay, I pick the broken leg scenario and I'll start calling the casting company."

"Right!" Frank said. "You guys get to work. I'm going home. Lena, we get this taping done and you have a month in Italy. Six weeks at the most. By the way, we start taping the ski accident day after tomorrow."

This should be a real adventure, because I don't ski.

64

This week, we would begin to introduce my ski vacation. I didn't know what to expect. The producers would write a script for me that introduced me to new the sport of skiing.

I was waiting for casting to call me regarding a guy with a "doctor-like" appearance. He could be early thirties or older. The last thing I needed was another man at my bedside to fall for.

I was doing a great job pretending that I wasn't thinking about Whitey, until Nana told me that his mom called her. Nana said, "What's a matta, you? Bianco and you *finito?* His Mama call-a me today. She worry that she no see you long-a time. I tell her that when I see Lena, I'm-a gonna find out."

"Nana, we are taking a break from each other. We decided that our families are very different."

"Oh." She looked very serious. "I think I maybe I understand. I'm very sorry for you, Bella. He's a good man. You are a good woman. Maybe too good for him."

"Thank you Nana. Maybe it will work out later."

I made that a short subject. We chatted over coffee and cookies. Zio came up from the basement and joined us. He kissed my cheek and said he was glad to see me.

He said he missed Ma and Dad and Bobby. "I see crazy Paulie when he comes to look for food every day."

When I got home, there was a note on the kitchen table. "Niko stopped by. He's at our house. Can you stop in?"

I couldn't say I was surprised. I knew he would be inquiring about my plans soon.

When I walked in Niko stood up and extended his arms to me.

He pulled me to him by the shoulders and kissed my cheeks. "Bella Lena!" he said. "I'm so glad I caught you. I know how busy you are."

"Thank you, Niko. It's good to see you too." *I have to play the game*, I thought.

"Have you had a chance to work out some time off from your job?"

"Yes. They are planning episodes for my absence from the show to begin this coming week."

"Do you need me to talk to your boss or put in an encouraging word to arrange this?"

I did a mental cringe at the thought of Niko and Frank Latmen in the same room. Could someone just shoot me first?

"No, Niko. It's all taken care of. I'll be filming some scenes that will look as if I'm having ski lessons. Then I'll conveniently break a leg. They'll show my recovery in a hospital bed and that will keep me out of the show for several weeks.

"Lena, I knew could count on you! I can't thank you enough for what you have done for Carlo and Penny. I'll get the ball rolling for your trip. You'll fly first class, of course. All expenses will be on me. You will be going to Sicily and arriving in Palermo. I'll have a car waiting for you at the airport. I'll tell Penny you're coming. She's going to be thrilled."

"Is Carlo picking me up?"

"No, I'll make other arrangements for you. Carlo has been very busy most days. I'm sure that Penny is lonely."

He kissed us all good-bye. My dad walked him outside. Ma looked at me with a forced smile.

"Ma, I'm fine with this. It's working out just great. Latmen has been very understanding."

"Whitey was right, wasn't he? It's ruling your life, Lena."

"It's part of who we are, Mom. I know we're getting in deeper. I see it happening, but it's our obligation."

Dad came in and hugged me. "You're a very special person, Lena. Other men have daughters your age who only worry about spending money and shopping and getting their hair done. None of them has accomplished anything compared to what you have done."

Ma was pulling rib tips and pasta out of the oven. "Sit, eat, Lena."

I ate with Ma and Dad and visited for a while. What else did I have to do?

I hadn't heard from Whitey. It was probably just as well. He understood that I couldn't walk away from my life and he couldn't accept that. If anyone ever came into my life again, they would need to accept me as I was.

When I got to the TV station, there was a huge machine blowing fake snow over a cardboard mountain. Huge chunks of foam board were glued to a plywood ramp. The snow was piling up on the plywood ramps. I was watching a backdrop unroll. The view was of a beautiful mountain covered with snow and a chalet in the background.

A ski lift was strung across the set with the chair lift above the snow pile.

"Hi, Frank! Is this all for me?"

"Lena, it's a good thing that I love you. This snow machine cost a fortune to rent."

"Frank, you are the best! I really mean that! Thanks for letting me have a life besides a job."

"Lena, don't think I'm blind to what goes on in everyone's life. I appreciate your devotion to our show. I know you are committed to making this show a success." He lowered his voice and said, "I know your personal life is a mess too."

I grabbed his face and kissed him on the lips. His face turned bright red. He made his voice as gruff as he could. "Oh cut that out, girl!"

"You're really wonderful, Frank!"

"Yeah, yeah. I know, babe. One month! Six weeks if you get desperate."

"I'm interviewing two men from casting after today's show."

Beth and Susan were a team before Susan had her baby. I was

hoping that they clicked again. I would suffer less guilt if they were a good team while I was in Italy.

I was getting a little excited about my trip.

I tried not to think about the real reason that I was going: to babysit Penny while Carlo goes on a seek-and-destroy mission.

I went to Sicily when I was ten years old. Ma and Nana took me to see the family there. I don't remember much, but Nana's family owned olive groves. I played in the groves while everyone was picking olives. They told me to pick the olives off the low branches and the clean ones off the ground. Mom would say, you can eat the ones off the tree, but don't eat the ones on the ground. I remember they were bitter and hard. I really didn't like them.

They sold most of that land. Too bad, because they had some beautiful stone houses on that property. Nana said that was her last visit because Papa died and there was nothing left for her or her family to go back for. Everything she cared about was here. Sure would be nice to have a little house and a few olive trees to go back to.

Me, Nana and Mama

65

My first interview was tall, dark, and handsome. He showed up wearing a doctor's coat and carrying a clipboard. He made me laugh. Frank didn't seem amused. I'm so easily influenced, and I'm spoiled from having such handsome men around me all my life. In a very professional voice the actor told me, "Angie, your break is lateral. It's serious. I'm afraid you'll be in traction for several weeks."

To this guy's credit, he was talented too. I didn't want to be so hasty. I would have him read for me again. The second time, I would have him read for Sophia and Eddie. They could make the final decision. I knew Frank needed me to move fast on this. I needed to "break a leg" some time next week in order to get this hospital scene set up.

Greg knocked and walked in. *Why does everyone think they can walk into my dressing room?*

"Lena, what are you doing tonight? Do you want to have dinner with me?"

"I'm interviewing another doctor type after the show. And what makes you think I'm available for dinner?"

"Quit playing games, Lena. I know you and Whitey are split up."

"Yeah, we are. Where do you want to go?"

He smiled a very happy smile. "How about my place?"

"NO! Dinner first!"

"Then what?" said the sly Greg.

"Oh, stop being a pervert, you little brat."

"Okay, I'll settle for dinner. For now."

Greg has always been my light at the end of the tunnel: Always easy to talk to, always ready to listen.

I asked Frank to sit in on the second interview for both the doctor tryouts. Mike Bosco was my favorite to begin with. We asked him to hang out in the employee lounge. The second guy, William T. Wagner, didn't read as well. His voice was slightly higher in pitch than Mike's. He read the same lines, but he didn't sound as believable.

Sophia and Eddie liked Mike better. Frank liked Mike's voice better also. Frank was concerned about him being a clown, because he showed up in the doctor's coat. "We're going to give pretty boy a chance. I hope he doesn't make me sorry."

Frank was such a sweetheart, and had such a way with words.

We had to get the new guy on board quickly. Frank went to the employee lounge to tell Mike he got the role. He took a script with him. He wanted to get this role started quickly.

Greg was waiting at my dressing room door. "Are you ready?"

"I thought I'd go freshen up a bit."

"Oh, Lena. You look just great to me. I made six thirty reservations at The Lamplighter."

"Okay. You might as well come in. I don't know what kept you from waiting inside this time."

"I didn't want to scare you when you came in."

"I'll dress behind the screen. I'm gonna call my ma first to tell her I'm going out."

"You have your own house, don't you?"

"Yes, but she still worries if she doesn't see my car by early evening."

I fluffed my hair and changed into one of my cute TV outfits. I brushed my teeth in my tiny bathroom.

Greg was standing at the door when I came out. "You always look so beautiful, Lena."

I felt myself blush. "Greg, you are such a flirt."

We were walking toward his car. "Greg, I thought I'd take my own car. Then I can just drive myself home."

"I'll bring you back here, Lena. Let's ride together."

When we got in the car, I put some lipstick on. I noticed Greg staring at me with that old moony look. "What? I miss Penny doing my makeup. Sometimes I even forget to wear lipstick. She does a much better job than I do."

"No, Lena, you are more beautiful than when I first met you. I think you're more comfortable in your skin now."

"Thanks, Greg. But if you are thinking about starting the old relationship over, you need to take it slowly. I've got a year's worth of battle scars to heal."

"I know, Lena. Let's have a nice dinner and catch up. We both have a lot of history."

The Lamplighter Restaurant was a very select and secluded place. The booths had extremely high backs with wraparound sides. Some of the booths in the back had velvet curtains. Not ours, thank goodness.

Greg though we should have steak and lobster. I hadn't eaten since breakfast, so everything sounded great to me.

My Italian fat cells suffered greatly when my last prince bit the dust. I told Greg to ask for the bread basket, just as the waiter placed it on the table. It was a masterpiece in itself. Beautiful chunks of French bread, lovely salted rolls, twisted buns, and more. They also brought a crock of garlic butter and plain butter. Greg poured the wine while I buttered my first chunk of bread. He was laughing at me.

"Lena, I forgot that watching you eat is second to having sex."

"How would you know that?"

"Well, I can still hope."

We had a wonderful evening. Dinner was outstanding. I ate too much, but then I always do. We were waiting for dessert. I was very relaxed.

"Lena, can I ask you about Whitey?"

I felt my face flush, but I answered him. "Yes. He couldn't handle my family ties. He felt my connections were too strong and they have too much control over me. I can't change that and he can't accept it."

"Fair enough, Lena. I thought you and Whitey were going to be forever. He looked at my face and said, "I shouldn't have said that. Do I dare ask about Gino? I guess not. Never mind."

"No, it's okay, Greg. I'll never get over Gino. But I can talk about it. He was promised to someone else years ago, when he was a child. It was a deal between families in Italy. He forgot to mention it."

"Holy shit! Lena, that's just awful."

"Yeah, it stinks big time."

"I've upset you. I'm so sorry. You seem to be handling it so well."

"I'm an actress, Greg. It's what I do for a living."

"You are a very special person, Lena."

Our dessert arrived. We shared a huge chunk of coconut cake with chocolate sauce. Needless to say, I had no problem eating my share.

Greg paid the check. He was helping me on with my coat and leaned over and kissed my cheek. "Thank you, Lena. It was a great evening."

"You're welcome, Greg."

We made small talk on the way back to my car. Once we were in the parking lot he laid a big wet kiss on me, like old times.

"Whoa, Greg! I'm not ready for this."

"I guess there's no chance of coming to see your new house, or you coming to my apartment?"

"Not tonight, Greg."

"Lena, you know I had to ask about Whitey and Gino."

"I guess you had to. But remember, Greg—you were the one whose family couldn't accept an Italian girl."

"I care a lot about you as a friend, no matter what happens between us."

"I know, Greg. Be careful going home."

66

Rigging up a fake fall wasn't an easy task. It has to be taped ahead of time and other reactions can be spliced in. I was wearing a full ski outfit: leggings, parka, boots, gloves, and skis. Now I had to go to the top of the snow mountain and fall down. Convincingly.

I went to the top of the ramp, threw the poles out sideways and dropped to my butt, while I screamed loudly.

"Let's do another take Lena!"

"Oh, for cripes sake," I mumbled.

I climbed the steps behind the fake snow mountain. This time my ski caught on a chunk of Styrofoam at the top step. The skis went out in front of me and the poles flew out to the sides, "Oh, Nooo!" I yelled. I fell on my ass so hard I was watching the sparkly stars spin like fireflies. *Gee,* I thought, *Just like a cartoon.*

Eddie was yelling, "That was great, Lena."

The stagehands were helping me up and removing my skis. I was busy rubbing my bruised ass.

Frank asked, "Lena, was that a real fall? Are you all right?"

"Yes, Frank. It sure was. I think I'm okay."

After tomorrow's show, we will film little old me in traction. I'll be in a hospital bed, attended to by the new Doctor Mike. We decided that calling him "Dr. Mike" would be easier than adding another name to the cast. I really don't think that I can remember any more names.

I planned to go home and soak in a hot tub of water.

When I got home, I saw my airline tickets on my table. This was all really happening. The note from Mom said, "Niko dropped these off today."

The reality of this was brutal. I was going to babysit Penny while Carlo iced, popped, or deep-sixed someone. There was no kind way to say it or phrase it. I felt a little sick when I thought about it. I was so squeamish about the trip. I wanted to be excited, but I was simply overwhelmed about what was happening.

I tried to keep my mind on the positive part of the trip. I was going to see Penny. I really missed her. I had to start packing. I had to lay out the clothes I was taking. Remember: lay out the skirts and pants, then the interchangeable tops over the first outfits. Put the jewelry in the shoes. Get some tissue paper.

I needed to go to the bookstore for a guidebook. I was trying to focus on sightseeing. I wanted to see everything I could in Sicily. I was sure Penny would be able to show me around by the time I arrive. Niko said that Penny was lonely. Carlo must be occupied elsewhere on a daily basis.

The flight was about fifteen hours. I'd have plenty of time to contemplate my visit.

68

I got to the studio early. I saw the snow set had been replaced with a hospital set. Dr. Mike was studying his script. A nurse, a girl I had never seen before, was sitting on the bed next to a fake cast. She was also reading her script. I introduced myself, and she told me her name was Pam.

Frank was pacing in front of the set. He smiled when he saw me—at least whatever passed for a smile in Frank's world.

"You ready for your broken leg, Lena?"

"Yep. I wore white shorts under my long flowing skirt today."

"Smart girl. Go easy on the makeup today. Remember you're supposed to look banged up and stressed. Can you do a bruise on you cheek or chin? I want you to look like the ski pole hit you in the face."

"I'll do both. I can do it out of the makeup box and use some eye shadow."

"Go do it! When you're done, have Greg take a Polaroid of it so you can duplicate it if you need to."

"Give me about twenty minutes."

I came out with my hair slightly messy and the two bruises on my face. I still wore my lipstick, but didn't wear blush or eye makeup. I got a few wolf whistles anyway because I had shorts on. Wardrobe was ready with a hospital gown. They slipped the cast over my leg with no problem. I could tell immediately that the inside was scratching the heck out of me.

"Hold it, Frank. I need a stocking under this thing,"

"Wardrobe! Find some kind of stocking for Lena."

That being done, they hooked my leg into a sling and began to hoist it up in the air.

I watched it go up. At some point, I said "Whoa! How high does it have to be?"

"This should be just about right," Dr. Mike said.

"What the heck do you know, hot shot? You've only been a doctor for about thirty minutes."

Everyone laughed. Mike looked a little embarrassed. "You're right, Miss Delatora."

The nurse had only two lines.

Nurse: "Are you in any pain, Miss?"

Angie: "Yes I am, Nurse."

Nurse: "Dr. Mike will prescribe something for you."

Dr. Mike enters: "Angie, your break is lateral. It's serious. I'm afraid you'll be in traction for several weeks."

Angie: "Oh, Doctor, This is very uncomfortable."

Dr. Mike: "Angie, I'll stop in to visit you as often as I can."

"CUT! Fade to credits! Frank yelled.

"Sounds great, kids! Tomorrow Dr. Mike brings Angie a book. Later we'll splice that into a future episode. I want him to ask some personal stuff. Lena, pick up your script in Eddie's office. Then we'll shoot a scene to ease into a "flowers" episode. This will be done next week while we shoot the regular show during the day. The extra stuff will be shot before the show or after. Study the spots and I'll let you know where they go. That's it!"

When he says, "That's it," he's done. Clear the set. He said all that without taking a breath.

I picked up my script from Sophia and Eddie and went to my dressing room. I had spent two hours in the leg cast. We did a couple of retakes. My leg was itching like crazy.

Greg knocked and walked in, again. It's a good thing that I kept my shorts on.

"Lena, how do you think it's going."

"However it's going, I'm going. One way or another I leave for Italy one week from today. I have my tickets already."

"Holy cow! How long will you be gone?"

"Four to six weeks."

"You feel like dinner, Lena?"

"Not really. My back is killing me from my leg being jerked up in the air for two hours, and my leg itches."

Greg looked down at my red leg. "Geez, Lena, let me put something on that."

He dashed out before I could say anything. I let him wash my leg and put some kind of medicated lotion on it.

"We've got to do something about that cast. I'll take it to the prop guys and have them drill some small holes in it for air. That will help keep your leg dry. I'll find a different kind of stocking for you, too. If we keep it dry, it probably won't break out.

"I have sensitive skin."

"Yes, I know, Lena."

"Greg, you can stop rubbing my leg now."

"Oh! Sorry. Of course."

We both stood up. I kissed his cheek. "Thanks, Greg. I really appreciate your concern."

"Any time, Lena. We'll take a rain check on dinner, huh?"

"Sure, we'll do it another night."

I drove home in silence. I didn't even want the radio on. Suddenly, I was lonely. I was doing a great job not thinking about Whitey. He had made up his mind that we couldn't work out our problems. Well, it was really his problem, not mine.

I pulled into my driveway and saw Mona and Paulie. "Oh, good!" I said out loud.

"Lena, I brought a bottle of wine," Mona said.

"Good! I have some salami and cheese."

"I'm glad you too are here. I really didn't want to be alone tonight."

Mona kept looking at me and raising her eyebrows. I knew she was asking if something was wrong.

"Paulie, go ask Ma if she has an extra loaf of bread. These crackers aren't cutting it."

"Lena, are you gonna tell me what's wrong?"

"Mona, I just don't know. I'm really in a funk. I felt lower and lower as the day went on. I'm looking forward to the trip, but I'm a little afraid."

"What are you afraid of, Lena?"

"What if I'm jeopardizing my job? What if I don't like what's happening in Italy when I get there? I keep pretending I'm stupid or blind to what's going on. I know what's going to happen while I'm there."

Poor Mona. It just occurred to me that she didn't understand the real purpose of my trip. "Mona, you need to come over without Paulie. I can't say anymore tonight."

With that, Paulie was tapping at the door. Mom had loaded him down with so much food he couldn't turn the doorknob. He had a tray with salami, ricotta, and black olives. Mom had cut some eggplant into squares and heated it with rib tips and pasta.

"Sorry it took so long. Your ma had to heat all this stuff up."

"Crying out loud. This is the reason my ass needs its own dressing room."

Mom came over a few minutes later.

68

I would have another scene with Doctor Mike today. Wardrobe brought me a different stocking for my leg. The first stocking was wool. That was my problem. This stocking was a silk blend. It was much more comfortable.

Nurse Patricia comes in. "Hello, Angie. Dr. Mike is on his rounds. He'll be in to see you this morning." She makes a slight adjustment to the pulley.

Angie: Thanks, Nurse Patricia.

Dr. Mike walks in: He hands Angie a book of short stories. "I hope you enjoy this. It was one of my favorites during my internship. My time was so limited and my attention was so focused on medical journals, I hand to keep all of my reading limited to short stories."

Our eyes meet. The voiceover says, "I felt something. It was a connection of some kind. A spark. I know he felt it too."

The scene cuts to the B and B: Beth says: Angie has a very handsome doctor. I saw him yesterday.

Sabra responds: Well, Beth, I think Angie is due for a new love interest.
The girls ramble on for some time about Angie's romantic

life, or lack of it.

It appeared that everyone on and off the set is concerned about who I'm steaming the sheets with. Makes me glad I'm going to Italy. This show's script seems to sink its teeth into my private life.

The daily scripts would be predictable if they didn't include the parts that seem like they were scripted from my private life. Considering the fact that I don't blab to anyone at the station, it's amazing that they can parallel my life so easily. Truth is stranger than fiction.

I went to the employee cafeteria for lunch. I usually bring something from home, but I got up late this morning. I got a ham sandwich and a bowl of soup. I sat at a table with the stagehands and set painters. "What kind of soup is this?" I said to anyone who was listening.

One of the guys said, "I think the sign said chicken soup."

"It tastes like the chicken just walked through it."

We were laughing about that, when Dr. Mike walked over and asked if he could join us.

I said, "Sure, have a seat."

He had the meatloaf *and* the chicken entrée. They both included potatoes and vegetables. Two hot rolls, four little cartons of milk, a chunk of chocolate cake, and a bag of chips.

We all stared at his tray, waiting for him to commence. Low and behold, he plowed through all that food in about fifteen minutes. He looked up and saw us all staring at him and looked embarrassed. "I think I'll save the chips for later."

"I hope you can button your doctor's coat after that lunch."

The stagehands were still staring at him with their mouths open. One of the painters said, "My ma would love this guy. She's always telling me to eat more."

"I go to medical school at night," Mike said. "I live alone and don't keep much food in my apartment because of work and school. I'm not home much, so I eat big when I can."

"Well that explains your large consumption of all food products when available."

Mike and the guys at our table all nodded while chewing.

"Lena, have you read your script? Am I attending to you tomorrow?"

"Yes, we need this script to move along pretty quickly. We'll start chatting and getting friendlier tomorrow. We'll need about two more shows before we can fall in love."

He put his arm around me and said, "It won't be difficult at all."

The stagehands had gone back to work and we were alone by this time.

I looked at this young guy with stars in his eyes. He was on cloud nine. He was thrilled with his new TV role; he was studying to be a doctor, was handsome and smart. I figured him to be about twenty-five years old. Just about a year and a half older than me.

"Mike, I don't want to discourage you. But a new romance isn't on my agenda. But I do want to apologize for my comment about your, *"Only being a doctor for thirty minutes."*

"Oh, that's okay. Lena, I hope I didn't offend you. I was trying to stay in my roll off camera."

I laughed and said as nicely as I could, "Thanks Mike, but stuff it."

I understood he was in the onscreen mode. He walked away looking a little forlorn.

After lunch we went back to the set. This would be Mike's third onscreen day as my doctor.

Dr. Mike: Angie, I thought flowers would brighten your room.

Angie: Thanks, Dr. Mike. Is that the same as saying, "Angie, I brought you flowers?" If you are bringing them for me, say so. If you are decorating the room, I'll try not to get excited over the flowers."

Dr. Mike: Okay, let me rephrase that. "Angie, these flowers are for you."

I thought, *Mike's smile is dazzling.* I felt myself softening up for this guy who worked all day and night and ate enough to choke a horse, because he went from this job to school. Whew, exhausting thought.

Angie: "Dr. Mike. Are you flirting with me?"

Dr. Mike: "Miss Angie, I believe I am."

Dr. Mike leans in a little closer. Angie can smell the aftershave and the breath mints or toothpaste. He takes her hand.

Dr. Mike: "Angie, I wish I could take you out to dinner. Or explain to you what sparks I'm getting. This is so unusual for me."

Lena thought: *Very ad libbed, Dr. Mike.*
Knowing the rush was on for her to let the romance to bloom, she took the next step.
Dr. Mike has her hand already. Angie pulls him toward her. He leans into her and kisses her full on the mouth.
This was a lingering kiss that the cast and crew wasn't expecting.
The camera faded out and the crew applauded.
Frank said, "Okay kids, glad no one had to push you into that last scene. You did a little ad libbing, but I guess that's just fine."
"That's it!" We were dismissed.
I went back to my dressing room and sat down. *"I will not have a crush on this guy,"* I said to myself. *"Just because I got a little zing from the lip contact, I'm not going to consider steaming the sheets with him."*
Greg knocked and walked in. Holy crap, it's a good thing I have a changing screen.
"What was all that lip action about?"

"Well, Frank wants me to fall in love with my doctor. I need to speed it along. I leave for Italy in a few days."

"That looked pretty convincing to me."

"I'm supposed to be convincing. I'm an actress, and that's part of the act."

"Yeah, I guess so, but you didn't have to look like you were enjoying it."

Now I was feeling sorry for him. "Greg, do you want to come over to see my new house tonight?"

"Geez, I thought you'd never ask. What time?"

"Let's make it 8 p.m."

"Sounds great! I'll be there."

When I don't stop at my ma's, she always calls me as soon as she sees my car in the driveway.

I answered, "Hi, Ma."

"How was your day, honey?"

"It was okay. I kissed Dr. Mike. We needed to move the romance along 'cause I'll be leaving for Italy next week. By the way, Greg is coming over tonight."

Long silence. "Oh, how did that come up?"

"I invited him, Mom."

"Nana always liked him."

"Well, I'm glad to hear that. He'll be here at eight."

"Okay, Hon, we'll see you later," and she hung up.

Did I ask her to come over? No! I said to myself. *I did not. But she will, won't she? And she'll bring Nana too, right? Yup! She will.* I answered myself.

I really had to get out of town. This family was driving me nuts. I lead two lives. Neither is private. The one on TV is open to the world, the other life has been created by my family. That's a lost cause, because they live it for me.

I decided to shower and get all dressed up cute: capris and a turquoise sweater. Maybe they'd think I was going out and everyone would go home.

Greg showed up at 8 p.m. sharp. He brought a box of donuts.

"That's nice, Greg. I don't get it. Why donuts?"

"Flowers seem too stuffy. I thought about a bottle of wine, but then it would seem like I had expectations."

"You don't?"

"I wondered if you still had the nightie and toothbrush in your purse?"

"Don't put the horse before the cart. Do you want Pepsi or should I open the wine? I've got pizza bread and some other snack stuff."

"I'll have Pepsi with the pizza bread."

I no sooner took the pizza bread out of the oven and the doorbell rang. "Oh, shit," I said.

It was Nana. She came in with Jojo the Wonder Dog.

"Gregorio! Josie tell me you visit tonight. I come-a to see where you been."

Jojo was very happy to see everyone. I don't ever remember Greg seeing Jojo before, but there was the dog, rolled over on his back letting Greg scratch his belly. Then Nana hugged Greg and kissed him on both cheeks.

I never got to sit down before Ma rang the doorbell. She came in carrying a roasting pan. My Dad came in behind her carrying a bottle of wine.

"What's that, Mom?"

"Oh, just a little baked mostaccioli with sausage."

Dad held up the bottle of his homemade red.

Greg smiled and hugged my dad.

Holy crap! Do they think Greg is here to stay? It's a visit, for crying out loud! Every time I bring a guy home my family thinks he's the one I'm going to marry. They act like it's a darned reunion. Well, I guess it's a little like a reunion.

I walked over to the kitchen counter and opened the wine. I poured a glass. I drank that and poured myself another glass.

Okay. I was better now.

Greg was enjoying all the attention. Nana was inviting Greg over to see the basil growing in the papa's wine press, because he and

Paulie carried it out of the basement for her. She also invited him to come for lunch, or *pranzo*, as she said in Italian. Greg was totally confused. He just kept nodding his head. Between Nana's broken English and her Italian words thrown in, he looked completely baffled.

I must have left the door unlocked. Zio came in looking for Nana. *"Rosina, avete Stupido con te?"*

"Yea. He come-a with me when I go."

Greg leaned over and asked, Lena "Who is this guy?"

"It's my dad's uncle, Zio Peppino. My nana is married to him."

"Lena, we need to talk."

"What?"

"Your Dad's uncle married your grandmother?"

"Yes. About two months ago."

"Where'd this guy come from? I never heard about him before. And what's a Zio?"

"Zio means uncle."

"Where did this guy come from?"

"Originally, from Italy. But he lived about six blocks from here when he broke his hip. Then he moved in with my parents."

"Lena, I'm really so confused about this."

"It's not a big deal, Greg. They aren't blood related. It's my mother's mother and my father's uncle."

"True. I must keep an open mind."

We ate and drank until after midnight. Nana and Zio were shocked when they saw the time. They couldn't believe they stayed out so late.

"Rosina, andiamo. Stupido, he's tired."

Mom and Dad took that as a hint to leave too. Greg was clearing the table. I was standing at the sink washing the glasses. He came up behind me and put his arms around my waist. He nuzzled his face into my hair.

"You really smell great, Lena."

I turned around and put my arms around his neck. "Well, here we are again. Same people, different place."

"This was a really nice evening. Like old times. I always enjoyed your family. Even when I don't know what the heck they're talking about."

Here I am, I thought. *I have to make a decision. Do I send Greg home—again? Letting him feel frustrated and used, or do I let him stay?*

He took the decision out of my head. Once we started making out in my kitchen, he lifted me on to the countertop and let nature take its course. He's taller than me and that worked out just fine. We worked our way into the bedroom for the second round.

Later, he said, "I never got to see the nightie you carried in your purse."

"No point in that now!"

"True. How did the courtship of Nana and Zio come about? Isn't he your grandfather now?

"No, I decided to keep calling him Zio. He came to stay with us when he broke his hip. He started having lunch with Nana and taking walks with the dog."

"Where did the dog come from?"

"That's another story. Greg?"

"Oh, okay."

"I'm glad you stayed."

"I'd say that was mutual."

"Not disappointed?"

"Oh, hell no, Lena. Worth the wait. Although some nights I wanted to bang my head on a wall when I got home."

"I leave for Italy next week."

"Yes, I know. This wasn't a commitment. Whatever it was tonight, neither of us has regrets."

Greg was a wise man.

69

Three more days before I left for Italy. I was flying into Palermo and going to my Nana's hometown of Marsalla. I decided to go see Nana tonight. I want to spend time with her before I go, and it will give me a chance to ask her about things I might want to see while I'm there.

I have a positive mindset. I don't think that having a man in my life is important right now. I'm going to have fun in Italy, try to stay out of any big decisions and enjoy my visit with Penny and Carlo. I always leave my Nana's house with a good feeling. I need to make it last until I come back from Italy.

When I knocked on the door, Nana said, "Whats-a-matta-you? Nobody knock if you family. Only strangers knock."

I kissed her and told her that I really missed her. "I been right here Lena. Why you stay away. I saw you two days ago with Gregorio. Where is he?"

"I wanted to see you by myself, Nana."

"Okay, you gonna eat?"

"Sure. I'll have something to eat; where is Zio?"

"He go to Pisquale store for bread."

"What are you making, Nana? I'll help you in the kitchen."

"Today I make cookies. Some cucidate and some-a plain."

"Where did you get the figs?"

"Peppino went to the market today. He go very early in the dark."

"How did he get there?"

"He go on the bus, what do you think? Why you ask so many questions? Get soup bowls, Lena. I make-a Minestrone today."

While she talked about what she made, I set the table. I got the cheese grater and a plate for the cheese to sit on. I put out some small glasses for Zio's homemade wine and got the silverware.

Zio brought home two loaves of bread and some pastries. Oh well, I'd worry about my diet tomorrow.

While we ate, I asked Nana about her trip from Italy to the America.

"I come to America in 1914. I was thirteen years old. I come with my sister Maria and my mama, Giusappa. I name-a you Mama after her. We left Marsalla onna train to Palermo. We sleep onna the train. Then we take a boat to Masina. We had to cross the small Strata Macina."

"Is that the ship that came to the US?"

"No, Bella. Then we take another train to Napoli. From Napoli we take a boat so big it scare me to death. For twelve days we were on this ship. Sometimes I got sick. We no like-a the food. My mama, she cry."

"What was the name of the ship, Nana?"

"We come here on the Colombo. I remember when we got to the Statue of Liberty. Ellis Island they call it. We were very happy, but very afraid. We only had a suitcase. Now we waited for my Zia, Antonia to come.

"You know I'm going to Sicily in a few days, Nana. I wanted to compare the way you had to travel to how easy my trip will be. It's only nine hours to Palermo."

Nana seemed to get very sad. I thought she would enjoy talking about her trip to America.

"Nana, do you think that you would like to go back to Sicily? I wonder if you and Zio would like to visit your families? I would pay for this trip as a wedding gift to you and Zio."

"No, this is my home now. When you were a *bambina* we went back. That was enough for me."

We cleared the table and brought all the dishes into the kitchen.

"Nana, did I make you sad? I only wanted to find out some things before I got on this trip."

"You didn't make me sad. Some-a-time, when I think about how fast all-a the years go, I get a little bit scared. You go on this trip Bella. Have a wonderful time and take a lot of pictures. You go to Marsalla and see my old house. I give-a the *infornazione* to you mama. Don't worry so much about me. I'm just-a fine.

Zio was tilting his head toward the door. I got the message what he wanted to speak to me.

"Nana, I'm going to get some other clothes out of my car to change."

I met Zio on the back porch. "What is it Zio? Is Nana okay?"

"We have a fight this morning. She no lika-a *Stupido* sleep in the bed with us. I try to tell her that the *cane* all-a time sleep with me before we get married. She say, 'Okay. Maybe you take-a you *cane* and go back to Josie house.' I dunno what to say to her. She no talk-a to me all day."

"Zio, I'll talk to her for you. I don't know what difference it will make."

I walked through the back door into the kitchen. I had to pass Nana and Zio's bedroom. I stopped short and peeked inside. They were sleeping on the same old double bed that Nana has had since I was a little girl. I've got to get her a queen size bed.

"Nana, I'll do the dishes."

After a moment, I mentioned that I noticed she seemed a little upset.

"I no marry Zio to sleep with a *cane*. The dog go in the middle. I don't wanna no dogs in my bed. Zio push-a the *cane,* then I move to the side and almost fall off-a the bed."

I almost laughed out loud. I was getting a mental picture of this threesome with the dog in the middle. No wonder she was so cranky. She wasn't getting any sleep.

"Nana, you need a bigger bed. Then if Jojo comes in the bed, he'll have room."

"What kind-a bed gets bigger? You think I wanna move out of my house so I can get a bigger bed?"

I went back to the bedroom and looked inside. If we moved the one nightstand against the wall, I think she could get the queen sized bed in there.

"Nana, I'm gonna buy you a new bed. Consider it a wedding gift. I'll take care of everything."

"You buy me enough stuff. Save-a you money!"

Well that won't stop me, I thought.

I called Ma when I got home. "Let's go to the furniture store. I want to get Nana a queen size mattress set. We'll get her new sheets and stuff too."

She was ready when I got home. She jumped in the seat next to me and said, "What brought this on?"

I told her poor Zio's story and she was laughing out loud. We got the queen sized bedding to match as closely to what Nana already as. After all, I now realize that she does not like change.

The mattress was being delivered day after tomorrow. Ma would be at Nana's for the delivery. I'll stop by after work and help put the new bedding on.

70

The following day I would do the regular show. When we finished, I would do two scenes with Dr. Mike. These would be the last scenes before my trip. The editors would chop them up, and use them to fill in all the romantic episodes with Mike.

There wasn't a lot of dialog. We held hands and looked into each other's eyes, while the nurses looked at us through the glass and talked about us.

Nurse Patricia : *"They are a beautiful couple, aren't they Nancy?"*

Nurse Nancy: *"Yeah, Patricia, they really are. They both have dark hair and eyes."*

Nurse Patricia: *"How much longer do you think she will have to stay?"*

Nurse Nancy: *"I don't know. I hope Dr. Mike doesn't sabotage the cast on her leg."*

Dr. Mike leans over and brushes his lips on hers. He loses his balance and ends up in Angie's lap.

Angie winces at first, then he draws her close while she tangles her fingers in his hair. This kiss is steamy. The camera shows Dr. Mike's shoes on the floor and the scene fades.

Credits begin to roll.

Some one in the stage crew yells, "Whoo Hoo!"

Everyone applauds.

I pushed Mike off me and slid over and motioned to the stagehand to get me out of the leg hoist. I couldn't exit the stage fast enough. The sound of applause and laughter followed me.

When I got to my dressing room I locked the door.

I knew Frank or Greg would be pounding to get in. Sure enough, Greg was calling "Lena, can I come in?"

Crap, I thought, *I knew this was going to be a big deal!*

I opened the door. "Don't make more of this than necessary, Greg."

Frank and Greg were both standing there. Frank was grinning from ear to ear. Greg was not grinning at all.

"Okay, what have you two got to say?"

Frank went first. "Lena, that couldn't have worked out better! Did you plan that?"

"No! Mike fell on top of me. He lost his balance."

"How did his shoes wind up on the floor?" he said.

I flopped down on a chair, "He was wearing loafers. They must have just slipped off."

Greg finally put his two cents in, "This romance with Mike is working out really well, isn't it?" He looked very glum.

Frank Latmen was a very serious guy, most of the time. Right now he looked like a man who was very pleased with the way things were turning out.

Another knock was at the door. It was Mona and Beth with flowers. Mike was behind them carrying cake. The cake said, "Bon Voyage."

"This is so nice of all of you. What a nice send off. I am coming back, you know?"

Mona was rounding everyone up, "Let's all go to the cafeteria! We'll have tables and chairs."

"I'll be along in a few minutes. I'll just change out of this hospital gown."

When everyone left, Greg was still standing there. "I'll wait for you Lena."

"Okay, you can be my escort. What's with the big party anyway?"

"Oh, Frank just wants you to know how much you'll be missed."

Greg put his arm around me while we walked to the cafeteria.

I think he was still hoping that he had some chance of a long-term relationship. I'm just not that open to anything permanent.

It was such a nice gathering. The entire cast and crew came to the cafeteria to wish me a great trip. Frank walked to the center of the room.

"Lena, I have an announcement to make. When you return from your trip, you will have top billing in the credits and be announced as "female lead." You've been performing that role for quite some time anyway".

Everyone applauded. A few moments later, Frank took me aside and whispered, "This role will come with a considerable increase in salary. You are the biggest draw for our ratings. Johnny will have the male lead billing. He's the only guy that we get lots of mail about, so far. I think Mike will steal that spot soon."

I gave him a bit fat smooch on the cheek. He blushed and wiped his cheek off while shaking his head.

How could I complain about this job? There aren't too many people who can have this much fun making a living.

71

When I got home, there was no doubt that my family was celebrating my trip as well. Auntie Lilly and Gemma were there with the babies. Nana and Zio were sitting on the porch. My dad was grilling steaks with Memo and Uncle Joey. I kissed my way inside and said to Ma, "This wasn't necessary. It's too much fuss."

"Oh honey, you deserve it! We all wanted to wish you *bon viaggio.*"

Secretly, I was hoping this shindig would end early. I needed to finish packing. I was thinking, *Matching outfits in layers; shoes and jewelry in the shoes to match each outfit.*

Yikes! Zio brought his concertina. I was never going to get out of here. Now baby Rosie and little Tony were dancing. They were doing a little tarantella.

Where did all this food come from? Dad was bringing up more wine from the basement. Greg's car just pulled up out in front.

I'm gonna go nuts before I leave for Italy.

I grabbed Gemma by the hand, "Come with me to finish packing!" Gemma was about eight months pregnant, so dragging her across the yard wasn't easy.

I had most of my clothes laid out on the bed in the spare bedroom. Gemma was sitting on the bed, placing the clothes and the tissue paper into the suitcase in layers.

"Lena, take some flat shoes. These are too fancy. You're gonna walk a lot while you're there. And you need more slacks."

"Penny said that women don't wear slacks so much like they do here."

"You only have three pair. Bring another pair of black slacks."

I pulled another pair out of my closed and handed them to her.

"I'm sure they have a washing machine."

"I don't know what they have, Gemma. They might wash their clothes on rocks for all I know."

Greg knocked at the door and walked in. He must have thought he was at the TV station.

"Hi ladies! Can I help with anything?"

"You didn't wait for me to ask you to come in, Greg."

"Well, I knew Gemma was here, so I knew you wouldn't be naked"

"Great of you to assume that, Greg."

"Really Lena, I came to help."

I know he's trying really hard to get the romance back into our relationship. That darned one-night stand got him all goofy.

"We're almost done. You can take this suitcase out to my dad's car if you wouldn't mind."

"Of course I don't mind."

"Lena, what about your makeup case?"

"I'll need that for morning"

"Walk me out to the car. I'm getting tired."

I walked Gemma outside; Greg was carrying baby Rosie out for her.

We said good-bye again and they drove off.

Greg followed me back into the house and put his arms around me. "Is this Gemma's second or third baby?"

"It's her third. I think they figured out how that happens now."

He laughed and kissed my neck, running his hands down my back.

"No, no, no, Greg. That's not going to happen."

"Can't blame a guy for trying. Can I kiss you good-bye?"

"Greg, please don't count on a long-term relationship. I don't know my own mind right now. My head is swimming with so much stuff, I can't give you what you need."

"I'd still like to kiss you good-bye, Lena."

"Can you control yourself?"

"I promise."

I let him kiss me goodnight and walked him to the door.

"I don't want to string you along, Greg."

"I understand, Lena. I'm always here if you need me."

Greg's a nice guy. I must be nuts not to latch on to him. My dad was coming across the yard as Greg was getting into his car. They waved to each other.

Dad came in and said, "Sit a minute, Lena."

Oh hell. Here comes the sermon about safety and the family.

"I want you to know how proud I am of you. There will be people watching out for you, so don't worry about anyone trying to muscle you."

Muscle me? What the hell does that mean? Do I need someone to watch out for me?

"Dad, get a good night's sleep. I don't want to discuss this trip anymore. I got the message; I'm aware of the pitfalls and the situation. I'm hoping to enjoy myself while I'm there, besides keep an eye on Penny."

"You're right, Lena. You get some sleep. Ma will give you a wakeup call."

Dad left, Ma called. "Do you want a big breakfast in the morning?"

"No breakfast, Ma. I'm flying first class. They serve lots of food."

"Oh, yeah. That's right. Goodnight, Bella."

72

I was finally on my way. Mama cried and hugged me like I was never coming back. It was raining. That complicated Mama's stress.

"How do they fly in the rain? I know they have all that electronic stuff. I'm still gonna worry. You should have eaten something. How long until they serve breakfast?"

"As soon as the plane leaves the ground, Ma."

"Oh, that's good. I put some biscotti in your purse if they take too long."

"When did she have time to sneak food in my purse?

We were ready to board. The agent was taking our tickets. As each person walked through the breezeway to enter the plane, the captain greeted each one personally. When he shook my hand, he said, "Miss Delatora, what a pleasure to meet you."

"Good morning, Captain. How did you know my name?"

"Ah, we get American soap operas in my town."

He was caressing my hand while the other passengers were waiting to board.

"Thank you. I'll find my seat now."

He kissed my hand before he released it.

He was very handsome, dark and elegant in his black uniform with all the gold decorations.

I thought his greeting was more familiar than it should have been. Maybe that's the difference in ethnic manners. After all, Italian men have quite a reputation.

The Alitalia flight was so elegant. Breakfast was served on beautiful china. It was a combination of breads, different egg dishes, and some fancy potato thing. Coffee, juices, and champagne were unlimited. The first class section was my new luxury in life.

The stewardess gave me little zipper bag with an eye mask, lotion, a hairbrush, and slippers. *Slippers!* I had no idea this was so fancy.

The rain sounded like chattering teeth tapping on the plane's widows. I really wasn't too pleased with that addition to my flight. I no sooner had that thought than piped in music started. That was better. I dozed restlessly in the reclining seats for a couple of hours. I was covered with a blanket when I woke up. The stewardess, whose name was Anna, came around at 11 a.m. with a snack cart. A plate with salami, cheese, warm bread, olives, and wine was placed on a cloth napkin on my mahogany pull-out tray. I'll be drunk by the time I get to Palermo.

How did they accomplish all this on an airplane?

She announced, "Lunch will be served at one thirty. You will find a menu on your snack tray. You can combine anything on the list or any of the complete lunches." She spoke perfect English with only a slight Italian accent.

"Thank you so much, this is lovely. I don't know if I can eat a full lunch. There is so much food here for the snack."

"I suggest you eat a light lunch. The captain has requested that you join him for dinner this evening."

"Oh, gosh! And where would he entertain a guest?"

"You will see a small area behind his seat. It has a folding panel for privacy. A table pulls down from the wall, bigger than this tray. It's very nice. Very private, you will see."

"Do I consider this an invitation?"

"He will stop to see you after lunch, to be sure that you accepted the invitation."

"Well, thank you for telling me in advance, Anna."

This flight was heaven so far. It was long, but everyone was so attentive that it was a very pleasant experience.

I was reading a book after lunch when I heard my name, "Miss Delatora." I looked up to see that handsome captain standing next to my seat.

"I would be pleased to invite you to dinner in my compartment this evening." He took my hand and caressed it, while running his other hand up my arm, giving me the chills.

I'm not sure if I liked the way he handled these parts of my body. Those aren't private body parts, but his hands were very sensual.

I found myself pulling my hand back while smiling at him.

Why not? I wondered. *How much trouble could I get into on a plane filled with people?*

"I would be pleased to dine with you, Captain."

"Tomas Benecase, at your service, Senorina. The stewardess will come to you around 6 p.m. to bring you forward."

"Thank you, Captain Benecase."

"Call me Tomas, please."

"Thank you, Tomas. I will see you this evening."

The lady in the seat across from me leaned over and said, "Oh, honey he's a hunk. You're a lucky girl."

"I'll let you know later, how lucky I am."

She laughed out loud at that. "My name is Louise Prince." She extended her hand across the aisle.

"Lena Delatora." I shook hands with her. She was older than I first thought. Once she turned her head toward me, I could see her more clearly, but she was very well kept and oozed wealth, from the looks of her clothes and jewelry.

"Yes, I recognized you when we boarded. I wanted to give you some privacy."

"How nice of you," I responded. "I'm glad for your company. It's been a long flight."

She told me that she was visiting her daughter in Palermo. Her daughter married a man from Italy while teaching here. She is expecting her first child.

"You must be very excited. Will you be staying very long?"

"Two months. At least that's what I planned. We'll see how well she copes with the baby and how long she can stay off her job."

We chatted quite a long time. I told her that my Nana was from

Marsala. I told her the story about my Nana marrying Dad's uncle. She thought that was very amusing. Then she asked about who was filling in for me on *Tortured Souls*.

"My scenes were filmed ahead of time. You'll be surprised at how creative they are with splicing it into existing episodes."

"Oh, now I can't wait to see what happens!"

Before too long, Anna came to tell me that dinner was ready in the captain's compartment. "I'll will escort you to the cockpit."

I had already freshened up and put on a different blouse. I was glad that I had packed two shirts and another skirt in my carry-on bag. I'd have another outfit to change into for my arrival in Palermo.

The captian was standing in front of the cockpit entrance. He pushed open the metal door that opened into a spacious, private area. The food looked beautiful, like all of the other meals on this flight.

Before we had the chance to sit down, the captain stepped toward me and pushed his body against mine. He was obviously very glad to see me. Well, this gave the word "cockpit" an entirely different meaning.

I put my hand against his chest and pushed him back. I made a sideways move to sit into the compact chair. He quickly took the seat across from me.

"Tomas, that was very forward and quite rude."

"Please forgive me, Miss Delatora. I was overwhelmed by your beauty."

Once again, I reminded myself of where I was. The cultural differences and expectations of male/female relationships were somewhat bent toward allowing this behavior.

"Please, let's continue with dinner. Forgive my rudeness. I often forget that Americans have different customs. I have ordered scaloppini with wine sauce, some garlic pastas, as well as lavish desserts."

I smiled and said thank you.

I was not immune to this handsome man, whose long legs and arms seemed to overtake the small space. I think I mentioned before, his smells were a real turn-on too.

He worked hard at being a gentleman throughout dinner. His questions were slightly personal, but not rude. We discussed my last relationship, although not in detail.

He told me that he was widowed and had grown children. In my mind, I thought this made him too old for me to entertain the thought of dating. He must have married very young. But then, I thought, he might not have dating on his mind at all. Perhaps he was thinking of different type of encounter entirely. An encounter of a lot less personal nature than dating, like a cockpit encounter.

We had coffee, and wine with dessert. By the time we were finished with the meal, I was more than ready to spend the next few hours alone with a good book.

Capitan Tomas kissed my hand, then both my cheeks. The hand would have been sufficient, but he was going to fly the plane, so I didn't want to make him mad. The copilot had been alone for long enough.

Louise had her nose in a magazine while she ate her dessert. Once I was settled in my seat, she raised her head just enough to peek over her magazine. "Well, your face is very flushed."

We both laughed. "Our captain is an awful flirt, made some very forward moves, and has extremely fast hands."

She really got a chuckle out of that. "I'd be disappointed if he were any different. This is Italy, my Dear. It's all very different. I think because you play a certain type of lady on your *Tortured Souls*, he may have expected you to be that same lady in real life."

"Louise, I thought about that myself."

Everyone seemed to settle in for some rest. We would be landing in about five hours. With the time difference, it would be morning when we got there.

73

The flight was descending. The captain announced our approach to the airport. It was a very smooth landing. There were only two slight bumps when the wheels hit the runway. Passengers exited the plane, thanking the stewardesses and flight crew. Of course, Captain Benecase bowed to everyone, but he kissed my hand, making him appear as if were much closer than we actually were. I was glad this flight was over. I don't owe anyone any more affection than I feel necessary. After all, this is the sixties and I am liberated.

I collected my luggage and looked for a sign with my name on it. I saw a man holding a large cardboard up that said, "LENA." Yep, that's me. I'm glad it didn't have my last name.

The driver smiled and said, "Good morning" in English. He said, "Please follow me."

Oh, I would be glad to follow this hunk. Stop right now, Lena! Don't even think about it.

As we got closer to his vehicle, Penny jumped out and ran to me. We jumped up and down like a couple of twelve-year olds. We were both chattering and asking a million questions, greeting each other with hugs and kisses.

"How are you? How was the flight? You look fantastic!"

We had to stop and catch our breath. I finally asked, "Where are we staying?"

"You're going to love it, Lena! It's an old villa. Some modern conveniences like a washer and dryer, a TV, and some air conditioning, mostly it's really ancient. The furniture is all antiques. It has about twenty-five rooms. I've only been in about ten of them.

We'll have to go exploring. I've been too afraid to wander around alone in this big house."

"It hardly sounds like a house. More like a museum."

"That's what it looks like. Wait until you see it! We have to drive about an hour, but we're going to stop for breakfast. Vince is our driver. He's taking us to a little family owned restaurant. The food is fabulous. I've been there before."

I was amused at how animated Penny was. She seemed to have come out of her shyness to a great extent. She was chatting with Vince, giving him instructions and requesting different stops to make on the way to the villa.

When we got to the little café, Vince went in ahead of us. I asked Penny why we didn't go with him. "You know, Lena. Someone always checks every place I go. Carlo calls him my escort, but he's really my bodyguard. I caught on to that right away."

Vince came out and said, "I've taken the liberty of ordering for you ladies. I hope that's okay."

He spoke perfect English. How nice.

"Thanks, Vince. That's just fine."

The little place was really the front portion of a house. It was probably the living room and dining room. They had little tables and chairs in the two rooms. I felt like I was in my Nana's house.

Penny acted like royalty. She has accepted the role of "pampered lady" with no problem.

We had fried bread with eggs in the middle, potatoes and eggs, hot rolls, homemade jelly pastries, and some of the strongest coffee I have ever had. I don't think I'll sleep until late tonight, so it's probably good to get this caffeine early in the day.

Vince took his plate and sat at a small table facing the door. That was a sure sign that he was looking out for us, no matter what you call him.

We stopped at an overlook and Penny pointed out the villa where we are staying. "If you look on the left side of the villa, you can see a huge garden. There is a pool in the back, but it's sheltered from the street. The front terrace has a beautiful garden and lawn chairs with tables and a big fountain. Sometimes I have dinner outside, mostly when Carlo gets home early enough."

"What does Carlo do, Penny?"

"He's doing some work for his father. He showed me the building once. He has a little office and he does some bookkeeping and manages the company."

I know Penny. She's not that naïve. Whatever helps her get through her days is just fine with me.

74

The villa was as beautiful as Penny said. The stone carving on the front of the villa said, "Villa Bazzoli by the Sea," in Italian. I guess it had been in the Bazzoli family for a very long time. I had my own room with a private bath. The bathrooms were added sometime in the twenties, but they were very nice. Heck, as long as they have a tub, toilet, and sink, what else do I need? The villa was over one hundred years old. They had tile all over the place. The walls and the floors were beautiful. No wonder it lasted so long. The garden area as well as the pool had beautiful tile on the ground. *I think I'm gonna like this place*, I thought to myself. The ceilings are so high! Some of the help looks like they have been here since the place was built.

Vanessa, one of the maids, was helping me unpack. She was ancient, but not as old as some of the help I've seen. They had wardrobe cabinets, no closets. She was mumbling something about. *"Too much clothes. Americans buy too much."* I pretended I didn't understand her. Actually, I only understood bits of what she said. Maybe she spoke a different dialect, or she was talking too fast.

I decided that I would ignore whatever Penny ignored. That sounded like a safe game plan, until I got accustomed to who was in charge of what.

"Lena, do you want to explore the villa?"

"Yes! I can't wait!"

"Let's go back to the entry hall. These walls are one-foot thick. The tapestries hanging are older than the house. All these portraits are of the Bazzolis. The one on the top right is Carlo's great grandmother. The stone steps are from the river at the back of the house. The river doesn't look like much now, but when the house was built, the riverbed had a ton of stone. Those stones were hand chiseled and fitted one by one.

We started on the first floor.

"Penny, I think I saw this kitchen in a Frankenstein movie."

"They haven't remodeled it since it was built. The stoves and ovens have been replaced, except for the stone oven where the 'bread cook,' Katarina, bakes. She wouldn't let anyone touch it." Penny said the long wooden tables had newer wooden tops. They had been placed over the old tops that were very damaged and scarred.

"The walls have not been painted in ages. It's hard to tell what color they started out as. I've seen the cleaning ladies tie white clothes on the ends of brooms and clean the walls."

Dozens of pots and pans hung from hooks. Most were copper, some were stainless, and others cast iron. Baskets of vegetables were lined up on another counter. A huge basket of potatoes was under the table. This kitchen was overwhelming.

"How many people live here?"

"Right now I think there are about ten—that includes the people who work here. Some of the help have a house in the back. Katrina and her husband live in the back of our house. He's the gardener. The cottage is as big as my house in Chicago."

"Penny, this looks like they could have made movies here!"

"They probably did!"

We went out the back door of the kitchen where vegetables grew and flowers climbed on trellises. Penny was right about the servant's house. It was like a guesthouse.

Vanessa, her daughter, and husband lived in the cottage. He helped Katrina's husband in the garden. Katrina baked all of the bread daily. Vanessa ran the house and they both cooked. They stay out of each other's way for the most part. You don't want two cooks in the kitchen.

Oh hell, I thought. *Fresh baked bread every day, right in this house. I'm really in trouble now.*

"Let's go to the back section of the house!"

Penny led me through the rest of the bedrooms downstairs. There was a huge living room with ceilings about twenty feet tall. There was enough furniture in the living room and dining room to fill my house several times. Then there was the library. Penny showed me where to find books in English. Jeez, this place was huge.

"Do you want to see the upstairs yet? I've never gone any further than the first floor."

"I'm a little overwhelmed already. I'm glad our rooms are on the first floor."

I have a bedroom and bathroom, but Penny and Carlo have a bedroom, bathroom, and a nice little sitting room. It was very cozy for them. Our rooms were down a long hallway to the right of the entry hall.

We decided to have a snack in the garden. The temperature had dropped a few degrees. Vanessa brought out bread with olive oil and grated cheese, cool wine, and fruit and sliced cheeses. I am just a big fat pig. I could enjoy living like this.

Penny reminded me that it stays light until nearly 10 p.m. "Do you want to walk to the plaza? Everyone strolls around the fountain."

"I would love that. Will Vince be joining us?"

"Yes. But we have to pretend that we don't know him. He keeps his distance. If we have gelato, he will come a little closer to be sure it's what everyone else is having."

"Holy cow, Penny."

"You'll get used to it."

We both freshened up. Penny wore a long skirt and a sleeveless blouse. I wore a sleeveless summer dress with a full skirt.

"Does this look okay?"

"Yep, it's perfect"

When we got outside, Vince was waiting for us.

"I'll walk with both of you tonight, Miss Penny. Miss Lena is new to town; it will look as if I'm with her."

Vince was pretty easy on the eyes, so I didn't argue that.

We strolled at a leisurely pace. I was surprised at how many people were on the streets. As we got closer to the main street, it seemed like everyone was outside. People sat on steps or walked in the streets. Clusters of friends and families gathered everywhere.

We found some stone steps to sit on near the fountain. I was happy people watching and eating my gelato.

Vince stepped back just far enough to let us have some girl talk.

Penny poked me with her elbow. "What do you think of Vince? He's single, you know."

"Oh, that's good to know. You know that Whitey and I split up?"

"Nooo! I'm really sorry to hear that. I was honestly joking about Vince. When did the breakup happen, Lena?"

"Just a few days before I left. Is Vince really single?"

"Yes!"

I gave her a condensed version of Whitey's feelings about the family involvement.

"Well, Lena, at least we know that Vince is in up to his ears already."

We both laughed at that. In my head, I was sorting Penny's behavior and comments. It seemed like she was very comfortable with the facts about Carlo and the family.

Suddenly, I was struck with jet lag. I was exhausted. We decide to head back to the villa. Vince asked if I wanted to take his arm. I thanked him and hooked my arm through his. He insisted on walking on my left, at the curbside.

Penny and I chatted while we walked. She told me that they were able to get special connections to American television. She watched me fall down in the ski scene.

As we chatted, I became focused on a couple across the street. It was an older man with a beautiful young woman. She was very pregnant. He was talking very loud and held her roughly by the arm. Penny and I both stared.

Vince placed himself between us and linked his arms with ours. "Turn your heads away ladies. It's best you don't acknowledge some things."

I looked up at Vince and said. "He must have paid dearly for that young bride."

He could tell that I was really upset by what I saw.

I looked over at Penny. "I've seen them before. He treated her like that before I knew she was pregnant," she said.

"Wow, what a creep. He got the young bride. You would think he could treat her better than that."

Vince said nothing, but hurried us along.

We entered the villa through the garden gate. Vince unlocked the kitchen door and walked each of us to our rooms, saying a polite goodnight.

I took a quick shower and fell into bed. I must have slept like the dead. I'm usually very sensitive to the bright morning light. Vanessa came in and opened the curtains, and it never woke me up.

"Miss Lena, *bunongiorno. Alzati!*"

She scared the hell out of me. I jumped straight up. I saw that she had brought coffee. I sat on the side of the bed and helped myself.

I was still trying to adjust to where I was, as well as the time difference, when someone knocked on my door. Vanessa said, "*Entrare.*"

What? I can speak for myself. She just told someone to come in—just like at the TV station.

Fortunately, it was Penny. She pulled up at chair and poured herself coffee off the bedside table.

"You can go now, Vanessa." Vanessa mumbled something about "*Americanos,*" and left the room.

"I didn't think she understood English."

"Oh, she understands a lot more than she lets on, so be careful what you say around her."

"Thanks for the warning. I'll remember that."

"Lena, do you want to swim this morning. It's going to get really hot later today. We'll come in after we swim, have lunch, take a little nap, and go to town tonight."

"Penny, where's Carlo?"

"He got in late last night and left early this morning. He's going to try to come home for lunch. But he has to go back to the office until later. Let's go swim."

I couldn't help notice how accepting Penny was of all things family. It seemed that she loved this life, loved Carlo, and was adjusting just great to her life in the villa.

"I'll change and meet you at the pool."

When I got outside, I looked in the pool area and didn't see Penny. I went in to the garden seating area. Penny was sitting in a chair next to a girl in a lounge chair. The girl had a cloth on her head and Penny was holding her hand.

As I got closer, I recognized the girl from last night in the town square.

"Oh, Lena, this is Mariella. I saw her holding on to the gate when I came out. She was leaning forward. I think she was about to faint."

Vince came out of the house with a glass of cold water and some cloths in a bowl of ice.

"Miss Penny, she can't stay here. You shouldn't have let her in."

"What the heck, Vince? She's pregnant and was alone out there. What was I supposed to do?"

My opinion of Vince just slipped down a notch on the compassion scale.

"I understand how you feel, Miss Penny. Let's get her feeling better and send her on her way."

"Shouldn't we pull the car around and take her to her house."

"I'll take her part of the way, but we can't be seen with her. You stay here with Miss Lena."

Penny didn't ask any more questions. It seemed like there was more to this pregnant girl's story than we both knew. I would bet that the old man she was married to was extremely possessive and didn't want her to have any contact with outsiders.

Mariella was feeling better. She drank plenty of water. Penny and I took turns switching the cold rags on her head. The heat was brutal again today. She shouldn't have been out alone.

Vince brought the car around to the front gate and we walked Mariella outside. Vince came around and helped her into the car.

"Grazie, grazie. Mia migliore." Thank you, I am better, she said.

Penny and I watched the car drive down the street. We looked at each other. "That's so sad, isn't it? That poor girl has a life of heartache to look forward to. That old husband must be a real jerk."

"Yea," Penny agreed. "There are so many stories in this town. I really have learned to mind my own business."

"You do a fine job of that, Penny. I don't know if I could do as well."

75

Mr. Latmen was in the studio looking at the TV monitor. He was watching the finished, cleaned-up section of my ski accident.

"Lena did a great job on that fall."

Eddie, the producer agreed.

"We'll show it at the end of tomorrow's episode. It will be interesting to see how viewers respond to her fall."

Frank must have had this type of experience before. Just as soon as the credit rolled the phones started ringing. *Everyone wanted to know if Angie/Lena was really hurt. Who's going to take her place? Is she going to leave the show?*

"Great fall. I knew this was going to boost those ratings as soon as her butt hit the ground!" Frank said.

Sophia and Eddie were thrilled as well.

"Tomorrow we'll tape some shots of Dr. Mike writing to Angie, telling her how much he misses her. Those will be saved for episodes after Angie leaves the hospital."

Beth was pacing in her dressing room. Greg was with her.

"Why are you so worried about your scene? Mona is very easy to work with. She'll help you in any way she can. Are you worried about your lines?"

"No. Not my lines. I'm just worried about everything else."

"What do you mean, Beth?"

"What if Lena doesn't come back?"

"She's gonna come back, Beth."

"If she doesn't come back?"

"People start rumors, Beth."

Greg decided to call Red. Penny needed someone to assure her about today's show. It had to be someone who had an emotional attachment. That's how Penny functioned.

"I called Red. He's going to keep you company until the show starts."

"Greg, what if Lena doesn't come back and we all need to take on more of a role in the show?"

"Oh! Here's Red. I'm going to go get some props ready for the show. He'll take care of you, Beth."

When Greg walked out of the dressing room, he heard Red telling Beth, "It's going to be just fine, sweetheart."

Greg knew that breaking up with Beth was one of the best things that could have happened in his life.

76

Penny and I were in the pool. Carlo and Niko were walking toward us. I was glad to see Carlo, but I wasn't expecting to see Niko.

Penny and I climbed out of the pool and wrapped ourselves in big towels. Carlo hugged me tight, got wet, and hugged Penny harder.

Niko held out his arms to me and put me in a bear hug. Then he kissed Penny on both cheeks.

"Niko! I didn't know you were coming." I smiled my best smile.

"It was easier to come and help out rather than keep giving Carlo instructions. He has had a lot on his shoulders since he got here."

"Carlo, why don't you spend some time in the pool with the girls this afternoon?"

"Dad, don't you need me at the office?"

"I can take care of this. It's more important that you spend time with these beautiful ladies in the pool."

Somehow, I got the feeling that this plan was already worked out earlier.

Vanessa brought a cold lunch to the poolside: meats and cheese and come caprisi salad and wine.

After lunch, Niko excused himself and kissed Penny and I good-bye. "Let's have a nice dinner tonight. Vince knows the place. Come around 8 p.m. Carlo, come to the office around two. We'll finish our business and meet the ladies there."

We sat around the pool and chatted for a while. Carlo asked, "Where's Vince?"

Penny, who was dozing in Carlo's arms, half asleep, replied, "He took Vanessa to town for groceries."

I sat up and said, "Let's all go with him next time. I would love to see all the stalls of food and clothes."

Carlo laughed. "You'll get your chance, Lena. You and Penny will need a full day for that."

Vince seemed to be the *"go to"* guy for everything. He was certainly the strong silent type. He seemed to be around all the time, but never in an obvious place.

Penny pointed him out at the pool. "Do you see that little wooden table behind those bushes."

"Yes, I see it."

"You can see his feet under those bushes. There is a convenient bare spot in the bushes at eye level. We are never out of his sight. He watches us like a hawk."

"Wow! I didn't realize that watching us was so critical."

"Well, it is. I don't ask why. He made me understand, very gently, that he is everywhere that I am, except for my bedroom and bathroom. Whether I see him or not. Now the same will apply to you."

"I never see him, Penny. He's really good at what he does. He must wear camouflage or something."

"Nope, he's just quiet and careful. He used to check my bedroom at night. But, that was before Carlo got here."

"What do you mean? Didn't you get here together?"

"Yes, but the first week, Carlo had to stay in town doing some business for his Dad."

"Well, it's good to know that someone is looking out for us. Penny, will Vince be joining us for dinner tonight?"

"Oh, he'll be our driver, but he'll have his dinner at a separate table. When we're finished, he will bring us home."

Carlo had gone into the house to get dressed for the office.

I went into my room to get clothes out and select my wardrobe for the evening.

I could hear two men's voices through the open bathroom window.

"The hole will be in the boat already. I'll knock out the plug with my foot when we get out far enough. You will have a boat nearby, ready to pick me up."

"How do you know he can't swim?"

"We've investigated that already."

I knew exactly what I was hearing. This was the culmination of Carlo's ceremony. It was the final act of his swearing in to be a made man. It was the killing.

My mind was racing. I sat on the bed and took deep breaths. I knew this was something that had to be done. I knew the family had determined this was a bad man who needed to be eliminated. Carlo couldn't erase anyone who had an ounce of goodness in his heart. I knew both voices.

When the men outside my window were gone, I got into the shower. I couldn't stop shaking and kept taking deep breaths.

I decided on a pink sleeveless dress with white shoes and a clutch purse. I am an actress. I can pretend that everything is just fine. I knew I could never repeat what I had heard but I could pretend that I never heard it, because that's how good I am.

I knocked on Penny's door. When she opened it, she looked so cute! She was wearing a full red skirt and a beautiful white sleeveless sweater. I gave her my best smile.

I said, "Let's go show off for these men!" We linked arms and walked to the front door.

Vince was waiting outside. He said, "Well, you ladies both look lovely," as he opened the door. He helped us into the car and closed the door.

As the car approached the center of town, I noticed a commotion in front of a yellow brick house. People seemed to be upset, and comforting each other.

"Vince, what happened? Is someone sick?"

"There was an accident. Someone drowned in an old boat this afternoon."

I felt my stomach flip over. I made the connection immediately. This was the plan I had heard through the bathroom window.

"That's just awful. How sad. Do you know who it was?"

"Yes. It was Mariella's father."

"Oh, no," Penny said. We were both stunned

"How is she doing, Vince?"

"She seems to be handling it pretty well, Penny. I saw her this afternoon when we were at the market. She has a big family. They will take care of her."

I said, "I hope her old husband is some comfort to her."

He got very quiet. "Lena, she has no husband."

There was no need for further discussion about Mariella. I realized that the father treated her badly because she was pregnant out-of-wedlock.

We got to the restaurant for dinner. It was a lovely old building that might have been a stone barn at one time. A big terrace had been added to the back. The party had spilled over to the outside, as well as the room between the eating area and the terrace.

Niko and Carlo were doing a lot of hand shaking and backslapping. They greeted us with open arms.

I was given this gift of acting. I am really good at it. I pretended that I was thrilled to be among these people who were celebrating. I was introduced to several people who joined our group.

I looked around at all these people. Most of them were men. I had a sudden realization that most of them were murderers. Not necessarily today, but they were all family members and had killed at some point, to be sworn in.

The subject of my TV show came up and the conversation focused on that for quite a while. I was glad to participate in a subject that I knew something about.

I just kept drinking more wine. It seemed that Vince was mingling with the group more than usual. He wasn't off to the side, or hiding like he usually does. I'm pretty sure that he was the person filling my glass with wine.

Our gathering broke up around 1 a.m. There was more backslapping and hand shaking. I couldn't help noticing that Carlo was at the center of this crowd.

Carlo rode home with us. Since Penny and Carlo were in the back seat, I rode in front with Vince. Penny was all snuggled up against Carlo, chatting up a storm. Wine will do that to a girl.

Vince looked over at me and smiled. I knew he was amused by Penny's chatter in the back seat.

I was a little surprised when Vince reached over and took my hand. I didn't pull away, but I felt a little strange. I'm usually pretty sure of myself in close situations. I guess I wasn't sure where Vince's loyalties belonged, or what my loyalties were either.

I'm not saying that Vince wasn't a good-looking guy. I found myself staring at him on more than one occasion. I didn't think he noticed me doing that. I thought about pulling my hand away and decided, *What the heck! Sometimes a girl needs a little attention.*

We dropped Penny and Carlo off out in front of the house. I started to get out, but Vince pulled me back. "Lena, can you wait? Come with me to put the car in the garage."

"Okay, no problem."

We pulled the car around the back and he came around to open the door for me. I was half expecting him to pull me to him in an embrace. He just held my hand and helped me out of the car.

What the hell? Now I was expecting him to make a pass at me! What's a girl gotta do?

He led me toward the backyard. His little table was set up with a cloth. It was under an arbor. I never noticed that before. The table was set with fresh flowers. A plate with pastries was on the table, along with some cheese and red wine with two glasses on a tray.

"Well, it looks like you were planning this."

He pulled out a chair for me and poured each of us some wine. I called Vanessa when we were leaving the restaurant.

I put my elbows on the table and my chin on my fists. He held up his glass and we said "salute."

"So, Vince what's this all about?"

"This is my attempt at a first date. It's the best I could do right now."

"I'm a little surprised, Vince."

"Why, Lena? Did you think I wasn't allowed? Wait! Before you answer, I talked to Carlo about your last relationship."

"Oh, do you mean the one who couldn't handle my family obligations or the one who dumped me for the little girl he was promised to when he was twelve years old?

Vince laughed, "Lena, was that a warning to me not to cross you?"

"I don't know how to handle this?"

"Lena, can we just enjoy each other's company and get to know each other?"

"Okay, Vince. Tell me about yourself. Start with *'When I was a little boy . . .'* "

"When I was a little boy, I grew up on the North side of Chicago."

"What's your last name, Vince?"

"Morreale. My dad owned a butcher shop on Cleveland Avenue."

I thought about this for a moment. "I remember you, Vince! I used to go in there with my nana all the time. I always thought you were so handsome."

"I wish I could say that I remember you, Lena. I would probably remember your nana. What's Nana's last name?"

"DeLuca."

"DeLuca! Do you have a bunch of uncles? Sammy, Joey, Paulie, Mikey?"

"Yes, Johnny and Pete too."

"I knew Paulie and Joey best. When I was thirteen, my dad sent me here to learn the family business. My dad thought the business was the same as his: groceries and meats. He couldn't have been more mistaken."

"Vince, this is really a strange coincidence."

"Lena, I don't believe in coincidence. I think some things are meant to be."

"Does your dad know what kind of 'business' you are in now?"

"We never talk about it. If he knows, he keeps it to himself. What can he do? The decision was made and now I live here."

I was beginning to understand what his family connections

were. He was more than a bodyguard. He had a set of skills that were still being developed. He took orders and he gave orders. He made some decisions on his own and he consulted higher-ups when he needed to. In his own words, *"I am an asset and a liability."*

I felt like Vince was a force to be dealt with. I understood that he was a lot more than he appeared to be.

I looked him in the eye and said, "Are you going to tell me about the man who died today?"

"It's ugly, Lena, but here it is: for your ears only. The young girl who fainted outside the gate, it is her father, just like I told you. He is also the father of her baby. Her mother died when she was eleven years old. He has been raping her since then. He made her do everything her mama did: that included housework, cooking, and everything a wife would do."

I felt a little sick when he told me this. That poor, poor girl.

"So, Vince, now that her papa is gone, will the her family take care of her? Did they all know what was happening to her?"

"Her aunt came to us. They knew, but he threatened them. He told them all to mind their own business. Now it's over, and maybe she will have some chance at a normal life."

"Vince, she's going to have a twisted, disgusting memory of her baby's father. What will she tell her baby about his or her father?"

"She will tell him that his father and his grandpa drowned in a fishing boat together. And that will be the truth for the most part."

We were both quiet for quite a while. I was lost in thought. "It's almost daylight, Vince."

"Lena, I wanted this to be a little romantic. But it didn't turn out that way."

"Maybe you didn't notice that I have my feet in your lap. That's a little romantic."

"Oh, but I did notice. I didn't mention it, because I didn't want you to move them."

"Vince, I need to go to sleep now. I mean by myself!"

He let out a loud chuckle. "Let me walk you to your room."

He kept his arm around me as we walked toward the house.

Vanessa opened the kitchen door when we passed. She started jabbering in Italian and Vince responded in a stream of words back at her. She called him Vincenzo, his Italian name.

When she closed the kitchen door he said, *"Pazzo."*

We stood outside my room and he kissed me goodnight. He nuzzled his face in my hair and said, "I want to remember your smells. I waited days to get this close to you."

I fell into bed exhausted. I didn't even take my makeup off.

I didn't know what to make of this guy. If I fell for him, I'd be leaving myself wide open to be hurt again. He lived in Italy. What kind of relationship would that be? Am I an easy mark? Maybe this would be different, or perhaps it would just be a vacation fling.

In the morning, it was business as usual. Vanessa woke me up with her usual grace and charm, pulling open the drapes and stomping around like a 250-pound truck driver. *Bunongiorno! Alzati!*

Wake up! Geez, I just went to sleep. She sure runs a tight ship.

"What time is it, Vanessa?"

"It's after breakfast. Almost lunch!"

"What? No coffee? Are you trying to kill me?"

Someone knocked at the door. I said, "Come in." It was Penny.

She had a little wooden cart with food and coffee. "I made this myself. Vanessa said that breakfast was over. It's only ten o'clock. I knew you would want coffee and stuff."

"Oh, Penny, you are an angel." She had fixed toast, eggs, and some fried apples with cinnamon and sugar.

"Vanessa, you need to be a little nicer to Lena. She misses her mamma and papa."

"Oh, Miss Lena, you live-a with your mamma and papa?" She walked over and pinched my cheeks.

"I think she was thinking that I'm a loose woman because of what she must have heard about my acting job."

"Yes, Lena. I don't think she expected you to be close to your parents. She'll have a different attitude now. I bet she'll treat you like a little princess."

"Oh, you mean instead of an intruder or a lazy cow?"

We both looked at Vanessa. She smiled and nodded, but we knew she understood most of what we said. I was looking forward to the new and improved treatment.

Penny looked outside, "Another hot day, Lena. Do you want to swim today?"

"Yes, but let's go into town while it's cooler, then we can swim after lunch."

"I'll let Vince know, so he can get ready."

"Oh, Penny, can I tell him? Where is his room?"

"Ohhh, Carlo and I thought we saw some unspoken looks between you two!"

"Well you were both on target, let me tell you! He had a little romantic table set up behind the trees with wine and cheese. We talked until it was almost morning."

"How do you feel about that? I mean him making a pass at you."

"I'm a little surprised. But I feel good about the attention. I've been a little blue since Whitey and I split up."

"Oh by all means, go tell Vince what you want to do today. It's the second door to the left of the kitchen. It has a lion's head doorknocker. Lift the jaw to tap the door."

I had no sooner lifted the lion's jaw when the door swung open and Vince pulled me inside. His lips locked on mine before I could say a word.

"Whew! I guess you're glad to see me."

He laughed. "Well, I thought you came to continue what we started early this morning."

"I wanted to ask you if we could go into town today."

I was wearing my bathing suit cover up over my two-piece bathing suit until we decided what we were doing today. He had that up and over my head before I knew where his hands were. How do men do that? I think it's some sort of genetic thing that happens with them. I haven't met one man who didn't have fast hands.

I managed to get my hands up in a motion to halt his advances. "How did you know it was me?"

"When you lift the lions jaw, there is a peep hole under it."

"Oh, I wondered how you managed to pull me in so quickly."

There was a knock at the door. Dear Vanessa announced in her gravely voice, "Vincenzo, *dire a Lena che ha fiori!*"

"Okay. Vanessa!"

"Did she say I got flowers?"

"Yup."

"Gee, I guess it's no secret that I'm in here. She seems to know everything."

"Carlo says that she has eyes on the back of her head."

"I guess I'll go see who sent the flowers."

Vince was trying to look unconcerned, but I could tell he was actually annoyed.

"Get dressed, Vince. I'll meet you in the front hall."

Penny was holding the flowers when I got into the kitchen.

"Who the heck is Captain Benecase?"

I started to laugh. "He's the captain of the flight that I arrived on."

"Let me see that card."

Vince walked up behind me and took the card out of my hand.

"Dear Senorina Delatora, It was my extreme pleasure to meet you. Thank you for sharing dinner with me."

"When did you have time to eat dinner with him? I brought you here directly from the airport."

"Well, Vinnie, Captain Benecase had a private dining area behind the cockpit of his plane."

"Penny, explain how a cockpit becomes a dining area."

"Well, Vince, I really don't know."

"Okay you two, it has a table behind the seats with a little partition that pulls down."

"Well,"Vince said. "Only an Italian airline would think of that. I see he has a phone number here. Are you planning to call him?"

"No, I wasn't planning to. I don't even know how he knew where I was staying."

Penny was laughing out loud. "Oh, you two sound like an old

married couple. I didn't know this was so serious."

Mumble, mumble, mumble. That's all I heard from Vanessa as we left.

We parked on the side street near the market. We crossed over to the shady side. The shops were so unusual. I could see this was going to be an expensive afternoon.

I glanced across the street and saw Mariella. She was dressed in a pretty flowered smock, walking like a little penguin. She walked with a little lady who could have been her grandma. The grandma-lady carried some net shopping bags. It was apparent that the bags had colorful baby clothes. They stopped at a sidewalk café and sat down.

"Vince! Çan we go across the street and say 'hello'?"

"Lena, it would be better if we mind our own business. She needs time to adjust to what's happened to her."

"I guess that's true."

"What happened to her?" Penny asked.

I kept my head down and let Vince explain. "Her father and her husband died the other day in a boating accident."

"Oh I thought I understood Vanessa saying something about that. She was married to that older man, wasn't she?

"Yes her father and husband went fishing together all the time. Terrible accident. Too bad."

"Yes, poor thing. Lena, do you think we should have a little baby shower for her?"

"No, Penny. I think we should let her family fuss over her for a while. She needs that."

Vince squeezed my hand while we were walking. I knew he approved of my comments.

We shopped until Vince couldn't carry any more bags. Penny and I were loaded down too.

"How will I ever get this stuff home?" I wondered out loud.

Vince offered the suggestion, "Lena, I can ship it for you. Penny has sent a lot of stuff home already."

"Oh gosh, Lena, I've sent huge crates of stuff to my mom and her husband."

"Okay, then I'll stop worrying,"

"We walked along the side street where our car was parked. I glanced to my left and saw Carlo with two other men. It looked like he was putting the muscle on some creepy looking guy. Vince glanced at me and gave me a subtle shake of his head.

"Ladies, let's turn at this corner. There's a little place that has the best gelato you will ever taste."

I don't think Penny saw it. If she did, she never acted as if she saw anything. Vince walked us to the little gelato stand and we picked our flavors. "You ladies rest while I'll get the car."

He left the packages with us and off he went.

77

had so much fun today, Penny. It's been a long time since we went shopping together."

"Yes, I know. Especially after I met Carlo."

"Penny, how long do you think you'll be staying in Italy? You seem very happy here."

"It's a different lifestyle, Lena. I have never been so happy or confident about myself. Carlo seems very happy here."

I wanted to say, *"How would you know. You hardly see him."* Instead I asked, "Will he always have these long hours?"

"We talked about this recently. He told me he wants some time off from his duties with his dad's company. He is trying to get next week off, while you're here, and go up to the mountains. We talked about a place where he stayed as a child. You could see the entire countryside down to the ocean, all along the coastline."

Vince pulled up with the car and we loaded all our packages. "Aren't you going to get any gelato?" I asked.

"I don't think I will. Vanessa is planning Eggplant Parmesan and tiramisu for dinner. I always stuff myself then pig out on the tiramisu."

"I wonder if she could broil some chicken and make a salad for me. I glanced at my backside this morning. It looks like dinosaurs still roam the earth."

Penny and Vince cracked up at that. Vince finally said, "It looks great to me."

I saw Penny's eyebrows go up.

When we pulled into the driveway at the villa, Vanessa was pacing and wringing her hands.

"Ho aspettato per voi. Mariella! Il suo bambino è in arrivo."

"Easy Vanessa. Slow down. "

"The bambino is coming. They have nobody with a car. They send a little cousin to tell me breech. The feet coming first."

Suddenly we all understood.

Vinnie's face took on a sudden calm.

"Ladies, go inside. I'll go to Mariella's house. I know she is staying at her grandma's house.

"Vince, I'm going with you."

"Lena, please stay with Penny. Vanessa, *andiamo.*"

"Vanessa will stay at the hospital with Mariella's family. I have to attend to some other things while I'm out."

"Oh, I understand."

Well I don't really understand, but I have a pretty good idea that the family is going to be more involved that I originally suspected.

Penny had a puzzled look on her face. She looked at me and shook her head as if to dismiss the thought

"Let's go raid the kitchen. I'm hungry."

Vanessa's husband, Savario, was sitting in the kitchen with a plate of food in front of him.

Penny said, "It's okay, Savario. We are going to help ourselves to some dinner. We can manage."

"Okay, signore." He smiled and nodded as he backed out of the kitchen.

Penny stuck her head in the fridge and pulled out a pan of baked chicken while I found bread and cheese and wine in the pantry. Savario already had the heated eggplant on the stove. I took some glasses and plates from the open shelving in the kitchen. We put the chicken in the oven.

I told Penny, "While we're waiting, let's get out of these clothes."

"Good idea."

I slipped into a long lounge dress and brushed my hair. I left my shoes off. The cool floor tiles felt good on my feet. We had shopped all day in cute shoes and the soles of my feet were burning.

Savario had left the kitchen when we got back.

I poured us each a glass of wine while we helped ourselves to the eggplant parm. We were both quiet. There was a lot to think about.

I got up to get the chicken out of the oven and put some on Penny's dish and mine.

When I settled back into my chair, Penny said, "Why is the family so involved in Mariella's life now?"

I thought about it before I answered. I had to decide if we were talking about the family or just Carlo's family who lives in this house. If she's talking about the Mafioso Family, it's the first time that she's mentioned that out loud.

Now I have to play dumb. I can't tell her about Mariella's father and the new baby.

"They probably feel really bad that she lost her husband and her father. The baby has no father or grandfather."

We cleaned up the kitchen and started back to our rooms.

Penny stopped me in the hall and put her arms around me. "Penny, is something wrong, I asked?"

"No. I don't know what I would do if you weren't here. You bring logic and calm to all this crazy stuff. How long do you think you can stay?"

"Well, the agreement was four or five weeks."

"Oh, thank goodness. This is only the end of week one!"

As I was walking past the phone in the hall, I saw a note stuck to the wall with a pin.

"Lena, El Captain Benacase call you two times. I tell him you got all the flowers."

I thought it was pretty funny that she wrote exactly the way she spoke.

Penny laughed when I read it to out loud to her.

I went back to my room and washed my face and brushed my teeth. I flopped into bed and tried to read. I tossed and I turned and finally put the light back on and picked up my book. I couldn't seem to focus on reading. I went into the bathroom, planning to take a warm shower to relax me. I froze and stood still.

I heard voices outside my bathroom window again.

"It's a girl, that should make it easier for her to accept the baby. If it was a boy she would only see her father's face."

"Is she doing okay?"

"Yeah, they had to do a cesarean. She'll have a scar, but she's glad it's over."

"Vince, let's have Penny and Lena shop for baby stuff. I don't want the girl to worry about anything like extra expenses."

"I'll tell the girls at breakfast. Will you be there?"

"Yes, Vince. How about we take off with them next week. Maybe we'll go to the mountains."

"I'd like that. Goodnight, Carlo."

"See ya in the morning."

78

heard footsteps fade and the same footsteps coming toward my room. I took several huge steps and jumped into my bed. I had no sooner climbed in when I heard my door creak open. Soft shoes shuffled across the floor. I knew it was Vinnie. He sat on the edge of the bed and slipped his shoes off. I flipped the covers off and he slipped in.

"Thanks, babe. That was a nice welcome. I really need to hold you. I thought about you all day. I had visions of you in bed with me.

I said, "Hang your clothes on the back of the door, and I'll let you use my toothbrush."

"Wow! I was just hoping for a goodnight kiss!"

"Well, you crawled into my bed!"

"I'll be right back, sweetheart!"

I slipped out of my pj's just as Vince practically jumped into my bed.

I slid one leg between his and wrapped the other one around his hip. As his kisses trailed down my neck, I began to relax. I missed being held. I loved having a man's arms around me. I was so glad that part of Vince wasn't relaxed at all. Good for me!

Getting to know him was really easy. "Lena, I've been waiting for you most of my life. There is no one I have met that I would like to spend time with. Every time I see you, my heart jumps into my throat and I have trouble breathing. Tell me if I'm wasting my time wanting you?"

"Vince, you're talking too much." He laughed, but never stopped exploring.

I whispered, "You are definitely not wasting you time."

Later, we were lying wrapped in each other's arms and legs. I said, "I'm going to take a shower."

"I'm coming with you!"

He soaped me up first. Then I soaped him up. Then we made love standing in the shower. Then on the floor of the shower, with my legs wrapped around his back.

We dried each other off and that led to more making love in bed. We fell asleep exhausted.

We woke up in a tangle of sheets and towels.

"Hey!" I shouted jabbing Vince. It's after ten o'clock. We probably missed breakfast."

"Oh, crap!" he mumbled.

We scrambled for our clothes. I pulled on my sundress and slipped into sandals. Vince stepped into his pants and shirt, without his jacket. We quick-stepped down the hall. I walked into the dining room ahead of him as casually as I could. I know my face turned red as soon as everyone turned to look at me. Vince came in behind me about thirty seconds later. "Good morning, all."

Then he took me completely by surprise. He walked over and planted a big wet kiss on my cheek and said, "Good morning, babe."

Many sets of eyebrows shot up. Vanessa mumbled in Italian, again.

I just smiled and batted my eyes.

Carlo smiled at me. "Listen, I've been thinking. Maybe we could take a week off and go to the mountains in Cefalu. I know a little place we can stay. There are streams where we can swim and find nice picnic areas. What do you both think?"

Vince looked at me and smiled, "What do you think, Lena?"

"I'm on vacation, I'll go anywhere!" I never took my eyes off Vinnie.

Penny said, "I think we should go pack!"

She dragged me into the hall. "Wow! You two have sex written all over you. No secret there! It must have been quite a night."

"It was an amazing night!"

"Lena, you have stars in your eyes. Are you falling for him?"

"I'm trying not to fall, but I am barely hanging on."

"You! Miss Lena!" I knew that voice.

I turned to see Vanessa standing with her hands on her hips.

"El Captain Benecase is here to see you."

"Oh, hell. I'd better go see him."

He was in the front vestibule, in full airline uniform. "Bella, Lena. I couldn't wait any longer to see you." He held his arms out toward me. "I thought I would come to pay you a visit."

"Captain Benecase, I am sorry if you misunderstood my silence for acceptance."

Those words were no sooner out of my mouth than I heard someone clear their throat behind me. I knew it was Vinnie.

He put his arm around me and said, "I am Vincenzo Polino." He extended his free hand to the captain. "Miss Delatora has recently accepted my proposal of marriage."

I know my face went pale and my knees got weak. As they stared each other in the eye, the captain's face got beet red, then he pumped Vince's arm up and down like an old water pump.

"*Bellisimo! Buona fortuna!*" He quit pumping Vince's arm and grabbed my shoulders to pull me forward, kissing both my cheeks.

He backed out of the vestibule without ever turning around. He jumped into his waiting car and drove away. He kept nodding saying, "*Buona fortuna, Buona fortuna!*"

I slowly turned to Vince and stared at him. 'Wa-What?" he stammered.

"That was pretty forward! Considering we have only done the wild thing a couple of times and never talked about commitment."

"Lena, don't be angry. I had to get rid of him. He would have been all over you like a fat boy on a cake."

"That might be true. I want you to understand that there is no commitment here. I'm recovering from some really crappy relationships. I don't want to fall hard this time."

He looked really disappointed. I didn't mean to hurt his feelings.

"Would you rather not go away with Penny and Carlo?"

I put my arms around him and said, "No, Vince, I want to enjoy what we have. If it grows from here, then it was meant to be."

"We get along really great, Lena."

"Yes, I know we do."

"And we are so compatible, Lena. And the sex is great."

"Yes, we are, Vince, and it is great. You practically read my mind."

"Does that mean you'll stay here and marry me?"

"Not so fast, *Pisano*! That's a decision for another day. I'm going to pack my suitcase and get ready for our little trip."

I knocked on Penny's bedroom door. She yelled, "Come in."

"Cripes! Did your closet explode again? Did you forget everything I taught you about packing?"

She giggled. "No, I had to sort through it anyway. You only need a few outfits and a bathing suit. There is only one restaurant, and it's owned by someone in Carlo's family. The food is supposed to be wonderful. Of course he hasn't eaten there since he was in his teens."

"Are you excited, Penny?"

"Yes I am. Can you tell? I want my husband to myself for a little while. I miss him so much."

"This is going to be a fun trip. It will be good for both of us."

Penny made her big innocent eyes at me.

I said, "What?"

"Okay sister. Sit down. I want all the dirty details about Vinnie. You have stars in your eyes. It must have been an amazing night."

"Well, I like him a lot. He's very affectionate."

"Does that mean the sex is great?"

"Yes it is. He's sweet and considerate. I can tell you more about the way I feel after we come back from our getaway."

"I think you're falling for him, Lena."

"I'm not sure I've fallen, but I'm not saying it couldn't happen."

79

The drive was beautiful. The mountain is called Pizzo Cobonara. Vince insisted I sit on the side facing the villages. They were small, with little clusters of houses and tons of flowers. I have never seen so many different colors. Carlo gave us a running narrative about the scenery.

"Those are olive trees. My family owns a lot of olive groves, but I'm not sure if this is part of it. Why don't we stop for lunch at this little hut down the road?"

We all agreed. I know the mountain air was really working on my appetite. The little hut turned out to be a tiny house. There was a sign out in front that said *"Alimentare Di Oggi,"* translating to "Food Today." Lucky for us.

There was no menu. You simply ate whatever was prepared that day.

We were served breaded, fried eggplant, and braised lamb chops. The lamb chops were cooked with basil, rosemary, and lots of garlic and onions. They brought the lamb chops to us in a large flat bowl with potatoes and tomatoes. I couldn't help glance at the peaceful sheep grazing on the little hill outside the porch. The eggplant was served in a basket lined with bread. Oh, the bread! Fresh and hot with homemade butter.

"Oh," I sighed. "I'll never loose weight while I'm here. Maybe I'll take a walk after we finish eating."

"I'll take a walk with you after we eat, Lena." The way his eyes met mine left no doubt about what he had in mind. He already had his hand up my skirt on my thigh so I said, "Yes, that would be nice." Those eyes held so much promise.

It was a wonderful meal. We ate so much it was sinful. Carlo kept complimenting the tiny Italian lady who prepared this feast. She really outdid herself.

Then Vince said, "Let's go for our walk, Lena." We followed a little path behind the hut. As soon as we were out of sight, he pulled me into his arms. First he just held me.

"Sex is like a drug with you, Lena. I can't get the taste of you out of my mouth or the smell of you off my skin. I don't know what's wrong with me."

He buried his face in my hair and took a deep breath. His kisses traveled all over my neck. He kissed his way back to my mouth and slowly sunk his tongue between my lips into my mouth.

The grass was soft and cool behind the rock formation. The little area was shaded from the sun. He pulled me down onto the grass next to him. His hands seemed to tremble slightly while he slid the shoulders of my sundress down. I unbuttoned his shirt to feel his skin against mine.

"Vinnie, why are you shaking?"

He almost looked as if he would cry. "Lena, I don't want you to go back to America."

His hands never stopped feeling my skin. He had great hands.

"Vince, I have a commitment. It's a contract for the next five years."

"What are they doing while you're here?"

"They prerecorded some episodes to splice into the ongoing scenes."

By this time we had gone too far to discuss my soap opera.

Vince's lovemaking was fierce and possessive. His desire for me was all consuming. We didn't think of anything but our bodies, pleasing each other, touching. "Yes, right there. More. Now!"

We held hands and walked back to the little clearing where Penny and Carlo sat in the sun. They were sitting close together, whispering sweet nothings and sharing a desert. They smiled when they saw us approaching.

Carlo said, "You two have a warm glow. I wonder why?"

"Keep wondering, wise guy," Vince said.

Penny smiled knowingly and said, "Are we ready for the rest of our drive?"

The little lady who cooked our delicious meal had packed a box of food for us to take with. Carlo told us that she was afraid that no one else would travel this road today and the food would be wasted. I know that Carlo gave her a generous tip.

I insisted that Vince sit in the front with Carlo. It would give them some time to bond. Penny and I needed time to plan our activities and coordinate our wardrobes.

We traveled down through the valley in *Porticello,* on our way to *Cefalu.* The ocean was turquoise and green with white sand. I could see bathers sunning themselves and children running in the sand. The road was along the hillside, giving us a full view of the water and the coastline. White houses dotted the hillside. We could see across the small beach to the other side of the water where taller homes nestled in the hills. This was more beautiful than anything I had ever seen.

Penny and I were so quiet looking at the view, Carlo finally said, "Hey! Are you girls asleep back there?"

I said, "No, we're both at a loss for words looking at this beautiful view."

"Carlo, can we stop and watch the sunset over the ocean?"

I could see Carlo smile. He knew that Penny was a sucker for sunsets.

The colors were all reds and oranges as the sun descended in front of the mountains into the ocean. As the sunlight reflected over the fields of purple and blue flowers, it looked as if the color shot straight up into the sun from the ocean.

I looked at Vince and said, "Where will I ever see this again?"

"You won't see it anywhere else. That's why you can't go back to Chicago."

"Oh, but I have to, Vinnie. I have a role to play in this show. I don't know how much longer they can drag the story out without my participation.

He put his hands up in front of him and said, "I can see it now! *LENA DELATORA LEAVES SOAP OPERA. SHE MEETS PRINCE CHARMING IN ITALY!*"

"Oh, would that Prince Charming be you?"

"You bet it's me! I've been waiting a long time to meet my Princess. I can't let you go now that I've found you."

I let him put his arms around me from behind, and we smiled at the setting sun. Inside, I knew were destined for heartbreak, because I couldn't stay here in Italy.

Carlo announced that we were very close to our destination. "When we go around the curve of this mountain, you'll see a grove of olive trees. When we pass them you'll see some grape vines on the left. That would be the first Bazzoli Estate. It's not a big house like the one in Palermo, but it's still very nice. We have a groundskeeper and a lady who takes care of the house. She'll cook for us too. Her name is Domenica. I haven't seen her in years. The groundskeeper is her son."

By this time, we were pulling into a stone shelter that looked like it once had some other purpose in a previous life. It had shelves built into the stone walls and old jugs and containers were lined up against the back wall.

Carlo was explaining that this had been the first building his great grandfather constructed. It was the original open front store where they sold wine and olive oil. His grandpa and great grandpa made cheese and dried salami here in this open front stone hut.

We heard a small cry of delight, then saw Domenica run from the house with her arms outstretched to Carlo. He picked her up in his bear-like arms and squeezed her.

"You such a big guy, Carlo! You always make-a me feel so small."

"You are small, Dominica, but you never look older. And you are still beautiful."

"Oh, go on!" She flapped her hand at him and turned her head, pretending to be shy.

Domenica looked at Vince. "I remember you too!" she exclaimed. "You not so skinny anymore, Vincenzo! I remember you come with Senor Niko and Carlo a long-a time ago."

Carlo introduced Penny as his new bride, and the old woman cried her eyes out.

Domenica spoke in Italian and Carlo translated. "She wants to know if we'll bring our babies here to visit."

Penny said, "Carlo, tell her we'll come back, but the baby won't be here for about six months."

He started to repeat what Penny said when he went pale and he stopped speaking. He looked dumbstruck. "Did you say six months?"

Penny's face turned red and she told him, "I was going to wait to tell you, but this seemed as good a time as any."

He pulled her into his arms and kissed her. "Oh, gosh! We'll have to be more careful. I've got a million questions. How do you feel, honey?"

"I'm just fine, Carlo."

Domenica didn't need a translation. She was exclaiming in Italian, "*Buona fortuna!*" How lucky we are! She was kissing Penny and congratulating both of them.

Vince introduced me as his lady friend. I was glad he didn't say fiancée. Domenica kissed me and welcomed me with open arms. I think Vince said something about my TV job, because Domenica was practically bowing to me.

We were finally escorted into the sprawling old building. The old stone walls were reflected on the inside as well as the outside. The home still maintained a semblance of dignity and fine elegance. The curtains on the windows were crocheted lace and the huge fireplace filled one wall of the large kitchen. I looked at it and said to Vince, "You could roast half a cow in there."

"I think it's been done," Vince whispered.

Domenica produced bread, cheese, olives, olive oil, fruit, and two bottles of some kind of liquor. We were all doing shots of this liquor and dipping chunks of bread into olive oil. Penny was drinking water.

When her son, Benito, came in with a case of wine, the hugging and kissing started all over again.

I saw Vince slip out to the front door. I followed him and thought that it appeared he was standing watch.

"Are you worried about something, Vince?"

"Not worried, just cautious. Everyone is eating and drinking in the kitchen. That leaves the front of the house with no one around."

"Tell me why you would be concerned about that."

"You see the brackets on the sides of the front door?"

"Yes, like an old fort."

"That's right. There were family feuds and lots of rivalry between families at one time. I'll probably find the 2x4 and use it tonight."

"Should I be worried, Vince?"

"I don't think so. I'm sure that Benito has spread the word that Carlo is visiting. That means that old neighbors and well wishers will want to stop by. Not everyone has been happy with the Bazzolis' success. They have been an important part of this community. When Niko's grandfather began buying all this property, not everyone was pleased. He wanted all this land and was willing to out-bid anyone to get it. That was nearly one hundred years ago. Families have a way of holding grudges. Why don't you go inside and enjoy the festivities. I'm sure Domenica is cooking up a storm. I can smell the meat roasting."

He kissed me and hugged me hard.

"I won't be out here much longer."

Before too long, Vince escorted two ladies and an older man into the kitchen. They stood in the doorway until Carlo recognized them. He finally smiled and extended his hands to them. They kissed each cheek and were invited to join us.

We were having conversations in broken English with these neighbors. Penny and I were doing pretty good at understanding them. I was practicing my Italian and they seemed to understand me. I told them to correct me if I was saying something wrong. They laughed and said I was doing just fine.

Vince finally left his post at the front of the house and joined us. The meal was fantastic. There was so much beef, roasted chicken, and lamb, we couldn't begin to do justice to the assortment. Domenica had also prepared vegetables and assorted fruit from the trees on the property. And then there was the bread. I'm really disgusting. I have no control. I will explode before my vacation is over.

It was late in the evening. I was beginning to help Domenica clear the dishes and put food away. I could see that Penny was beginning to get tired. Maybe it was because I knew she was pregnant now. Our visitors picked up on the signal that the evening was winding down. They helped clear the long table and we all began to say our good-byes. Domenica was proud to show us her new dishwasher. It had a wooden front next to the sink, and I didn't even notice it.

Carlo took Penny by the arm and said, "I'm sure you won't mind if I take my pregnant wife off her feet a little early."

We all agreed that it was a fine idea. Carlo was so delighted with the fact that Penny was pregnant, he was practically giddy.

Vince was doing a walk-through of the house after everyone went to bed. I went along because I'm nosey.

He checked every door and window. "Too many damn doors in this house," he mumbled.

"Why is that, Vinnie?"

There's a kitchen door that was for groceries, vegetables from the garden, and milk; another door on the east side for the bushels of olives that went to the workroom to be pressed. The west side has a door because of the vineyard. After the grapes were pressed, the bottles were brought inside to ferment. Then there's the front door. I closed that off with the 2x4. Last of all is the trap door on the roof."

"What the hell was that for?"

The ladies dried the sunflowers that they grew in the big garden in the back. They used them for seeds and oil. They also dried other flowers for soap and perfumed oil."

"Wow! This was a busy house!"

We had worked our way back to the kitchen. I was looking up at the old trap door in the ceiling. Vince was behind me. He wrapped his arms around me and buried his face in my neck.

"I can't even concentrate when you're near me. How will I survive when you leave?"

Vince said stuff like this all the time. I'd like to think that he meant it, although I'd heard this type of romantic bull many times recently. While Vince was nuzzling my neck and his hands were roaming everywhere, I thought about the men in my life. Gino hurt me the most. He broke my heart. He was long gone and never to be forgotten. I think I loved him with all my heart. We were like a drug to each other. I think Greg wanted me and he thought he loved me, but I wasn't Jewish. Whitey said he loved me, but he couldn't handle the family commitment.

And now there was Vince. He made my blood rush to my head and my heart pound. While I was letting my past loves romp through my head, Vince was busy undressing me in the kitchen. I finally felt the chill when he started to pull my dress over my head.

"Hold on, *Pisano!* Whadda ya doin' here? Let's go find our room."

He picked me up in his arms keeping his hands strategically placed under my dress that was nearly off my body.

"Vince! Get my panties off the floor!"

He flipped them up with his foot and caught them with one hand.

"You're a very clever guy."

"Yeah, that's one of my many talents."

He bumped the bedroom door open with his hip.

"How do you know this is our room?"

"I put the suitcases in here."

"Clever and smart, too."

"And so hot for you, Lena."

He took his clothes off and slid in bed next to me. The only light was from the narrow window in the corner of the room. The moonlit room was full of shadows.

Breathing together, mouths and hands everywhere. "We should take a shower first. We've been driving in the car all day."

"Not yet. I need to be inside you first."

We had such passionate sex that I saw colors. I know I saw a red explosion when I climaxed, followed by blue fire.

"I think we just had mind blowing sex, Vince."

"Baby, I'm trying to figure out where we are. I swear you intoxicate me."

We stayed wrapped together for quite a while. I finally said, "I'm getting in the shower now."

"I'm coming with you. I don't think I can take a shower alone, ever again."

We opened the bathroom door. I started laughing and couldn't stop. Vince simply stared like a dummy.

"It's a copper bathtub," he whispered.

It was obviously well taken care of. It was as shiny as a new penny. We were worried that there was no running water. Vince said that old tubs like this had to be filled with buckets heated on the stove. We tried the faucets and were pleased to find hot and cold running water.

We wrapped our legs around each other in the small tub.

"Lena, tomorrow I'll see if any of the other rooms have a shower."

"I don't know, I kind of like this."

He looked a little puzzled, but smiled.

Vince fell asleep before me. I lay in the dark, still pulsing from our lovemaking. I could hear the night sounds of the house around me. I could hear the shrill cry of a bird. Small creatures made the brush rustle outside our window. Then I heard Penny giggle, followed by Carlo's quiet throaty laugh. I was so happy for them. Carlo had nearly burst with joy when he heard about the baby. Niko will probably have another big party when he finds out. I fell asleep wondering, *When was the last time I laughed out loud? I know I've had a lot of serious sex, but what happened to fun?*

Morning brought a beautiful, sunny day. The smell of Domenica's cooking floated through the house. I pulled the covers off Vince's head. "You hungry? I'm starving. I'm going into the kitchen."

"I'll be there in a flash," my sleepy prince said.

"Good morning, Domenica!"

"Buongiorno, Miss Lena! Did you sleep well?"

"Yes. This food smells wonderful."

"Sit, please. I'm gonna give-a to you."

"I can help myself, Domenica. You don't have to wait on me."

"It's a pleasure to have-a people here. Let me do this."

Carlo and Penny came out to the kitchen next. They looked very happy.

Vince staggered into the kitchen like he had been drinking. While he poured himself a cup of coffee, Carlo said, "Did you take wine back to your room last night?"

"No, I'm drunk on love."

Carlo and Vince toasted with cups of coffee.

Penny and I rolled our eyes at them.

I said to Vince, "I'd like to see the roof garden this morning."

Domenica smiled, "I would be happy to take-a you up to the garden after breakfast."

Vince frowned, "I'll check it out first. I want to be sure that the roof is safe."

"If Domenica has been up there, Vince, I'm sure it's fine."

He looked at me like I was foolish. "It's my job, Lena." He got up from the table and put his plate in the sink.

"My Prince Charming seems to be a little grumpy this morning."

Penny replied, "I got the same impression."

We heard some movement on the roof, then some footsteps. Suddenly we heard a loud crash. We looked up and saw Vince's leg hanging through the kitchen ceiling. We could hear him swearing and banging around.

Domenica said, "I forgotta tell him he gotta walk on the boards."

We all started laughing so hard. I was doubled over holding my stomach. We could hear Vince swearing and thrashing in the corner of the kitchen above our heads. We couldn't stop laughing. Finally Carlo caught his breath and said, "I'd better go see if he needs some help getting his leg out."

When the men came back into the kitchen, Vince said, "I'm glad you were all amused by my efforts to check for safety."

Carlo said, "Looks like we have some work to do today. I think there is some wood and shingles in the barn."

Domenica was making herself busy cleaning the corner of the kitchen where Vince's leg came through. No one mentioned that, *"He gotta walk on the boards."*

I said, "Vince, don't be so upset about this. It's an old house, how were you to know that the roof was so soft?"

"I could have gotten hurt. You guys were so busy laughing that you didn't think about that."

"You're right, Vince. Are you okay"?

"Yes, I'm okay. I just hurt my pride."

The men were in the barn looking for wood and shingles. The rest of us lesser beings were helping Domenica clean and rearrange her kitchen. We moved the table to the other side of the kitchen and cleared off the countertop. They started pounding the wood over the big hole in the roof, and dust was falling all over everything. Domenica was talking to herself in Italian. Some of it wasn't nice. All I caught was, *"Shoulda walk on the boards."*

This day was going to be used up already. I asked Penny why Carlo didn't call into town to have a carpenter take care of the roof.

"We talked about that, Lena. He said that nobody moves too fast in this little town. By the time the arrangements could be made, we would be gone. The rain would come in and Domenica would have a nervous breakdown."

"I could imagine her climbing on the roof trying to fix it herself."

"Lena, what do you want to do today?"

"Well, we're too far away from town to walk. Do you think we could take the car?"

Penny smiled at my bright idea. "When the guys come down for lunch, I'll ask Carlo. I don't think he'll say no. I think I can have anything at all that I want, now that I'm pregnant."

"I think you're right, Penny."

80

We had been sitting on the veranda that surrounds the house, thinking it would be best to get out of the way. We decided to see how Domenica was handling all the dust and pounding.

She looked pretty glum before she saw us. The she broke into a smile.

"Domenica, we want to help you clean up and start lunch."

"*Oh, Grazi, giovani donna.*"

Penny and I began washing off the table and chairs. I happened to look up and I realized they would have to do some patching on the inside of the ceiling too. I could see other patches and discolorations on the ceiling. It added to the ambiance of the old world charm. The house itself was easily one hundred years old. Domenica had her new appliances and marble countertops, but the tables and chairs and storage facilities were all original to the house. She loved her fireplace and the old wood and brick walls.

We started pulling food out of the large refrigerator. Domenica had quite a selection. The leftovers alone would be enough, but she had prepared roasted chicken and potatoes as well as an assortment of vegetables at some point during the early morning hours. We had pans in the oven and pots on the stove in no time at all. I felt like I was at home. "Geez, I miss my nana!" I said out loud. All of a sudden, I started to cry. Penny and Domenica were shocked. They stopped what they were doing and put their arms around me.

"What's wrong, Lena? Oh, my gosh. Are you okay?"

Domenica was beside herself with stress. She chattered away.

Half English, half Italian: "Oh, poor bambina! What's wrong-a with you?"

I finally said, "I'm really okay. I suddenly got homesick. I miss my parents, my nana, and even Zio." Domenica didn't need a translation for that. She opened the kitchen cupboard and pulled out the bottle of liquor that everyone was drinking last night. She poured us each a shot, which Penny declined. I drank mine and Domenica drank hers and Penny's. We all laughed and got back to work.

After we had the table set, we heard the guys climbing off the roof. They must have smelled the food. Carlo looked amused and Vince looked like a big bear with a grumpy face. They washed up and sat down with no words spoken. Carlo finally said, "I think we'll finish up pretty late. I want to patch the ceiling too."

Penny said, "Honey, can we take the car into town? Maybe we can see some sights. At least walk around town a while."

"Oh sure, babe. No reason to stick around here."

I said, "Domenica, would you like to come with us?"

She looked pleased and surprised. "Mostly I go to town in-a the old truck with-a my son, Benito"

"Hey!" I said, "Where is that guy? He could be helping you."

"Oh, he gonna show up when-a the work is fineto," Domenica said.

Carlo laughed out loud. *"So Domenica. Il suo bene.* I didn't expect to see him."

I got the impression that Benito is a lazy bum, but I didn't say it out loud.

When Domenica left the room, Carlo said, "Benito has some kind of radar. He knows when there's a party or lots of food. His radar also works when there is work to be done. He goes in the opposite direction.

Vince has stepped out the back door to see how much lumber was left. When he came back into the kitchen, we were all laughing. "What's so funny?" he said.

"We were talking about Benito," Carlo explained. "It's amazing that he always disappears when work needs to be done."

Vince behaved as if he thought we were talking about him.

Carlo tossed the car keys to me as he walked back outside. "Have a nice time, my beauties. Be careful."

Vince said, "I don't really think they should be alone, Carlo."

"Nobody knows who we are, Vincenzo"

Penny and I went to change our clothes. Domenica was headed for her room to do the same. She was very excited to be going out with us. I was glad to have someone who knew where they were headed.

We were all ready at just about the same time. Domenica had on a purple dress and a little hat. She had a shopping bag for each of us, and several for herself.

"Today is market day. You gonna see lots of stuff. They gotta lotta clothes and purses and jewelry for you to take home. Maybe you get some *ricordo.* How you say? Souvenirs. We get all our food today and I gonna put it in the car, okay?"

"Oh, sure," I said. "That will be fine. We'll all be together. It's gonna be fun!"

Talk about sensory overload! The colors and the smells were overwhelming. We walked along the narrow streets looking at all the stalls. The area was a little different than the streets of Palermo. The stalls were more rustic and the people seemed smaller. I know that sounds strange, but it was a smaller town, so I think the people grew smaller here.

I saw a beautiful handbag for my mom. It was light-colored genuine leather with beautiful hand-tooled pockets in the front. I got my dad one of those donkey carts that's painted red with flowers. I know that's really cheesy. My nana has one that's small. I got dad one that's about a foot long. I knew he'd get a kick out of it. My brother Bobby was always a tough one to buy for. I got him a shirt that was all embroidered down the front. He'll look like one of the older guys in it.

We were selecting fresh vegetables with Domenica along one side of the street. She was smelling bunches of greens and squeezing the produce. I was watching the people milling around and bargaining with the vendors. I looked across the street, just taking in all the sights. I know I saw Carlo duck into a doorway. I've got pretty good eyes. It was broad daylight and he wasn't that far away. He's a pretty tall guy, easy to spot among all these little people. I have to remember that he leads many lives. That first one is the most secret life. You know, the one where he likes other guys? The second one is the wonderful husband that he has become for Penny. Then third life is the one that he leads with his dad, Niko I realized now that this little side trip from Palermo had a hidden agenda.

I turned on my brain filter. I have to be one of those monkeys. Hear no evil; see no evil; speak no evil. I guess I'm all those monkeys. I have to pretend all those things all the time. Geez, I was getting tired of this secret spy stuff.

I was in deep thought when Domenica said, "Hey, Miss-a Lena. You okay?"

"Oh yes. I guess I was daydreaming, Domenica."

Penny was either blind, or perfectly content with everything around her. I needed to be more like her.

Domenica was showing me some escarole. "You like-a dis?"

I said, "I like everything you cook, Domenica!"

"Okay, ladies I think I got enough food. Let's have a snack."

We stopped at a storefront café. I ordered soup. I thought that's all I would get. Nooo. It came with a huge bread basket, some breaded and fried vegetables, and a pot of cappuccino. We all ordered something different and shared the bread and vegetables. We talked and relaxed for quite some time. We were finishing up and paying the waiter, when I saw Carlo getting into a car across the street.

This time, we made eye contact. *Oh, shit,* I thought.

I stood up and gathered some of our bags. "I'll get the car and pull it over here. Domenica, you stay with Penny and I'll be right back."

I heard a horn beep when I was walking down the hill toward

the car. It was Carlo.

"Hey, Lena! How was your shopping expedition?"

"Hi, Carlo," I said, as chipper as can be. "What are you doing in town?"

"I had some last minute business to take care of for my dad."

"Your secret is safe with me."

"Thanks, Lena. I knew it would be. I'm heading back to the house to finish the hole in the kitchen ceiling."

Well, I'm the see-no-evil monkey right now, I said to myself.

We were unloading the car in the little carport, bringing the groceries around to the back door.

Domenica said, "I think somebody lock-a this door from inside the kitchen."

"I'll go around and open it." I volunteered.

When I got inside, I stood looking at the door like a dummy. I tried the door, but it was pretty obvious that someone had nailed a 2x4 across the door.

I went back around to the outside and said, "Domenica, why is the door nailed shut?"

"I don't know why. I don't wanna nail it shut. Maybe Vincenzo do it?"

"I'll go find out."

I walked around the to the back of the house and found Vince in the little tool shed.

"Hi! Do you know anything about the back door being nailed shut?"

"Yes, I nailed it shut," Vince said.

"It there some reason for that?"

"There are too many doors in this house. It makes me uneasy. I can't watch them all."

"Well, Vince, maybe we should live life in a little rat hole with only one entrance."

"That's not a bad idea, Lena. It would be safer than this old house."

Suddenly I was fuming mad. So many thoughts were running

through my mind. Finally I said, "This is insane, Vince. People can't live life so afraid all the time. I'm sure that Carlo wouldn't want Domenica nailed into this house. It's unsafe."

"Lena, my concern is for all of us. There is a lot of bad blood in this area regarding Carlo's family. It's up to me to keep everyone safe."

"Carlo mentioned that no one knows who we are. Will you take the 2x4 off the door when we leave?"

"If Domenica wants it off, that's what I'll do. Every village has a gossip system. Benito has a big mouth. I'm sure everyone knows one of the Bazzolis is here.

I walked away from Vince with a bitter taste in my mouth.

Domenica and I brought the groceries in through the old carport door. Vince and Carlo were out in front of the house, so we got no help with the bags.

I was peeling eggplant and Penny was roasting peppers over the fire to peel them. Domenica started braising steak on top of the stove. We were all chatting and going about our business. When Carlo and Vince came in, I asked, "When are we planning to go back to the villa?"

Carlo shrugged his shoulders and Vince looked insulted. Carlo said, "I thought we would drive back on Sunday morning."

Today was Thursday. I wasn't too keen on staying several more days.

"I thought that if we leave tomorrow morning, it will give me a full ten days to stay here in Italy before I have to go back to the States. I would like to spend more time at the villa."

Carlo said, "What's everyone think about leaving tomorrow morning?"

Sweet Penny said, "That would be nice. Maybe we can have a pool party or a picnic in the garden when we get back. We didn't get to use the pool very much since Lena came."

Silently, I thanked Penny.

"It's settled then! We'll leave in the morning."

I could see the mixed emotions on Domenica's face. "We gotta have a special party in the garden tonight for dinner. Maybe Benito can bring some wine up from the cellar and I will make sausage with wine sauce."

I saw Carlo roll his eyes. Benito had been missing in action for several days. I'm sure there was a story behind this Benito fellow.

We ate lunch for nearly two hours. All the meals take a long time. I've discovered that to eat too fast is an insult to the cook. We take our time at home, but in Italy it's a ritual. Dinner is always after dark and it takes even longer.

That night we were helping Domenica set up the long boards on top of the sawhorses for our feast in the garden. She was an amazing cook. The oils, wine, and spices she combined were close to perfection. Penny brought out the long flowered tablecloth that Domenica had made many years ago for such occasions. Carlo and Vince hooked up a string of lights.

Benito showed up when all the work was done. "Mama! I smell your cooking all the way down to the town!"

That was a slight exaggeration, but Domenica looked pleased with the compliment. Neighbors came from all the surrounding houses.

The wine flowed all evening. The food never stopped coming. Old Fabrizio brought his concertina. We danced a tarantella in a circle. Then he played some sweet waltzes. Carlo danced with Domenica and she grinned ear to ear.

Vince was sitting next to me. He put his hand over mine and asked, "Lena, can we go for a walk?"

I stood up and followed him without answering.

"I got the feeling that I really screwed up the last couple of days."

"Vince, being around you too much is like living in a bubble. There is too much tension. I feel like the walls are closing in on me."

"Lena, that's my job. I tried to explain that to you. I'm responsible for security. It's what I was trained to do."

"Vince, I think we both know this isn't a long-term relationship. It was wonderful while it lasted."

He looked a little dumbstruck. "I was hoping it was going to be long term. I'm apologizing for my attitude this afternoon. I hope that's not why you want to leave early."

"I want to spend more time in Palermo. I want to be able to tell my Nana what I saw. She was born there."

We walked back to the house. The ladies started bringing the food inside. The men were relaxing with wine and cheese.

I was in deep thought when Penny said, "Trouble in paradise?"

"I just had this conversation with Vinnie about our relationship. I started out thinking it was a vacation fling. Last week I was in serious 'like.' Now I don't want to think about it because my head is going to explode."

"Lena, I wanted this vacation to be fun. You don't seem happy."

"He's not a fun guy. There were a few moments of laughter, but most of them had to do with being naked or looking for a place to have sex. He is one fine hunk-o-man, without a doubt. He's skilled in many ways, but fun isn't one of them."

I proceeded to tell her about the night we had sex in the old copper bathtub. Vince and I both had our legs over the end of the tub facing each other. Penny had her hands over her mouth, she was laughing so hard. He face was beet read and she was bent in half.

"I'm trying to picture this, Lena."

Vince happened to walk inside and saw is. Penny and were laughing so hard I nearly wet my pants. He shook his head smiling and said, "Somehow, I get the feeling I might not want to know what you chicks are talking about."

"No, you really don't want to know!"

It really felt good to laugh. It made me remember how much fun Whitey and I used to have together. Even when he got shot, he could still make me laugh during his recovery.

Penny and I walked down the hall toward our bedrooms, still laughing.

I managed to pack all of my clothes before Vince came to bed. I left the closet light on so he could have enough light to pack. Hopefully, by the time he came to bed I would be asleep and no conversation would be necessary.

81

Domenica packed a banquet filling two huge baskets. I would miss her.

We hugged and kissed all around. Even Benito stayed overnight to say good-bye to us.

They stood on the gravel driveway, Domenica was crying and waving. Benito was doing a double-handed fist pump over each shoulder. Who knows what that meant?

I was riding in the back with Vinnie. I was choking back tears with my arm waving out the window. I was feeling very melancholy.

Vince was keeping up a good stream of chatter. Carlo was talking about directions and a little side trip to a small town he remembered along the way. I settled in, ready to enjoy the scenery. I didn't feel like talking much. I would answer when anyone addressed me personally, but I was burnt out. I felt emotionally drained. I was anxious to get back to the villa. I pretended to doze and let the chatter fade into the background.

"Let's stop and eat some of this buffet that Domenica packed," Carlo suggested.

We had only traveled about twenty-five miles at that point, but they were slow miles winding through the mountains. Food always made me happy—especially if there was bread within reach.

We found another perfect patch of grass near the sea. We spread out blankets and pulled food out from the baskets. No one would ever go hungry in this family. I don't think anyone would go hungry in Italy.

I'm always amazed at how many foods can be packed without refrigeration. This was an ancient country that hasn't always had an efficient means of keeping food fresh. Penny and I unpacked the food and spread it out on the blanket. We had dry tomatoes, olives in oil, artichokes, and crushed eggplant with garlic and onions. Of course we had bread. That in itself was glorious. We also had panforte, a sort of flat cake with fruits and nuts. I lay down in the sun and was dozing.

Vince put his hand on my arm and said, "Lena, will you walk with me?"

I was half asleep. I opened my eyes and gazed at him. Immediately, my guard was up. I was trying really hard to contain my emotions. My brain filter turned on to defensive mode.

We strolled hand in hand. I really didn't want any physical contact, but what could I do? We were traveling together in such close quarters.

"Lena, I really screwed this up, didn't I?"

"Not so much screwed up, but simmered down."

"Oh, Lena, but the sex was great, wasn't it?"

"Yes, Vince. No doubt about that."

"Why are we letting this go?"

"I can't commit to a permanent arrangement here in Italy."

He began telling me that Paulie was being sent to Italy to learn about how the family functions. Vince would begin teaching him about the family business. Paulie was going to learn much of the security that Vince does. This decision was made because of Paulie's incident with heroine. They decided to ship him to Italy for his own good. I smiled and said, "Vince, this will be a big change for you and Paulie. Let's not make any lifelong decisions. We don't even know if Paulie is going to be able to adjust to life here."

All I could think about was the two weeks left at the villa. I missed my family. I even missed my job.

Penny suggested that we ride in the back for the remainder of the trip back. She wanted to talk about baby stuff.

Eventually she dozed off. I watched the scenery, all the while planning what I would do with my mixed up future.

Have I learned anything from my life so far?Yes!

1. Turn the brain filter back on. Before you do anything else, stupido.

2. Quit sleeping around. You don't need to hop between the sheets with every good-looking man who flirts with you.

3. Keep your panties on. Oh, wait . . . that's the same as #2.

4. Think about this TV job. Do you want to do this for the rest of your life?

5. Maybe I should go school. I mean, really learn something like nursing or teaching before it's too late and my brain goes dormant.

Carlo announced, "Home is in sight, ladies."

82

We came around the curve onto the driveway of the villa. I saw two black cars off the front of the main drive.

I figured Niko and some family members must have come to greet us and discuss some pending family business.

That's when I saw the little old lady coming around the side of the house. I stared for a moment. I thought it was Vanessa. Then she turned her head. "Nana!" I yelled. By the time Carlo parked the car, I was flying out of the back seat. I ran to her and threw my arms around her. I was squeezing her so hard she said, "Bella! I no can breath."

That's when I saw Mom, Dad, Zio, and Paulie coming out of the house. Bobby came out behind Paulie with a big grin on his face.

Through her tears, Ma said, "We missed you so much, Lena. One night we were sitting around talking about you when Niko stopped by to tell us about Penny and Carlo's baby. I already knew that Paulie would be coming to Italy. I told him how much we missed you. He said, 'So, go see her. It's my treat!' These limos picked us up at the airport."

"Ma, how did you know we would be back today?"

"Carlo sent a message while you were traveling. He called us, and we packed our stuff and Niko sent a car for us."

Vanessa said, "Everybody come inside. I gotta lotta food ready."

The women here must always have food prepared ahead of time. There was enough for a small town. I recognized some of my nana's food prepared along with Vanessa's.

People began to arrive. Some must have traveled all day to get here. There was a lot of hugging and kissing and crying.

When things settled down a bit, Dad took Ma by the arm and walked outside to the backyard.

When they came back in, I could tell Mom had been crying. I knew he had told her about Paulie staying in Italy, and now he told her what his duties would be.

I glanced down the long hallway toward the bedrooms. That's where the phone was on the wall. I could see several pieces of paper tacked to the wall by the phone. I walked a little closer. The all said things like, *"Call Frank," "Call TV station," "Greg say call station."* Nice to know that I was missed. I half-heartedly thought perhaps Whitey might have called. I even let myself think that he might be here somewhere, waiting to surprise me. I gave myself a mental slap and said, "Get over yourself, Lena. He's done with you."

When we all sat down, my dad said, "Paulie has something to tell all of you."

I glanced at Nana. I could tell she knew already. It wouldn't have been fair to surprise her in front of everyone.

Paulie sat up straight and said, "I have been asked to stay here in Palermo to learn about the family business."

We all acted surprised, even though we all knew, except maybe Mariella.

We all kissed Paulie and congratulated him. He was in for some serious growing up, really fast

Vince was standing at the kitchen counter eating. He never blinked or said anything about being Paulie's training buddy. I caught his eye and he gave me one of his famous head nods that said, "Follow me."

I excused myself as if I were going to the bathroom, because I am a floozy and a pushover.

I walked around the side of the house and met him at the back door. He pulled me into his arms and planted a wet fiery kiss on me that made the back of my neck break out in a sweat.

I said to myself, *Lena, you are a slutty mess.*

Then, after more passionate kisses and some groping, I said to myself, *Lena, sex is like chocolate for you. It can't be saved for later.*

Once have it, you got to have more.

"I can't be in the same room with you without wanting you. Can you come to my room later, Lena?"

I thought, *You can say no, Lena, you tramp.*

"I have to see where everyone is sleeping first, Vince."

When I got back to the kitchen, Mom came over and sat next to me.

"Are you all right, Lena? Your face is all flushed, honey."

"I'm just excited to see all of you, Mom."

At that moment Vince walked back into the kitchen. Ma looked from Vince to me. Her eyebrows shot up and she tilted her head like a doll. My ma doesn't miss anything. She has radar like a World War II commando.

I knew she would be paying me a visit in my room later. Vince could just simmer and wait for me.

The party moved into the garden. Penny and I went into the pool. The men talked and smoked cigars. Mom came out in her red bathing suit. I saw Dad roll his eyes at her. Maybe she wouldn't have time to visit me tonight. Maybe they would turn in early due to jet lag and the red bathing suit.

We ate outside and drank wine and ate more food. My dad said, "Lena, you look terrific."

"Yeah, Dad. I probably gained ten pounds."

"No, babe. You really look thinner."

Only my loving dad could say that.

It was after midnight when we all turned in. I put on some slutty silk pajamas. I couldn't be sleeping naked in case my Mom visited me.

I must have dozed off. I heard, "Honey, are you awake?"

It was my ma. For just a second I forgot that they were here.

"Come in, Mama."

She climbed into bed beside me and put her arms around me. What could be better than hugging your mom?

Then she got down to the serious discussion. "Are you messing around with 'Tall, Dark, and Brooding'?"

"Ma! You don't expect me to answer that, do you?"

"Okay. I'll take that as a yes."

"So, what's your next question?"

"Are you still carrying a torch for Whitey?"

"What difference does that make, Ma? He walked out on me. I need to forget my past and try to channel all of my energy into my future."

"Wow, Lena. That sounds mystical. I don't know if Vince is the right person for you to be messing around with. He looks dangerously handsome, Lena."

"Yes, I know. He reminds me a lot of Gino. I know I'm over him for sure."

"You know Vince might wind up in Chicago."

"I've heard that, Ma."

"Well, go to sleep sweetheart. You might want to lock your door until you decide who your heart belongs to."

That's my mom. Always has words of wisdom. *Who does my heart belong to?*

My big hunk-o-love would be sleeping alone tonight.

The next thing I knew, someone was pounding on my door, yelling in a hoarse whisper, "Lena, Lena!"

I opened my door to Vince. "Why are you yelling?"

"I thought something might be wrong. You never lock your door."

"My mom and I were talking until really late. She must have pushed the button lock when she left."

He was climbing into bed with me. "Holy Cannoli, Pisano! You can't stay in here and play hot potato. My whole family is in the house. There're going to want to do stuff today. Probably go into town and see some sights."

"Oh, yeah. I didn't think about that. You know, Lena, I haven't been around family for years. I forget about stuff like that. I don't know how to react to this togetherness."

It never entered my mind that Vince didn't have that mechanism. He wasn't raised by wolves, but he was raised by men who didn't have the sense of what's proper for family bonding.

"You're right, Vince. I apologize. We need to be very discrete if we have any more meetings."

"I got it, Lena. I do understand."

The next morning, we packed up all the women into the car and Vince drove us all into town. Vinnie parked the car and we all walked around. He bought us all gelato and we sat by the fountain. I swear that Ma and Nana both looked younger today. I guess it did them both a lot of good to be away from home on a real vacation. Nana and Zio were going to take one of the cars and go off by themselves for a few days. Nana insisted that Zio drive around town today and tomorrow because he hasn't driven a car for so long. She was afraid that he wouldn't be able to navigate the narrow streets and the mountain roads. Nana said that she didn't want to die in Italy.

We went into a little jewelry store where Mom flirted with the owner and got a real bargain on a pair of gold earrings. Nana was chatting with the wife about the little town she grew up in and they knew some of the same people. Penny walked down the street. She smelled cookies and bread. Her homing device was on overdrive when it came to food these days.

I walked outside to wait for them and sat on the wooden bench by the door. I was people-watching when I saw Mariella walking toward us. This was the young girl with the bad daddy. She was pushing the baby in a buggy, coming directly toward me.

"*Buongiorni,* Mariella. How is your baby?"

Mariella turned the buggy around so I could see her. I was afraid to look at the little girl. I thought she might look like a she-devil, or maybe a miniature of the bad daddy.

The baby girl was beautiful. She had a mess of curly chestnut hair like Mariella.

Mariella said, "She looks like my mama when she was a baby."

"She's really beautiful, Mariella."

"Do you want to hold her?" she asked.

She handed her to me before I could answer.

I have been around babies all life. I think this was probably one of the most beautiful babies I have ever seen. Her big brown eyes focused on my as if she knew me.

My mom and Nana came out of the store while I was holding the baby. Nana asked who she was. "She's a neighbor from the town. Penny introduced us."

Nana and Ma fussed over the baby. Nana said she looked like baby Angelo with more hair.

Vince came walking toward us from the location where he had stationed himself to spy on us. Mariella tried to hand the baby to him, but he was having none of that. My mom held the baby while Vince walked with Mariella a little distance from us. I wondered what he could have to talk to her about. I realized that they could be discussing a number of things. The family was probably looking after her financially. They tried to do things like that without the recipient knowing where the money was coming from. Mariella was smart and beautiful. I am glad that someone could help her get away from her father. I pretended that I didn't know the details. I'm getting really good at that.

When she came back for the baby and the buggy, Vince announced that he invited Mariella to the house tonight for the party. He said that Vanessa was planning a huge celebration for my family's arrival, and our return from Palermo.

We were strolling along at a leisurely pace. Mom and I were arm and arm. Penny was holding Nana's elbow, because some of the cobblestones were uneven.

My mom gets a twinkle in her eye when she has something to say. I could see it coming. "So, Lena. Did you do any thinking about our talk?"

"Ma, I kept my door locked."

"No, silly. Did you decide who Mr. Right is?"

"I didn't know I had to make a decision today."

"Lena, you have a lot of men in your life."

"Mom, I do have had a lot of men in my life. Most of them are in the past. I don't know if I'm in love with any of them right now."

"Fine. Keep you door locked until you decide."

"Ma, I don't know if that's going to work for me. It's not like a lottery."

"It really is like the lottery. You just pick one."

"The others aren't here. Gino is out of the picture. I'm not sure what's going on in my head, so don't make me nuts."

We both laughed.

When we got back to the villa, there were lights strung in the trees. Long tables were set up with bright blue cloths. I smelled food—a lot of food. A whole pig was roasting in a pit. There were people walking down the driveway with baskets and plates of food. When I think of the celebrations we have had at home, I know where this custom comes from. The excessive food is expected at all times. I looked around at all the people here. What a great turnout.

This also gave me the opportunity to look at other women my age. Geez, they all had big butts. It's not just me. My mom has a smaller butt than me, and Nana has a big butt. This group had an assortment of butt sizes. All the women were with good-looking men, so I guess they were used to big butts. Enough with the butt obsession.

I guess I obsess about my body too much—probably because of the TV thing. I have always heard that TV makes you look ten pounds heavier. I was torn between this beautiful place where I was vacationing, and my job that I love so much. Wait until Frank sees my butt. I can just hear him now: *"Good to see you Lena! About time you came back! What the hell happen to your rear end?"*

Time to eat! Niko was hoisting the pig out of the pit. He would carve it on a huge wooden table at the side of the pit. It smelled wonderful. I'm not sure I can eat that nasty-looking skin with all the fat. The meat itself looked good. Trays were lined up on the table for the pork to be cut off the bone. Vanessa was putting platters of vegetables on the long tables. Wine was placed along the tables. I recognized the bottles and small casks from the little shed next to the house.

Carlo was sitting with Penny and Mariella and Paulie. Guests were socializing and kissing and patting each other on the back.

I was stuffing my face and daydreaming. Some small tables were at the edge of the garden. I saw Paulie and Mariella get up from the table where they sat with Carlo and move to the small table. After a few moments, she handed him the baby. He was cooing and babbling to the baby as if he had never seen one before. They were having an intense conversation, smiling and nodding at each other.

Paulie's Italian was like pig Latin. It was part Sicilian, mushed up with English. Mariella looked amused, pleased, and confused, alternatingly.

This was the biggest gathering we'd had here since I arrived. It was a pretty big deal having all these people from America in this little town. It was almost like a wedding, without the bride and groom. I shudder at the thought.

Dad was helping Niko slice more meat off the pig. He was holding it with two giant spikes while Niko was wrestling with the poor animal. As the evening wore on, the poor pig looked less and less appetizing. In the process of hacking it apart, the head finally got turned around. Now his face was looking at me. I didn't like the animal eyes staring in my direction.

I was looking around the gathering and beyond, where the few animals were in the back of the house. I saw some sheep and chickens. I saw one horse and about half dozen pigs. I glanced over at the sad pig relative on the table. Poor pig.

As I sat observing the crowd, I wondered where Vince was hiding. It's unusual for him to not be present, scanning the crowd and watching like a hawk for the bad guys who obviously stalk the Bazzoli family.

I finally spotted him sitting on a picnic table, close to the driveway. He was half hidden by some trees. He sat on top of a wooden crate on the tabletop. The only thing he was missing was a tommy gun. He was wearing the traditional flat pancake hat. His head was scanning back and forth watching the crowd and the driveway leading to the road.

Cripes, I was really sick of this cloak and dagger stuff. It made me goofy.

I looked over at Paulie, sitting with Mariella. Holy shit, he was kissing the baby. I did a mental head slap. What goes around, comes around. This was payback. Getting a husband for Mariella and bringing the new mom into the family was bringing things full circle. Mariella would be obligated to marry Paulie. Paulie would feel the same about Mariella. Suddenly my stomach felt sick. It made me instantly break into a sweat. I pushed my plate away. I felt exhausted. I wanted to go back to my job. I want to be sheltered and in the dark about some things. I want to go out for lunch and get my hair done. I was tired of this family stuff. I wanted to go home. One more week, and I'd be out of here.

Vanessa came over to the table. "Miss Lena, you gotta lotta messages on the wall by the telephone. Did you see?"

"No, I didn't see. I'll go check now Vanessa, *Grazie.*"

I went to the phone in the hall and saw the notes stuck all over the wall. Most of them were from Jack Latmen. In broken English, of course. Vanessa made a good attempt at translating.

"Lena, you call me now. Frank" No date or time.

"Lena, why you no calla me back. When you comma home."

No punctuation or signature.

"Lena I miss you."

No signature.

"Lena call me when you can call me. Mona"

I went outside to ask Vanessa about the message with no signature.

"Too longa time ago. I no remember."

I decided to call Frank. Even with the time difference, he would be awake. I don't think he ever sleeps anyway.

"What?" he said. Typical of Frank to answer this way.

"Hi Frank, it's Lena."

"Holy crap, Lena. Where the hell have you been?"

"I'm in Palermo, Frank. Just like I told you."

"How much longer will you be gone?"

"I'll be back in one week."

"Lena, people are calling and writing. They are afraid that you won't be back from your ski accident."

"Frank, did you have enough footage to fill in, so far?"

"I have one more good shot of you and a nurse discussing physical therapy when your cast comes off. You are very emotional in the script. Can you walk with a limp?"

"Yes, Frank. I'll make it work. I'll practice before I get home."

"Okay, Lena." And he hung up. What a guy. That's Frank. He never says hello, good-bye, or knocks to come in.

It sounds like everything is going well at the studio. Everyone is showing up for work and getting along. I'll know more in a week or so.

I went out to say goodnight to my folks and kiss Nana goodnight.

"You going to bed so early, honey?"

"Yep, I'm exhausted. I'm turning in. I want to call Mona before I go to bed."

83

Mona answered on the first ring. "Holy crap, Lena! I'll be so glad when you get back. I don't think anyone understood how you pulled everyone together. I'm so glad to hear your voice."

"Good to hear your voice too, Mona. Is everything okay?"

"Oh, gosh? Johnny and Susan are hot and heavy again."

"I thought he was in love with his wife again. He wanted to have a baby, the last I heard."

"I think he has too much testosterone. I think that's what it's called. Some men are never satisfied with one woman. Beth is trying like hell to seduce Dr. Mike Bosco. Frank is loosing his mind, He's slapped himself in the head so much that his forehead is always pink! Oh Lena, we miss you lots! I'm so worried I can't keep it together. We've been giving Mike more hospital scenes. He says his medical training is really coming in handy with the script."

"Whoa! Mona, slow down. Do you know that Paulie is moving to Sicily?

"Yes. Lena, I'll always have feelings for him. He needs more help than I can give him. You know he couldn't stay away from 'Helen From Hell'? Are you okay, Lena?"

"I met a man here that I though I was in love with. I think I was just lonely and boy did I love his body. He didn't have anything more to give me. I'm trying to break it off. Well, I'll have to by next week. I've been calling him Tall, Dark, and Brooding."

"It's not the same without you. We'll talk more when you get home."

We said our good-bye's and hung up.

I though about going back outside. I woke myself up talking on the phone. I got to the door leading to the yard. There was Paulie, still holding Mariella's baby. The baby was fast asleep and Mariella was asleep with her head on Paulie's shoulder. I know I shook my head I disbelief. I thought about the word *disbelief,* but I believe anything since I've come here.

Stupid Paulie. He falls into any trap that is placed in font of him. He's such a dunce. He fell for Helen's crap then he was using heroine like it was a flu shot. Now he's going to marry Mariella. I wonder if he was aware of the situation before he came here? I'm going to try to talk to him tomorrow. I want to make sure that he knows the story before he gets in any deeper.

Suddenly, I felt tired again. I didn't want to be in a bad spy movie any more. I turned to go inside and Vinnie was waiting outside my room.

I took one look at him and said, "NO!"

"Lena, It would relax you if you let met make love to you."

"Yeah, that's probably true. I am very tense. But I don't need any more emotional crap. I'm done."

As I was talking he was backing me into my room. He's a wizard at taking my clothes off. My shirt was first. He had it pulled over my head at the doorway. He shimmied my slacks and my panties down with one hand.

The last thing I remembered was saying, "Lock the door."

84

"Lena, get up! Come to breakfast."

I looked next to me. Yup, Vinnie spent the night.

"I'll be there in just a few, Mom!"

Vinnie was sleeping like the dead. Oh, I shouldn't even think the word "Dead."

He looked like a Roman warrior. He was really a beautiful man.

I slapped him in the arm, "Vince, wake up!"

"What the hell?" he said.

I slapped my hand over his mouth so he wouldn't yell again.

"My mom is at the door. Go in the bathroom."

"I gotta go anyway."

"Well don't pee."

We both started laughing. "Well, don't flush."

"That's disgusting, Lena."

This guy was so sure of himself.

By the time I finally opened the door, Mom had gone into breakfast.

Breakfast was a gigantic buffet. That's not unusual, but this spread was bigger than usual. I walked along the tables in the kitchen. I realized that some of this food was refrigerated from last night. People brought so much stuff that Domenica and Nana had to bring some of it inside.

Some of the guests stayed overnight. It would make sense because they traveled so far to get here. Hell, this place was like the Holiday Inn anyway.

In the afternoon we went into town. I spend so much money last week, but I still wanted to bring a little something to everyone at the studio. I decided on belts for the men and small handbags for the ladies.

I had Paulie on my mind. I was planning to corner him later and discuss Mariella.

I bought some shoes. Ma bought a cute dress. I bought an extra suitcase.

Vanessa was eyeing a huge buffet sideboard with a granite top. It was at least six foot long, maybe more. "This would be a good table for baking bread and rolling dough," she said.

The table was on a wagon with a two-horse team. When she finally got the owner down to a price that she thought was fair, she said, "You bring to my house?"

"Si, signora! Everyone knows the Villa Bazzoli."

She gave him the location anyway, and we continued shopping.

By the time we got home, the horse and wagon were in the front yard.

We unloaded our packages, expecting the old man to be inside having espresso in the kitchen.

Vanessa said, "Where did the man go?" to no one in particular.

We put our things away and came back to the kitchen. Vanessa was at the stove preparing dinner. "Hey, I dunno where the guy go from-a the wagon."

I said, "He'll probably be back later. Maybe he wanted to give us time to take the buffet off the wagon."

We changed our clothes and decided to go in the pool before dinner.Vanessa came outside and said. "The horses are gone."

"Where did they go?"

"I'm-a no sure, but the wagon is still here with the table."

We all trouped outside. Yep, he came for the horses, but he left the wagon. "The horses are probably worth more than the wagon."

"He's gonna want the wagon though, right?"

"Ma, we have to get the buffet off the wagon, then he'll come back for it."

Lunch came and went. As the dinner hour approached, Vince and Carlo came home.

"Hey! What's that wagon doing in the front yard?"

Vanessa, how are you going to get that thing off the wagon?"

"I think-a the men take it off the wagon," Vanessa responded.

They both started laughing. "Vanessa, this thing must weigh about 1000 pounds with the marble top."

"Cosa si sta parlando. Ferro e mettere il carro."

"Vanessa, the man didn't put it on the wagon himself. He had to have help. He must have had a hoist to get that thing up there. It's not going to be easy to get that monster into your kitchen."

"Why he no come back for the wagon?"

"Probably because he knows that we can't get this thing off the wagon."

The women went back into the kitchen. Vanessa was so sure that she was going to have that buffet in her kitchen that she was busy moving tables and making room for it.

I was thinking of a way to move that buffet, but I'd have to keep it to myself and let the men work it out. I didn't want to steal the show.

We went outside the next morning after breakfast. The wagon was backed up to the kitchen door. I guess that was a step in the right direction.

We brought the coffee out to the picnic bench to watch the guys brainstorm the issue while eating biscotti and drinking lots of coffee. Close to noon they switched to wine.

Paulie finally showed up and I pulled him into the side yard

"What the heck are you doing, Paulie?"

"Well, I'm going to stay here and work for the family for a while."

"Not that, *stupido*. I'm talking about Mariella and her baby.

"Well, the baby's name is Eva. Actually, her full name is Eva Maria, after Mariella's Mama.

"Listen, you little shit, you're avoiding my questions. What do you know about her and her baby?"

Paulie looked like he didn't want to discuss this. He also knows that I won't back off.

He said, "I know that her dad and her husband were drowned in a fishing accident. The real story: her Dad was raping her for years and we had to take him down."

"Thank God, Paulie! I thought you were knee deep in uncharted territory."

"You know, I'm not stupid, Lena. They are paying me big bucks to marry a beautiful girl with a baby, become part of the family. I know whatever I have to know, Lena."

I hugged him so hard and kissed his cheek.

"What are you getting so mushy about, Lena?"

"Oh Paulie. This pushes you right into being a grownup."

"Yeah, yeah. I'm on fast forward now."

We walked around the side of the house. The sides were off the wagon now, and

I couldn't keep my mouth closed any longer.

"You guys are going to need a hoist to get that thing out of the wagon. You'll need a big pulley . . . strong rope and some 2x4s.

"And how do you suppose we'll get it into the kitchen once we hoist it off the wagon?"

I looked at Vince and said, "Logs, gentlemen. Logs."

"How does that work, Lena?"

"You hoist one end of the buffet, put a log under it. Put another log under the backside and roll it on the logs. Put another log in front of that one and keep rolling it toward the house."

Now, I never used this method, but I was sure that it worked, from everything I had read.

Vince and Carlo were very quiet for a moment. Then Vince said, "Wow, how did you figure that out?"

'I didn't figure it out. The Egyptians did. That's how the moved the big stones that built the pyramids."

"Wow, I should marry you because you're so smart," Vince said.

"I think that option is off the table."

This was such a big project. The two men made it an all day ordeal. They finally cut the 2x4s, pounded them into the ground, and rigged up the pulley.

They were cutting the logs, after I reminded them to leave the logs a little bigger than the width of the buffet.

Nana came into the yard grumbling about something Zio had done.

"He's a no good for driving. He all-a time looking left and right and he no see some-a thing in front of him. He almost kill a lady."

"I saw her, Rosina. I don't know why she stop to look at me in the middle of the street."

"She look-a you because you drive like a stupido."

"Hey! Whaddaya doing with that big thing on the wagon?"

"They're going to put it in Vanessa's kitchen."

"I can help them," Zio said.

Nana had a holy cat fit. "Oh no! Peppino! You no gonna help. This is gonna kill you."

Zio shooed her with his hand.

"Okay, I'm gonna help Vincenzo guide this thing off the wagon. Carlo you turn-a the handle on the hoist."

They had rigged up a double rope around the middle of the buffet and put the big hook through it.Vanessa ran outside with a blanket to put under the hook so it wouldn't damage the precious marble.

It worked! They got it off the wagon with no damage. They flipped it on its back so the legs wouldn't interfere with the rolling process.

They were headed for the kitchen! The rolling logs worked just great.

Vanessa decided to put it closest to the back door where it came in. She had already moved all the other kitchen furniture out of the way.

She was delighted. Now she busied herself polishing the wood and rubbing oil into the marble top.

My mom, Penny, and I helped get the kitchen back in order.

I fell into bed exhausted around midnight. I slept alone, finally.

I woke up feeling like I had slept all day. I put a shirt on over my pajamas and wandered into the kitchen. It was eleven thirty.

Mom was having coffee in the garden with Penny and Vanessa

when I walked outside.

"Good morning, sleepyhead," Mom said.

"I didn't realize it was so late. I might as well have lunch."

No sooner said than done! Vanessa jumped up and brought a tray with bread cheese, melon, and sliced meat.

We were all very quiet today. I wondered where the men were this early in the day—more secrets and lies, probably. It's just as well that I don't know. I was going home soon, so I didn't care where anyone was.

Finally, Mom said, "Are we going anywhere today?"

"I hadn't thought about it, Ma."

"Can we walk to town? Is that permitted?

"I don't know," Penny answered, "Sometimes they say yes, sometimes no."

Mom looked at Penny, "Penny, why don't you rest today. Sit by the pool and nap in the shade. You've been really busy since we all invaded your home."

"Sounds like a good idea, Josie. I think I will."

"Is Paulie out, Ma?"

"No, he's getting dressed. Carlo is picking him up at one."

"I'm going to get dressed, too."

The last door on the right side was Paulie's room. I knocked.

I said, "Paulie, it's Lena."

"Come in, babe."

He hugged me and said, "Sit down. What's wrong?"

"I'm worried that you don't know what you're getting in to."

"They told me Lena. Nobody sugar coated Mariella's past. I have to make her my own and become a father to Eva."

"Give yourself a chance to get to know her, Paulie. Don't jump into it too fast."

"Lena, they have the wedding planned. It's going to be the night before everyone goes home. I didn't want to have a wedding without my family. You know if I try to get out of it, they would probably kill me."

I was speechless. I knew my mom seemed a little distracted this morning. She must know. "Who knows about the wedding, Paulie?"

"Everyone except Nana. The men told Zio last night. He seemed to understand."

Paulie hugged me. "I'm going to miss you, Lena. We've been like brother and sister."

"I guess that's going to make Mariella my sister-in-law. Well, I don't feel like her aunt."

"I think she's gotten attached to me already, Lena. The baby is beautiful, isn't she? She looks a lot like baby Rosie, doesn't she?"

I smiled, "Yeah, she does Paulie."

85

This would be the last time I could poke my nose into Paulie's life. I realized that as I started to get dressed. I was feeling a little blue about it.

Ma and I walked to town—probably against the rules, but what the hell.

Nana and Zio were out driving to a small town south of here. Zio couldn't get into too much trouble driving there. The streets were narrow and the car was the size of a shoebox. Nana never stopped yelling a Zio. She started shouting when they got in the car and we could see the car jerking and swerving as she yelled while he was going down the street.

Dad would be busy today bonding with the boys. He would be with the family most of the time that he was here.

We were pretty much on our own. We strolled along at a snail's pace. We walked down the many side streets leading to town. One street we turned down was a complete surprise. It was long and narrow and nearly the entire front yard was a vineyard. It was smaller than the vineyard at Villa Bazzoli, but beautiful, just the same. I could smell the sweet grapes and the sour fermenting smell. It reminded me of Nana's basement where Zio made wine and Papa Joe before him.

While Mom and I stood gazing at the garden, we heard a man's voice, *"Bongiorno buon pomeriggio, signore, vi piacerebbe assaggiare qualche vino."*

Mom flashed her winning smile, "We would love to sample your wine from the garden."

"Grazie, that would be very nice."

This handsome man extended his hand and welcomed us into his garden. He was movie-star handsome. We followed him like love-struck zombies. He had black hair, slightly greying at the temples, and was wearing a fitted white shirt, rolled at the sleeves. He had on dark blue pants with a kerchief tied around his neck. Mom followed him like she was in a trance.

"Okay, Mom, wait for me!"

He led us into his beautiful garden. Long tables were set with typical checkered

tablecloths and bottles of wine with glasses.

"Are you expecting company?" I asked.

"No signora. We are having a wine tasting this afternoon. Always on Wednesday."

"Oh, that's why you were so welcoming," Mom commented.

"Signora, I would have welcomed you any day of the week." He offered his arm and Mom followed him, grinning from ear to ear.

I followed like a dutiful daughter. He seated us at one of the long tables. A younger version of our host came out of the house with trays of cheese, grapes, and bread. It was as if we had walked into a garden party and we were the guests of honor.

It didn't occur to me that he knew who we were until he asked, "Will you be staying at Villa Bazzoli long?"

Mom told him, "We will be leaving on Tuesday morning."

The younger version of the host came over and introduced himself. "I am Stefano Androtti, Jr. This is our vineyard."

More people came into the garden for the wine tasting. We were ready to leave. When we stood, Mr. Androtti, Sr. walked over to us.

"Thank you for visiting us. Perhaps we will meet again before you leave."

"It was a pleasure to meet you, Signore Androtti."

He kissed our hands and bowed as we exited.

"Well, I'm glad you enjoyed flirting with that nice man all afternoon, Mom."

"I wasn't flirting, Lena. I was simply being polite."

"Ha! I saw you batting your eyes at him."

"Well, Lena, it's just a good thing that I haven't lost my touch."

I looked at my watch. "We still have time to go to a few shops if you want to."

"Oh yes! Let's do that, honey."

We shopped until nearly dinnertime. I found a white peasant dress that was very traditional with a full skirt and embroidered bodice. Mom found a similar dress in black and red.

When we got back to the villa, everyone was home. I wasn't hungry, but it was nice to sit with everyone. Nana and Zio got back in the afternoon. She had so much to talk about. Some of the ladies she saw remembered her from her childhood. She was proud to show off her new husband. It was nice to see her so excited.

As the evening wore on we moved into the garden. Paulie left and came back with Mariella and the baby. Everyone welcomed her like family and we passed the baby around to play with her.

We heard a car drive up and a man walked toward us. Vince came out from his post behind the tree with his hands outstretched.

"Stefano, good to see you."

"Hello, Vince. I brought an invitation from my dad to your family." He handed the handwritten invitation to Vince and they walked toward us.

"I would like to introduce everyone to Stefano Androtti. He has a vineyard not too far from here."

Stefano Jr. shook everyone's hand and mentioned, "I met the ladies this afternoon when they stopped at the wine tasting at our vineyard. I would like to welcome all of you by inviting you to my home for a garden party this evening."

Everyone was delighted at the invitation. The invitation said to be there at 8 p.m.

When Stefano shook my hand to say good-bye he stared into my eyes a little too long. Vince tapped him on the shoulder and steered him toward Nana and Zio. I knew I'd hear about this later. I really thought that Stefano was gorgeous. I only had a few more days in Italy. I could keep my mouth shut and my knees together—

no problem.

Needless to say, Vince was in my room waiting for me that evening.

"NO! Go away, Vince!"

"Lena, I just want to talk."

"Okay, so talk."

"I want to be sure that Stefano doesn't push his way into my territory."

"Ha! Don't make me laugh, Vince. I am not your territory."

"You know what I mean, Lena."

"Yes, I do. You want to be sure that if you can't have me, Stefano doesn't have me either."

"Yea, that's pretty much what I mean. You were mine first."

"You Italian men are a pain in my ass. I can't wait to go home."

"Do you have an Italian man waiting for you at home, Lena?"

"I have several men friends that are interested in me. I don't feel the need to sleep with everyone I'm attracted to."

"You could have fooled me."

As soon as he said it, I knew he regretted it.

I narrowed my eyes and stared at him. "We are through, Vince."

"Lena, I didn't mean that to come out the way it did."

"You don't need to explain, Vince. We had our fling. It's over."

"I really care about you, Lena. It wasn't a fling."

"Leave now, Vince. We are finished talking."

He could tell I meant it, and he turned and left.

I sat on the bed and buried my face in a pillow. I cried my dirty little cheating heart out.

"There. Now I feel better," I said out loud to nobody.

I knew that I was finished with Vince. I wanted to go home. I couldn't leave soon enough.

86

I got dressed for the party with Stefano in mind. I wore my white sundress and thin strap sandals. I put on red lipstick. Penny had trimmed my hair the night before. I was putting out my Gina Lollobrigida look for the evening, and the final touch was the gold hoop earrings.

Dad gave me a wolf whistle when I walked out to the car. He rolled his eyes at Mama. She was wearing the black and red summer dress she had bought that afternoon with red high heels. He loved it when Ma wore red. We wanted to walk because it was a beautiful evening. Dad said, "No way." Carlo and Vince took us in the other car and we all arrived in style.

The wine was flowing freely when we arrived. Someone handed me a glass of red, which I drank promptly.

Vince walked up behind me and said, "You look beautiful tonight, Lena." I said, "Thanks Vince." I didn't turn my head to look at him because I'm a sucker for sad eyes.

We were the guests of honor. The Americans, who where visiting, and staying at the Villa Bazzoli. There was food everywhere, and meat was cooking on open fires in several places. Baskets of bread were on the tables as well as cheeses and sweets. A little group was playing music. They had a concertina and a harmonica and mandolin. Later a man joined in with a flute.

Team Androtti, the father and son, were working the crowd, kissing cheeks, shaking hands and passing the babies around, including Mariella's baby Eva.

Mom and Dad were talking to Mr. Androtti, Sr., and Mom was flirting shamelessly. Dad didn't seem to mind. Vince was following me around. I could feel his eyes burning through the back of my head.

Someone kept filling my glass. The wine was going down really easy. Nana and Zio were doing a little two-step to the concertina music.

The Androtti's had put down plywood for a dance floor. Stefano and his brother Jake were putting down additional sheets because everyone was dancing and they needed more room.

My glass was full again. Like magic.

My mom and dad were doing a little tarantella. Mom was holding a white handkerchief and Dad took the corner and danced all around Mom. Everyone made a circle and clapped.

When the applause got louder, I thought is was for my folks, but it was because Niko Bazzoli had arrived.

There was more kissing and hand shaking and greetings all around. More wine was poured. My glass was full again. This wine was a little sweeter and smoother.

My dad brought me a plate of food. "I think you'd better eat something, Lena."

So I did. I sat between two handsome men, Stefano and Jake, and I chowed down. After that I don't remember much.

What I tell you now is what I found out the next day. My mom told me that I got up to dance with them both. It started out as a tarantella and quickly turned into a dirty boogie. I had my sandals in my hand and flipped my skirt all around. She said I was the star of the show, until I threw up in the rain barrel next to the house.

Oh, but the show was not over. Vinnie tried to help me by putting a cold cloth on my forehead. I yelled at him and said, "Oh no you don't, cowboy. I'm not riding that horse again." Paulie finally picked me up and put me in the car to take me home.

I found all this out in the morning, after I woke up in my sundress smelling like a wet dirty dog.

Thank goodness, Paulie had washed my face and cleaned me up a bit.

Mom and Dad laughed when I came into the kitchen after I showered.

Paulie put a cup of coffee in front of me with some dry toast. I said, to no one in particular, "I think I died. I don't ever remember getting that drunk before."

Dad said, "I'm not surprised. I didn't think you'd remember anything."

"I don't remember much."

"Yeah, Dago Red will do that to a person."

I drank my coffee and went back to bed.

Later that day, I stumbled out of bed and showered. I went out to the pool area to find Mom, Penny, and Domenica. It was unusual to see Domenica sitting down. I think she partied pretty hard too. Everyone was feeling sorry for me, but not as sorry as I felt for myself. I felt like I'd had brain surgery with no anesthetic.

I wondered about today's activities. Mom reminded me that Paulie was getting married day after tomorrow. "We have a lot to do, Lena."

"Cripes, Mom. Where is the wedding?"

"It's going to be at the Androtti Vinyard."

"Oh, great. I'll have another opportunity to make a fool of myself."

"Nana and Zio have their fancy clothes from their wedding. I can wear the white suit that I brought. What are you going to wear?"

"I'll go into town with Penny later and help her pick out a dress. Maybe I'll buy something new. What is Mariella going to wear?"

"Her aunts found her mother's wedding dress in the old house. They are putting some new lace on it, and making a dress for baby Eva."

"I feel so bad for Paulie. How is he going to handle this mess of a marriage?"

"Don't underestimate Paulie. I think he's got a little crush on Mariella already."

"I hope they fall in love. It would be awful to have to live here and not have a wife who loves you, wouldn't it Ma?"

"Mariella never knew what it meant to have a man love her, Lena. Paulie knows how to treat a woman. He's had serious relationships before. Mariella was afraid at first, but I had a talk with her about how a man should treat a woman. I don't think she's afraid anymore."

"I had no idea that you have had a talk with her about such serious stuff."

"When the arrangement was made for Paulie to marry her, Niko asked me to talk to her like a mother. We had lunch in town and had a nice talk."

"Ma! Did you make her blush? I'll bet you explained things pretty clearly."

"What could I do, Lena? I don't think her old aunties would give her much insight. They should have taken her away from the father years ago. She has no uncles alive anymore. That's how her dad got away with this all these years."

"It makes me sick to think about her life. Where will they live?"

"Niko invited them to live here at the villa. Mariella doesn't want to begin her marriage at that house where she grew up. This will be a fresh start for her. Domenica is thrilled. She will have baby Eva, and Penny's new bambino to take care of. I know you're anxious to get home, honey. You have your friends and your job to look forward to. I know you miss Whitey."

"Ma, I can't believe you said that. How could you mention his name? He walked out on me, remember?"

"Lena, I think you belong together. He could change his mind."

"Why would you think he would be waiting for me? He can't take the family connection—remember that too? Just forget him, okay Mom. That part of my life is over."

87

The Androtti Vinyard was being prepared for the wedding. Niko was sending a catering company to arrange everything. The dance floor would be similar to the plywood that was there the other night. The food would be prepared on large open grills. Lights were strung from the trees and pink and white paper flowers were tied everywhere.

Paulie was bringing Mariella and her cousin Anna to the villa with baby Eva. We would help her dress for her wedding at the villa. The remainder of Mariella's belongings were at her aunt's house. Paulie would get them later.

When I left Chicago to visit Palermo, I never expected any of these things that happened. I was overwhelmed and exhausted by the amount of change and activity that had taken place. In a million years, I never expected Paulie to be getting married, nor did I expect that he would be staying in Italy. My world was changing and shifting. My Chicago life was calmer. I could live with that.

I thought Penny would be coming home with me. Now I knew that she might stay here indefinitely.

Penny was doing Mariella's hair and makeup. She was doing a beautiful job. Mariella looked like a movie star. Penny wove fresh flowers into her hair in a halo. A little netting was attached to the flowers. The dress was simple, in an off-white color. I think it was white originally; the silk and lace had aged over the years, but it looked very pretty. She was a beautiful girl. The makeup just enhanced her natural beauty.

I wore my white dress from the party at the Androtti Vinyard. Domenica hand washed and starched it. She put a pink sash at the waist. I guess I was in the wedding party, although I didn't know I was going to be. Mariella's cousin carried the tiny Eva, who was six weeks old today. I was in charge of flowers and making sure the bride's dress was in perfect order.

We paraded to the church as was customary in small towns. The bride was arriving by car. The old church was beautiful. Niko was arriving at the church with Mariella. There was Paulie, standing at the altar with Carlo. He was wearing a black suit. My handsome Paulie, who I thought would live near me all my life.

The music started and the bride was walking down the aisle with Niko Bazzoli. Paulie was getting married in a foreign country to some beautiful girl that he hardly knew. He would be a made man eventually. What an awful thought on his wedding day. That's the rule, and I won't be sorry to miss that.

The Bazzolis are in charge of this whole situation. I was drawn back to the ceremony when I heard, in Italian: "Ladies and gentlemen, I present to you Mr. and Mrs. Paul DeLuca." I missed the vows. The couple was walking toward me. Mariella had tears running down her face. They stopped to kiss Nana, Mama, and then turned to me. Paulie kissed me on both cheeks and said, "I love you, Lena."

We were all leaving the church. Paulie and Mariella both had tears streaming down their faces. I think Paulie's were for a variety of reasons. This might be too much too soon.

The procession was beginning through town. People applauded and sang as we walked to the vineyard. This was an open wedding. At some point the entire town would pass through the gates. The streets leading to the vineyard were decorated with streamers and flowers. When we got to the vineyard, it was beautiful. Anything connected to the Bazzolis was always over the top.

I was holding a glass of wine, but I was not planning to drink it. The flashbacks from the other night were still too vivid.

Someone tapped my shoulder. It was Mariella. "I am afraid without you, Lena."

"Don't be afraid, Mariella. Paulie is a good man. He will make you happy. Penny will be here and she will stay close to you. It will improve your English, because she doesn't speak much Italian."

I looked around for Paulie. He was in deep conversation with Niko and Carlo. When Paulie looked up and saw Mariella and me talking, he excused himself and came over.

"I think Mariella is a little worried, Paulie. She is overwhelmed by all the decisions that have been made."

"She doesn't need to worry about anything. A month or so ago, she didn't know how she was going to manage her life. Now it's all being done for her."

"Paulie, did anyone ask her if she wants to live in Niko's villa?"

"No. I guess I thought that would be the best place because Penny is there. She doesn't want to live in the house where she grew up with her rotten father."

"Just make her feel like she's part of the decisions, Paulie. This package was arranged by Niko and the family. You're going to be married to her, so make her feel like a wife instead of an arrangement."

"Lena, what am I gonna do without you? I don't think right. I know you keep me straight."

"You have to figure out what's right and what's wrong. I can't be here for you, Paulie."

"But I can phone you, Lena. And I will!"

As the party progressed, the bride and groom disappeared—probably off to some secret honeymoon place.

I asked Mom, "Isn't the baby too young for Mariella to . . . you know."

Mom just rolled her eyes as if to say, "You have a lot to learn, Lena."

I got to my room to find cousin Anna asleep in my bed. A laundry basket sat on two chairs next to her with baby Eva sleeping peacefully. I went to sleep in Paulie's room.

The next day, I finished packing. Time for me to go home. Happy days!

I went in to the kitchen to find Niko having coffee with my folks and Nana with Zio.

"Good morning, Lena. I want to thank you for everything you've done for Penny and everyone else since you've been here."

I thought, *Don't ask me Niko, please don't ask me.*

"Lena, I don't supposed you would consider staying on to help Penny with the baby?"

"Oh, Niko, I really can't. As much as I have loved being here, Frank has called several times sounding the alarm about the TV show. He's afraid the ratings have dropped off since I've been gone."

"Oh, that's what I figured, Lena. Maybe you could arrange to come back here after the baby is born?"

"I was hoping to do just that, Niko. I can't wait for the baby to be born."

"Well, I'm glad that's settled."

Niko arranged for two cars to take us to the airport. I was just as excited to get home as I was to come to Italy. The pilot was *not* Captain Bennicase.

We were treated like royalty. The crew was outstanding. I slept on and off most of the way home. Mama kept chatting about Paulie. She kept trying to get me to eat. I could live off this body for another five weeks. Nana seemed very quiet. She asked a few questions, mostly about time of arrival. Paulie was her baby boy. It was going to be hard for her to live with the fact that he is going to stay in Italy permanently. Paulie's problems kept getting the best of him. This was where he belonged. Niko and the family would take good care of him. I don't like to think about what he will have to do to become a made man. I hope the person he has to eliminate will be rotten like Mariella's father.

Our flight was uneventful. Dad and Zio were sitting together. Men don't talk much. Mama woke me when we were getting ready to land. The drive from the airport to the house was about an hour. Now everyone wanted to talk. We were in a limo—thanks to Niko, again. The driver must have thought we were all crazy.

When we got home it was twilight. Mama wanted me to stay with her tonight. I said no. I wanted to sleep in my own bed. The driver dropped my suitcases inside my door. I tipped him. Dad tipped him too.

The house smelled musty. I opened a few windows, changed into a tee shirt, and hit the bed.

88

The phone was ringing. It took me a few seconds to decide what to do and where I was. I answered.

"Hello."

"Hey babe, It's Greg."

I was having a flashback of our encounter just before I left.

"Hi Greg. How are you?"

"Hi Lena. It's good to hear your voice. I thought I might stop by in a little while. I'll bring some lunch and the script for the show."

"That's a good idea. Lunch too, because I don't have anything in the house. Give me at least an hour. What time is it?"

"It's nearly three."

"Wow. Good thing that you called. See you later."

Back to normal. Thank goodness. I jumped in the shower and pulled out some clothes—pants and a white shirt. Good enough. I towel dried my hair and put some lipstick on. Not too bad. I had a little color from being out in the sun. I could see the remains of too much wine and too many parties in the wrinkles around my eyes.

The doorbell rang. Hell, Greg already?

It was flowers. The arrangement was huge; it looked like it should be for a wedding or a funeral. The card said, "Glad you are home safe. I miss you." No signature.

What the heck? Let's see—it could be Frank, or Mike Bosco, Greg, or even Whitey. Can't be from the TV cast. They would have said *we* miss you.

The doorbell rang again. This time it was Greg. He brought flowers and sandwiches. So I guess the other flowers weren't from him. He stood there and stared at me for a long time. He broke out in a smile.

"I couldn't decide how much I missed you. Now that I see you, I know I missed you a lot."

He put his arms around me and held me close. He slid his arm under the back of my sweater.

"Greg, you aren't going to let this go, are you?"

"Oh no, Lena. I thought I'd get more aggressive in my quest to win you over."

"Oh, boy. Stop looking toward my bedroom. We aren't going to wind up in there."

"We started in the kitchen last time."

"Back off, buddy. You're pushing too hard."

He laughed and sat down. "I guess you need to get yourself acclimated to being home first."

"I want to hear all the latest gossip about the cast and crew. I'm starting out with a clean relationship slate. No men in my life for a while."

"You're not one of those Born Again Virgins, are you?"

I poured us a glass of wine, since I didn't have anything else to drink in the house.

The doorbell rang. Greg said, "I'll get it."

It was Dad. "Hey, Greg! You don't waste any time, do you?"

"Strictly business, Mr. D."

Greg took one of the two bags of groceries out of Dad's arms. They unloaded them onto the counter.

"I knew you wouldn't have anything in the house. I went to the store for Ma, so I got some stuff for you."

He had milk, bread, butter, cheese, and some cold cuts.

"Dad, let me pay you."

"No, when did I ever take your money?"

As an afterthought, Dad said, "Greg, when did you get here?"

"Just a few minutes ago. I brought some lunch and the script for this week."

Dad came over and kissed me good-bye.

I wonder if he thought Greg came over during the night?

"So long, kids."

"Good-bye Mr. Delatora."

"Call me Sam, Greg."

Greg filled me in on all the news at the TV station. "Johnny and Susan are back together. Mona didn't seem too broken up about it. Johnny's wife said he should stick with his baby's mother. Beth is doing her best to win Red over. I think he was falling for her, but then she started acting a little loopy."

"Has she been taking her meds?"

"Yeah, but I think she must have skipped a dose here and there. She has those containers that say MON, TUES, WED, but seems to have leftovers by the end of the week."

"Who fills those for her?"

"I think her family has a visiting nurse or something who comes on weekends to fix her up."

"How's Frank?"

"Oh, he's a wreck as usual. Worse since you're not there. He'll be so glad to see you. He says that you're the person who keeps everyone on track."

"How is little Sabra doing? She only had a few days on the set being my kid sister, when I left."

"They have given her lines almost every day. I think she's a natural. No hitches or glitches. She does her lines and she's very good."

"How about Dr. Mike?

"Well, I thought you'd never ask. He hasn't had many lines, but they have written a minor car accident into the script for Mona. He has been her attending physician. I think he's attending to her on and off the set."

"Oh, that's very interesting."

I think I hesitated a moment too long. Greg picked up on that really quick.

"Oh, Miss Delatora, do I detect a little something in your voice about Dr. Mike?"

"Oh, hell no Mr. Neuman. I barely know the man. I plan to

keep my distance from any attachments to anyone of the male persuasion."

"Does that include me, Lena?"

"Business only, Greg."

"I know you, Lena. You are a very passionate person. You won't be alone very long."

"We'll see about that, my friend."

89

I went in to the TV station a little early the following morning. I parked and walked in just like I usually do. It seemed awfully quiet. I opened the double doors that led to the set and the dressing rooms. There was a huge banner: "WELCOME BACK, LENA." Everyone yelled, "SURPRISE!"

I took a quick look behind me, just in case this welcome was for someone else. Nope, it must be for me. Everyone hugged and kissed me.

Mona came over and took me by the arm, "Come and see the cake, Lena."

There was a huge cake with the same welcome back message. There were sandwiches and bags of chips and mountains of cookies.

"Oh my gosh, I can't believe this is all for me."

Latmen came over and hugged me. "Cripes, I'm glad you're back. I thought I was gonna lose my mind with all these big babies working here."

This was my life. Italy was exciting. I'd had a fling with Vince. It was wonderful that my family came too. The day flew by. I got my new script.

The phone was ringing when I walked into my house. I picked it up and said, "Hello."

The voice said, "Did you get my flowers?"

"Lena," he said, "I'm coming to Chicago. I promise I won't complicate your life."

It was Vince.

I hung up the phone without saying anything. I poured myself a glass of wine. I should have finished beauty school. My heart was fractured. My brain was like soup. I think I needed to step back and get my life in order. I didn't know if I wanted Vince to come here. I didn't want a man to control me anytime soon.

The phone was ringing again. I didn't answer it. What's a girl gotta do to get her life back?

My nana once told me, "Don't let a man take so much of your life for himself." That's loosely phrased, but *you* get the message. *Now* I get the message.

CPSIA information can be obtained
at www.ICGtesting.com
Printed in the USA
LVOW08s0144300517

536250LV00002B/343/P